Tamara McKinley was born and raised in Australia. Adopted by her grandmother, she was eventually brought to England to finish her education. Tamara McKinley lives on the south coast of England, and writes full-time, but travels back to Australia frequently to visit her eldest son and do research for her books. She is the author of *Matilda's Last Waltz*, *Jacaranda Vines*, *Wildflowers* and *Summer Lightning*, also available from Piatkus.

Undercurrents

Tamara McKinley

PIATKUS

Author Note

There is a small seaside town in the far north of Queensland called
Trinity Beach. The residents may not recognise it as it is presented in
Undercurrents for I have taken certain liberties with its geography and
character and for that I apologise. The Trinity of *Undercurrents* is an
amalgam of Bluff Beach in Devonport, Tasmania, and Palm Cove and
Trinity in Queensland – my idea of heaven on earth – for each repre-
sent a special time in my life.

Tamara McKinley

Copyright © 2004 by Tamara McKinley

First published in Great Britain in 2004 by
Judy Piatkus (Publishers) Ltd of
5 Windmill Street, London W1T 2JA
email: info@piatkus.co.uk

The moral right of the author has been asserted

A catalogue record for this book is available from the British Library

ISBN 0 7499 3512 X

Set in Times by
Action Publishing Technology Ltd, Gloucester

Printed and bound in Great Britain by
Butler and Tanner Ltd, Frome, Somerset

For Daireen Eva Liefchild McKinley and all the women who raise other people's children and love them as their own. They truly understand the meaning of motherhood.

The cruellest lies are often told in silence.

Robert Louis Stevenson 1850–1894

Prologue

The SS *Arcadia* had left Liverpool six weeks earlier. Now it was the 10th of March in the year 1894, and the storm came off the western shores of Australia with little warning.

The Captain fought to keep his ship bow on to the hurricane winds and titanic seas, but he was beginning to suspect it was a losing battle. He'd already watched, helplessly, as three of his crew were washed overboard as they attempted to repair a hatch cover, and now two of the three masts had been snapped off like matchsticks. The decks were leaking, the cargo scattered to kingdom come, but the funnels had held and the mighty engine still throbbed in the engine room. He knew his ship had seen other storms and survived them, just as he had done, and he refused to give in. There were 1,500 passengers in his care as well as his crew. It was his duty to bring them safely to land.

He peered through the rain-lashed window into the black night. This storm could have tossed them miles off course, and with no moon, no stars, it was impossible to fix their position. Riding the shifting, rolling deck beneath his feet, he took a firmer grip on the great wheel and began to pray. This coastline was littered with submerged islands of coral and pinnacles of rock. Even *Arcadia*'s steel hull couldn't survive being battered against them.

In the first-class stateroom on the upper deck, Eva Hamilton clung to Frederick. It was dark. So black she couldn't see his face or the gleam of her new wedding ring. Yet her fear was laced with excitement, a dreadful thrill that they were at the height of a great adventure. Nothing could have prepared her for this.

The great ship plunged with stomach-churning ferocity, lifted her bow and tossed them both from the bed to the floor. 'This can't go on,' shouted Frederick above the banshee wail of the wind and the thunder of the ocean. 'Three days we've been riding this storm. The hull won't take it.'

'She's lasted this long,' Eva yelled back as they again found one another in the darkness. 'We have to keep faith in the Captain.'

He didn't reply, merely tightened his grip around her waist.

Eva sat on the floor, her face pressed to his chest, her back hard against the oak panelling. The storm had begun as a darkening of the skies to the east. The Captain had assured the passengers all would be well, and that this was merely a routine hazard off these western shores. Yet, as the wind picked up and began to howl and the waves towered so high they blotted out the horizon, the passengers had sought refuge in their cabins – no longer exhilarated but terrified.

Her own fear was beginning to surface and she hastily turned her thoughts to more pleasant things as she attempted to remain rooted in one position. They were on their way to a new life in a new country. Frederick would take up his role as Her Majesty's Land Surveyor and she would settle down to manage his home and take part in whatever society Melbourne had to offer.

Their first home would be gracious once the furniture was unpacked from the hold, and she'd daydreamed all through the long engagement of the time when she could hold soirées and tea parties with the ladies of that region. Her trousseau was carefully packed away in trunks, the dresses and tea gowns folded in linen to protect them from the sea air. What a swathe she and her handsome husband would cut amongst the colonials, for no doubt they were hopelessly out of touch with London fashion.

Her pleasant thoughts were interrupted by a fierce crash that seemed to shudder right through the ship. The *Arcadia* plunged, then lifted her bow, rising higher and higher until it seemed as if they were suspended from the sky itself.

Eva screamed as they were sent slithering up the wall and thudded against what she guessed was the ceiling. Crockery smashed all around them in the darkness. Furniture crashed and splintered and the chandelier shattered in a million pieces as it hit something hard. All excitement for the adventure was swept away in a moment of pure terror.

'Freddy,' she screamed as she clutched his lapels. 'We're going to sink!'

'Hold on to me!' he yelled in her ear. 'Whatever happens, don't let go.'

Eva didn't need telling twice. Frederick was warm and solid and the only anchor she had. She wasn't about to lose her hold on him.

The bow crashed back into the heaving sea and came to a shuddering standstill. A thousand-ton wave towered over the *Arcadia*, now helplessly caught in the jaws of the reef.

2

The captain looked up at it, knowing this was the end. His last thoughts were for the poor souls in steerage and the men in the engine room as the wave released its full force and fell with a giant hammer blow on the helpless ship and broke its back.

Eva screamed. Water was pouring in. The storm plucked at her with icy fingers, trying to rip her away from Frederick into the howling blackness beyond the cabin.

'We've got to get out of here.' Frederick yanked her to her feet. 'We must stay together,' he shouted above the wind. 'Hold on tight and don't let go.'

Eva grasped his hand. She was soaked through and chilled to the very bone for she was still in her dinner gown. She couldn't see, and didn't know which way they were going. She had to have faith in Frederick's sense of direction,

The ship lurched and writhed, grinding ever further into the reef as they stumbled knee deep in water into the passageway. The wild night was full of terror. Passengers fought, clawing and trampling each other in the darkness to reach the boats. The screams mingled with those of the wind giving them a vision of hell.

Eva grabbed Frederick's belt and hung on as he pushed and shoved and fought his way through the chaotic stampede. Her long skirts were hampering her, but to survive was all. The instinctive urge to reach those boats, to get out before the sea claimed the ship and took her down made Eva strong.

She heard children screaming for their mothers. Felt the fanatical clawing of another passenger as he was dashed from the deck by a monstrous wave. She clung on to Frederick, blind with panic, no longer caring who or what she was trampling.

They reached the lifeboat station and Frederick managed to grab Eva and pin her against an iron stanchion just as another wave hit the deck. Eva gasped as the force of it took her breath. It had struck hard. Washing the length of the ship in a fury of spume, it had taken every-one who had reached here before them.

'Come on. Make a run for it.' Frederick tried to wrest her from her hold on the stanchion.

All was blackness, all confusion. Eva had been numbed by the cold, the howling of the wind and the crash of the sea. Blinded by the sting of salt, she was frozen, incapable of moving. She knew only that she was clinging to something solid – something that had saved her from that terrible wave and the blackness that was all consuming.

Frederick pressed his body over hers as another wave battered the dying ship. It tore over them, wresting fingers from their hold, snatching their breath and any courage she might still have had.

3

'Now, Eva,' he yelled. 'Come on.' He tore her fingers from the stanchion and swept her up into his arms just as another wave poured over the bows and smashed in a hatch. Water tumbled into the forward holds. Acting as ballast, the bow momentarily righted itself.

Eva heard the faint sound of a creaking pulley as Frederick stumbled along the deck past the shattered remains of the funnel. A boat was being swung over the side. 'They're going without us,' she yelled. 'Stop them.'

The davits swung. The boat inched away from the tilting deck. If they didn't do something before the next wave hit then they would be lost.

Frederick lunged as the *Arcadia* gave a vast, dying shudder and the lifeboat began to swing outwards – away from the ship.

Eva found herself flung from his arms and flying into the maelstrom. She opened her mouth to scream, but her breath was viciously knocked from her as she landed with a thud in the bottom of the lifeboat. Hands reached for her, helping her up, jamming her between the others who'd made it in time.

She looked up. They were dangling clear of the *Arcadia*. Frederick was still on deck. She could see the outline of him as he leaned against the railings. 'Freddy,' she screamed. 'Jump, jump.'

He couldn't hear her. The words had been ripped away by the wind. Drowned in the angry sea.

She fought off the restraining hands and grabbed the nearest sailor. 'You've got to go back,' she screamed. 'My husband's up there.'

He shook her off as the little boat rocked dangerously on the davits. 'If I don't get this rope unjammed we'll all die,' he shouted into her face. 'Sit down.'

She had no time to berate him for she was sent crashing once more to the bottom of the little boat as it collided against the side of the ship. Hands no longer reached for her. The other survivors were too intent upon clinging to the sides of the boat. In despair she looked back at the *Arcadia*. She was breaking up fast, the rocks and coral ripping great gouges below the waterline as the sea lashed over her tilting decks.

'Freddy,' she moaned. 'Oh my God, Freddy.' Tears mingled with the rain and the sobs were dredged from deep within her as she watched a wall of water race from stem to stern. It swept the remaining passengers away into the night, their screams lost in the wind.

The lifeboat was also in trouble. With ever-increasing force it was being rammed against the side of the *Arcadia*. Soon the bow would be smashed to pieces. It was imperative the umbilical cord was cut from the mother ship.

4

While the seamen struggled to clear the wreckage that had become entangled in the davits, Eva strained to pierce the darkness for sight of Frederick. She could hear the screams of those in the churning water below, and feel the sickening lurch as once again the lifeboat crashed against the *Arcadia*.

But it was too dark. She could see nothing.

With no warning, the stern of the lifeboat plunged several feet towards the water. Eva's screams mingled with the others, but they were cut short when the bow did the same. Like the other survivors, she clung to the side, eyes tightly shut, breath shallow as they swung level.

The boat hovered there for an instant, then plunged with breath-taking suddenness towards the maelstrom below. They landed with a bone-jarring crash and were immediately flung away from the dying ship by a gigantic wave. But the seams of that little boat held and the surviving men pulled hard on the oars to get as much space as possible between them and the stricken *Arcadia*.

Eva moaned in fear and grief. Out there, in the blackest of nights and in the vast, angry seas of this foreign ocean a ship had died, and along with it had gone her husband and every dream they had shared.

Chapter One

Australia 1947

Home. It was an emotive word, conjuring up warmth and love and security. Yet, here she was, at thirty-two, back in a place that had remained only a provocative memory. A memory of eternal sunshine, of childish pleasures – a memory of something dark behind the brightness of the sun – something that only now, after twenty-two years, she was beginning to understand.

Olivia shivered, touched by something far colder than the light breeze coming off the sea. Those long-lost days of childhood had returned full force now she was here, and as she watched the children playing on the beach, she was drawn to one in particular.

The little girl was absorbed in making sandcastles, her fair curls glinting in the sun, her mouth pursed in concentration. It was as if time had stood still in the intervening years and she'd been granted a glimpse of how she had once been. As if she was the child, innocent, unaware of the tangle of secrets and lies that bound her to the people she trusted. And yet Olivia knew that innocence was priceless, for the truth, when it was finally revealed, could shatter everything she had believed in.

What kind of future did that little girl have, she wondered, as the child emptied the small metal pail and resumed digging. What secrets will overshadow her life? She hoped there were none. Hoped she was loved.

Olivia blinked away the tears that threatened and made a concerted effort to remain calm. The years of war had taught her it was pointless to feel sorry for herself. A waste of energy to let the rage surface and take over. She had learned there was little profit in letting the fear of the unknown waver her resolve. Better to use these still moments to garner strength and courage for what lay ahead. For the truth was here in Trinity, and she was determined to find it.

She tucked the handkerchief into her belt and brushed sand from the narrow shantung suit that had been considered the height of fashion in post-war London, but made her feel overdressed amongst the cotton frocks and swimwear of the others on the beach. Her white gloves, handbag and peep-toed high heels were all wrong too, and her smile was wry as she continued to watch the child at play. She hadn't waited to book into the hotel. Had been too impatient to change first before coming here. For this beach, this tiny corner of northern Queensland encompassed all the memories.

Despite the bewildering and painful reason behind this trip, she had gleaned some fun from choosing a new wardrobe. It had almost been a relief to hang up her uniform for a while, to forget the horrors of what she'd seen and all the other responsibilities she'd shouldered as a nursing sister and become a woman again. Even though it meant using all the clothing coupons she'd saved.

With a deep sigh she leaned back on the wooden bench and took in her surroundings. She'd forgotten how much space there was. Forgotten how extraordinary the light after the darkness and chaos of London in the Blitz. Time, for once, seemed to have no meaning, each day following another at a leisurely pace, without the hustle and bustle she'd become so used to in England. It was as if the years of war had never been. As if this corner of the world had merely woken from a long sleep, the nightmares forgotten in the healing warmth of the sunlight the Australians almost took for granted.

As she looked around her, she saw that warmth reflected in the easy way of the people and in their cheerful attitude to life and welcoming smiles. She closed her eyes for a moment and breathed in the scent of pine and eucalyptus that was tinged with sea spray. The magic of this special place had begun to work on her. How quickly she'd forgotten its force.

Olivia's gaze swept over the familiar scenery. It was familiar because her dreams were of this place. Familiar because the memory of it had lived with her, deep in the yearning part of her being ever since she'd had to leave. Now the wonder of this homecoming filled her with such deep emotion she could barely catch her breath. Nothing had changed, she realised. It was as if this special corner of the world had been waiting for just this moment – like a precious gift, it seemed freshly unwrapped and sparkling – and she drank in the sights and sounds and scents she had once thought were forever lost to her.

The beach curved in a crescent of pale yellow sand that was lapped by the milky froth of the warm Pacific. At the furthest reaches of this arc lay sheltering cliffs of black rock that tumbled into the turquoise sea. These rocks were streaked with red, the colour of rust – the colour of the vast outback, which sprawled only a few hundred miles west of this peaceful bay. Pine trees and bright yellow wattle jostled for position along the cliff tops, their roots buried in a thick carpet of pine needles, cones and rich black soil.

Olivia breathed in the fragrance that had been so much a part of her childhood, and as she watched the elegant pelicans glide across the water, she listened to the cries of the curlews and plovers. Home. This was home, regardless of the painful memories, regardless of the secrets she had still to uncover. Her time away had been short in the wider scheme of things, but in truth her spirit had never left. For like the native trees, her roots were buried within this black soil. She prayed only that they were deep enough to withstand the coming storm.

Giles ran a finger around his collar and wished he'd worn something more suitable. His tropical suit was rumpled and travel-stained, the collar too tight on his shirt, the tie strangling him. He pushed back the panama hat and wiped his brow with a handkerchief. The heat reminded him of Italy, and the interminable weeks he'd spent in the POW camp after being shot down. Escape had come at a price and even in these peaceful surroundings he thought he could hear the echoes of gunfire beyond the seabirds' cries.

He tugged his hat forward and smoothed his moustache. He was doing this for Olivia, he reminded himself. It didn't matter if he suffered a little discomfort. She was worth it.

Giles eyed the young woman sitting on the bench by the shore and although she was set apart, not only by her clothing, but by her demeanour, he knew instinctively she was content to be alone. Her thoughts had to be in turmoil, and he felt he understood what coming home had to mean to her. He'd experienced something similar when he'd finally left hospital and returned to Wimbledon, but if he'd been asked to describe the overwhelming emotions of that day he'd have been hard pressed. For they were legion.

He loosened his tie and collar and after a moment's hesitation slipped off his jacket. The empty shirtsleeve would always be a reminder of his war, but he had to learn to come to terms with it. At least he was still alive. Placing the jacket on the ground beneath a pine tree he sat down and leaned against the rough bark. Lighting a cheroot, he watched Olivia through the drift of smoke.

She had been a part of his life for twenty-two years and he could still clearly remember the day she and her mother had arrived in that quiet street in Wimbledon. He closed his eyes and watched again as the crates and cases were carried into the house from the removal van.

8

His eleventh birthday was a week away and he'd been hoping their new neighbours had at least one son young enough to play with. It was lonely being an only child.

Giles opened his eyes, his gaze immediately seeking out Olivia. He smiled at the memory of the sharp pang of disappointment he'd experienced when the little girl had emerged from the taxi. How wrong he'd been to think she couldn't be a friend.

Olivia had intrigued him from the start, for she was different from anyone he'd ever met. Despite being a year younger, she enjoyed the rough and tumble of his boyish games, and positively thrashed him at climbing trees and riding their ponies full tilt across the common. She was brave and energetic, never bursting into tears or telling tales, and would wear the grazes and bumps of their adventures with a bravado he'd admired.

Giles felt the laughter bubble up as the snapshots of memory flashed before him. He'd poked fun at her accent once. He'd never done it again. For he'd soon discovered she could deliver a stinging punch as good as any boy.

He looked across the expanse of sand to the young woman on the shore, and felt the old familiar surge of love. Olivia's rougher edges had been smoothed by the years at a girls' boarding school, and the accent was gone, but there were still flashes of that famous temper, of the little hoyden who'd admitted in a quiet moment to feeling out of place in what the English termed 'society'.

Olivia had come into her own during the war years, if the gossip on the wards were anything to go by. No-one could drive an ambulance quite as fearlessly, or deal with stroppy air-raid wardens and surgeons quite so effectively. Her energy and no-nonsense approach had served her well, and yet her gentler side had come to the fore when caring for the maimed and screaming as they had been disinterred from the burning rubble of the East End and brought into the wards.

Giles watched as she sat deep in thought. Small and slender, the straw hat shadowing her face, there was no hint of the passion he knew was encompassed in that little body – no clue to the experiences she'd had, or the bewilderment she must be suffering over the events of the past few months. The casual observer would notice only the aura of stillness that surrounded her, the neatness of her dress and the deceptive delicacy of her frame. On closer observation perhaps they would note the depth of fire in her dark eyes and the way the chin was held so defiantly – and garner a hint of the strength of will behind the elfin facade. Perhaps get a glimpse of the lustrous black hair she had refused to cut despite fashion and matron's orders and which lay coiled neatly at her nape.

9

He flicked ash from his cheroot and sighed. How many times had he been tempted to unfasten the pins so he could run that curtain of ebony through his fingers? How many times had he wanted to kiss those dark winged brows and sweet mouth, to cup her face in his hand and feel the softness of her skin?

He dipped his head and grinned. Olivia would box his ears for taking such liberties – and quite rightly. For he'd never told her how he felt – had never dared risk the deep friendship they had shared over the years. Now it was too late. What woman, let alone one as beautiful as Olivia, would want him now?

Giles dismissed the fleeting moment of self-pity, recognising it for what it was, but acknowledging the truth behind it. Yet he was all too aware of the spark of hope that would not be extinguished. The hope that one day Olivia would come to love him.

He ran his fingers over the empty sleeve. The ghost of his left arm was still there, still aching, itching, tingling with a life it no longer had, and he supposed he would eventually become used to its absence. In a way, he mused, his missing limb was like his relationship with Olivia. There, but not really in the form and solidity he wished it to be. He'd had to settle for friendship – second best – and forget all the plans he'd made at the beginning of the war for marriage, children, and a home in the country.

He suspected she didn't share his passion, but regarded him with deep affection as the elder brother she'd never had, the closest friend and keeper of her secrets. To speak of love would change things between them; bring an awkwardness that had never been there before, a shifting and withdrawal of their shared intimacies that would ultimately destroy what they prized. So he'd remained silent.

He stubbed out his cheroot, careful to make certain it was well and truly dead before getting to his feet and retrieving his jacket. He was being selfish, he admitted. Thinking only of himself when Olivia was obviously deeply troubled. She had made this journey for a reason – a reason, which unusually, she had so far not shared with him. He had no doubt she would tell him when she was ready, and he must be prepared to put all thoughts of love aside and be her anchor. For he had a nasty feeling they were heading for stormy waters.

Chapter Two

'Wait on a minute, why don't ya?' yelled Maggie Finlay as she struggled through the narrow door into the bar with the crates of beer.

'A bloke could die of thirst,' grumbled the shearer, who was in town for a few days to spend his hard-earned money before moving on to the next sheep station.

'You'll die of something far nastier if you don't stop your whingeing,' Maggie muttered as she stacked the crates beneath the counter and plucked out a bottle. She looked the shearer in the eye. He was a grizzled individual, with leathery skin and bloodshot eyes. 'Money up front, mate. You know the rules.'

He pulled a ten bob note out of his pocket and slammed it on the counter. 'Strewth, Maggie. What's bitin' you today?'

Maggie tucked back the wisps of brown hair that had escaped the bristle of pins she used to keep it neat, and blew out a breath. 'The heat, the flies – having to run this place on me own while Sam goes fishing. So what else is new?'

She left him to his beer, turned back to the shelves behind the bar and began to run a damp cloth over them. Despite living so close to the shore, the outback dust still lay in a red film over everything, and Maggie wondered if she would spend the rest of her life trying to get rid of it. She caught sight of her reflection in the mirrors behind the shelves and sighed. The clean cotton dress was already sticking to her, and there was a smear of dirt where the beer crates had left their mark. Her hair, freshly washed that morning, already looked limp and dull, and there were dark shadows beneath her eyes. She was too skinny – more like a boy than a woman in her thirties, and the lack of decent make-up didn't improve matters either. There seems to be no time to myself any more, she thought crossly. I look a sight.

Yet she liked living in Trinity. It was a nice little town, with enough passing trade to keep things fairly lively. Shearers and drovers came in from the Big Wide to spend their money, and the homesteaders left the awful heat of their remote stations and came to relax at their beachside cottages. All in all, she mused, she was glad she'd come here, even if the reason for the long journey north hadn't quite been fulfilled. At least a part of her curiosity had been satisfied, and knowing what she did, she'd had to acknowledge that some things just weren't meant to be.

I really shouldn't grumble, she thought as she dusted. I have work, a roof over my head and the sea to swim in – to hell with everything else.

She looked in the mirror, gazing past her reflection to the room behind her. The hotel stood on the corner of the main street, which ran directly down to the shore. It was almost a hundred years old and had so far managed to escape fire, flood and the pestilence of white ants, but it needed a coat of fresh paint and some of the windows were webbed with cracks. Painted brown, it had two storeys, both surrounded by wrap-round balconies where the guests could sit in the shade and watch the world go by. The old hitching rails were still embedded along the kerb, but most of the hotel patrons arrived in utes and cars these days.

The bar was similar to any other in Australia, dark and sombre with fly papers hanging from the ceiling and a rickety old fan stirring the hot air in an attempt to cool the patrons down. There were a couple of rough wooden benches set against the walls, but most of their customers preferred to lean against the polished pine bar with their boots resting on the brass railing that ran just above the floor.

Maggie would have liked tables and chairs and vases of flowers about the place. Gingham curtains would have looked nice at the windows, and perhaps a bit of carpet to deaden the noise. Yet she knew this was out of the question. This was a man's world and not even a second world war could alter that. They liked things unchanged, and probably didn't even notice just how run-down and shabby the place was.

Women and their fancy ideas were still relegated to the lounge or the verandah, and after almost a year of working here, Maggie approved. After all, what lady would want to hear a load of blokes swearing and boasting, the volume rising in direct parallel to the amount of beer consumed? Fights broke out regularly – never anything too serious – but it was why the furnishings were kept to a minimum, and women kept out.

Maggie grinned, gave the shelves one more swipe and began to wash the glasses. She knew why she was having a bit of a blue – Sam. Impossible man. Impossible to deny her feelings for him. If only he would notice her – see her as more than a good manager and barmaid – see her as a woman. But she suspected that Sam thought of her as just someone to clean and cook and take care of his business. A companion at the meal table, someone to chat to when the bar was closed and they could rest for an hour before retiring to their separate rooms.

Samuel White was the owner of the Trinity Hotel. A war hero who'd returned from Europe to find his wife and son had perished in a bush fire. He had turned away from life in the outback and had invested in this place. At forty-two he was ten years older than Maggie, but still had the energy of a man half his age. Tall, lean and tanned by the sun, his dark hair was winged with grey. He wasn't handsome in the ordinary way, not until he smiled. Then his face lit up and warmth struck the startling blue of his eyes and emphasised the blackness of his lashes. Maggie was in love with him, God help her, and she would often lie awake at night and wonder what it would be like to share his bed.

'Any danger of another jar?'

The shearer's voice broke into her thoughts and she thankfully pulled another bottle from the crate and opened it. There was no point in wishing things were different between her and Sam, and thoughts like that were doing her no good at all.

The bar was slowly filling and the noise level was rising as an argument broke out on the possible winner of the Melbourne Cup which was due to be run in a week's time. Maggie was sweating profusely as she served drinks, mopped up spills and tried to keep the peace between the warring factions. Her feet were hurting and her back ached, and there was still no sign of Sam. Love him or not, Maggie would give him a piece of her mind when he did show his face.

She was bent double, wrestling with a heavy barrel that needed to be attached to the pump and didn't notice the drop in the noise. 'Can one of you blokes get round here and help me with this flaming thing?' she yelled. 'Stuck tighter than a cork up a goanna's arse.'

The silence that greeted this plea for help was so unusual she left the barrel and straightened her back. Maggie was met by a sight and sound she'd never before experienced. The silence was so profound she could hear the cricket chirruping in the drainpipe, and the wall of backs pressed against the bar made it impossible to see what had brought about this phenomenon.

As she stood on tiptoe and tried to see what was going on, the wall in front of her parted like the Red Sea. The silent men shuffled back, their glasses held tightly against their chests, their eyes wide in suspicion and horror.

13

The woman stepped into the bar and let the door swing behind her. She seemed unfazed by the reaction of her audience and actually smiled and nodded to a couple of the younger men who'd apparently forgotten how to shut their gaping mouths.

Maggie reddened, aware of how she must look to this cool, elegant woman in the beautiful suit and white shoes. Aware of the coarse language she'd used only moments ago, that had surely been overheard. She ran a hand over her hair, tucked back a few stray wisps and attempted to smooth the lapels of her cotton dress. The lady had courage, whoever she was. But she wasn't a local, that was for sure, for no respectable Australian woman would be seen dead in here unless she was working behind the bar.

'What can I do you for, luv?' she asked. 'Ladies' lounge is out back, or you can sit on the verandah and I'll bring you something.'

All eyes followed the woman as she approached the bar and placed her handbag on the counter. They began to mutter as she pulled off the gloves and dabbed her top lip with a pristine handkerchief. 'I was wondering if you have a room?'

A Pom, realised Maggie. No wonder she could waltz in here like that. 'Come with me and I'll see you right,' she said hastily.

'I'd like a drink first,' said the woman who seemed determined to remain on the other side of the bar. 'A cold beer would be just the ticket.'

The muttering grew and Maggie could distinctly hear the comments now being bandied about. 'I'll get you a drink in the ladies' lounge,' she said with a firmness that belied the laughter bubbling up inside her. Whoever this woman was, she was one tough sheila, because she had to be aware of the stir she'd caused. Good on her. About time this place was shook up a little.

Maggie flipped back the panel in the bar and almost pulled her towards the side door. 'In here, luv. Before you put my customers off their beer.'

They entered the cool parlour, the light dimmed by the closed shutters, and turned to face one another. Of similar height, Maggie found she was staring into a pair of wide brown eyes that were several shades darker than her own. 'Sorry about that,' she said. 'But the blokes can be a bit crook when a woman comes into the bar. Makes 'em nervous.'

'Why ever should they be nervous of me?' The tone was soft, the vowels rounded. 'I often go into the pub in England.'

'It's different here, luv. You'll learn.' Maggie grabbed the visitor's book. She was feeling uneasy, gauche, all too aware of her grubby clothes and reddened hands. This woman had an unsettling effect on

14

her, and she could only think it was the stillness of her, the complete confidence in the way she did everything. 'One night, was it?'

The handbag was placed on a side table, the gloves alongside it. The hat was removed and the black hair smoothed back from the flawless face. 'We seem to have got off on the wrong foot. I'm sorry if I've caused trouble.' A slender hand was thrust forward. 'The name's Olivia Hamilton.'

Maggie shook her hand, noting the polished nails, and the absence of a wedding ring. 'Maggie Finlay. Manager and general dogsbody of this place,' she said with a nervous laugh. 'It ain't much, but it's home and the sheets are clean.'

Olivia's smile seemed genuine. 'Then we shall look forward to staying here,' she said softly. She must have noticed Maggie's look of surprise. 'I'm travelling with a friend,' she explained. 'We'll need separate rooms of course, and I don't really know how long we'll be here.'

Maggie hid her knowing smile as she watched Olivia fill in the reservation docket. Separate rooms or not, she'd been in this business long enough to know 'friends' often shared a bed. It would be interesting to see what kind of man this cool, composed Olivia favoured. And even more interesting to discover just what the hell she was doing so far off the tourist track.

'Maggie said you'd be in here,' said Giles as he came into the upstairs parlour that connected their bedrooms. 'I hear you caused quite a stir. They're all talking about you.'

'At least they're leaving some other poor bugger alone,' she murmured before taking a sip of the ice cold beer Maggie had brought up earlier.

Olivia noticed he'd changed into light slacks and a fresh shirt. He was a handsome man, with his light brown hair, hazel eyes and trim moustache, but she could see he was tired. The darkness under his eyes told of sleepless nights, and possibly some pain despite the medication. Yet Giles had never complained, and seemed to be slowly coming to terms with the amputation.

She smiled and sank further into the softness of the armchair. She too had washed and changed, and had even snatched a half hour of sleep while Giles had a drink in the bar. Her loose-fitting cotton dress and sandals were far more comfortable than that silly suit, and she didn't feel quite so out of place. Yet she was exhausted. It had been a long journey from Sydney to Trinity and she still couldn't quite believe she was here. She took another sip of the beer and sighed in satisfaction. 'Makes a change from the warm brew back home.'

15

Giles placed his glass on a nearby table and sat down. 'So,' he began, as he often did. 'Has the old place changed much?'

She shook her head. 'Not really. There are more cars about of course, and the road has been covered in bitumen, but on the whole it's just the same.' She took in her surroundings. The dusty aspidistra in the corner, the worn sofas and chairs, the scratched tables and dull paint were all so familiar. As was the squeaking fan on the ceiling, the dusty French doors leading out to the verandah, and the dangling fly-papers covered in black bodies. 'In fact, if I didn't know this was a hotel, I could have sworn it was the old house. We had a flowerpot just like that one in the corner.'

She saw Giles was restless and knew, before he spoke, what he was going to say. Yet she needed to absorb everything that had happened today. Her senses were filled with the sights and sounds she'd thought she'd never experience again. Her mind almost overloaded by the enormity of what she was doing.

'Are you going to tell me why we've had to come to the other side of the world?'

Olivia silently admitted she hadn't been fair to him. Dear Giles. What would she have done without him these past months? He was such a brick, and she'd been taking his warmth and kind heart almost for granted. 'Did Mother ever tell you the story of how she came here?'

Giles shook his head. 'Eva was a mystery to me, Olivia. Actually, I don't think she liked me very much. Never really talked.'

Olivia nodded. 'She could be like that,' she admitted. 'But I think it was shyness on her part, rather than anything else.'

Giles snorted. 'I'd have said Eva was the least shy person I've met. Despite her lack of height and her tiny frame, she had a glare that still made me quail long after I was out of short trousers. Afternoon teas at your house were positive purgatory.'

Olivia laughed. 'Yes, they were a bit much.' Mother liked to do things properly. Afternoon tea was served promptly at four, with cucumber sandwiches, scones and cake. No crusts on the sandwiches of course, and lemon in the tea. Milky tea was regarded as common.

Giles grimaced. 'It was dreadful trying to balance plate and cup and saucer and carry on polite conversation. I never did get the hang of it.'

Olivia laughed and had a fleeting remembrance of Giles as a young man, sitting awkwardly on the edge of the couch, cup and saucer in one hand, plate piled high with sandwiches in the other, napkin on his knee. He'd rarely managed to eat much despite Mother's urging.

16

'Mother's Victorian upbringing was deeply ingrained, unfortunately, and I think that was her main problem. She often said she never felt she fitted in over here. There was no class system, you see, nothing tangible she could hold on to. And when she finally went back to England she found so many things had changed she was at a loss as to how to deal with them.' Olivia sighed. 'Bless her heart. I do miss her, you know.'

'Of course you do,' he said softly. 'It can't have been easy to watch her die. I don't know how you did it.'

Olivia looked out of the window and saw how the sky was now darkening, streaked with purple and red. The sunset was going to be spectacular and she wished she could escape this room and the memories and return to the beach. Yet, she had come so far, now was not the time to back off and wish things were different.

'Years of nursing gives you a tough shell. But nothing prepares you for the death of a loved one.' Her voice broke and she blinked. She could remember Eva from those early years. She'd been full of life and nothing had seemed to get her down. Yet, Eva had never been a tactile mother. Never one to suddenly sweep her up in a hug and rain kisses on her. There had been many times when Olivia had yearned for her to break from the stilted constraints within which she was imprisoned and show some emotion. It had taken a long while to understand it didn't need kisses and hugs to prove she was loved.

'In the end it was a release for both of us. She had so much pain, and hated being helpless.'

'Quite so,' murmured Giles. He paused for a moment and fingered his moustache. 'I admired her in a way, even though she terrified me. She always seemed so strong, so in control. That's why I was surprised she packed you off to boarding school. One would have thought she'd have appreciated your company. Being alone, as she was.'

Olivia grimaced. 'Ghastly place. Still, Mother thought she was doing what was right. I needed educating, refining and to be taught to behave like a young lady, not a tomboy. They did that for me alright.' She gave a wry smile. 'But I can't pretend I wasn't lonely, and if it hadn't been for Priscilla, I don't know if I'd have lasted.'

'Ah, yes. Priscilla.' Giles smiled, the teasing sparkle in his eyes not lost on her. 'Still around, is she?'

Olivia laughed. 'Only now and then. We've grown up and don't need one another quite so much any more.' She cleared her throat and took another sip of the beer. She felt calmer, ready to begin this frightening journey into the unknown. It was time to tell him something of the history behind this extraordinary journey.

17

'When Mother died last year I had to deal with all the bumph that goes with winding up the estate and so on. I was clearing out her bureau when the drawer became jammed.' She grinned at him. 'You know how impatient I am. Can't bear being thwarted. I stuck a screwdriver under it and practically ripped it out. Damaged the drawer, of course, but once I'd seen what was hidden behind it, it no longer seemed to matter.'

Giles sat forward in his chair, the empty shirtsleeve dangling. 'Always loved a good mystery,' he enthused. 'What did you find?'

Olivia smiled despite the turmoil of her thoughts and the images that were haunting her. There was still so much of the boy in Giles, despite the horrors he'd been through. Yet how to describe the appalled shock she'd experienced when she realised what she had found. She could see herself now, sitting in the middle of the floor, the broken drawer upended beside her, the tears rolling down her face unheeded as the grandfather clock chimed one hour and then another. Her world had been turned upside down. She hadn't known what to believe.

Olivia emerged from her dark thoughts and realised Giles was still waiting for a reply. Yet she didn't want to spoil this first day home by recounting those terrible hours. Better to start right back at the beginning. That part of the past didn't have the power to hurt her, so it was safe. 'I'll tell you soon enough,' she murmured. 'You'll have to be patient with me,' she pleaded. 'This isn't going to be easy for either of us.'

Giles frowned as he leaned back in his chair, his hazel eyes searching her face for some sign of what was troubling her. But Olivia was determined not to be rushed. She wasn't yet ready to voice her true concerns, and if he was to understand why they were here, then she had to put things in order. She and Giles had always been close – he would understand eventually.

She made a concerted effort to relax. Her quest for the truth had begun, and like Eva Hamilton all those years ago, she had no idea where this journey would take her.

Chapter Three

Olivia was exhausted. The retelling of Eva's story was too much after such a long journey. She looked at her watch. 'Time for dinner,' she said. 'Come on, Giles. I'm starving.'

Giles looked at her in horror. 'You can't leave it there,' he protested. 'What happened to Eva? Was Frederick drowned?'

'You'll find out soon enough,' she said through a yawn.

Giles hauled himself out of the chair. 'You're being unfair,' he grumbled. When he got no response he gathered up his cigars and lighter and stuffed them in his pocket. 'I don't suppose I'm expected to wear a tie and jacket, am I?' he asked with an edge of impatience.

'Shouldn't think so. It's hardly the Ritz.' She tucked the empty sleeve into the belt around his trousers. 'Do come on, I'm famished.'

His irritation with her vanished. 'Yes, Matron,' he teased. He earned a soft cuff on the chin as a reminder not to push her too far, then she linked her arm with his and they went downstairs.

'Tea's ready,' shouted Maggie as she hurried past the bottom of the stairs with overloaded plates. 'Follow me.'

Like the rest of the hotel, the dining room had seen better days. But the floor shone with polish and the tables glimmered in snowy cloths. The last of the sunset was streaming through the lead-light panes at the tops of the windows, painting a golden glow over the diners. Shabby it might be, but it was obviously popular.

Olivia and Giles took their seats at a table laid for two, fully aware of the curious stares and the drop in the noise level at their arrival. Olivia smiled and nodded in acknowledgement of the muttered 'g'days'. She realised immediately they were objects of curiosity, but managed to keep any exchanges polite and fairly uninformative. She didn't want everyone knowing her business, and old habits died hard. She'd been in England too long to relinquish information at the drop of a hat.

19

'Here you go.' Maggie placed two heaped plates of food in front of them. 'That'll put colour in your cheeks and no mistake,' she said with a grin at Giles.

Olivia smiled silent thanks, and was rewarded with a nonchalant shrug before Maggie moved on to the next table. Without being asked, Maggie had cut the meat into manageable portions for Giles, and Olivia was warmed by this thoughtful gesture. Then she looked down in horror at the meal before her. Four, no five lamb chops, a piece of steak, a mound of potato and a fried egg, all liberally covered in a thick onion gravy. Two thick slices of bread and butter were balanced on the side of the plate. 'How on earth am I supposed to eat all this?' she whispered to Giles.

He winked. 'You said you were starving. Prove it.' He loaded his fork and began to chew. 'It's very good. Nice to have decent meat again.'

Olivia sighed. It was still hot despite the sun casting the last of its light and the darkness fast approaching. Her appetite had been curtailed by rationing, and combined with the weariness and the awful heat, she doubted she'd make much headway with this gargantuan feast. But the smell of mint sauce and onions was tempting. She tucked in and was amazed that she managed to eat at least half of it. Giles was right. There was obviously no rationing here, and it had been a joy to eat a lamb chop again.

She finally pushed the plate away and sat back in her chair, her stomach pleasantly full. As she waited for Giles to finish she took the opportunity to survey the other diners. They were all male, some of them obviously rather more wealthy than others, and she guessed these were the graziers – the nobility of the outback. These men didn't share tables with the drovers and ringers and shearers, but they talked across as if there were no class barriers and seemed totally at ease with themselves and each other.

What a strange place Australia is, she thought. No wonder Mother found it puzzling, for there seemed to be none of the strict codes of English society. Yet she found that cheerful informality heartening, and acknowledged that things had begun to change in England too. It had taken a war to do that – perhaps now they could all move on.

She looked up as Maggie fetched the dirty plates and replaced them with bowls of steaming sponge pudding and custard. 'I shall get very fat if I eat this much every day,' she said with a smile.

'Don't reckon you will,' replied Maggie as she put the plates on a tray. Her gaze swept over Olivia and she grinned. 'You're like me. Born skinny.'

Olivia digested this bit of wisdom and wasn't quite sure how to take it. Years of rationing and hard work had made her thin – it was nothing to do with being born that way. 'I really haven't room for this,' she said as she handed back the pudding.

'Give it to Giles. He could do with fattening up after what he's been through.'

Olivia saw Giles redden and guessed he and Maggie must have had a long talk while he drank in the bar. 'Are you the only one working here?' she asked as Maggie polished a spoon and placed it carefully next to Giles' right hand.

Maggie tossed her head. 'There's Lila and her daughter in the kitchen and someone comes in the mornings to clean the place and to help in the bar at weekends. Sam is supposed to be here – he's the owner – but he's gone walkabout as usual.' Her brown eyes flashed gold in the reflected light of the lamps she'd lit earlier. 'I'll have his guts for garters when he does show,' she threatened. 'He knows Saturday nights are busy.'

Olivia drank a cup of tea and watched Giles plough his way through most of the two puddings. She laughed softly when he finally leaned back and wiped his mouth on the napkin. 'I'll be surprised if you can move after eating that lot,' she teased. 'But it's good to see you've got your appetite back.'

'Comfort food,' he replied with a smile of satisfaction. 'Reminds me of boarding school and the officers' mess.' He patted his stomach and lit a cheroot. 'Now that's what I call a proper dinner.'

Olivia grinned and as Giles began a long involved conversation with a nearby grazier, she watched Maggie stride in and out with trays of plates and cups and saucers. Her expression was stormy, her mouth set. There was obviously still no sign of the errant Sam, and Olivia was beginning to feel rather sorry for this anonymous individual. Maggie was obviously not someone to cross.

Giles had been asked to join the other men for a drink, but he wasn't really in the mood and Olivia could tell that all the travelling was beginning to tell on him. They finally took their leave and decided to take a stroll down to the beach. They needed the exercise after such a meal, or it would be impossible to sleep.

Olivia breathed in the soft scent of night flowers, and the crisp salty tang of the sea. It was so still, so silent, the road so empty. She linked her arm through his, enjoying the peace and the light breeze coming off the sea. Enjoying the familiar companionship.

The beach was bathed in moonlight, the water sparkling beneath a black sky strewn with stars. Olivia kicked off her sandals, peeled down her stockings and wriggled her toes in the sand. It was still warm from the sun. She lifted the hem of her skirt and waded into the velvet coolness of the water.

21

After struggling with his shoes and socks, Giles joined her. They stood ankle deep in that balmy water, gazing in awe at the enormous sky. The Milky Way splashed a majestic white cloud of a million pinpoints of light that seemed to have no beginning and no end. The Southern Cross and Orion twinkled coldly and clearly against the backdrop of endless darkness, and the moon was a perfect silver sixpence reflected in the ripples on the water.

Olivia once again felt the calming influence of this place that had once been home. As a child she'd never been permitted to stay out after dark, but she'd sat for hours at her bedroom window watching the heavenly display. The stars were old friends – and like old friends they seemed to be welcoming her back.

Sam rubbed the mare down, made sure she had enough feed and water and quietly bolted the stable door. Gathering his fishing tackle and catch, he turned to look at the lights blazing from the hotel and grimaced. It was late, much later than he'd thought, and he would no doubt catch an earful from Maggie.

'It's my bloody hotel,' he muttered. 'I can come and go as I please.'

Yet he knew it was only bravado. He felt bad about letting Maggie cope alone and wished he had a proper excuse for his lateness. But the truth was he'd forgotten the time. Had sat there by his favourite fishing pool up in the tablelands and dreamed away the day, relishing the solitude and the peace the rainforest always brought to his soul.

He was getting old, he thought as he decided to roll one last smoke before facing Maggie. What had happened to the tough grazier who'd fought fire, flood, drought and bullets? He'd become a dreamer, that's what. An old bludger trying to make sense of a changing world that had moved too fast for him. He grimaced. Without Stella and the boy none of it mattered anyhow.

His hands cupped the match as it flared in the darkness. This simple action still had the power to chill him, for it was a reminder of the war – a reminder of sniper fire fixed by the gleam of a carelessly guarded third strike of a match. A reminder that one single spark had the power to wipe out everything he'd known and loved.

The images of that burned-out shell when he'd returned home to Leanora Station after the war still lived with him. He could still see the simple gravestones in the little cemetery. They had already looked abandoned and were terrible reminders of nature's power. A man could fight all his life against that power, but it always won in the end. It had been a harsh lesson.

With a sigh he stuffed the dead match back in the box and eased his shoulder against the rough wood of the stable wall. The will to fight had been knocked out of him then. He'd had to accept that resilience was for younger men. They had the strength for it – the hunger to keep going. His war was over in every sense, and now here he was, the owner of a shabby hotel in the far northern reaches of Queensland.

Sam pushed the gloomy thoughts away and watched Maggie through the lighted window. She was moving swiftly as always, mouth going nineteen to the dozen as she talked to the lubras in the kitchen. He grinned. She was a dinkum sheila and no mistake. Skinny as a rake, but not bad looking when scrubbed up for a special occasion, Maggie had proved she was the perfect choice to run his establishment. But he'd guessed a while back that poor old Maggie had had it rough all her bloody life, and admitted he wasn't exactly helping matters by staying out late and leaving her to cope on her own on a Saturday night.

He finished his smoke and ground it beneath his boot heel. His absence hadn't been totally selfish, he acknowledged, for it was in Maggie's interest that he kept his distance. He'd noticed how she looked at him and had understood what it meant. He'd been flattered that someone so much younger should find him attractive – though why this should be confounded him.

Not that he hadn't been tempted, he thought with a grin. Maggie had fire in her and he'd always admired that in a woman. Yet his instinct told him Maggie wasn't the sort to accept a fling and then forget about it. They lived in the same hotel, in a tiny town where gossip was rife and everyone knew your business and he was reluctant to enter into any kind of relationship that might cause complications.

Sam picked up his tackle and catch and loped towards the back door. If he was lucky Maggie would remain occupied in the kitchen and wouldn't hear him come in. He reached for the latch, but the door was snatched open.

'Where the hell have you been?' she snapped, arms akimbo, feet planted squarely in his path.

Sam stood in the stream of light pouring out through the open door, his fishing gear dangling from his hands. He scuffed the dirt with his boot, his face hidden by the brim of his hat. 'Forgot the bloody time.' He looked back at her and grinned, hoping this would better her mood. 'Sorry, Maggie.'

She laid the flat of her hand on his chest and pushed him back out into the darkness. Slamming the door behind her, she faced him. 'Sorry ain't good enough, Sam,' she snapped. 'I've been on me own since six this morning. The bar's heaving and we've got eight rooms rented out.'

23

He felt the embarrassment heat his face as he tried to avoid her accusing glare. 'Fair go, Mags,' he drawled. 'I got a nice bit of fish for tea.' He held up the catch, his smile winsome.

'I'd like to tell you where to shove it,' she said angrily. 'But I'm too much of a lady.'

Sam knew he shouldn't grin, but just couldn't help it. Maggie was so comical when she was angry.

'Don't you bloody dare,' she hissed, her index finger inches from his nose. 'This isn't funny, Sam. I've been on me feet all day, and I've had enough.' She threw the tea towel at his face and stormed into the enveloping darkness. 'I'm taking tomorrow off,' she said over her shoulder. 'And might very well not come back. So put that on your line and go fishing.'

Sam bit his lip and tried not to laugh. He turned away and pushed through the door into the light of the passageway. She'd be back. She always came back. Yet, as he deposited the fish in the kitchen and left for the bar, he had a sneaking suspicion he'd pushed her too far this time. One of these days she'd carry out her threat, and the thought of running this place without her wiped the smile from his face. However would he cope?

'Looks like the workers are revolting,' murmured Giles as they heard the last of this exchange and watched Maggie storm into the night.

'Good for her,' replied Olivia. 'She's entitled to let off steam.'

They made their way up the broad staircase with the shabby red carpet and crossed the square landing to their adjoining rooms. 'Nightcap?'

Olivia nodded. 'I'm absolutely whacked, but my mind is still on full alert. Perhaps a brandy will help me sleep.'

Giles poured them both a hefty slug from the bottle he'd bought earlier and they sat in companionable silence listening to the squeak of the ceiling fan and the soft thud of insects hitting the screens over the window.

Olivia relaxed into the soft comfort of the faded armchair and closed her eyes. The sounds and scents of her childhood were returning, their persuasive allure drawing her ever closer to the reason behind this homecoming. She would soon have to face the consequences of this journey, of the events that had been out of her control and beyond her understanding when she'd been a child. The images of those early years were vivid, and she frowned as she remembered that not all of those days had been filled with sunlight – but rather with fear.

'What are you thinking about? You look very solemn.'

24

She opened her eyes and gave him a wan smile. 'Ghosts,' she replied.

He lifted a brow as he fumbled with the top button of his shirt. It was still warm, despite the lateness of the hour. 'Sounds ominous.'

Olivia looked away, her gaze finally settling on the doors leading to the verandah. She could just make out the glow of the moon through the screens, and she was once again the little girl at the window, watching the stars, listening to the terrible arguments that went on in the other room. 'Why do we only remember the sunny days?' she murmured. 'Why do we never remember the rain, the clouds, the wind that cut like a knife?'

'Because we don't want to,' he replied gruffly. He shifted in the chair. 'Talk to me, Olivia. Tell me what's really worrying you.'

She plastered on a smile she knew wouldn't fool him, but helped her to overcome the dark thoughts. 'Later,' she said. 'I haven't finished telling you about Mother's awful introduction to her new life in Australia.'

He cocked his head, his gaze thoughtful. 'You're tired, and obviously troubled. Perhaps we should leave it until tomorrow?'

She shook her head. 'I won't be able to sleep. Mind's too active.' She took a drink of the brandy and her good mood was partially restored. 'Besides,' she added, 'there are things I have to do tomorrow, and there might not be time for story-telling.' She saw the curiosity gleam in his hazel eyes and laughed. 'One thing at a time,' she teased. 'You'll know as much as I do soon enough.'

Eva sat shivering and crying in the bottom of the little boat as the storm raged and the men struggled to wield the great wooden oars and keep them afloat. Eva thought their labours in vain, for how could mere mortals keep them from drowning in such a ferocious sea? How could any of them survive this terrible night?

For the first time since leaving England she was sick. So sick the spasms eventually exhausted her and she slumped in the icy embrace of the water that sloshed around her in the bottom of the boat. The cold had robbed her of the spark of will that had seen her defy her parents and marry Frederick. Had robbed her of the thirst for adventure that had brought her across the world. She'd had enough and no longer cared what happened to her. If Freddy was gone, then she was prepared to go with him. Her eyelids were heavy as her head drooped and the water seeped into her nose and mouth.

'Come on, ducky. No sense in drowning before you have to.'

Eva heard the woman's rough, cockney voice and was only vaguely aware of the strong hands gripping her beneath her arms, tearing the fabric of her dinner gown. Only vaguely aware she was being hauled along the bottom of the boat and manhandled until she was sitting propped up between what felt like two stout legs. She tried to open her eyes to see who was misusing her so roughly, but the lids seemed glued together by the salt and the wind. 'Cold,' she shivered. 'So cold.'

'I know, darlin', we're all cold.'

The boat lurched and rolled and the stinging salt lashed her face as the strong arms enfolded her and held her close. Eva could smell the wet wool of the woman's dress and the strange musty scent of her skin. She felt a vague resentment for this stranger and her almost insolent familiarity, but was too ill and downhearted to protest. Her neck bowed and she rested her head against the protective arm. Her last thoughts before she fainted were of Freddy and that terrible wave that had swept him away.

Eva came round sometime later, startled to find herself still in the bottom of the boat, still within the woman's embrace. There had been no let-up in the storm. The waves were thunderous, the rain and spume sharp needles that battered her exposed face as she looked around. The men were still bent over the creaking oars, pulling in ragged unison, their faces contorted with pain and fear. The other survivors huddled in groups, heads bowed against the lashing sea and driving wind.

As she watched, one of the seamen collapsed over the oar and it was only the swift reaction of one of the other men that saved the oar from being lost overboard. With an unceremonious shove, the passenger took the seaman's place. 'If you can row, then give these men a rest,' he yelled into the wind. 'If you can't then start bailing out.'

The weary seaman stumbled over them to reach the locker in the bow. He fell as a giant wave crashed against the stern, landing heavily at Eva's feet. She reached across and helped him up before taking her place at the oars. The survival instinct had returned more forcefully than ever. She had survived this far – she wasn't about to give in.

The seaman passed down two buckets and a collection of tin mugs which were stored in the locker. The remaining survivors grabbed the mugs and began to scoop. It was a miracle they were still afloat, for there was at least a foot of water in the bottom.

Dawn eventually arrived. It was as grey and cheerless as the sea beneath it. Yet the storm appeared to have blown itself out, for the waves, although towering, no longer fought for supremacy. They rolled like muscular leviathans, each following the one before with only the occasional ruffle of wind to stir a creamy crest.

Eva was resting after her stint at the oars. She sat back on her heels and watched the sky lighten. Her back was aching, her lips were dry and salt-encrusted, but the spark of life still burned brightly within. She had kept faith they would survive the night – and they had. Now she had to believe they would soon see land and find other survivors.

She turned to the cockney woman who'd been so kind to her and was shocked by the great weariness in her faded blue eyes – at the lines etched so deeply into her youthful face. Jessie had also taken her turn at the oar and had remained there for hours. Had insisted she could pull as strong as any man after her years of working in a rope factory. Now she was slumped on the floor of the boat, all energy gone, all spark extinguished.

'We're safe, Jessie,' murmured Eva as she gathered the damp shawl around the other woman's plump shoulders. 'The storm's over.'

'And the ship?' Jessie's voice was a rasp between cracked lips. None of them had had a drink for hours.

Eva looked out at the swell of the ocean, hoping that at each rise of the boat she would spot some sign of life, of land. But there was nothing. She turned back to Jessie and after a momentary hesitation, put her arm around her shoulders. 'Gone, my dear,' she said, her voice breaking with emotion.

'What about the others? Any sign of other boats?'

Eva shook her head. If there had been other boats they could easily have missed them in such titanic seas. It didn't need words to convey the tragedy of it all, and the two women sat together in the bottom of the boat deep within their own thoughts, their gaze trawling the endless, heaving ocean for some sight of humanity or redemption.

The watery sun was ebbing fast and as the boat rose on a swell a cry went up. 'Land! I see land!'

With hope restored, Eva and Jessie struggled to their knees in the bottom of the boat and tried to catch sight of this miracle. 'There,' shouted Jessie with excitement as she pointed a grimy finger towards the setting sun.

Eva peered into the brightness, her hand shielding her eyes. She saw only the golden glow of a tropical sunset. Saw only the endless sweep of an empty ocean. Then, as she watched, she realised she'd been mistaken. It wasn't a sunset at all, but a vast hill of yellow sand that seemed to stretch along the horizon. She turned to Jessie and they fell into one another's arms, the tears warm on their faces, the relief immense – all barriers of class and status forgotten momentarily in that one instant of euphoria.

The men pulled even harder on the oars. They were close to

exhaustion, their shirts darkened with sweat, their hands ruined by the unaccustomed labour. Yet the sight of land seemed to have given them a burst of energy and they bent their backs willingly.

It was dark when the boat finally ground into the sand with a bump. A full moon lit their way as they stumbled through the few inches of water and collapsed on the beach. Eva found a rock and sat down. She stared up at the sky in awe. Never before had she seen such stars. It was as if the heavens were putting on a show to celebrate her survival.

The tears came again, hot and heavy, rolling down her face. She was alone. Freddy would never see the stars again. Would never hold her again and call her his precious girl.

'No time for all that,' said the seaman gruffly. 'Pull yourself together and start collecting wood. We need a fire and shelter.'

Eva's famous temper flared. This particular man had insulted her before, yelling orders, pushing her aside as he organised the other passengers in the little boat. 'How dare you talk to me like that, you dreadful man,' she spat. 'I am not your servant.'

He grabbed her arm and pulled her from the rock. 'On yer feet,' he growled.

Eva was about to protest when he swung her round and made her take in their surroundings. 'There ain't nothing here but sand. We need water and warmth and somewhere to sleep, 'cos tomorrow we gotta start walking.'

Eva wrestled her arm free and looked up into his grizzled face. He was the most loathsome creature she'd ever encountered and smelled simply appalling. 'Walk? Why should we walk?' she demanded. 'Someone must know we're here.'

'We've been blown miles off course,' he snapped. 'No one will think of looking this far south and walking is the only way outta here.' He pushed her from him and walked away.

With gathering horror, Eva finally realised what he meant as she slowly turned and took in their landing place. The beach stretched for miles in either direction. Littered with jagged black rocks, it was otherwise naked of any other feature. Dunes glimmered in ghostly grandeur behind her, the frail vegetation clinging to their sides, drooping towards the sea. There were no buildings, no friendly light-house out by the rocks, no signs of civilisation at all.

She turned to Jessie, who'd come to stand beside her. 'We had better do as he said,' she muttered. 'We're going to die of pneumonia if we don't get these clothes dry.'

The night passed quickly for the fifteen survivors were all exhausted and soon fell asleep in the warmth of the enormous fire they had built above the tide mark. Eva woke to find the heat was now

28

coming from the sun. It struck her like a furnace, burning her face and exposed shoulders. She ran her tongue over her dry lips, wishing she could have another drink from the evil-tasting canvas water bag one of the sailors had brought ashore. But there had been enough only for each of them to take a sip. Now it was empty.

She looked longingly at the sea. Surely it wouldn't hurt to take a little drink of that? It might be salty, but at least it would slake this awful thirst. She gathered up her skirts and waded in. As she cupped the water and bent to drink, her hands were roughly slapped apart.

'Don't drink that!'

Eva whirled to face him and almost lost her balance in the water. It was that obnoxious sailor again. 'I'm thirsty,' she rasped.

He grabbed her wrist and hauled her, struggling, out of the water. He released her only when they had advanced up the beach to the others, who were still huddled around the fire despite the sun's heat. 'If you drink the seawater you'll be mad before the sun sets.'

'Don't be ridiculous,' snorted Eva.

He turned and faced her, his expression having lost the earlier belligerence. 'I beg your pardon, lady, for treatin' you kinda rough, like. But I seen it 'appen and it ain't a pretty sight.' He grimaced. 'Screamin' and hollerin', frothing at the mouth. Death's slow. But inevitable. Better to be thirsty.'

Eva's temper deflated and she looked around at the other seamen who were nodding their agreement. She returned her attention to him. 'But I'm so terribly thirsty,' she said with a plaintive cry.

'It'll get worse,' he mumbled. 'Better get moving while the sun's still low.'

Eva eyed the other survivors. Out of the fifteen there were six sailors, five women and four men. She recognised none of them and surmised the other passengers must have come from the lower decks, possibly even steerage. Realising she needed to lead by example, she picked up her salt-stained skirts and began to tramp after the seaman. The sooner they climbed the dunes, the sooner they would find water and civilisation.

The sun beat down mercilessly as they slithered and sweated up the ever-shifting dune that seemed determined to keep them on the shore. Seabirds wailed overhead in mournful accompaniment to the moans of exhaustion as they struggled onwards towards what they all hoped was deliverance.

Eva tore a strip from her petticoat and covered her head as she and Jessie scrambled on their hands and knees from one tenuous purchase to another. Despite the makeshift veil, Eva felt the sun burning her exposed shoulders. Felt it hammering on her skull, bringing an almost blinding headache to thud behind her eyes. Yet she knew the sailor had been right. For when she looked behind her the sea was empty. There would be no rescue. Their survival was in their own hands.

One by one they reached the summit. Hands reached down to help those lagging behind, and once they'd caught their breath they dared to look around them.

The land stretched to every horizon. Blood-red, hostile and silent, it shimmered beneath the vast sky. Pale grass formed a shifting, endless sea against the alien earth, the few trees bent in arthritic torture from their exposure to the wind. And high above them soared the dark, circling presence of great birds of prey.

The little group was silent as Eva fell to her knees and stared around her. She didn't know what she'd been expecting. But it wasn't this awful desolation. In a daze of pain and despair, she watched the seaman stride out. Watched him carefully pluck the thick leaf from a spiny bush and put it to his mouth. Watched his throat as he swallowed. 'Water,' she rasped. 'He's found water.'

They gathered around him and followed his lead. The water was brackish, but Eva thought she'd never tasted anything as wonderful. 'How did you know it was here?' she asked in awe.

'Native trick,' he replied shortly. 'Seen 'em do it many a time when I were here afore.'

'You've been here before?' Eva carefully licked the final few drops from her cracked lips. 'Do you have any idea of where we are? Of how far we'll have to walk?'

He stared out over the land for a long moment before his gaze settled back on her face. 'We're lucky,' he growled. 'Nearest town's about a hundred miles away.' He pointed north, then must have read the horror in her eyes. 'We'll make a shelter and stay here during the day and travel at night. Moon's up, it'll light the way.'

The little party of survivors made a rough shelter by hanging coats and petticoats and shirts over the drooping branches of a nearby tree. They huddled in silence all through the interminable day, moving only to wave away the worrisome flies that hovered and buzzed and settled. They crawled over mouths and eyes and explored every inch of exposed flesh until Eva thought she would go mad. How could she ever have thought Australia would be an adventure? Why on earth did anyone choose to live here – and how did they survive this fearsome, deadly sun? Yet far more terrifying was the thought she would have to walk so far. A hundred miles, he'd said. A hundred miles. It was surely impossible.

Night fell swiftly and the breeze coming off the sea cooled burned flesh and brought a measure of relief. Then they were walking, their feet lifting the red earth in clouds of dust, the women's skirts hampering every step as they dragged in the dirt and caught on the spiny needles of unseen scrub. There was silence within the group. Strengths were found where once there had been weakness. Courage dredged from wells of resilience never before realised. For the will to live was the most powerful emotion of all.

Eva walked beside Jessie, gaze fixed to the horizon, each step bringing her closer to what she prayed was a safe haven. She would not be beaten despite the chaffing of her shoe against her heel – despite the burning on her shoulders where the sun had seared them almost raw. She looked across at the other woman and saw the determination on her face that surely mirrored her own. Their eyes met, and with a brief smile that barely touched their tortured lips they returned once more to their inner thoughts.

Dawn had lightened the sky with streaks of pink and orange when the cloud of dust was spotted far off towards the horizon. They stumbled to a halt, each shielding their eyes against the glare, peering intensely at this phenomenon.

A murmur rustled through them as they puzzled as to what it might mean. The murmur grew as they began to trek towards it. Speculation was rife, fear almost tangible as someone suggested it could be a dust storm, or marauding black fellows.

The cloud grew nearer and the wavering form of something moved within it. Yet it was too far away to discern what it could be and their steps were less sure as they set off again. Fear slowed them as they straggled across the rough terrain, but their gaze never faltered from that looming, ominous cloud.

Eva stumbled alongside Jessie as the cloud grew and tiny, dark forms wavered at its heart. She stopped walking, her hand shielding her eyes as she tried to believe what she was seeing. 'It's a wagon,' she breathed. 'A horse and wagon.' Tears began to stream down her sunburned face and for once she didn't bother to wave away the flies. 'We're safe. We're safe,' she sobbed.

The survivors stood and waited as the cloud drifted on the wind and the wagon drew near. Now they could hear the shouts, the crack of the whip and the thunder of the hoofs of the outriders. Now they could make out the jingle of harness, the rattle and jolt of the wagon as it sped across the rough terrain.

Eva took Jessie's hand and gave it a squeeze. 'I never did thank you for saving me,' she said quietly. 'I would have drowned if you hadn't pulled me out of the bottom of the boat.'

Jessie returned the pressure on her fingers. 'We helped each other,' she said gruffly. 'You kept me going, you know,' she said with a wan smile. 'I weren't about to let you beat me – not a lady who never walked further than the 'ouse to her carriage.'

Eva nodded and silently accepted the truth of her words. She had kept going because she felt it was her duty to set an example to the lower classes – but in truth she didn't want to show any weakness in front of this tough, determined little cockney – and that had given her the will to go on when she thought she was finished.

The wagon was nearer now, the dust rising from beneath the wheels and the horses' hoofs, swirling in choking clouds around the onlookers. Eva pulled the makeshift veil over her mouth and nose and closed her eyes to slits as the rescuers came to a thundering halt.

She was about to join in the joyous greetings when she caught sight of a figure at the back of the wagon. She stilled, her pulse racing, her mind confused.

The man jumped down from the wagon and strode towards her, arms outstretched and so wonderfully familiar.

'Freddy?' Her voice broke as he swept her into his embrace. 'Oh, Freddy,' she sobbed. 'I thought I'd never see you again.'

Chapter Four

Maggie's temper evaporated as she strode down the street towards the beach. She had said her piece and made it plain she wouldn't be messed about any longer. Yet they both knew she would never leave – for where else would she go? She had no family waiting for her. No home to return to. Nothing.

Kicking off her shoes she began to tramp along the sand, relishing the warmth on her bare feet and the tug on the backs of her legs as she forced the pace. The night air was velvet, the breeze from the sea refreshing after the awful heat of the kitchen. Her smile was wry as she remembered the sheepish look on Sam's face, and the hopeful look in his eyes as he presented her with the fish. Typical man, she thought. As if a bit of fish could make up for anything.

She finally eased off the pace. It was no surprise to discover where her walk had taken her, and she regarded her surroundings with little emotion. Things could have been so different, she thought wistfully. If only. She squared her shoulders and turned away, determined not to let those thoughts take over. There was no profit in wishing for something that would never happen. No point in dreaming. For there was nothing here for her, and never had been. The lesson had been a harsh one and she wouldn't make that mistake again.

Maggie began the long trek back to the road. Her lack of emotion was a sign she was healing. A sign, that no matter what, she would remain here and make the best of things. She had to stop running sometime. Had to put the dark years behind her and begin again.

The hotel was in darkness when she finally returned, and after living in Sydney for so many years she still found it strange that people went to bed so early up here in Queensland. For she'd forgotten how she used to rise before the sun each day. Forgotten the long hours spent working on the cattle station and the weariness as the sun finally set. It was a different way of life from the one she'd had in the city, and she was thankful to be a part of it again.

The slab wood cabin was set in the far corner of the plot, well away from the stables and the noise of the hotel bar. Consisting of one room that had been divided into three, it was nevertheless furnished comfortably. Maggie had set the double bed in the far corner, and had placed her favourite trinkets on the dresser. The rather rickety table and two chairs stood in the centre of the cabin, the couch and armchair on either side of the stone fireplace. A curtained-off area served as a bathroom, but as water had to be pumped from the bore, this consisted of an enamel sink, a jug and bowl and a chamber pot stored away in a cupboard. The dunny out the back was dark and spider infested, and after the luxury of indoor facilities in Sydney, she'd refused to use it.

Maggie opened the door and lit the kerosene lamp. The cabin felt like home, and it was a luxury not to be sharing a dormitory like she had in the city. She looked around in satisfaction at her pictures pinned to the wooden walls, and her china ornaments laid out on the polished pine mantelpiece. With a vast yawn she dragged off her clothes, pumped water into the sink and began to wash. The water was from the bore and had a faint aroma of sulphur, but it was hot and welcoming.

With a towel wrapped around her, she took the pins from her hair and let it fall around her shoulders and down her back. She was too tired to wash it again tonight, and as she was determined to take the next day off she had plenty of time. Sitting on the bed, she began to brush away the tangles of the day, her thoughts drifting to the English visitors.

The cinema had been her passion when she was down in Sydney, and she and the other girls from the clothing factory would sit in the darkness and be carried into a world far distant from the one they knew. Maggie grinned as she thought of Giles. He reminded her of Laurence Olivier, and she loved the way he talked – all plummy and terribly stiff upper lip. She giggled. Olivia was just the same, and she wouldn't mind betting she was a stickler on the wards – just like those overseers in the factory.

Maggie tossed the brush aside and pulled on the cotton nightdress. Climbing into bed, she pummelled the pillows until she was comfortable. Olivia's clothes were expensively tailored, her hands manicured, her make-up flawless. The two of them must have a lot of money to come all the way over here, but they didn't have the look of holidaymakers. It was a puzzle, she thought, as she watched the lamplight flicker on the ceiling. One that she would probably never solve, for

34

Olivia, as nice as she was, was a bit daunting, and Giles had not been forthcoming when they chatted in the bar before tea.

She lay there and allowed her thoughts to drift. It had been a long journey to this northern town, and some might have said it was wasted. But ever the optimist, Maggie saw it as a success, for the journey had supplied some of the answers to the questions that plagued her, and had resulted in a new beginning – a feeling of being settled again and safe for the first time in years. If only Sam would notice her, then her happiness would be complete.

Maggie's gaze settled on the photograph on the dresser. The silver frame was tarnished, the images of her beloved parents faded behind the scratched glass. Yet they brought back the memories of a brief, but happy childhood. A childhood that was to be torn apart by tragedy.

Maggie loved Waverly Station with a passion. It sprawled across the rich farm belt north of Adelaide, swept over gentle hills and down into grassy valleys. The birds always seemed to be singing, and the cattle looked sleek and polished beneath golden skies. Yet she understood the hardships and sacrifices that had to be endured to make Waverly as beautiful as it was, and from the moment she could walk, she'd willingly done her share of work.

She sat on the fence, legs dangling, wondering when she'd be able to wear the dress her mother had made for her eleventh birthday. It was weeks until the next country fair, and she was impatient to show off the lemon muslin with the puff sleeves and frothy petticoat that swirled around her legs as she danced in front of the long mirror in her parents' bedroom.

Yet she'd overheard Mum and Dad talking last night, and realised this was not the time to be thinking about dresses and dances. Dad was worried about the feed bills, the stockmen's wages and the next payment on the land lease. Mum was fretting about the news in the papers – something to do with Wall Street in America. Maggie had gone to sleep the night before puzzling over this. How could some street in America affect Waverly? But she didn't like to ask, because she shouldn't have been listening in when she was thought to be asleep.

With a deep sigh she climbed down and went to fetch the last of the feed buckets. Filling the troughs was her final chore of the day, and although she hated hearing the calves bellowing for their mothers, she knew they'd soon calm down. The sounds and scents of Waverly were so much a part of her that she had learned very early on there was little time for misguided sentiment. The animals were well cared for

35

on Waverly, but they had to be rounded up, castrated and spayed and either sold for slaughter or kept for breeding.

Maggie fed the calves, checked their water and waved to her father as he eased off his boots and collapsed in a chair on the verandah. As she finished tidying up, she repeatedly glanced across at the old house that had taken on a golden glow as the sun began to die in the west.

The homestead had been built almost a hundred years ago by her dad's grandfather. It had settled into the earth, the slab walls and corrugated-iron roof weighed down with creeping flowers and ivy. Any breeze could blow through the cracks between the slabs and under the roof where the joists were buckled. Cool in the summer, the homestead was freezing in the bitter nights of the outback winter. The wooden steps leading up to the verandah had been replaced recently, but the termites had already started to chew them away. The roof was patched and undulated like a swayback horse, and the screens on the windows and doors needed a coat of paint and a touch of oil. The verandah railings had been bleached by the sun, and the planks on the floor needed nailing more firmly down. Yet it was home, and Maggie could never imagine living anywhere else. She finally joined her dad in the shade and sat in her favourite rocking chair.

Harold Finlay rolled a cigarette as he narrowed his eyes and peered from beneath the brim of his hat out to the spread of land. He was a man of few words, but Maggie knew he loved her. It was in the smile that creased the corners of his eyes and enhanced the etching of lines on his face. It was in the gentle touch of his hand that was encrusted with years of ingrained dirt and callused by a lifetime of labour.

'Yer ma's late getting back,' he murmured as he struck a match.

'I'll get tea,' Maggie offered. 'She's probably yarning with Betty Richards and forgotten the time.'

Harold Finlay nodded and continued to stare out over his land as the cigarette burned between his lips. 'Reckon you'd be right, luv,' he muttered.

Maggie's gaze swept the horizon. The sun was almost gone and it was a long ride back from the Richards' place. Not wanting to voice her concern, she patted her father's shoulder and left the verandah to prepare the evening meal.

The potatoes were cooked and mashed, the salted beef sliced, the bread warmed in the range and filling the homestead with its mouth-watering aroma. Maggie smeared the sweat from her face and returned again to the verandah. The kitchen was like a furnace. 'Tea's ready,' she said.

'I'll eat when yer ma gets back,' he replied as he stood and searched the surrounding hills.

36

Maggie saw how his knuckles whitened as he gripped the railings. Saw how set his expression was, how deep the lines running either side of his mouth. A shaft of fear drove through her and she struggled to contain it. 'She'll be here any minute,' she said with forced brightness.

He looked down at her, his eyes mirroring his unspoken fears. 'Think I'll ride out and meet her,' he murmured. 'You stay here.'

She shook her head. 'I'm coming too,' she said firmly.

Harold Finlay regarded her for a long moment, his expression unreadable. 'Reckon you'd be better off here, darlin',' he said finally. 'Not good for you to be out after dark.'

Maggie frowned. Dad must really be worried. She had often ridden at night, and had joined the annual round-up at eight years old. She was used to riding her tough little pony through the hot days and bitter nights. Used to sleeping on the ground under the stars with only a saddle as a pillow and a thin blanket against the chill. Used to being far from the homestead for weeks on end with only the men for company. She didn't bother to reply, merely left the verandah and began to saddle her pony.

Harold followed her, and as they rode out through the first of the gates that would lead them to the track, he touched her elbow. 'Thanks,' he said softly. 'Reckon I needed the company after all.'

Maggie saw the dread in his eyes and swallowed. Mum had to be all right. She just had to. Yet the Richards' homestead was over thirty miles away, and Mum had been there enough times to know she had to start the journey back by mid-afternoon, or it would be dark before she reached home. Maggie knew there had been no calls over the two-way, so Mum must have left. But where could she be?

They rode out across the paddocks as the darkness gathered and the moon rose in a clear, star-studded sky. They rode through the great herd of cattle, which shifted and complained about being disturbed from their night forage. Picking up speed, they left the cattle behind and galloped along the track that was rutted from the wagon wheels and hardened by the constant beating it took from horses' hoofs. This track wound through the vast grazing land and bush and was the shortest route to their neighbours' property.

The horse galloped out of the darkness, eyes wild, mane flying. It reared up as Maggie tried to catch the trailing reins, and her pony propped and skittered out of the way of the flashing hoofs.

'Leave it,' yelled Harold. 'She'll find her way home.' He kicked his own horse into a gallop and tore down the track, with Maggie close behind him.

Maggie's fear was in every breath, in every beat of her pony's hoofs. Mum's horse was far behind them now – but where was Mum?

37

They found her beside the track, almost hidden by a fallen tree and the long buffalo grass. Her neck was broken. Death must have been instantaneous.

Maggie blew out the lamp and lay there in the soft glow of the moon, the tears warm on her cheeks. The death of Elizabeth Finlay had cast a long shadow over the haven that was Waverly. Yet that shadow was only a precursor of the profound darkness to come.

Olivia felt rested after a good night's sleep, and although she dreaded the forthcoming meeting, was eager to get on with things. It was still very early, only just after sunrise, and the sky was already blue and cloudless. As she dressed she looked out of the window to the street below. Despite the hour, the shopkeepers were sweeping the board-walk and hauling out their wares, and a few early risers were strolling in the sunshine or sitting on one of the benches that had been placed at intervals along the grass verge. The pace of life was gentle. There was no bustle, no rush, no traffic fumes clouding the azure sky. It was another world, far removed from London's smog.

She finished dressing and opened the door into the lounge. Dust motes floated in the sunlight streaming through the shutters and she flung them open and unlatched the screens. The air was fresh and still cool from the night. The scent of exotic flowers mingled with the tang of salt and the hot, dry aroma of the vast, empty lands beyond this green oasis.

Olivia dug her hands into the pockets of her cotton trousers as she stepped on to the hotel balcony and took in her surroundings. Palm trees shielded all sight of the beach, but far out over the rooftops she could see a line of impossible blue, and the hazy outline of a tiny island. The town itself was sheltered by palm trees and ferns, and tangles of ivy entwined with beautiful flowers. There were one or two buildings that hadn't been here twenty years ago, she realised, but on the whole not much had changed.

Leaving the covered balcony, Olivia went to Giles' door and listened. She smiled, for she could hear him snoring. Better to leave him to sleep. She could bring his breakfast up later.

'G'day, Miss Hamilton. How ya going?' He grinned and stretched out an enormous hand. 'The name's Sam White.'

'How do you do,' she replied, painfully aware of how English she sounded. They shook and Olivia's hand was swamped in a firm grip. He was a handsome man, she realised as she took in the broad shoulders, the muscular arms and friendly smile. No wonder Maggie stayed on.

'Breakfast is on the go,' he said cheerfully as he led the way into the dining room. 'Help yourself to tea or coffee while you wait.'

Olivia couldn't help but smile back. All this cheerfulness in the morning was catching, but she couldn't quite resist the temptation to prick his bubble of enthusiasm. 'No Maggie this morning?' she asked with feigned innocence.

A glimmer of something akin to panic clouded those startling blue eyes then was gone just as swiftly. 'Day off,' he said shortly as he turned and left the room.

Olivia pressed her lips together as she helped herself to coffee and sat down. The dining room was empty, but she didn't want to risk him overhearing her giggles. So Maggie had stood firm, and by the look of things, her threat to leave had hit the spot. Sam was obviously a worried man under all that bonhomie.

Breakfast arrived and Olivia inwardly groaned. A piece of steak was accompanied by two fried eggs, fried potato, bacon and something unidentifiable – it was unbelievable that anyone should be expected to eat all this.

Sam deposited a large bottle of tomato ketchup on the table and stood there grinning. 'Set you up for the day. Enjoy your tucker, Miss Hamilton.'

She poked the object of mystery on her plate. 'What is this?' she asked.

'Snag,' he replied. Then he must have seen her frown, for he stroked his chin and thought for a minute. 'You call them sausages,' he said finally.

Olivia eyed the fried lump of what looked like something you stepped in on the pavement and decided it bore no relation to any kind of sausage she'd ever had. She grimaced and dipped her fork in the potato.

'Snags look rough, I know,' he said apologetically. 'But they taste fair dinkum.'

She looked up at him, hoping he wasn't planning to spend the entire time watching her eat. For the sake of peace she cut a small piece off the lump and gingerly put it in her mouth. The flavours sang and she cut another piece. The lamb was mixed with onions and mint and pepper, and a hint of parsley. The unfortunate-looking snag was delicious.

Sam nodded as if to confirm he'd been right and returned to the kitchen.

Breakfast was usually a cup of coffee and a slice of toast, snatched on the run as she left for the hospital, and after last night's feast, she just couldn't cope with so much food. Even the sight of it defeated her. She collected Giles' breakfast on a tray and carried it up to him.

39

He was up and sitting in his dressing-gown on the balcony, his cigar smoke drifting on the early morning breeze. His eyes widened as Olivia explained about the snags and cut up the meat, but he didn't seem put off and happily chewed his way through most of it.

Yet Olivia could see the dark shadows under his eyes, the weary slant of his shoulders and knew the travelling and the heat had taken its toll. 'Stay here and rest this morning,' she said quietly as he relaxed back into his chair. 'I've a couple of things to do, but they won't take long, and we can go to the beach this afternoon.'

'Where are you going?'

'To visit the old house,' she said shortly. There was no point in worrying him by telling him any more. 'And to lay a few ghosts,' she added with a soft smile.

'You take care, old thing,' he said. He caught her hand as she stood up and prepared to leave. 'I know you too well, Ollie,' he murmured. 'There's more to this than just seeing the old house again, isn't there? Are you sure you don't want me to come with you?'

She couldn't quite meet his gaze, and bent down to kiss his cheek. 'Just rest,' she muttered. 'I'll need you much more later on.' She picked up her handbag and left swiftly before he could change her mind.

Olivia left the hotel, and instead of turning towards the beach, she kept straight on, down the sandy lane that wound between two rows of little wooden houses that would have been called bungalows back in England. Most of them had been painted white, the window frames and screens adding a touch of bright colour. The ones on the left had unbroken views of the sea, the ones on the right were placed so they had a glimpse between each house. Rowing boats, fishing nets and children's toys littered the back gardens, and beach towels and bathers hung from washing lines. Sea grass poked through the sand and the scent of wattle filled the air, mingling with the rising warmth of the sun. Olivia felt a strong sense of déjà vu. Time had indeed stood still, for this was exactly how she remembered it.

The house she sought was on the end of the row, overlooking the beach. It was the same as all the others, set apart only by the large plot of land that surrounded it, and the addition of a shady wrap-around verandah. An attempt had been made to soften the rather severe lines of the house, for someone had planted bougainvillea at the side; now it scrambled up the walls and over the roof in a profusion of purple and pink and white flowers.

Olivia swallowed and her legs began to tremble as she reached for the latch on the back gate. Her hand touched the familiar, weathered timber and the rusting latch, and she froze. She wasn't ready for this. Not ready at all. What on earth did she think she was doing?

She felt her pulse race as she stood there, and despite the loose cotton blouse and thin trousers, she could feel the sweat trickle down her ribs. This is madness, she silently berated herself. Yet, as she remained frozen outside the gate, she knew why she hesitated. The swing still hung from the gnarled tree in the corner of the garden. The shed still leaned precariously against the back fence, and the cluster of banksias still bloomed in the flowerbed that ran along the side. The ghosts she'd come to lay were alive and calling her, drawing her back to the times when Eva had not been there to protect her.

'Are you looking for someone?'

The voice, so near, startled her, and Olivia turned sharply, almost stumbling in the sand. 'I . . .' She swallowed as the suspicious blue eyes regarded her from over the neighbouring fence. The woman's thin face was tanned, her hair pulled tightly back into a ragged knot. 'I don't suppose Irene Stanford still owns this place, does she?' she finally managed.

The eyes lost their chill and the woman smiled. 'Jeez,' she breathed. 'What's a Pom doing all the way up here?'

Olivia's legs were still unsteady, her nerves shot. 'I've come to visit the Stanfords,' she said, rather more sharply than she'd intended.

The gate was unlatched and the woman came out into the sandy lane. She was wearing a red cotton dress liberally sprinkled with bright yellow flowers. Her feet were bare and her skin was the colour of mahogany. A small child clung to her bare legs and peeked around the garish dress. 'The name's Debby, good to meet you,' she said as she stuck out a hand.

Olivia shook the hand and smiled as she introduced herself. 'The Stanfords?' she tried again.

Debby shook her head, her mouth pursed. 'They still own the place, but we don't see much of them,' she said as her gaze trawled over the house and yard. 'Mrs Stanford prefers to fly down to Sydney when it's too hot.'

Olivia experienced an almost overwhelming sense of relief as the tension left her. 'Are they coming down this summer?' she asked.

The thin brown shoulders shrugged. 'Who knows? Mrs Stanford's not one to tell me her plans.'

Olivia didn't miss the note of sarcasm. 'Do they still live out at Deloraine Station?' she asked.

Debby squinted in the sun as she cocked her head. 'Reckon they do,' she replied. 'Are they relations or something? You've come a long ways to find them.'

'I'll go out there then.' Olivia could feel the tension rising again. She no longer wanted to talk to this woman. No longer wanted to stand here in the blazing sun outside the house that had once been home.

'Best of luck, mate,' Debby said cheerfully as she picked up the small boy and straddled him on her bony hip. She leaned forward, her tone confidential, her eyes glittering with malice. 'I could be speaking out of turn,' she muttered. 'But watch yourself. Irene Stanford isn't the easiest person to get on with. Thinks she's better than any of us.'

So, thought Olivia, she hadn't changed. 'I know,' she replied. 'We go back a long way.' She saw the curiosity, the yearning to gossip. Thanking her for her time, and not wishing to linger, Olivia strode out and hurried down the lane. She was aware of the woman watching her, aware of those blue eyes following her until she turned the corner and was out of sight.

The beach called to her and she couldn't resist. Sitting on a rock, her bare feet immersed in a pool, she stared out to sea and waited for her pulse to slow. A line of pelicans foraged at the water's edge, their gait ungainly and full of self-importance. The tiny island on the horizon had come into focus now the early mist had cleared, and she could just make out the golden arc of beach and the pine-covered hill. Yet her mind was fixed on Irene Stanford and the journey she would now have to make to find her.

Chapter Five

Olivia walked past the entrance to the bar and let herself in through the side door. After the reception yesterday, she had no wish to ruffle any more feathers despite that, in her opinion, it was ridiculous that a woman couldn't go into the bar.

The square hall was central to the hotel. Doors led to the dining room and ladies' lounge, and there was a hatch through to the bar. The staircase swept down from the first floor, and would have been quite a grand affair, if it weren't for the shabby carpet. Sam was polishing glasses behind the bar, his back turned to the hatch.

Olivia cleared her throat. 'I was wondering if you could help me,' she began.

Sam flipped the cloth onto his shoulder and turned, his smile broad, making him very handsome. 'Glad to do what I can,' he drawled.

Olivia was almost mesmerised by his eyes. The direct gaze held her and she had to blink to break the spell. 'Is there anywhere I could hire a ute?' she said finally.

'Going up north to Cooktown, are you?' he asked as he leaned on the counter between them. His shirtsleeves were rolled up and his muscular arms were deeply tanned beneath the dark fuzz of hair. 'Bonzer place. Used to be a thriving pearl fleet up there.'

Olivia dug her hands in her trouser pockets. She was far too aware of his magnetism, of how, if she just reached out her hand, she could have run her fingers along those sturdy brown arms. She cleared her throat. 'I thought it was Broome where they did the pearling.'

He laughed, showing straight white teeth. 'Common mistake, luv,' he said. 'Cooktown was bigger than Broome – now they're both gone.'

She frowned. 'Gone? I thought Broome was still thriving?'

He shook his head and ran his fingers through the thick black hair that was enticingly threaded with silver at the temples. 'Japs knocked seven bells out of it. Doubt it will ever be the same.' He sighed and folded his arms. 'I can let you borrow my ute,' he offered. 'It's not much, but the engine's good, and you'll need something sturdier than that hired car to get you over the tracks to Cooktown.'

Not wishing to disillusion him about her true destination, Olivia thanked him. 'But won't you be needing it? I could be gone for some time.'

He grinned and she had a glimpse of the young boy he might have once been – full of mischief and cheeky with it. Goodness, he was handsome.

'Reckon I'll be stuck here for a while,' he drawled. 'Maggie's gone walkabout.'

Olivia found she was grinning back and had to pull her thoughts together. 'I'm going to need a map,' she said as she avoided his gaze.

'Reckon we don't have any,' he said regretfully. 'Not much call for tourists up this way, and the roads to Cooktown are only tracks anyways.'

Olivia realised she would have to tell him the truth. She'd been out to Deloraine years ago, but Eva had been driving and as a child, Olivia had taken no notice of her surroundings. 'I'm actually going out to Deloraine Station,' she admitted. 'I don't suppose you could draw a map or something?' Her voice faded as his blue eyes widened.

'That's a ways to go,' he muttered. 'And if you don't know the track, you could easily get lost.' He thought for a moment, his gaze resting on her face. 'I could take you there, but it won't be for a day or two.'

Olivia stood there, the impatience beginning to build. 'But I have to go now,' she blurted out. 'It's important.'

The gaze was steady, holding her there, the unspoken questions almost tangible between them. Then he reached under the counter and tore a page out of a notebook. Licking the end of a stub of pencil, he began to draw. 'You leave the town and head west,' he began.

Olivia leaned forward to follow the lines he was drawing, all too aware that their heads were almost touching. All too aware of the heat and fresh clean smell of soap emanating from this attractive man.

Maggie had frittered away the morning. The early swim had chased away the dark dreams and left her tingling as she sat in the sun and dried off. She had seen Olivia come down to the beach and had been on the point of approaching her when she realised the other woman was deep in thought. Whatever the reason for her being here, she decided, Olivia was obviously a troubled woman.

After washing her hair and cleaning up the cabin, she was at a loss

44

as to what to do next. She could have caught the weekly bus into Cairns, but it was a long slow journey, and not much fun in this heat. Borrowing Sam's ute was not an option after she'd almost totalled it a few months back, so she was stuck here. She could have mooched around the shops, but there was nothing she needed, and the shops in Trinity were mostly practical. No department stores and fancy little clothes shops like in Sydney. No coffee houses and tea shops. Just feed merchants, grocers, butchers and hardware.

She eyed her reflection in the mirror and flicked a few stray strands back over her shoulder. Her hair was loose for once, shining from the shampoo, falling in soft, light brown waves around her face and shoulders. She leaned forward and performed the tricky act of brushing on mascara, then added a dash of lipstick to celebrate her first day off in months. With a nod of satisfaction she stepped back and eyed the full effect. The cotton dress was pale green and freshly ironed, the sweetheart neckline disguising the lack of bosom, the narrow belt emphasising her tiny waist. Her sandals were tan leather and showed off her long, slender legs. All in all, she decided, she didn't scrub up too badly.

'Right,' she breathed. 'Sam White, here I come.'

There were already a couple of utilities parked in the back yard, and Maggie could hear the lubras gossiping in the kitchen as they prepared yet another gargantuan meal. She pushed through the door, and instead of going into the kitchen, she headed for the hall. Sam would be in the bar, but for once she would not be in there to help him, she decided. She would order a drink from the hatch and go and sit in the lounge. It was about time she started behaving like a lady, not a doormat.

The door opened on silent hinges and Maggie was about to make her entrance when she caught sight of Sam and Olivia. They were learning over the bar in the hatch, their dark heads almost touching. Her determination ebbed as a sharp pain of anguish ripped through her. The two of them were smiling and talking, looking into one another's eyes, completely oblivious to everything around them. The electricity between them was almost tangible. They made a handsome couple, she admitted with a bitterness she could almost taste.

She watched the two of them laugh at something. Noticed the fleeting touch of Olivia's hand on Sam's arm before she took the piece of paper from him. There was no doubt about it, thought Maggie. They were flirting. Why, oh why, didn't Sam look into her eyes like that? The longing was an ache she could hardly bear.

Olivia turned from Sam, her eyes widening in surprise, her smile friendly. 'Hello, Maggie. You do look nice. Decided you couldn't stay away from the old place?'

45

Maggie's face was stiff with resentment as she attempted to smile back. 'Something like that,' she muttered.

Olivia grinned. 'Enjoy your day off and don't let him bully you,' she said with a tilt of her head towards the watching Sam. 'Perhaps we'll see you on the beach later?'

Maggie stood in the doorway and watched the other woman run lightly up the stairs. Even in cotton strides and a shirt she looked elegant and cool, she thought bitterly. She had everything. Why couldn't she just leave Sam alone?

'How y'goin', Maggs?' Sam was leaning on the counter and grinning. 'Coming back to work?'

Maggie was galvanised into action. She let the door slam behind her and strode across the hall to the hatch. 'No. It's my day off,' she snapped. 'And as you seem to have nothing better to do than flirt with our customers, I'll have a gin and tonic with lots of ice.'

A dark eyebrow shot up. 'Jeez, Maggs. What's biting you? She only wanted to borrow the ute.' He poured out the drink and put it in front of her.

Maggie took a hefty swig, which almost took her breath away. Being a beer man, Sam had always been heavy handed with the gin. 'What's she want with your ute? It's not as if there's anywhere to go, and there's that fancy hire car out back.'

Sam dipped his chin in an obvious attempt to hide the smile that was tugging at his lips and sparkling in his eyes. 'She and Giles want to go out to Deloraine,' he muttered.

Maggie's hand stilled. The cold glass touched her lips, but she didn't notice. 'Why?' she asked softly.

Sam shrugged. 'None of our business, I reckon,' he murmured. His eyes were no longer sparkling, but were clouded with concern as he looked at her. 'You all right, Maggs? Gone a funny colour there, mate.'

Maggie swallowed the drink and ordered another. 'I'm fine,' she lied.

The bar was finally closed, the doors locked behind Kenny, the part-time barman, and the lights off. Sam covered the crates with damp cloths and wearily came through into the main hall. It had been a busy night, and he could fully understand why Maggie had put her foot down and refused to do any more. He would give her some slack from now on, he decided. He hadn't been fair, and it was his hotel, after all.

He was about to make his way up the stairs to his room when he noticed the lights were still blazing in the lounge. Swearing softly under his breath, he retraced his steps.

Maggie was sitting in an armchair, her face turned towards the dusty paper fan in the empty fireplace, her hair falling in a soft veil over her shoulders. An empty glass was on the low table beside her, and the room was full of cigarette smoke.

'Since when did you smoke?' he asked as he opened a window and let the cool night air clear the fug.

'Since I started drinking,' she muttered. Holding out her glass, her face still turned from him, she ordered another gin and tonic.

Sam eyed the empty glass, and after a swift calculation reckoned she'd had more than enough for one night. 'Time for bed, Maggie. Work tomorrow.' His tone was soft.

'Yes,' she said wearily. 'That's about all I'm good for, isn't it, Sam?'

She turned towards him and Sam tried unsuccessfully to hide his shock. Maggie's face was streaked with the black stuff she'd put on her eyelashes, her lipstick smeared, nose shiny. His heart went out to her and he perched on the arm of the chair, and placed his hand awkwardly on her shoulder. 'Come on, luv. What's wrong?'

'Everything,' she said with a sniff, her voice muffled by his shirt.

He knew he shouldn't, but he couldn't help smiling. '*Everything*'s a lot to be wrong,' he said gently. 'Come on, Maggs. This isn't like you.'

She jerked away from him and blew her nose. With angry swipes she attempted to clean the mess from her face. 'So what is?' she rasped. Turning bloodshot eyes to him she glared through fresh tears. 'Good old Maggie,' she snarled with a toss of her head. 'Want something done? Maggie will do it. Need a cleaner and cook, a barmaid? Good old Maggs will come up flaming trumps.'

Sam stared at her in amazement. He had no idea she was this angry. But what on earth could have brought it on? 'Reckon it's the gin talking,' he said.

'No it flaming isn't,' she snapped as she wrested from his hand and stood up. Leaning heavily on the solid mantelpiece, she drew up her chin and with admirable dignity attempted to appear steady on her feet. 'It's me talking, Sam. Margaret Finlay. The gin has only given me the chance to see things clearly.' She hiccupped and almost lost her balance.

Sam caught her elbow. 'Come on, Maggs, I'll walk you home. You're in no fit state to leave here on your own.'

'But I'll still be alone, won't I?' she snapped as she tried to get her elbow free. She stumbled as she stepped back from him and looked up into his face. 'I've always been alone, Sam,' she said with heartbreaking simplicity. 'Why is that?'

47

He was at a loss. This wasn't the Maggie he knew. Not the Maggie who was tough and seemingly able to cope with anything. Not the Maggie he admired. He tried to think of something to say – but what words could heal the obvious pain she was going through? 'Maggs,' he began.

'I'm sorry,' she said with a sniff. 'Perhaps you're right. I've had too much to drink and made a fool of myself.' She looked back at him. 'But the loneliness suddenly became all too much,' she explained. 'I just couldn't bear the thought that everyone I've ever loved has shut me out, left me behind – forgotten me.'

He put his arm around her, his chin resting lightly on the top of her head as she sobbed into his chest and soaked his shirt. Maggie felt surprisingly tiny in his arms, so frail and helpless. It had been a long time since he'd held a woman like this. A long time since he'd experienced that wonderful sense of protecting someone small and defenceless.

'I don't know what to say,' he admitted. 'I never realised . . .' He faltered to a halt, not really knowing where the sentence was taking him. The memory of Stella was sharp and this was a delicate situation. Emotions could easily get out of hand, and poor Maggie had obviously been hurt enough without him trampling all over her feelings with his size elevens.

She sniffed back her tears and stepped from his embrace. 'Come with me,' she said softly as she took his hand. 'I want to show you something.'

He hung back. 'Maggs. I don't think that's wise, do you?'

Her tear-streaked face was lifted towards him and she gave a ghastly smile. 'No worries, Sam. I'm not about to leap on you.' She tugged his hand again. 'I just want to explain things, that's all. Come on.'

His reluctance made him resist. The last thing he needed now was for Maggie to bare her soul, or whatever it was women did at times like this. Experience had taught him it was dangerous, and often led to things they would both regret in the morning. 'Can't you tell me here?' he asked, as he stood firm.

She shook her head. 'I'll make coffee, and we'll sit in separate chairs and be frightfully respectable,' she said in a mockery of Olivia's plummy voice.

Sam reluctantly allowed her to lead him through the back door and across the yard. He held on to her as her legs almost gave way and she stumbled over a rough piece of tarmac. He was beginning to realise this had something to do with the Englishwoman – but couldn't fathom what. There had been no sign of animosity this morning, and he'd have expected them to become friends, for he guessed they were about the same age, and there were few enough women here not to be falling out for no reason.

Maggie tugged at her skirt and straightened her hair as she weaved across the cabin and put the kettle on the gas hob. Then she pulled out a drawer, grasped a thick book and fell into a chair. 'Sit down,' she ordered. 'It's time you and me had a long talk.'

'It's late,' he said as he hovered just inside the door. He glanced over his shoulder at the dark and deserted yard. 'I really should be going.'

She cocked her head. 'What's the matter, Sam? Afraid I might declare undying love for you? Afraid I might muck up your comfortable little life by making a scene?' Her expression softened. 'You've got a lot to learn about women, Sam. Sit down, luv. This won't take long.'

The kettle was whistling and he made them both a strong cup of black coffee before he sat in the chair opposite. He was exhausted and needed the coffee to keep him alert. They drank in silence and he glanced around the cabin. Maggie had made it homely and it was far removed from the squalor the last manager had left behind. 'What's that?' he asked finally, nodding towards the book in her hand.

She looked at it, her fingers running over the tooled leather in a caress. 'This is my life,' she said softly. 'This is all I have to prove who I am and where I came from.' Her eyes were golden in the lamplight as she looked at him. 'But even that was a lie,' she added.

Sam swallowed the lump in his throat. Maggie was getting to him, and he felt the overwhelming need to hold her. To hold her and shield her from whatever it was that tormented her. Yet he was wise enough to resist. For Maggie's very posture spoke of needing space around her – of that singular, invisible barrier of resistance all women seem to put up when they are determined to be heard.

Maggie watched him, and saw the different emotions flit across his handsome face. In that moment she loved him more than ever, for he was trying his best to console and be patient despite his reluctance to be here. She was mortified at the scene she'd made. That was definitely the last time she'd hit the gin bottle, she vowed silently. She looked at his face, and at his large hands clasped loosely between his knees and remembered how they had felt when he held her. Perhaps, after she'd told him about her life, they would reach a closer understanding. Perhaps then he might see her as more than just a skivvy.

She looked down at the first photograph and gently slid it out of the little corner pieces that held it in place. 'This is Waverly,' she

49

explained. Her hand was remarkably steady as she passed the photograph over, her voice soft and loving as she recounted those early years and the death of her mother.

Elizabeth Finlay was buried at Waverly. The small family cemetery was in a far corner of the property, surrounded by a picket fence that was bleached by the sun. Crows cawed in the surrounding trees and the light breeze sifted through the long grass with a mournful sigh. It was a peaceful place – a place of refuge – a fitting resting place for one so loved.

Maggie came every day to lay fresh wild flowers and pull weeds and ivy from the grave. She would sit beside that little wooden cross and stare across the valley to the hills beyond in silent communion with the woman who now slept beneath that warm, scented earth. Home just didn't feel the same any more. There was no laughter. No vigorous tap, tap, tap of Elizabeth's feet on the wooden floor. No soft kiss at night. Harold had withdrawn into his own world, his own mourning, and there seemed to no longer be a place for Maggie in his sorrow.

Maggie should have been lonely, for there were no playmates, no brothers or sisters. But she had Ursula, her constant companion. Maggie knew Ursula was a figment of her imagination, and now she was almost grown up she should have ended the friendship. But Ursula remained steadfast and true. Her friend listened to her secrets, colluded in adventures and consoled when there were tears. They had grown up together in the adult world of Waverly, and now, in her darkest moments, Ursula was her solace and more real than ever.

The drought had taken hold and the beef cattle were rounded up and sold, the men paid and sent on their way. Silence fell on Waverly throughout that long dry summer and the following winter. The rains still hadn't come during the next summer and as another winter approached the remaining stock was slaughtered. The paddocks were empty, and so were the kennels. The horses and tack and all the farm equipment were sold off at auction and Harold stood to one side, his expression morose as he watched the hammer fall and another piece of Waverly was carried away by strangers.

Maggie watched, tears in her eyes as her father shuffled back to the homestead after the auction. His step was slow and unsure, his shoulders slumped in defeat. He was lost without Elizabeth and it seemed to Maggie that he'd given up on Waverly, even life itself.

She followed him as the last of the trucks left the Station, the clouds of dust rising over everything. It was as if the dust was just another smothering blanket of silence – another shroud to be laid on this dying, desolate place that had once been home.

'We have to do something, Dad,' she said quietly as she sat beside him on the verandah. 'Waverly's dying. Mum wouldn't have wanted that.'

His sad eyes peered out from beneath his hat brim, taking in the desolation. 'I . . .' he began as a tear slowly trickled down his face.

Maggie moved swiftly and knelt at his feet, her hands on his knees as she looked up into his face. 'It's all right, Dad,' she said. 'We'll manage somehow. You and me together. Make Mum proud of what we can do.'

'It's too late,' he said gruffly.

Maggie grasped his knees. 'No it's not,' she persisted. 'We can buy more stock. Do the repairs. Borrow some machinery and a couple of horses from Betty Richards.' Her enthusiasm was growing. 'We could paint the old place up, and before you know it, we'll be right again.'

He smeared away the tears with a work-roughened hand and finally looked down at her. 'I've failed, Maggie. Failed you and yer ma.' His hands covered her fingers and held them tightly. 'I'm sorry, darlin'. I haven't been much of a dad to you over the past two years, have I?'

The relief that he still loved her took her into his arms. They held one another as Harold finally cried for his wife, and Maggie's heart ached at the sound of this once strong man's tears.

He eventually eased away from her and after blowing his nose and wiping his eyes, he stood at the verandah railings and looked out over the land he and his father and his grandfather had worked all their lives. 'It's all gone, Maggie,' he said finally.

Maggie frowned. Her father's tone was so final, the words a puzzle. 'No, it isn't,' she protested. 'It's all still here. We just need to love it again, to look after it properly.'

Harold dipped his head, his hands clutching the railing as if his very life depended upon it. 'It's all gone,' he said again. He ignored her interjection with a dismissive shake of his head. 'I owe too many people too much money. The auction was to settle some of the debts, but I'll never be able to pay them all.'

Maggie felt the breath being punched from her as she took in what he was saying. 'But how? Why? Waverly has always been a good station.'

'It is,' he said flatly. 'And will be again in the right hands.' He turned then and Maggie saw the bleakness in his eyes and etched in the lines on his face. 'I took risks, darlin'. Thought me and yer ma could ride this depression out. But it's getting worse. Every day there's another bill, another demand for lease payments. Our savings are gone – all of them. We have until next week to get out.'

51

Maggie sat there, stunned into silence. She'd had no idea of how bad things had got. Couldn't possibly imagine what it would be like to leave this place that was the only home she'd ever known. 'Where will we go?' she whispered.

Harold's rough hand gently stroked back the light brown hair from her face and tucked it behind her ear. 'I've been offered a job up in the Territories,' he said. 'It ain't much, but it's work and board and will see me through until I can find something more permanent.'

Maggie felt a rising tide of panic as her father's gaze slid away from her and he stepped back to the railings. 'What about me, Dad?' she demanded. 'Have you found me a job up there too?'

'No, darlin'. I've arranged for you to stay with some nice people until I get settled.'

'I don't want to go anywhere without you,' she burst out. 'I'm nearly thirteen. I can cook and clean and be useful around the place.' She rushed to his side, grasping his arm, forcing him to look at her. 'Take me with you, Dad,' she begged. 'Don't leave me.'

He held her close, his rough hands stroking her head as if she was a young, frightened colt. 'Can't do that, darlin'. The Territory's no place for a girl.' He eased her from her tight grasp at his waist and looked down at her. 'I'll see you right, Maggie,' he said firmly. 'And when I'm settled, I'll send for you.'

'But how long will that be?' The tears were flowing and she did nothing to stop them. Her world was falling apart. She had already lost her mother, now she was about to lose her home and her beloved father.

'Can't say,' he replied, the sadness darkening his eyes. 'But I'll make sure it won't be too long.' He kissed the top of her head. 'I love you, Maggie. Never forget that.'

A week later they were riding on the wagon behind the plodding, aged Hector. They had left almost everything behind, and the flatbed of the wagon was nearly empty. Maggie had been determined not to look back at the homestead. But she couldn't resist saying one last goodbye.

Waverly homestead already looked small and isolated, empty and abandoned, she realised as her gaze drifted over the familiar paddocks and outbuildings. She remembered playing in the barn, riding out on round-up, swimming in the creek. And there was the rope swing Dad had fixed from one of the trees. The ache was deep as she thought of another little girl swinging there.

Maggie blinked away the tears and turned purposefully forward. It had been a mistake to look back. She must steel herself for what was to come. Closing her eyes, she felt the warm, welcome presence of Ursula. She'd been afraid her friend would stay on Waverly, but she was here beside her on the buckboard. Yet the time for childish things was over. How long would Ursula remain with her once she'd begun her new life?

She opened her eyes and looked down at the things in the flatbed of the wagon. There wasn't much, for the furniture had been sold or left behind for the new tenants. There was a bedroll, pillow, saddle and tack and Dad's spare riding boots. The rest of his clothes were in the holdall, his blacksmith's tools in the roll of canvas tied to the swag along with cooking pots and a tin mug.

She thought about her own small bag beneath the tarpaulin in the back. The yellow muslin dress was carefully folded beneath the moleskins and work shirts. It was too small for her now, but it was the last thing Mum had made and she couldn't have left it behind. Just like the photograph album, she thought as she held it tightly to her chest.

Her fingers traced the ornate tooling in the leather as they jolted and trundled over the impacted earth. As long as she had her memories she and Dad would come through this. As long as she believed he would find work and come back for her, she would survive. The thoughts were a mantra as they slowly crossed the shimmering, dying plain and headed north into an unknown future.

Sam sat in silence as Maggie's voice drifted away. He could hear the clock ticking on the mantel and the sound of the crickets in the trees at the back of the yard, but in his imagination he could feel the heat and dust of that lonely trek, and the heartbreak of a lonely child.

'I reckon you must think I've got a screw loose,' muttered Maggie. 'With my imaginary friend.'

Sam sat forward in his chair. 'Is she still around?' he asked, his voice tender.

Maggie shook her head. 'She left when I finally took my destiny in my own hands.' She looked back at him, her gaze steady, as if defying him to make fun of her.

Sam shook his head, his slow smile loosening the tension in his tired face. 'She was around when you needed her,' he said softly. 'That's all that matters.'

Maggie looked away from him and stared into the empty fireplace, and he wondered what she was seeing, what her thoughts were. Her childhood was so far divorced from his own that he couldn't really understand how it must have been for her. With four brothers and two sisters he'd never felt the need for an imaginary friend. There was too much work to be done, too many people jostling for space in that overcrowded homestead. They too had struggled through the depression, but they had survived.

'Where did you end up?' he asked as the silence grew. 'You said you finally took charge of your own future. What happened?'

Maggie stood and ran her hands down the creased dress. 'It's late,' she said. 'And we both have work in the morning. I'll tell you another time.'

Sam glanced at the clock, amazed at how swiftly time had passed. He stood and took her hands. 'Will you be all right?'

She nodded. 'Thanks for listening. I needed to talk.'

He squeezed her fingers and stepped back. 'Any time,' he said – and meant it.

He left the cabin and ambled back to the hotel. His thoughts were legion, his emotions strangely jumbled. Maggie had surprised him tonight, and he had surprised himself at how easily he could be drawn in by her. She had triggered off something in him that he thought had been lost when Stella and his son had been killed in that bush fire.

He remembered being in love. Remembered the joy of holding his newborn son. Remembered the devastation when he'd returned to the homestead to find nothing but burned-out trees and black ash underfoot. It had taken five years to bury those emotions, but as they emerged now, he realised they were as raw as they had ever been. The need to hold someone was overwhelming. The need to lie next to someone, to talk through the night and make love was an ache within him. The yearning to belong – to be a part of someone else's life – was all.

He would have to be careful, he thought as he let himself in through the back door. The last thing either of them needed was the illusory comfort of a physical relationship that would most likely peter out once the passion was gone. They were too vulnerable, and he instinctively knew that neither of them could risk being hurt again.

Chapter Six

It was Monday morning. Maggie heard Sam's ute leaving the yard as the sun came up and momentarily panicked. Surely he wasn't going off again? Then, through the haze of a dreadful hangover, she remembered Olivia's plan to drive out to Deloraine. She slumped back on the pillows. She felt terrible and knew she must look a sight, but it was time to get up – to get on with the day.

Avoiding her reflection in the mirror, she brushed her hair and realised even that was lacklustre. With a sigh she gave up trying to improve things and steeled herself for the moment when she would see Sam again. Whatever had she been thinking of? This wasn't Sydney, and she could have caused all kinds of problems for both of them, for the people of Trinity could forgive most things, but a drunken woman was not one of them.

Monday mornings were usually quiet in the hotel during these summer months until lunchtime. The graziers would bring their families in for lunch and then the men would get down to some serious drinking while the women and children spent the afternoon on the beach. Maggie shut the cabin door, squared her shoulders and squinted into the glare. Her head was bad enough without the sun bouncing off every glossy surface, she thought as she hurried into the welcome shade of the hotel. If only there were a few clouds to mar the perfection of the sky, a hint of rain, or even a haze over the sun – but then this was Queensland, God's own country, where such things were rare.

'G'day. Looks like you could do with one of my special hangover cures,' said Sam as she stepped into the passageway.

Maggie had a sneaking suspicion he'd been waiting for her, and was thankful he'd decided to take charge of what could have been an embarrassing moment. 'I could do with something,' she said, her eyes firmly avoiding him. 'My head feels like it's about to explode.'

Sam made her sit down before he handed her a long glass. 'A little something I prepared earlier,' he explained. 'Looks like hell, but it'll do the trick.' He grinned, his dark blue eyes gleaming with mirth. 'Go on, Maggs. Down in one, then you won't taste it.'

She eyed it with suspicion. It smelled even worse than it looked. Taking a deep breath, she downed the concoction and almost gagged. Something slimy had slid down her throat. 'What the hell's in this thing?' she gasped.

He grinned again. 'Tomato juice, Worcester sauce, pepper and a raw egg. No worries, Maggs. It'll do you a power of good.'

'Debatable,' she muttered.

He took her hand and pulled her to her feet. 'Take the rest of the day off,' he said kindly. 'In fact – take the week off. About time you had a bit of a holiday.'

'But the hotel's full,' she protested once she'd got over the shock.

He shoved his hands in his pockets and shook his head. 'Got help in the bar, and Lila's brought in her cousin to wait tables.' He leaned towards her and smiled. 'You are indispensable, Maggie. I want you in one piece and happy. I've taken the rip too many times and this is my way of saying sorry.'

Maggie blushed and looked away so he wouldn't see the gratitude and love in her eyes. 'Thanks,' she said, her voice a little unsteady. 'Though what I'll do all week I have no idea.'

'Go on the beach. I expect Debby will be down there with the kids. Be company for you.'

Maggie nodded, but knew she wouldn't seek out Debby. They were of an age, and got on well, but Debby had three children and a husband. It was summer, a time for families, and she would only feel she was intruding. Besides, she realised, she was still feeling frail after last night. Still haunted by the dreams that had followed her confessional talk with Sam.

She looked back at him and smiled. 'I'll leave you to it then,' she said with false brightness. 'And don't forget Billy Weaver hates gravy. Whatever you do don't let Lila smother his dinner with it.'

Sam slapped her bottom playfully. 'Get on out of here, woman,' he said in mock severity. 'Before I change me mind.'

Maggie blushed again and hurried off, yet she could still feel the warmth of his hand where it had touched her so fleetingly – and it filled her with a sense of well-being.

As she prepared for the beach she thought about the man who was capable of stirring up so many emotions and knew that after last night she would have to tread carefully. Sam was not a man to be rushed. Not a man easily swayed by tears. She would have to keep her emotions under control and take it slowly. For he was a prize worth winning, and she didn't want to risk damaging the tenuous understanding they had reached.

Half an hour later the headache was gone and she was walking down to the beach. The straw hat had seen better days but it kept the glare off her face, and the cotton dress she wore over her swimsuit was faded. Armed with a towel and a book and a bottle of soda, she found an isolated spot over by the rocks where the palm trees gave a measure of shade.

The beach was crowded and rang with the sound of children playing in the sand and the water. Couples stretched out in the sun, umbrellas were bright and cheerfully coloured and picnics were being devoured.

Maggie tamped down on the longing to be a part of a family and busied herself by laying down her towel and pulling off her dress. She lay on her stomach and determinedly made herself relax. As the sun warmed her skin she felt the tension leave her and the soft lap of the water on the fine, golden sand soothed her into blissful sleep.

Giles and Olivia had left Trinity before sunup on the Monday, and after a long day of driving, camped out overnight.

It was almost noon of the following day and Giles watched Olivia's face as she steered the utility over the dusty track. There was a hard edge to her jaw, and a pulse jumped in her neck. Her hands gripped the wheel, the knuckles white beneath the light tan. 'I don't see why we had to leave so soon,' he said quietly. 'You're still exhausted from the long drive up from Sydney.'

'This is something that can't wait,' she replied, her gaze fixed to the seemingly endless track that curved in front of them and disappeared into the horizon.

'I do wish you'd tell me what all this is about,' he said finally. 'You've been mysterious right from the start.'

She momentarily took her attention from the track and flashed him a smile. 'I'm sorry, Giles. It's not that I don't trust you. I just have a lot to think about, and until some of it is clearer, it's probably best to keep you in the dark.' She grinned and swung the utility around a deep pothole. 'Besides, you always said you loved mysteries,' she added.

'One would appreciate some clues to solve this particular mystery,' he said flatly. 'So far you've told me nothing.'

Her hand rested lightly on his knee. 'Sorry, Giles. I know I'm being unfair, but after today things will probably begin to make sense. And I promise I'll tell you more when we get back to Trinity.' She

57

flashed him another smile and concentrated on the driving. 'But for now, please just let me be. I need to prepare.'

Giles knew when he was beaten. He so desperately wanted to help Olivia, for she was obviously troubled, but experience had taught him she was best left alone to work things out. She would ask for help when she really needed it.

He tried to find a comfortable spot in the sagging seat as Olivia drove with her usual lack of restraint. This had to rate as one of the most uncomfortable rides ever, he thought as the utility bounced and shuddered and rocked over the rough terrain. Even beats flying through enemy flack with the Spitfire bouncing about like a wasp in a bottle.

The loss of one arm made it difficult, for he was off-balance, and he held on to the edge of his seat with grim determination. Sam had supplied them with tools and spares as well as water. Yet, if they got a flat tyre, or punctured the sump, he'd be worse than useless. The old bitterness rose as the stump of his left arm began to throb, and he had to concentrate hard on tamping that bitterness down, dismissing it. For it served no purpose other than to remind him of what he'd become.

He kept his thoughts to himself as he stared out at the empty land that shimmered in a heat haze beneath a furnace-white sky. Dark-red earth stretched away on either side of them, relieved only by pale, drooping gum trees, scrub brush and enormous termite mounds. Boulders littered the ground on either side of the track, obviously in an attempt to mark out some kind of road to the station. They had already passed through three gates, and there was another up ahead. Just how far was this place from civilisation? And what the hell were they doing coming all this way?

He climbed out of the car and opened yet another gate, then stood entranced as a mob of kangaroos came bounding out of a stand of trees. They were bigger than he'd expected – what he'd heard the locals call red boomers. He watched them bounce past him, their joeys peeking out of their pouches. It was the first time he'd seen kangaroos in the wild, and he turned towards Olivia with a grin of delight.

Olivia nodded and smiled and gestured for him to hurry up. Giles watched until the animals had disappeared into the long grass, then climbed back into the car, the joy of the moment lost because Olivia hadn't really shared it.

The heat was intense, evaporating the sweat on his skin, making his neck itch where it rubbed against the soft collar of his shirt. There was little relief even with the windows open, for the dust blew in, flies

58

and insects were swept against the windshield and even the wind was hot. They were too far from the coast to garner the salt breeze – too far from anything in his opinion.

This section of track ran through an area of tough, silver grass and dark-green scrub. The trees were sturdier, with thick foliage that had obviously been chewed by the cattle sheltering beneath them. These cattle were dusty and fly-ridden, tails and ears twitching constantly as they meandered from one tussock to the next. Giles could just make out horses and riders in the far distance, and realised they must be approaching the homestead at last.

He looked in approval at the sturdy fences that surrounded these paddocks, and the brightly flowered trees that offered welcome shade to the travellers of this rough track. A flash of green and blue heralded the flight of a dozen parakeets from their roost in one of the trees and he was busy watching them when Olivia drew the utility to a halt.

Olivia peered through the cloud of dust that swamped them as she brought the ute to a skidding standstill. As the cloud dispersed, she could see the homestead and the surrounding buildings that lined the home yard.

Deloraine homestead was a single-storey building that had obviously been added to since her last visit. The original house was square and squat, the wood bleached by the sun, the corrugated-iron roof much patched. The wings had been added with wider windows, shingled roofs and a covered-in verandah. Roses clambered everywhere and mingled with ivy and bougainvillea.

A vegetable garden had been dug beneath a canopy of netting, presumably to keep the birds off the produce, and there were dog kennels off to one side, where the pack of Queensland Blues had set up a ferocious welcome. Home pasture spread in front of the house, lush from a bore, shady with trees. Horses slumbered beneath these trees, their withers twitching from the worrisome flies, their tails languidly swishing. It was a pleasant, peaceful sight.

Olivia sat there as the engine ticked and cooled and the dust settled. Now she was here, her rehearsed speech had been forgotten. She wanted to turn around and go back to Trinity. But it was too late. There was someone coming out of the homestead and on to the verandah.

She climbed out of the utility and pulled on the sun hat. 'Hello, William,' she said as the man came down the steps.

Short of stature, but lean and tanned, the man looked younger than his sixty years. His grey eyes inspected her, the puzzlement clear as they shook hands. 'I'm sorry,' he said, finally. 'But have we met?'

59

Olivia wanted to smile, but found her face muscles were too tense. 'A long time ago,' she replied. 'I'm Olivia.'

'Well, strike a light and blow me down,' he breathed. 'Olivia.' He eyed her again. 'Jeez, you've grown a bit since I last saw you and yer ma. How y'a goin'?' His smile creased the lines around his eyes as his warm hand once more grasped hers and pumped it with vigour.

'Good,' she replied as she tried not to wince at his fearsome grip. She introduced Giles and the two men shook hands.

'Come and sit here in the shade and have a cuppa,' William said. 'Irene's about the place somewhere, I'll give her a shout.' He strode back into the house, calling to someone to make tea and find his wife.

Giles sat down with obvious relief in one of the battered cane chairs and began to fan himself with his hat. Olivia was too tense to sit. She paced back and forth on the verandah, her hands flexing, damp with perspiration. At the sound of light footsteps she turned, her pulse racing.

The two women stood and faced one another, and Olivia realised Irene hadn't changed much despite the passage of twenty years. At fifty, her hair probably owed more to peroxide than nature, but it was beautifully cut and dressed. The face was lightly made-up, the nails long and polished with red varnish. She was wearing white moleskins that emphasised her slender hips and long legs, and the tan of her shirt was the exact colour of her eyes.

'Hello,' Olivia said breathlessly. 'I'm . . .'

'I know who you are,' came the cold response. 'What do you want?'

She had so much wanted this to work, but the greeting swept away any such illusion. Olivia felt the trembling begin in her legs but was determined to finish what she'd started. 'I've come from the other side of the world to see you. Surely, after all this time you could at least be civil?'

'Why?' Irene's expression was unreadable. 'We have nothing to say to one another.'

Olivia desperately wanted to sit down. Her legs were about to give out on her, but she was determined to show no weakness in front of Irene. 'Mother died eight months ago. I thought you should know.'

A glimmer of something momentarily touched those cold eyes then was gone. 'So?' was all she said.

The anger was beginning to well. Didn't this woman feel anything? 'She hadn't been well for a long time,' she said, her voice breaking with the intensity of her emotions. 'The doctors diagnosed disseminated sclerosis, and coupled with brittle bones, her last few years were very painful. I was alone with her when she died.'

'Poor you.' The tone was flat, the lack of sympathy insulting.

'Poor Mother,' exploded Olivia. 'She wanted to hear from you.

60

Wanted to heal the breach before it was too late. But you never wrote back to her. Never tried to make things up between you.'

'I have a busy life. She chose to go to England. Why should I be the one to make amends just because she was crook?'

Olivia stared at her, the words for once lost by the sheer arrogance of the woman standing before her.

Irene shot a glare at the silent Giles before folding her arms and returning her attention to Olivia. 'I haven't heard from her solicitors,' she said coldly. 'No doubt they are still working out probate.' Her eyes took on a cold gleam. 'How much did she leave?'

Olivia finally found her voice. 'Probate came through quickly, and the solicitors asked me to give you these.' She handed over the velvet boxes, glad to be rid of them.

Irene took the boxes and with a cursory glance through the contents turned her gaze back on Olivia. 'Is that it?' Her tone was icy, the suspicion and avarice battling in her eyes.

Olivia nodded. 'There's a copy of her will. Clause fifteen makes everything quite clear. So there's no point in trying to change things.'

William had emerged from the gloom of the house accompanied by an Aboriginal girl laden with a tea tray. He must have sensed the frigid atmosphere, for his smile was uncertain. 'Good to see you again, Olivia,' he said awkwardly. 'There's plenty of room here if you both want to stay a while,' he offered. 'Long drive back to Trinity.'

'They're leaving,' said Irene.

'Aw, come on, Irene. It's been years since you two have seen one another. Let bygones be bygones and lighten up for once.'

She turned on him, her voice a hiss. 'Stay out of this, William.'

Olivia touched his arm. 'Good to see you again, William, sorry we've intruded.' She smiled at him, seeing the confusion in his face. 'By the way, is Jessie still alive?'

'What do you want her for?' Irene's eyes had taken on a guarded sheen, her mouth thinned to an ugly line.

William frowned and looked from one woman to the other. 'Who's Jessie?' he asked.

'She's dead,' snapped Irene. 'Went a couple of years back.'

Olivia stared at Irene and felt the loathing return. There had been a glimmer of hope that things could have changed between them. Now she knew they never would. For the loathing was mutual. Yet it was a blow to learn Jessie had died. She'd hoped for so much, now it looked as if she would never learn the truth.

Irene's gaze was cold and penetrating as they stood facing one another. Olivia swallowed. She'd come this far – it would be stupid not to at least try and gain some answers. Pulling a sheaf of papers from her trouser pockets, she held them up. 'Do you know anything about this, Irene?'

The papers trembled in Irene's hand as she quickly scanned through them and handed them back. Her expression was inscrutable. 'News to me,' she snapped.

Olivia searched for some sign of prevarication in that cold face and saw only disdain. Whatever secrets Eva had shared with Irene had died along with Jessie.

With an offer to William to visit them in Trinity during their stay, Olivia and Giles climbed back into the utility. Her hands were damp on the steering wheel as she turned the ute and headed back towards the first gate. She was trembling so badly her foot was jerking on the clutch pedal, and she nearly stalled the engine twice before she got herself back in control.

Olivia drove as if the horsemen of the apocalypse were after her. Drove so the cloud of dust shrouded the view behind her and blotted out the woman on the verandah. '*Bitch*,' she spat. 'Two-faced, self-indulgent, arrogant *bitch*. God only knows how I didn't slap her bloody face.'

'I think you'd better tell me what all that was about,' said Giles as he calmly lit a cigar.

She finally slewed the ute to the side of the road and killed the engine. They were in the heart of the outback, miles from the home-stead with still miles to go before they reached Trinity. The sun was setting and the purple and pink lit up the sky and drenched the land in a soft glow. The harsh reality of this outback world was achingly beautiful – with a sense of peace and tranquillity that washed through her and calmed the trembling. Yet the anger remained, cold and hidden deep inside her, making her more determined than ever to find the answers she'd come here for.

She stared out into the dying sun until the trees were mere black silhouettes and the birds had finally come back to their roosts. Then she turned to look at Giles. His woeful expression made her smile. 'Sorry,' she murmured.

He shrugged. 'As long as it made you feel better,' he replied. 'But give me some warning next time and I'll strap myself in. You're more dangerous than bandits at twelve o'clock, and without the old Spitfire, I feel somewhat vulnerable.' They smiled at one another as the tension immediately eased. He lifted an eyebrow, his expression quizzical. 'I must say, Ollie, you don't pick your friends wisely. Who the hell is that awful woman back there?'

Olivia turned from him and concentrated on the surrounding beauty of the dying day. 'She's no friend,' she said bitterly. 'Irene's my sister.'

Chapter Seven

Darkness fell and once again Giles helped Olivia erect the tent Sam had lent them. He knew she'd tried to take on the more difficult aspects in order to save his embarrassment, but had firmly refused to be given any quarter even though he found it heavy going with one arm. Combined with the ache in the stump and his own frustration, he was exhausted when they finally had it firmly tethered. Yet he refused to give in to it.

'Now for a fire,' he said. 'Can't have a camp without a camp fire.'

Olivia laughed. 'An old boy scout never dies,' she teased. 'Dib, dib, dub.'

They collected rocks and wood from beneath a stand of trees and Giles guided her as she made up the fire to the specifications he'd followed the previous night. The rocks surrounded the shallow pit he'd scooped out and the flames leaped hungrily through the bleached wood as he snapped off his lighter. As they'd learned the night before, it was surprisingly cold out here in the middle of nowhere and they stretched out their hands to the warmth.

Giles watched the firelight flicker over Olivia's face and thought she had never looked more beautiful. There was a smudge on her nose, her hair was coming loose from the tight coil and strands of it curled and snaked down her neck. It was going to be another long night, he thought wistfully. Knowing she was so near and yet out of reach was almost unbearable.

Olivia caught him watching her and giggled. 'Two nights alone. We will cause a scandal. We're hardly children any more, so I hope you're going to continue to behave like an officer and gentleman?'

Giles grinned at her teasing and tried to appear nonchalant. 'Don't worry, Ollie. I'm almost 'armless.'

Her giggles stopped and she looked stricken. 'Don't, Giles. It's not funny.'

He shrugged and looked into the flames. 'At least I can joke about it now,' he said lightly. 'There was a time when I couldn't bear to even think about it.'

Needing to change the subject and the mood, he decided it was time to eat. Sam had instructed him in the art of 'bush tea making', but he still wasn't sure if he'd got the hang of it. He picked up the tin contraption Sam called a billy and filled it from the giant container of water they carried in the back of the utility. Tossing in a handful of tea and a eucalyptus leaf he set the billy in the heart of the fire.

Olivia fetched the last of the packets of sandwiches from the utility and unwrapped the greaseproof paper. The bread was stale after being in the heat, and the tomatoes were warm and soggy, but they ate with relish as their backs froze and their faces burned.

Giles chewed the sandwich and looked out over the silent, moonlit landscape that was so alien to anything he'd ever known. It was a powerful place, this Australian outback, he acknowledged. Unchanged since time began, it echoed something primal within him that he couldn't ignore, and sitting here in the silence beneath a canopy of stars that dominated and enthralled, he thought he could understand how the aboriginal myths had come about.

'It's a wonderful sight, isn't it?' said Olivia as she leaned against a log and looked up. 'I wish I knew more about the stars, but we so rarely see them in London one almost forgets they're there.'

Giles was for once thankful for the hours he'd whiled away in the library during those interminable months of recuperation. 'When I knew we were coming here, I did some research,' he said. 'There are a lot of books on the Aboriginal Dreamtime, and the sun, the moon and the stars play an important part in their folklore.'

Her face was beautiful in the flickering light, her eyes shining with enthusiasm as she hugged her knees like a schoolgirl. 'I love stories. Do tell.'

He looked up, trying to think where to start. 'The Aborigines believe that during the creation, the stars and planets were once men, women and animals who flew up to the sky and sought refuge in the forms we see now. The moon is male, and associated with many stories about the origins of death, for the moon dies and is reborn each month. The sky itself is believed to be the home of the spirits, and a shooting star is seen as a spirit canoe carrying the soul of a dead man to a new land.'

'So it's male dominated, just like down here,' said Olivia with a touch of asperity.

Giles chuckled. 'Not at all. The sun is female and much revered. She wanders across the skies spreading light and warmth, taking a

64

long road in summer and a much shorter one in winter. She is usually called Mother Sun, for she brings comfort and warmth and life. In some myths, Mother Sun was actually the creator of life on the earth.'

'What do these myths have to say about Orion?' she asked as she tilted back her head and looked at the great constellation. 'I know about his belt, and his dogs, but not much more, and I'd forgotten one could see it here in the Southern Hemisphere.'

He was glad she'd chosen Orion, for the myths about the Southern Cross were few and almost incomprehensible. 'No belt or dogs in the native story,' he said quietly. 'Look at Orion and see if you can make out what they believe.'

He cleared his throat. 'In the early times there were three hunters. Birubiru, Jandirngala and Nuruwulping.' He stumbled over the tongue-twisting names he'd taken an age to memorise and which were probably pronounced quite differently from his poor attempt.

'In the dry season they spent days fishing from their canoe, which they called Julpan. They managed to catch only kingfish, which was unfortunate, for being of the totem of the kingfish they were forbidden to eat it. Eventually they were so hungry they agreed they would have to eat whatever they caught. Their children and wives were starving. So they fished and again only pulled in three kingfish, which they prepared to take back to camp to eat.

'The sun saw what they were doing and called up a great storm to stop them from breaking the most sacred Law. The clouds, the sea and the wind combined to make a great waterspout over Julpan, the canoe. Julpan's nose turned upwards and they all flew round and round and up and up within the spinning column of water. The three men clung on to their fishing lines as they were spun high into the sky and left there for all eternity.'

He leaned closer to Olivia and pointed out the stars. 'The canoe and the three fishermen form the stars of Orion. Their fish are the tiny stars below the canoe, still trailing on the lines of string.'

'That was lovely,' she breathed. 'And so believable in these ancient surroundings.'

'Tea's up,' he declared as the water bubbled in the billy. He took the smoke-stained tin can off the fire and was almost tempted to swing it round as Sam had demonstrated, but discretion being the better part of valour, he decided not to risk getting them both scalded, and poured out the tea into thick china mugs. They drank it without milk, but with a lot of sugar as was the traditional way. It was dark and strong, the mixture of eucalyptus and smoke giving it a strange, but not unpleasant flavour.

'So,' he began once they'd settled back against the log. 'Are you going to tell me about this sister of yours?'

Olivia sipped her tea, her gaze fixed to the awesome display above her. 'I don't really know much about her,' she admitted. 'We left here when I was ten, and I haven't seen or heard from her since.'

'Despite the years apart, there's obviously ill feeling between you,' murmured Giles. 'Could have cut the atmosphere with a knife back there.'

Olivia remained silent. The ill will had been so much a part of her childhood it had almost become natural and therefore accepted. It saddened her, for Irene was the only relative she still had, and it would have been a comfort to be able to talk with her, to share the worrying revelations in those pieces of paper she'd found.

Giles poked the fire and added the last of the wood. 'I must say, Eva kept very quiet about Irene. Never knew you had a sister at all until today. Came as quite a shock.'

Olivia smiled. Darling Giles. So English, so predictable. It was only since coming back here that she realised just how different he was from the Australian men – but it was a good difference, for Giles would always be dependable. Would always do the right thing. Not like Sam, who was handsome and devilish and swaggered through life as if it owed him something.

'Mother and Irene fell out years ago. I never knew why. Perhaps it was something to do with Irene marrying William.' She glanced at Giles over her shoulder and smiled. 'He wasn't gentry, you see. Just a dirt farmer without much education or class as far as Mother was concerned. I think she had high hopes of Irene doing rather well in the marriage stakes.'

She giggled and poked the toe of her boot against a fallen branch and pushed it back into the fire. 'We both disappointed her there,' she added. 'But at least I had the war as an excuse for not hitching my wagon to some handsome flying officer – I was far too busy working and having fun to get serious over some man. Too many of our nurses ended up marrying Yanks, and I bet they're regretting it.'

'You'd have thought Eva would have changed her mind as the years went on,' Giles murmured. 'After all, the marriage obviously works. They are still together.'

'Once Eva made her mind up about something, nothing could shift her,' Olivia replied. 'You know how she was. Totally unreasonable, and wouldn't have dreamed of admitting she could have been wrong.'

Giles remained silent and they both stared into the flames. 'That's what is so sad, really,' Olivia sighed. 'Mother tried to make amends

66

towards the end, but the damage had been done. It was too late. Irene never answered her letters.'

Olivia listened to the crackling wood and watched the sparks drift up towards the night sky. The memories were haunting, and she wished she hadn't stirred them up by visiting Irene.

'I've told you a story. Now it's your turn,' Giles said. 'Tell me what happened after your parents found one another again.'

Olivia's smile was grateful. Giles always knew when she needed to be taken out of her dark thoughts. What would she do without him if he went off and married someone? The thought was startling and she pushed it away. They were close friends, surely nothing would change that?

She stared into the fire and thought she could hear Eva's voice again. They had done a lot of talking those last few months, and Olivia had learned a great deal more about her parents than she'd ever done before.

'My father had been swept overboard and managed to cling on to a lifebelt all through that terrible night. He was washed ashore just before dawn along with several others and taken in by the people of Ranjimup. My parents stayed in the little settlement on the western coast until Eva's sunburn had healed and she felt strong enough to travel again. Father tried to book passage for them, but Eva flatly refused to set foot on another ship.' Olivia smiled. 'I can hardly blame her, not after what she'd just experienced.'

The Nullarbor Plain was a waterless, endless desert where there were no trees, no birds and only the sturdiest of grasses and scrub could survive. Eva had learned from their guide that the word Nullarbor was the Aboriginal for place with no trees, and she could see why. It was desolate. Like the rest of this raw young country it was surely a test of survival?

Their guide was a cheerful, carroty-headed young man called Bluey MacDonald. The son of a pioneering Scotsman, the eighteen-year-old Bluey seemed to relish the silence of this awful place. He told the small party of survivors about the vast cattle herds he was used to droving across this desolate land, and of the waterholes that became clay pans and treacherous.

His eyes were slits beneath the brim of his hat as he stared out across his homeland and told them how the poor beasts had to be forced to continue to the next waterhole, and the next, until they could find water. Thousands of animals died on these treks, but the adventure was to get through, to survive with as many alive as possible.

67

He saw the whole enterprise as a personal battle against the land and the elements. Saw it as a yardstick to his bravery and resilience. Men who had survived the Nullarbor were legends, to be talked about endlessly in the hotels in the outback towns by their peers – and, despite his tender age, Bluey MacDonald seemed determined to be counted amongst them.

Eva and Jessie listened in horror to his stories, and Eva wondered what it was about these men of the outback that made them relish it so. For she could hear the love in his voice as he talked about the empty, endless miles they were travelling. And could see the lust for adventure in his eyes that already had the deep etch of lines surrounding them from the infernal sun.

It was soon obvious that Frederick was enthralled by the stories, and held the young man in awe as he asked endless questions. Eva felt a tremor of misgiving when she was forced to admit her husband was the sort of man who would take to this life with vigour. Her own future was less certain, for life would change once Frederick took up his post as surveyor, and she had a nasty feeling there would be months of loneliness ahead of her.

The days passed and turned to weeks as the horses and pack-mules plodded across the arid wastelands where the earth was almost white from the salt beneath it. They slept by a fire each night, a saddle for a pillow, a rough blanket the only protection against the cold. Meals were unappetising hunks of what Bluey called damper bread, and salted meat that meant she was constantly thirsty. Tea was boiled in a billy and was digestible only because of the liberal amount of sugar Bluey added.

They had been travelling for almost two weeks. The sky was still bleached of colour in the furnace blast of heat, but now and again they could hear the seagulls cry as they hovered in the hot wind above the distant jagged coastline.

Eva had thought when she saw the sea that their journey was almost at an end. But when she climbed down from the horse and stood on the very edge of the cliffs, her spirits tumbled. They were still miles from civilisation.

The empty landscape came to an abrupt halt and glistening black rocks towered up from a brilliant sea, which splashed thunderously against them. There were no small settlements here. Only the lonely cries of the sea birds and the almost blinding glitter of an empty, treacherous ocean.

'Just thank gawd we're not out there, no more,' puffed Jessie as she came to stand beside Eva. 'I might not take much to sitting on an 'orse all day, but it's gotta be better than bobbing about on that,' she added with a firm nod as she rubbed her back and buttocks. 'My arse is killing me.'

Eva struggled to keep her hat on against the wind coming off the sea and cleared her throat to cover up a fit of giggles. 'Riding to hounds was certainly never as exhausting.' She stared out to sea as she tried to overcome the giggles. Jessie certainly had a way of putting things succinctly, and she had to admit to feeling the same discomfort – yet her strict upbringing meant she was rather shocked by the other woman's bluntness, and certainly couldn't express herself in such a manner.

Their tenuous friendship had grown during this long trek because of circumstances. They were two women battling to overcome the harsh conditions they found themselves in. Two women who understood the discomforts they suffered because of their gender. The men hardly seemed to notice, they realised, as Frederick and Bluey rode alongside one another and discussed male concerns, their respect and liking for one another growing with every tortuous mile.

Yet Eva had grown to like this woman, and appreciated her company. She might be rough, with the awful dropped aitches and cockney whine, but she had accepted her husband's death with stoic realism and maintained a positive outlook. She was tough and indomitable and if anyone could get through this awful journey it would be Jessie.

'Wouldn't know about 'unting, luv,' replied Jessie as she screwed up her eyes and looked out to sea. 'But as my 'arry used to say. You never knows what you can do till you have to do it.'

Olivia nodded and patted her shoulder. Jessie was always quoting her dead husband, but it seemed to bring her comfort to talk about him.

Jessie looked down at her skirts blowing against her sturdy legs. 'Gawd, I miss 'im. Don't know what I'm gunna do when we get to Adelaide. 'Arry was gunna work for this bloke in somewhere called the Barossa. We was gunna 'ave an 'ouse and everything, but now 'e's gorn, I'm gunna 'ave to sort meself out.'

Eva looked across at Jessie and remembered the firm, protective arms around her in that dreadful little boat. Remembered her tough resilience as they helped one another up those sand dunes, and her cheerful chattering that kept Eva's mind off the terrible trek towards the nearest settlement. She would need someone like Jessie when they arrived in Melbourne, she realised. For there would be a great many things to do before they were settled. 'How about travelling on to Melbourne and working for me?' she asked.

Jessie's eyes sparkled momentarily then her expression grew glum.

69

'I ain't had no training,' she said gloomily. 'Wouldn't know an 'atpin from an 'airpin.'

'I can train you as a housekeeper,' said Eva quickly before she could change her mind. The task would be enormous, but at least she could trust Jessie, who was almost painfully honest. 'It won't be too complex, and I'm sure you know how to run a household and look after clothes properly.'

Jessie's eyebrows shot up. 'That won't be too hard,' she said with a mischievous twinkle in her eyes. 'Neither of us has a stitch to call our own anyhow.'

'Quite,' said Eva. It was time to teach Jessie about decorum, and she certainly didn't need reminding of her lovely trousseau lying at the bottom of the sea. Or that she was wearing another woman's very shabby cast-offs.

'Thanks, Mrs Hamilton,' said Jessie, her expression unusually solemn. 'You're a diamond.'

'That's settled then,' said Eva, her voice brisk to disguise the lump in her throat.

Olivia hugged her knees, garnering the last of the warmth from the dying fire. 'They arrived in Melbourne almost six weeks after they set off from the western coast. Eva was surprised at the elegance of the house they had been given, and astonished that servants were already hired and furniture bought to replace what had been lost. Jessie rolled up her sleeves and took over managing the house and the maids with a vigour that came as no surprise to either Eva or Frederick.'

'This is the same Jessie you asked about back in Deloraine?' Giles swallowed a yawn. It was very late and he was obviously exhausted.

Olivia nodded. 'She worked for mother until she remarried and settled further north. I always thought of her as old, but she was only a year or two older than Eva.' She poked another stick into the dying embers and watched it flare.

'Life was good for Eva in those first few months. As Her Majesty's Surveyor, Frederick was on first-name terms with the Governor. As survivors of a wreck, and "new chums", they were swamped with social invitations. Mother was in her element and once replacement clothes had been sent out from England, she flung herself into Melbourne society.'

Giles sat deep in thought for a while. 'She was more like Jessie than she realised,' he said eventually. 'Tough, resilient, prepared to begin a new life in a country she must have found very strange compared to what she'd been used to.'

70

'Melbourne might have had pretensions of grandeur, but it was certainly nothing like London,' Olivia agreed. 'It was still being developed, and most of the houses were simple wooden shacks. Society of course was totally alien compared to that of London, and Mother had to compromise a great deal.' She grinned. 'You see, society in Melbourne meant that if you were a merchant, a sea captain, explorer or ex-convict made good, you were acceptable. Mother found it very difficult to adjust to talking to men and women with dubious pasts who had prospered in their vineyards or cattle stations and whose convict background was accepted and sometimes even boasted about.'

Olivia fell silent again and looked at the moon for a long time before continuing. 'The time came for Father to leave. He was to survey the land further north and into the Territories, and would be gone for almost a year.' She smiled. 'Bluey McDonald went with him of course – the challenge was too tempting for him to ignore. Eva and Jessie settled down to a routine and life moved on with Father returning for a few weeks at a time before leaving again. Mother had two miscarriages, but three years after they arrived in Melbourne she gave birth to Irene.'

Olivia closed her eyes and took a deep breath. 'It was 1897, and this longed-for child became the centre of her lonely existence. Jessie adored her and they both spoiled her rotten. When Father came home he fell immediately in love with this golden-haired child, but the lure of the outback was a temptation he could no longer resist, and although he was sad to be leaving his little family, he still disappeared for months on end.'

'There's a big gap between you and Irene. Must have been tough for her as an only child to suddenly have a new baby in the house?'

Olivia grimaced and stood up. She rammed her hands into the pockets of her trousers and dipped her chin into the warmth of her jacket collar. 'Eighteen years is a long time to be the spoiled only child. I can't blame her for resenting me. I must have come as a huge shock.' She opened the tent flap and wriggled inside the sleeping bag.

'Your father must have been delighted to have another child after so long,' said Giles as he threw the butt of his cheroot in the fire and struggled to his feet.

Olivia bit her lip and the silence stretched. She snuggled into the sleeping bag, garnering comfort and warmth – yet she remained cold. 'I don't think Father ever knew of my existence,' she murmured finally.

Irene wasn't hungry and certainly not in the mood for an in-depth

71

discussion with William. She pushed away the plate of food and scraped back her chair. 'I'm going to see to the horses,' she muttered.

'Reckon you ought to sit down and tell me what all that was about today,' he said as he caught her arm.

She jerked away from his grip and glared. 'It's none of your damn business,' she snapped.

'It is when I have to look at that sour face of yours across the table,' he drawled. 'Expecting a bigger slice of your mother's inheritance, were you?'

It was closer to the truth than she would admit. She didn't bother to answer him and slammed the door on her way out. Dragging on her boots, she left the homestead and tramped across home yard to the stables. The welcome scent of fresh straw and hay and oats all mingled with the aroma of horse was soothing as she walked down the line of immaculate loose boxes and greeted each animal by name.

How typical of Eva to die and leave her nothing but a few pieces of old jewellery. How typical of that little bitch Olivia to come out here and rub her nose in it. Her hand was trembling as she checked the bolts on the stable doors and tidied away the feed bags. Olivia had always been the cause of all her troubles, and Irene hated her. Mum had fussed over her and spoiled her, making Irene feel neglected and in the way. Serves Mum right if she died in pain and alone with the saintly Olivia. That would teach her to abandon her and leave her nothing worth talking about.

Irene's hand stilled as her heated thoughts whirled. But surely there had to be something she could do to get her rightful inheritance? Surely some way to contest the will, and get her hands on Eva's money? Why should Olivia have anything at all? It wasn't as if she deserved it.

Feeling a little calmer, Irene stood in the darkness and thought about the terms of the will. It had been clear as to why Eva had left her only the jewellery, but that was neither here nor there, she decided. She would drive up to Cairns tomorrow and get some legal advice.

The thought of Olivia's face when she'd denied all knowledge of those papers made her smile. 'Silly bitch,' she muttered. 'As if I'd tell her anything.' She smiled as she left the stable block and headed for the single stall in the far corner of the yard. It was a powerful feeling to know a truth that would never be revealed – a powerful weapon to have in her armoury should she ever need it.

Pluperfect's head was poking out above the half-door, ears pricked, eyes gleaming with malice. Eighteen hands of black, glistening strength, the stallion shook his head and showed his teeth in a snarl.

72

He was a bastard, a bad-tempered, evil bugger, and had to be isolated from all the other horses, but Irene adored him. William had wanted him sold and had even threatened to shoot him after he wrecked the stable in a fit of temper and nearly killed one of the jackaroos, but Irene was having none of it. Pluperfect was her horse and they understood one another.

She ran her hand over his velvet nose and felt the warmth of his breath on her palm as she rested her cheek on his and breathed in his dusty, horsy smell. 'Good fella,' she murmured. 'We won't let that bitch get under our skins, will we?'

Pluperfect tossed his head and stamped. His eyes rolled back, and his ears flattened to the finely sculptured head.

Irene backed off, knowing he would bite if she stood too close. 'That's it,' she encouraged. 'Show her what we're made of.'

She checked the bolt and fastened the top door. Stuffing her hands in the pockets of her moleskins she began to make her way back to the homestead. The lights were off and she hoped William was asleep. She needed time to think, to put a plan in place. For despite her brave words to Pluperfect, the shock of seeing Olivia today had been nothing compared to the shock she'd received almost a year ago.

William had known nothing, thankfully, and she wanted to keep it that way. But something had to be done about Olivia – for her presence here could only cause trouble.

Chapter Eight

'Maggie.' The voice was soft, tugging her from a pleasant dream. 'Maggie, wake up. You're burning.'

She opened one eye, reluctant to leave the dream, edgy at being disturbed. Her mouth tasted foul and there was sweat running down her face, but as she turned to see who had woken her, she realised her shoulders were indeed feeling rather tight after the two blissful days of baking in the sun.

Olivia was kneeling beside her on a colourful towel. She smiled. 'Sit up and I'll rub this in for you,' she offered as she opened a bottle of sun cream. 'Otherwise that's going to be painful.'

Maggie, still half asleep, did as she was told. 'When did you get back?' she muttered as she tried to bring some order to her hair and brush the sand and sweat from her face.

'This morning,' replied Olivia as her cool hands gently massaged the soothing cream into Maggie's shoulders. 'Looks like you've been getting a gorgeous tan, but you must be careful, Maggie. The sun's very strong.'

Maggie nodded as she attempted to regain her equilibrium. I must look a fair old sight, she thought as the capable hands went to work. Sweaty, covered in sand and almost drunk with sunshine and the last vestiges of sleep. Bloody hell, she swore silently. What must this cool, elegant English woman think of me?

She sneaked a glance at Olivia whose skin was lightly tanned and enhanced by the white costume Maggie suspected had cost a lot of money. Her legs were long and slender, the ankles and wrists delicate. The long dark hair beneath the straw hat was plaited in a thick rope, which hung over one shoulder. The sight didn't make Maggie feel much better, and she couldn't quite forgive Olivia for being so sophisticated.

'That's better,' said Olivia as she sat back on her towel. 'But I'd keep your shoulders covered. They look pretty sore.'

'Thanks,' Maggie muttered, then realised how churlish she was being. Just because Olivia was everything Maggie had dreamed of being, and was nice into the bargain, she didn't have the right to be rude. She pulled a thin cotton blouse over her shoulders and shot a sidelong smile at the other woman. 'That's lovely stuff,' she said as she watched Olivia smear the cream into her skin.

Olivia smiled at her, finished with the cream and handed it over. 'You keep it. I've plenty more.'

Maggie eyed it, sorely tempted, but reluctant. She hadn't meant Olivia to give it to her – she was just trying to make amends for her rudeness. 'I dunno,' she began.

'Nonsense,' retorted Olivia as she firmly placed it by Maggie's hand. 'I enjoy giving presents. It's been a long time since I could afford to.' She grinned. 'Take it, enjoy it. Every girl needs a bit of pampering.'

Maggie eyed the pale lavender bottle with the gold cap and ornate writing on the label. It looked very expensive and smelled wonderful. She grinned back. 'Thanks, and by the way, sorry I was rude the other day.'

Olivia eyed her for a moment and then shrugged. 'I didn't notice,' she admitted. 'Had my mind somewhere else.'

Maggie felt a stab of jealousy. No doubt Olivia's mind was occupied by her flirtation with Sam. She thrust the idea away. Nothing was going to spoil this beautiful day. Olivia was actually very nice, and there were so few single women of her age in this little seaside town, it would be a shame not to be friends.

Yet there were questions she burned to ask. She glanced across at Olivia, who was leaning back on her elbows, face lifted towards the sun. 'I'm surprised to see you back so soon,' she began. 'Deloraine's a fair ways to go.'

Olivia's dark eyes stared back at her, the expression enigmatic. 'It doesn't take long once you realise what a fool you've been to even attempt it,' she said, her tone flat. 'Giles and I camped out again last night, otherwise we'd have been back sooner.'

Intrigued, Maggie couldn't help herself. 'Got relatives up that way, have you?'

'Not that you'd notice,' retorted Olivia. She stretched out on the towel and pulled her hat over her eyes.

Maggie could take a hint. Yet Olivia's secrecy made her even more intrigued. Of course there could be a logical answer to the mysterious trip out to Deloraine, but she knew of no other English people in the area, so who on earth had she been visiting?

Maggie eyed the woman beside her and wondered what was going

75

through her mind. She appeared so calm and in charge, yet there were obviously things troubling her. She followed suit and stretched out. The sun warmed her, but sleep was far off. Her mind was far too active.

Olivia closed her eyes and relaxed in the warmth of the sun. From their short acquaintance she found she rather liked Maggie, and was tempted to confide in her. Yet they were still strangers and Olivia had never been one to share confidences easily. Especially ones that were so close to her heart.

She listened to the children playing on the beach and the cries of the gulls that muffled the soft roll of the waves on the sand. This was home, she reminded herself. She had every right to be here. And yet why did she feel like a usurper? Why did she feel so out of place – so adrift? The anchor of childhood had been swept away by the visit to Deloraine; now she was struggling to make sense of it all.

Her thoughts and the memory of that visit were making it impossible to relax. She opened her eyes and looked across at Maggie, the need to talk too great for this protracted silence. 'Have you been in Trinity long?'

Maggie rolled her head to one side and squinted in the glare. 'Just over a year,' she replied. 'It's a bonzer place, isn't it?'

Olivia nodded. 'In a way I wish I'd never left,' she said with a sigh.

Maggie rolled on to her side and raised herself on an elbow. 'Left?' she asked. 'But you've only just arrived.'

Olivia saw the curiosity in her eyes and smiled. It was easy to talk to Maggie, so why not unbend and share her thoughts? After all, it could do very little harm. 'I was brought up here,' she explained. 'We lived in one of those little houses down the beach, and I went to the school in Adelaide Street.'

Maggie's eyes were round with surprise as she sat up. 'But you're English,' she gasped.

Olivia laughed. 'I have dual nationality,' she explained. She smoothed the hair back from her face and gazed out to the island that shimmered in the heat. 'I was ten when I left Trinity, so the accent's gone and I'm probably more English than Australian now.' She sighed. 'I do regret that, because I've always considered myself to be Australian and I think it's important to be your true self, don't you?'

Maggie nodded, her mouth pursed in thought. 'Too right,' she replied. 'But sometimes it's not always that easy – not when you have no point of reference to begin with.'

Olivia watched as Maggie dug her fingers into the sand and let it drift from her palm. There was something rather sad in her expression, a

76

wistfulness that spoke of yearnings she had yet to understand. 'You're happy here, though, aren't you?' she asked.

Maggie's smile seemed forced. 'I reckon,' she replied. 'It's the nearest thing to home I've been for a long while.'

Olivia heard the sadness behind those almost careless words, and the desire Maggie obviously felt to belong somewhere, and as it echoed her own longing, she felt a strong empathy for this other woman. 'The war does that to people,' she said gently. 'I spent years living in tiny bedsits, or sharing with other nurses in places no-one would dream of calling home. Got bombed out twice, lost every-thing.'

Maggie tucked her hair behind her ears. 'I lost everything when I was eleven,' she said with such simplicity, Olivia knew she still carried the scars of that time. 'Been on the move ever since. But this place is special, I felt it right from the start.'

'Some places are like that,' she replied thoughtfully. 'It's as if you belong there – as if you've spent all your time trying to find it. And when you do, you know it's where you should be always.'

Maggie watched the sand trickle through her fingers. She squinted in the sun as she looked across at Olivia. 'I don't have the skill to express it as well as you,' she said finally. 'But you're right. I do feel I belong here, even though this is the first time I've travelled this far north. Strange, isn't it?'

'So, what brought you here?' Olivia set her own concerns aside. She knew instinctively that Maggie needed to talk, to unburden what-ever it was that troubled her. She'd seen it so often amongst the soldiers, sailors and airmen on the wards and in the nursing homes. Troubled and afraid for their uncertain futures in the months of recu-peration and prosthetics, they were nevertheless determined to remain silent in case they were thought to be weak. The British stiff upper lip had a lot to answer for – and it had been the devil's own job to get the men to talk, to air their fears – now, here it was again, transposed to the other side of the world, where a stiff upper lip was rarely witnessed.

Maggie continued to sift the sand through her fingers, her gaze misted in thought. 'Coming here was a mistake, really,' she said flatly. 'Like your journey out to Deloraine.' She looked across at Olivia and grinned. 'But at least some good's come of it,' she said. 'I've got my work at the hotel, my own little place – and of course there's Sam.'

'Sam is certainly very charming.' Olivia smiled back, warmed by Maggie's simple offer of friendship.

'I dunno about charming,' Maggie retorted. 'He's the most irritat-ing, frustrating man I've ever met.' She giggled. 'But I wouldn't

77

change him.' She shot a glance at Olivia. 'He'll come to his senses one day, so long as he isn't distracted.'

Olivia silently acknowledged the veiled warning. 'I can see why you like him,' she said. 'But he's far too good-looking in a rough, dark sort of way. I like my men fair and rather less rugged.'

'Like Giles?'

Olivia thought for a moment. Giles was certainly handsome in an understated kind of way, with his light brown hair and trim moustache. He had good eyes as well, she realised, and quite a sensuous mouth. She stared out to sea, surprised she hadn't really thought about him that way before.

'We go back a long way,' she explained finally. 'He's my best friend, the brother I never had, but that's as far as it goes.' She looked back at Maggie, a smile twitching the corners of her mouth. 'The trouble with Giles is, I can remember him as a rather bossy little boy in short trousers. With jam smeared all round his mouth and a tin of worms in his pocket. Hardly the stuff of romantic heroes.'

They both laughed, and in that moment Olivia realised a deep friendship was possible between them. They opened the bottles of fizzy drinks and made a toast. 'Here's to the men in our lives,' said Olivia. 'May they learn to understand us.'

Maggie giggled. 'Fair go, Olivia. What bloke ever understands a woman? We find it hard enough to get the hang of ourselves most of the time.'

'True. But you have to live in hope, don't you?' They smiled at one another, at ease in the knowledge that as women they understood one another perfectly.

The water was cool and welcoming and after a refreshing swim they ran swiftly over the hot sand and pulled the towels further into the shade. The sun was high, the sky clear and an impossible blue. Heat shimmered on the ground and above the trees, and even the gulls sounded weary of the endless days of sun.

Maggie felt good. The two days' holiday had worked wonders, and she was finding Olivia's company surprisingly enjoyable. Feeling relaxed and in tune with the world after the swim, she realised she was starving. She looked at her watch, amazed at how swiftly the day was passing. 'It's a bit late, but I'll go back to the hotel and try and get us a cut lunch,' she said as she towelled off.

'No need.' Olivia reached into a capacious beach bag. 'I asked Lila to do us some sandwiches once Sam told me where you were.'

Maggie grinned. She'd avoided Sam these past two days in case he changed his mind about her having so much time off. 'How's he going?'

Olivia nodded as she bit into the chicken and beetroot sandwich. 'Good,' she replied finally. 'He's busy, but he's got enough help. I think he's only just appreciating how much you do, Maggie. Won't do him any harm to sweat it out until you're ready to go back.'

'I'd get bored if I didn't work,' Maggie admitted ruefully. 'There's not much to do around here, and although these past couple of days have been dinkum, reckon I'll soon be itching to get behind that bar again.' She gave a short laugh of derision. 'Shows a lot for my imagination, doesn't it?'

'I disagree,' said Olivia as she finished her sandwich. 'If you enjoy what you do, then why not?' Her brown eyes were dark in the sunlight. 'Just give yourself a break now and again – there's more to life than pulling pints.'

'Maybe,' muttered Maggie. She finished her sandwich and joined Olivia by the rock pool, where they washed their hands. She didn't give voice to her thoughts – of how to explain she felt safer in the pub – safer in the environment she knew best? It was ridiculous, but the pub had become home – her first real home for years, and she didn't like being away from it.

'You said it was a mistake coming up to Trinity,' said Olivia once they'd settled back into the shade. 'What brought you here in the first place?'

Maggie leaned against the cool, black rock, her feet dangling in a sandy pool. 'Curiosity,' she said, her tone flat. 'I was searching for something, but when I found it, I realised I didn't really want it after all.'

She gave a sigh and dabbled her feet. 'There's a saying, isn't there? Be careful what you wish for, because one day you might actually get it.'

Olivia nodded. 'I know exactly what you mean,' she sympathised.

Maggie looked across at Olivia in surprise. 'What more could you possibly want? You're pretty and elegant and confident. You're obviously rich, and Giles is besotted.'

Olivia's eyes widened, then she tipped back her head and roared with laughter. 'Oh, Maggie,' she spluttered. 'If you only knew the half of it.'

'Go on,' Maggie urged as she hugged her knees. 'Tell me.'

Olivia eyed her for a moment before returning her attention to the shells she'd collected, and Maggie wondered if the other woman felt comfortable enough to share some of her experiences. She acknowledged that she'd evaded the question about her coming to Trinity, but perhaps, once Olivia had bent a little, those shared confidences would come more easily.

'I don't deny that my upbringing was better than most. Mother was a wealthy woman and I had the best of everything.' Olivia stared out to sea. 'But appearances are deceptive. I wasn't spoilt with money and presents and was expected to earn my own living and make my own way. Mother was a firm believer in women being independent. I make my own clothes, cook, clean and do all the things any woman does when she's on her own. I have no husband, no children, no living relatives at all.' She tailed off. 'Well, not ones I'm proud to admit to, anyway.'

She grinned at Maggie who recognised it as an attempt to take the bitterness out of her words. 'I'm a nursing sister, and during the war I saw sights that gave me nightmares. Heard things that made me doubt my sanity, and that of the crazy world we were living in. Whole communities were wiped out during the Blitz. People were homeless, alone, trudging from one place to another, looking for anyone they could call family. I've lived in awful bedsits, shared dormitories, slept on the floor and underground in the tube stations where the rats come out and walk all over you.'

Maggie shuddered. 'It's like that up here in the cane fields,' she said. 'Rats as fat as butter, skittering about everywhere.'

Olivia fell silent and Maggie saw the conflicting emotions flit across her face. 'Sorry,' she said. 'Didn't mean to make light of your experiences. It must have been terrible in London.'

Olivia shrugged. 'If one was lucky, one survived. I was in the hospital when they brought Giles in. It was always the worst fear amongst the nurses that one of their patients would be someone close. He was thin to the point of emaciation, covered in sores, his arm crudely bandaged and filthy.'

Maggie saw the gleam in Olivia's eyes as she blinked away the tears, and wished she'd kept her mouth shut. Yet Olivia seemed to want to talk, so she remained silent, knowing the healing quality of a good listener.

'He'd been shot down, you see,' explained Olivia. 'He was captured by the Germans who did nothing about the appalling break in his arm. Gangrene set in, and by the time he and two others managed to escape and get back to England, the surgeons had no choice but to amputate.'

'He seems to be coping, though.'

Olivia nodded. 'Yes, he gives a good impression of that, but I know him too well. It's all a front. He's still in a lot of pain, and the loss of his arm has taken away his confidence. He was about to begin his career when war broke out; now he feels no-one would take him seriously as a lawyer with only one arm.' Her smile was sad. 'Silly boy,' she murmured. 'I'd want him in my corner if I ever had to go to court. Tenacious as one of your cane rats.'

Maggie wasn't surprised to hear Giles was a lawyer. He had a certain air about him, a solid dependable air that made him approachable. 'There's a lot of boys whose lives have changed because of the blasted war,' she muttered. 'Education interrupted, jobs lost, things changed forever. Sam doesn't talk about it much, but he came home to find his sheep station burned to the ground and his wife and boy buried in the Station cemetery. It must take a lot to get over that.'

'What about you, Maggie? What are your demons?' Olivia touched her arm. 'I know you have them,' she said softly. 'They're in your eyes.'

Maggie looked into those clear brown eyes, the need to confide so strong, she felt it well up inside. 'I came here to track a particular demon down,' she began. 'But soon realised it was pointless. Now I have to accept I'll never know the answers to the questions I needed to ask. Yet the past refuses to go away – and I wish I could forget everything and start again.'

'Go on. Let it out, Maggie. It's obviously haunting you.'

Maggie told her about Elizabeth dying and the loss of Waverly Station. Then she told her about the long journey north in the wagon. 'I had no idea where we were going,' she said. 'But Dad promised they were good people who would take care of me until he got a permanent job.' She took a deep breath. 'If I'd had any idea of what was waiting for me, I would have jumped off that wagon and run as far away as I could.'

The land owned by the Catholic order of The Sisters of Our Lady sprawled in splendid isolation to the west of the Great Dividing Range. Miles of silver grass stretched in every direction beneath the shadows of the hazy blue mountains, and the cattle looked sleek.

Water was abundant, even in these years of drought, for there were rivers, waterfalls and lakes in this great grazing part of the country. Elegant egrets picked their way through the long grass as squabbling, screeching parakeets and sulphur-crested cockatoos vied for perches in the wilga trees that offered shade to the cattle and mobs of kangaroos.

'It's good country out here,' murmured her father. 'Sort of place I'd like to settle.' His gnarled hand patted her knee. 'You'll be right,' he said. 'This is a good place, and the sisters will take care of you.'

Maggie eyed the imposing iron gates and the high brick wall

surrounding the house they were approaching. It didn't look welcoming. The house was enormous, the bricks too red, the paint too white. The gravel driveway leading up to the steps had been weeded and raked and the white columns on either side of the front door were pristine white.

'Do I have to stay here?' she asked. 'Can't you ask if they've got a job for you? We could find a shady place by the river and make camp.'

His chin sank to his collar. 'There's nothin' here for me,' he said. 'I asked.' He was silent for a long moment as they slowly approached the gates.

'But I don't want to stay here, Dad,' she said with growing dread. 'Surely there's somewhere else I could go?'

He shook his head and slapped the reins over Hector's broad rump. 'Sorry, darlin', got no choice.'

She sat beside her father as the gates were pulled open by a man who tipped his hat as they passed by, and stared in awe at the smooth, green lawns and beds of flowers. Wondered at the snowy statues of Mary that stood in the lee of drooping, shady trees. And puzzled as to why she should feel so reluctant to be here. For it looked so green and peaceful, a dream place that was far beyond the reality of any outback station she'd ever known.

Yet there was something eerie about the windows that overlooked the splendour with blind eyes. Something too ordered in the cold perfection of those silent statues.

Hector came to a halt opposite the steps. He was an old horse and they had come a long way. His neck drooped as Harold dropped the reins and climbed down. Maggie followed him and fitted the feed bag over Hector's head. She stroked his neck and rested her cheek on his and closed her eyes. She would probably never see him again.

'G'day, Sister. Harold Finlay. You were expecting us?'

Maggie turned and saw the nun standing in the doorway of the big house. Her white wimple was tight to her thin face, cutting right into her cheekbones. The starched guimpe was snowy over her shoulders and chest and in sharp contrast to the dead black of her habit. The rosary beads were also black, interspersed with the same silver as the ornate crucifix that dangled almost to the nun's knees.

'Good afternoon to you, too,' said the nun gaily, her Irish accent making it sound as if she was singing. 'And this must be Margaret. Welcome, my dear.'

'Sister,' replied Maggie as she gave a small bob of respect.

'Come in, come in.'

The door was opened wide and Maggie and her father followed the nun into the cool shadows of a vast hall that smelled of incense. Maggie heard the echoes of children reciting their tables, and realised the floor was marble, the ceiling high and domed. The sheer size of it captured every little sound and enlarged it. There were no carpets, no flowers, only a statue of a sad-eyed Christ bleeding on the Cross, and an enormous painting of the Holy Mother clasping a tortured heart.

Maggie looked away. Brought up a Catholic, she had attended the tiny wooden church in the next town. The walls had been bare but for the Stations of the Cross, the altar adorned only by a simple iron Crucifix and glowing tabernacle. She'd never been faced with these terrible images – and she found them too graphic.

'Come along, dear, don't dawdle. Reverend Mother is waiting.'

Maggie realised the others had moved almost to the end of the hall and hurried to catch them up. It might be exciting to attend a real school, she thought as she heard the children begin their singsong recital of the tables again. She'd only worked at the kitchen table from the books sent up from Melbourne, and often wondered what it would have been like to sit in a classroom with a teacher.

The double doors were as high as the ceiling and elaborately carved. They opened on silent hinges and Maggie's terror returned.

Reverend Mother was seated behind a large desk, her back straight, her whiskery chin dimpled by the constricting wimple. Grey eyes looked out of the grey face and showed no life, no laughter – nothing but disapproval.

Maggie looked up at her father, who nudged her forward. 'She won't bite,' he whispered.

Maggie wasn't so sure. The Mother's teeth looked pointed as she opened her mouth to speak.

'Come in, Margaret,' she ordered in a voice that extinguished Maggie's glimmer of hope that living here might be bearable.

Maggie realised she had no choice. She flicked back her hair, lifted her chin and squared her shoulders, determined not to show this woman she was terrified.

The emotionless grey eyes trawled over her, the mouth twitching in disgust, the hairs on her chin almost bristling with dislike. 'Proud, I see. Wilful, too. We'll soon put that right,' she said.

'Maggie's a good girl, Reverend Mother,' said Harold as he stood there in his dusty old clothes and screwed up his hat. 'She knows how to behave.'

'I'll be the judge of that,' the older woman snapped. The grey eyes found Maggie again. 'Go with Sister Claire. Your father and I have things to discuss.'

Maggie looked up at her father in bewilderment. He rested his hand awkwardly on her shoulder. 'I'll catch you later, no worries. I'm not leaving without saying goodbye.'

Maggie gave a tremulous smile to Sister Claire, who smiled back and led the way back out of the room. But just as the door was closing behind her, she heard the Reverend Mother say something that would haunt her for years to come.

Chapter Nine

Giles wasn't feeling too good. The phantom arm was aching, tingling, dragging his spirits low as the heat sapped him of energy. He had stripped and lain on the bed for most of the day after their return to Trinity, with the shutters closed to block out the merciless sun. Yet sleep eluded him except for a few snatched moments.

The day finally began to draw in, the heat ebbing to a temperature only slightly more bearable. Tossing back the sheet, he struggled to wash and dress and then made his way downstairs in search of a long cold beer.

'Look a bit rough there, mate,' said Sam as he poured him the beer. 'There y'go. That'll soon put hair on yer chest.'

Giles lifted his glass in salute and downed half the pint in a couple of swallows. Nothing had tasted this good in a long time, he decided. The beer was light and golden in colour with a thin head of white foam. It was nothing like the beers back home, which were mostly bitter, dark and faintly warm.

He looked around the bar as Sam moved away to serve another customer. That too was unlike any pub in England, for there was no attempt to pretty the place up. No decoration, no copper pots hanging from oak beams, no leaded-light windows and framed lithographs of ancient farming scenes on the walls. Just linoleum on the floor, brown paint on the walls and a few rickety stools placed at the bar that no-one seemed to use. The Australians seemed to prefer standing with one booted foot perched on the highly polished brass railing that ran along the bottom of the wooden bar.

'Reckon the ladies should be back soon,' said Sam as he cleaned a glass and put it back on a shelf.

'Any idea of where they've gone?' asked Giles who'd gone in search of Olivia earlier that day to find he was alone. She hadn't even left him a note, and that rattled him.

'Beach, I reckon. Olivia asked Lila for a cut lunch, so reckon they've made a day of it.' He grinned and rested on the bar. 'Why don't you get your bathers on and join them? Reckon they must have said about everything by now and could do with some company.'

Giles thought wistfully of Olivia in her white swimsuit. The cut of it enhanced her shape and emphasised her long legs, and he'd seen how the other men on board ship had eyed her as she swam in the canvas pool. But it was too hot to contemplate going out in that blazing sun, let alone divest himself of his clothes in front of so many people and have a swim.

He drank some more beer and tried to relax. There had been a time when he'd thought nothing of going for a swim, and had in fact represented his school as well as his university in the swimming pool. Now, he was ashamed to be seen half naked, and a little afraid of how he might not cope in the water. 'Cooler in here,' he murmured when he realised Sam was waiting for a response.

'No worries about the arm, mate,' he replied cheerfully. 'Smokey Smith and Wally Burns both lost a leg in the war and they swim each day.' He grinned. 'We call Wally "Hopalong", but he don't mind. Couldn't be bothered to wait until a proper leg could be fitted and made up a peg leg instead from a bit of old timber he found out at their sawmill.' With a chuckle he picked up another glass to polish. 'Got carried away and cut it too bloody short, but couldn't be bothered to do another one, silly bugger.' He put the glass on a shelf. 'I know, I'll have a word with them in the morning and you could all go down together.'

Giles swallowed. This Australian had read his thoughts, but despite his tales of locals who had been mutilated, he still hadn't come to terms with exposing himself to others. And certainly wouldn't dream of inflicting the sight on Olivia, who was bound to want to come with him. 'Better not,' he murmured.

'Still feeling crook, eh?' Sam nodded, the understanding clear in his eyes. 'No worries, mate. Tell me when you're ready and then I'll have a word.'

An hour later he was introduced to Hopalong and Smokey, who swung into the room with a great clatter. After Sam had shouted a round of beers, Giles fell into easy conversation with these two men who understood what he'd been through.

'Reckon we're a trio of bloody old crocks,' drawled Hopalong, who was in his thirties.

'Speak for yerself, mate,' laughed Smokey, whose hair was grey at the temples despite being still a young man. 'Get a tin leg like mine instead of that wooden peg before the termites work their way up into your bloody brain.'

'Reckon they already did,' said Sam dryly.

They all laughed and had another beer and Giles began to relax and enjoy their company. His accent and missing arm seemed to make no difference, and it was almost as if he was back in the nursing home with the other amputees. They shared something no-one else could understand, and the relief was immense.

As the gong sounded in the dining room and Giles caught a glimpse of Olivia and Maggie through the hatch into the lounge, Smokey touched his arm. 'Hear you might like a swim in the morning, mate,' he said quietly, his gaze steady. 'Reckon if you was to be down on the beach early enough we could all go together?'

Giles slowly shook his head. 'I . . .'

'Look, mate,' interjected Hopalong. 'We've all been through this, and me and Smokey know it ain't easy. But we've been like this longer than you, and no worries, mate. If people don't like it, then they can look the other bloody way.' He swung from the bar, lifted his trouser leg and tapped his wooden appendage. 'I got nice shiny medals at home, but this is the only medal I'm really proud of. It shows the bastards could take a leg and still not kill me.' He grinned. 'So, what you say, cobber? You on for tomorrow?'

Giles laughed. 'Put like that, Hopalong, I can hardly refuse.'

They shook hands. 'Tomorrow it is, then. Six o'clock, so set the alarm. C'mon, let's get some tucker. I could eat a horse.'

Maggie had enjoyed having tea in the dining room. It made her feel she was really on holiday. Smokey and Hopalong had kept the talk up as usual, telling yarns that were barely believable, but entertaining enough to keep the whole dining room amused. Sam had joined them for a cup of tea when they had finished eating, and it was quite late when she said goodnight and made her way back to her little shack.

As she undressed and washed off the sun cream and sand and shampooed her hair, she thought of Giles. He'd obviously relaxed in the company of the other two men, and it was kind of Sam to suggest they swam together. Olivia had wanted to go with them, but a quiet word from Hopalong had made her see how important it was Giles did this on his own, and both Maggie and Olivia had felt warm with gratitude for his surprising understanding and uncharacteristic tact.

The sheets were cool as she slipped between them and rested back on the pillows. It had been a strange day, she thought. Giles was beginning to regain his confidence and Olivia had proved to be a good and understanding listener. She couldn't remember the last time she'd unburdened herself to anyone about the convent – in fact she never had before, and had surprised herself at how easy it had been – and how much better she felt for doing it.

She closed her eyes and the images flooded back. Not that she had told Olivia everything. There were some things she could never speak about. Some things that were so deeply embedded in the darkest part of her being that she would never reveal them. Yet the images were there, chasing away the need for sleep, bringing a deep sadness to overshadow what had been a lovely day.

The dust had barely settled behind her father's wagon when Maggie heard the clang of a bell. She sniffed back the tears and lifted her chin. Dad would be back soon, she told herself defiantly. She just had to make the best of things until then.

The clatter of many feet echoed through the great house and she was suddenly surrounded by girls and boys hurrying out into the quadrangle. There was a strange, grim silence, an almost desperate air in that surge of humanity that Maggie found confusing and not a little frightening. Adrift and uncertain of what was expected of her, she remained frozen on the doorstep.

The Reverend Mother swept down the hall, her veil billowing, the rosary beads clicking against her swirling robes. 'Outside,' she ordered.

Maggie turned on the step and was faced with lines of silent, watchful children. She looked for some sign as to where she should go, but there was none in those still faces.

The hand grasped her arm in a vice and pulled her down the steps. 'This is Margaret Finlay,' the Reverend Mother boomed. 'She is guilty of the sin of pride.' The silence was electric as the grey eyes swept over the still lines. 'What is the punishment for this sin?'

'Humiliation, Mother,' came the dull response.

Maggie looked into the sea of faces, but all eyes remained fixed on a distant point above her head. She turned to the Reverend Mother. 'I'm not proud,' she insisted. 'I'm just new to all this.'

The eyes were flint as the vice-like grip hardened and she was thrust round to face the lines of children again. 'Humiliation and Service is what you will learn here,' the woman said grimly. 'And you will learn, Margaret Finlay. I assure you of that.'

Maggie looked fearfully over her shoulder as another nun joined the Reverend Mother. She saw the flash of scissors and flinched as her long hair was roughly released from the plaits. Tears blinded her and rolled unheeded down her face as the Reverend Mother wielded the scissors and hacked at her hair. Soon it lay in glistening coils at her feet.

'Pick it up,' she was ordered.

Maggie knelt and gathered the hair, her hands trembling, the tears splashing darkly on the red earth of the quadrangle. Then she was hauled to her feet and paraded along the lines of silent children, the hair clutched in her fists, her eyes downcast. She felt naked and humiliated, and terrified of what else was to come. The sun beat down on her head, drying her tears, but barely warming the frozen core of her being during that seemingly endless walk.

The torture was not yet over, she realised, when the other children were dismissed and sent back to the classrooms. For she was ordered to remain standing in the courtyard until she was told otherwise.

The silence surrounded her as the door was closed behind her. The dust cloud on the horizon was gone, her father out of sight. Maggie stood there, legs trembling, head buzzing as the sun hammered down. She was thirsty and frightened and more alone than ever. 'Ursula?' she whispered. 'Are you there?'

The presence drew near and she took comfort in her imaginary friend. As long as Ursula had not deserted her, then she would survive this terrible place.

Maggie was left in the courtyard until long after the sun had dipped behind the roof of the great house. She hadn't dared move. Hadn't dared to faint even though her head swam and she could see dark spots before her eyes. She tried to run her tongue over her dry lips, but it felt swollen in her mouth. Her legs ached and she shifted her weight from one foot to another, but nothing seemed to ease the tingling, dead sensation that was slowly creeping up from her ankles.

'You are to come in, now,' said the soft voice.

Maggie eyed the nun through swollen lids and followed her into the blessed cool of the house. She could barely focus on her surroundings as she followed the gentle swish of the sister's robes down the endless corridors to the kitchen.

'When you've finished eating, you must wash the dishes and put them away. You will sleep in the dormitory through that door.' The sister folded her arms, her hands disappearing in the copious sleeves of her habit. 'Don't take too long. The last bell is about to sound and all children must be in bed.'

Maggie slumped into the chair as the nun swept out of the room. She eyed the plate of bread, the hunk of mutton and the tin mug of water. She had no appetite, but the water didn't come close to quenching her thirst. Taking the mug to the sink she filled and refilled it until the thirst was finally vanquished. The bread and mutton were stuffed into her trouser pockets for later – she had no idea when she would next be fed.

With the plate and mug washed, she looked around the kitchen for somewhere to put them and caught sight of her reflection in the window. Her eyes widened in horror as the pinched little face stared back at her. The thick, brown hair stood in tufts like a demonic halo, her eyelids were puffy and red, and the tracks of her earlier tears were still visible on her cheeks. Maggie Finlay no longer existed.

'I see you still haven't learned.'

Maggie whirled to face the Reverend Mother. 'I . . . I . . .'

'Sins of the mother,' said the nun as she grasped what was left of Maggie's hair and pulled her out of the room, 'must be purged.'

'Mum wasn't a sinner,' Maggie sobbed. 'Neither am I. I was only . . .'

'Silence,' hissed the Reverend Mother.

Maggie's fear and pain were overwhelming. The nun's bony fingers were yanking at her tender head and she was terrified of where she might be taking her.

The door was thick and studded with iron. The Reverend Mother turned a large key in the lock and thrust Maggie into the darkness. 'I will pray for you,' she said with icy contempt, then slammed the door and locked it.

Maggie huddled in the corner. The footsteps faded into the distance and she was left in a profound, black silence. She buried her face in her hands. Only Ursula's presence in that dark, demonic place kept her from going out of her mind.

Maggie drew her knees to her chest, the chill of that first night chasing away the heat as her memories demanded attention.

She had suffered more punishments as time wore on – more solitary nights in that dark punishment cell that all the children dreaded. Yet she'd eventually become almost immune to the Reverend Mother's cruelty. Become stronger and more resilient as she realised she was not the only one to suffer in this living hell. Life had taken on a strange kind of order once she'd understood more clearly what had been expected of her, and although she resented every moment she was there, she realised she must work with the system rather than try to beat it.

The mornings were put aside for lessons, the afternoons for work. The boys were sent out to the fields, the girls to the laundry and the vegetable garden. Friendships were tenuous and not encouraged and Maggie had soon realised why.

The children were at the convent because no-one else wanted them.

90

They were mostly orphans, or had been abandoned as babies. When they were of an age they were hired out to graziers or city folk who needed servants, and Maggie had begun to look forward to her fourteenth birthday. For it would mean escape.

Her father's letters were irregular. But as the months wore on in that hateful place the letters became fewer, and then they stopped. She'd discovered years later that work had dried up during those terrible years of the Depression, and Harold had taken to the road.

Waltzing the Matilda, the swagman with a bluey on his back and all hope eclipsed by poverty and the endless miles he had to tramp to get his dole ticket, he became like thousands of other drifters. Eventually he was nameless and faceless, merely a bundle of rags sleeping beside the track, a filthy, impoverished man with no hope and no-one to turn to.

She had no idea where he was, or even if he was still alive. The idea of him dying, alone and impoverished still brought a lump to her throat as she remembered the kind, gentle man who had been her father. Yet as the years had passed she couldn't fail to recognise the similarity in their lives, for she too had become rootless and drifting after her time at the convent. For there was somewhere far more unpleasant waiting for her outside those austere walls.

She was just fourteen when the nuns found her a place working as a kitchen help on a big station out near Wirra Wirra. Benny Granger was the youngest of five sons and not the brightest of boys at the best of times. He was fifteen when Maggie arrived at Granger Hill Station.

Maggie realised she was expected to work from sunup to sundown. The kitchen was a furnace in the merciless heat of that summer of 1929 and Mrs Granger was a stickler for things being done properly. Tall, fat and unpleasant, she seemed determined to make the servants' lives a misery, and the only redemption came in the tenuous friendship Maggie struck up with Mia Mia, an Aboriginal girl who worked alongside her and shared the mean accommodation.

Maggie's job was to prepare the vegetables, do the laundry and ironing and help Mia Mia clean the homestead. When the shearers came they would clear out the bunkhouse and help the cook prepare the gargantuan meals needed three times a day to feed the hungry men. There was no time to play. No time to sit and think, and the two young girls would collapse into their narrow beds each night and fall into a dead sleep.

The days turned into weeks and Maggie fretted that her father wouldn't know how to find her. The nuns had said they would inform him next time he wrote, but she didn't believe them. She was more use to them working here than going off with Dad, for they took half her wages. Yet she had some faith in Sister Claire, who had proved to be friendly and kind and just as frightened of Reverend Mother as the children.

Maggie had been on Granger Hill Station for eight months and was busy in the washhouse. She was alone, for Mia had gone walkabout a couple of weeks before and no-one knew when she'd be back.

The copper boiler was bubbling, filling the tiny wooden shack with clouds of steam as the fire roared beneath it. The wooden tongs were awkward and the heavy sheet kept slipping and splashing back into the water. Maggie's arms were scalded, but she knew better than to complain, for Mrs Granger believed firmly in ignoring injuries and letting them heal on their own. Doctors cost money.

The sweat was pouring down her face and making her simple cotton dress stick to her. She wrestled with the sheet and finally managed to guide it through the mangle. Turning the wooden handle she puffed and strained as the sodden sheet slowly came out the other side dry enough to hang on the line.

'Reckon you'll be right, there, Benny. Fair target, mate.'

Maggie whirled around, red-faced and furious. The boys had been plaguing her from the day she'd arrived. They seemed harmless enough at first, but the older ones had begun to take liberties, like surreptitiously running their hands over her bottom when she served at table, or sneaking up to her window to try and catch her undressing at night. 'Clear off,' she shouted with more bravado than she felt.

The four older youths smirked and nudged one another. 'Fiery, ain't she? Needs to be taught a lesson, Benny. Go on, mate. Get in there.'

Maggie was almost knocked off her feet as the youngest boy was shoved inside the shack and the door slammed behind him to a chorus of encouragement and laughter. She found she was in a tight embrace as they teetered and staggered in the restricted space, trying to avoid the fire and the copper boiler.

'Get your hands off me, Benny Granger,' she hissed. She put her hands against his chest and tried to loosen his grip.

But Benny, like most farm boys, was strong for his age. Squarely built, with large hands and feet, Benny was enjoying the game, and his sloppy smile merely emphasised the half-witted gleam in his eyes. 'Go on, Maggs,' he drawled. 'Give us a kiss. You know you want to.'

Maggie felt the heat of his rough hands around her waist, saw the slack lips and thick tongue and tried not to show her fear or her disgust. She knew he wasn't quite all there and realised she would have to be careful how she handled this. One wrong move and Benny would think she was happy to play this dangerous game. 'No,' she said sternly. 'I'll tell your mum. She'll be very cross if you muck about in here, Benny.'

Benny drew away from her, his large round face the picture of contrition. 'SSSSorry, Maggs,' he stuttered. 'Don't tell Ma. She'll fair wallop me.'

Maggie nodded. His fear of his mother had been enough. 'Go now, Benny,' she said with great calm despite the trembling in her legs. 'And then I won't tell.'

Benny grinned his silly grin and opened the door. His brothers swore at him in disgust and strode away back to the paddocks with Benny loping after them.

Maggie found she was shaking. Benny was easy to handle as long as you remembered he lived in fear of his mother and the big stick she kept in the corner of her parlour. But his older brothers were mean-minded – taking after their father – and she had a nasty feeling this wasn't the last of it.

The room she shared with Mia Mia was just big enough for two iron bedsteads, a chair and a rickety chest of drawers on which sat a bowl and jug to wash in. The shack stood apart from the rest of the outbuildings, its timber walls and tin roof mouldering from years of neglect and the elements. She had nailed a hessian sack over the single window, and tonight she pushed the back of their only chair tightly under the iron doorknob. Mia's disappearance meant she was alone, and for the first time since she'd arrived she missed the girl's snoring and the strong smell of the animal fat she rubbed into her skin and hair.

Maggie lay awake, her heart thudding so hard it felt it would come right through her ribs. She watched the light from the moon slowly cross the narrow window and disappear. The darkness filled the room, making her aware of every creak and every rustle.

She slept fitfully, startled awake by the least little noise, and as dawn began to lighten the room, she breathed a sigh of weary relief. They weren't coming. She was safe.

Climbing out of bed she poured water from the jug into the basin and then stripped off her nightdress. The water was pleasantly cool against her fevered skin and she closed her eyes for a moment to try and prepare herself for another long day.

The door crashed in, sending the chair skidding across the little room.

Maggie was about to scream when she was overwhelmed and thrown on to the bed. The hand over her mouth stifled all sound, the weight of his body meant she was completely helpless. Her eyes widened in fear as she realised all five boys now surrounded her. The door had been slammed shut, the chair replaced. There was evil in their eyes and she was old enough to realise what it was they were after.

'No,' she mumbled through the hand. 'No, please. Don't.'

'Shut up,' hissed the eldest as he pinned her to the bed.

She could feel the roughness of his working clothes as he shifted against her nakedness. Could smell his sweat and the heat of him as he flipped her over on to her stomach and almost smothered her by pressing her face into the lumpy pillow.

He took her roughly, his hands forcing her buttocks apart to ease his entry. He took her as no man should take a woman, and when he was done he climbed from her and his brother took his place.

Maggie was crying silent tears as she tried to move, to call out, to escape the terrible things they were doing to her. The pain was incredible – nothing could compare with it. And yet it went on and on and on.

Benny was the last. Blubbering and incoherent with a mixture of fear and excitement, he was debagged by his brothers and thrust upon her.

Maggie bit the pillow, eyes tightly shut, the scream roaring through her head and filling her throat as she prayed for oblivion.

Then they were gone. The door slammed and she heard them laugh and joke about what they had done. Heard them threaten Benny with a beating if he told anyone. Maggie was to be their entertainment and their secret.

Maggie lay on the bed, too exhausted and in too much pain to do anything. Her tears had dried, the sobs were hard nodules in her throat which nothing could shift. The cold realisation that they would come back and repeat the torture made her shiver uncontrollably. She had to escape – and soon.

The sound was soft, coming from the doorway. Maggie whimpered and pulled the rough sheet over her battered nakedness as she drew up her knees to her chest.

'You alonga me, Maggie,' whispered Mia Mia as she sat on the bed. 'Bad men come alonga you again.' The almost amber eyes were soulful in the black face as she looked down at Maggie. 'Mia know. They hurt her too.'

Maggie struggled to sit up. She ached everywhere and there was blood on the sheet and smeared on her body. 'But where can we go?' she whispered urgently. 'We're miles from anywhere and they'll soon realise we've gone and come looking for us.'

Mia began to wash off the blood, her dark hands swift and sure and yet tender. 'You alonga me. They not find us,' she replied as she helped Maggie to dress and bundle up her few belongings.

They crept out of the shack and Maggie was stunned to realise how swiftly things had happened. Stunned to realise what had seemed like an eternity could only have lasted minutes. For the sun had barely risen above the horizon.

There was already smoke drifting from the cookhouse chimney, and a few of the men were sauntering out of the bunkhouse for their early morning smoke and cup of tea, but they paid scant attention to the two girls on the far side of the yard. They were merely a part of the scenery and of no interest.

Maggie stumbled, her legs still shaking from the attack, her head thudding with an almost blinding ache.

Mia grabbed her arm. 'You gotta be quick,' she hissed as she swiftly glanced over her shoulder towards the homestead. 'Missus come soon. Hurry, hurry.'

The thought of Mrs Granger wielding that stick sped Maggie on. Soon they were in the paddock where the resting horses had been put to grass. She cowered behind a tree and watched Mia softly whistle to a proud-headed chestnut.

The horse pricked its ears and came trotting over to snuffle at Mia's open hand. She caught his mane and in one liquid movement was on his back. 'Come. Quick,' she hissed as she brought the horse closer to a tree stump and held out her hand.

Maggie limped out of the long grass and stood on the stump. She eased the knotted cloth that held her belongings over her shoulder, took the proffered hand and with an enormous effort of will made it on to the broad back of the chestnut. Clinging tightly to Mia, she closed her eyes and tried to block out the agony that shot through her as the horse took off at a gallop.

The sun rose and the heat hammered on their bare heads. The horse was eased into a canter and then to a walk as they left the homestead far beyond the horizon. Both girls were silent during that long ride, each busy with their own thoughts and fears.

Maggie's agony continued, both physically and mentally. She realised the Grangers would know she had run away by now, and would come looking for her. She knew that if they were caught they would be beaten. She also knew that Mrs Granger would never believe what her boys had done – for in her eyes, they were perfect.

As noon approached and the heat sweltered and shimmered on the vast plains, Mia brought the horse to a standstill and climbed down. Maggie slid from the horse's back and bit down on the groan as the agony shot through her and made her head swim. Mia led her to the shade of a wilga and began to dig at the root of a spiky cactus with a stick until a pool of water emerged. She cupped her hands and drank, indicating that Maggie should do the same.

Maggie drank gratefully, even though the water was cloudy with dirt. 'Where are we going?' she asked finally as she stepped back to let the horse drink.

'Mia go walkabout. Find spirit cave,' she said as she trawled the horizon for any sign they had been followed. 'Men come soon. You alonga me. Spirits help us.'

Maggie stared at her. Mia's skin was so dark she was almost a silhouette against the sun. She guessed they were of a similar age, but Mia was skinny and small-boned, with a halo of red brown hair that stood out in a tangled mass. She wore a cotton dress Mrs Granger had given her five years ago, and it hung loosely around her, tied at the waist with a piece of string. 'You knew they would do it, didn't you?' she whispered. 'You knew all along.'

Mia shrugged. 'They alonga me many, many time. Mia afraid, so find spirit place.' She grinned, showing fine teeth. 'Spirit help to find tribe,' she said. 'Mia no go back.'

Maggie watched as the Aboriginal girl gathered leaves and seeds and made a thick pulp which she smeared over the cuts and bruises. She felt little embarrassment as the girl plastered the wounds around her backside, only the relief this cool green mess brought to her insides.

They wearily climbed back on the horse, Mia's capable fingers entwined in his mane, her bare feet nudging his sides to get him moving again. Maggie eased the bundle on her shoulder and once more held tightly to the other girl. She was at last beginning to hope they had managed to escape.

The land began to change as they rode east. The grass plains were giving way to thick bush and tangles of great trees and ferns. Out of this green soared hills of rock and jagged pillars that threw long shadows across the earth. Maggie looked at them and shivered. They were dark, ominous and looming, their black facades scarred with a red so dark it resembled dried blood. Yet Mia seemed unafraid and perfectly at ease in these alien surroundings.

As the sun began to sink, Mia slid from the horse. 'Stay there,' she ordered as she pulled a long vine from a tree and used it as a make-shift leading rein.

Maggie eased her weight forward and rested her cheek on the horse's neck as they began to pick their way over the rough scree and tumbled, jumbled boulders. She gripped the mane, her whole body trembling from the effort to stay on board as they followed a meandering path only Mia could see and climbed further and further into the forbidding hill.

The sun was a glowing arc on the horizon, the great, empty sky streaked with orange and purple as they stopped. There was silence on the hillside but for the horse's laboured breathing and her own heartbeat. Maggie sat up and looked out over the land they had crossed. It stretched away into the distance in every direction, the hazy shimmer of the eucalyptus tingeing the gathering darkness with blue.

She turned to look at the hill they had climbed and scanned the jagged outcrops and tumbled falls of rock. 'I can't see any cave,' she said. 'Are you sure this is the place?'

Mia grinned and clambered up the rockfall. She approached a tangle of scrub and a spiny bush covered in bright yellow flowers and wriggled out of sight.

Maggie slid from the horse and led him up the fallen rocks. She still couldn't see where Mia had gone and started as the Aboriginal girl suddenly appeared from behind the bush.

'Come,' she said. 'This good keeping place.' She took the vine rein and eased the wary horse through a gap between the bush and the rock wall. His hoofs skidded and he propped and shook his head, but slowly and surely Mia coaxed him through into the narrow tunnel.

Maggie followed, the bundle clutched tightly to her chest. It was pitch black in the tunnel and she reached out and felt the damp walls that seemed to close in on her before Mia's fingers caught her own and led her with shuffling steps through into the main cavern.

Staring up in wonderment, Maggie realised she could see the purple and red of the sunset high up in the cavern's roof. It sent a pink glow into the darkness of the cave, touching the rough floor, gleaming on the ancient clay and ochre drawings on the walls. She looked at the stick figures chasing kangaroos with boomerangs, nulla nullas and spears. Admired the tiny white handprints that must have been put there hundreds of years ago, and wondered at the giant painted snake that wound its way along the walls and disappeared into the darkest corners. Yet, despite this rather ferocious serpent, Maggie felt the sense of peace and security that could only come from a sacred place.

Mia was busy collecting dried sticks that must have blown down through the hole in the roof. She had stripped off the cotton dress and was wearing only a dilly bag around her waist and a tiny pubic covering. Her breasts were small, her waist slender beneath the arch of her ribs. Sitting cross-legged by the pile, she swivelled a thin stick between her palms until a blue tendril of smoke wreathed its way through the kindling and was swiftly followed by a spark and then a flame.

Maggie watched her and realised this was a scene she would have witnessed hundreds if not thousands of years before. Mia was a part of this cave, a part of its history and myth. She edged closer to the

97

fire, for it was chilly now the sun had gone and the circle of sky above them was darkening. 'How did you find this place?' she asked.

Mia's eyes were topaz in the flickering light of the flames as she regarded the ancient drawings on the cavern walls. 'Spirit of the Rainbow Serpent bring me,' she said. 'Is my totem.' She reached into the woven bag at her waist and pulled out a few berries she'd collected earlier and handed some to Maggie.

Maggie was about to ask more about the snake when she heard a noise. Both girls froze, senses alert.

There it was again. It was the sound of horses' hoofs on rocks. The sound of men talking as they stumbled over the scree. The smell of cigarette smoke and sweat, and the warmth of hard-ridden horses drifted in to them from outside.

Mia smothered the fire with the soft dirt on the cavern floor and they were plunged into darkness.

The men were nearer now, moving about close to the mouth of the tunnel. Maggie could make out what they were saying, could recognise each voice as the Granger sons searched for them. Then she heard another voice, one that was unfamiliar.

'Women not come this far, boss. Bad place. Bad spirit.'

'Don't give me that bullshit,' yelled the eldest Granger boy. 'You tracked them this far. They've gotta be up here somewhere.'

'No boss,' the Aborigine was firm. 'Mia from Wombat tribe. Enemy of Rainbow Serpent. She never come here.'

The sound of boots scrabbling over the boulders made Maggie shiver and she felt the comfort of Mia's hand on her shoulder. 'Manuwa not tell,' Mia whispered in her ear. 'We same totem. He know spirit sing 'im if he break law of Rainbow Serpent.'

Maggie didn't understand. She knew only that the men were close and that any moment now they would find the hidden entrance to the cave. She shivered and clamped her teeth together to stop them chattering, as she and Mia sat huddled in the profound blackness.

'I reckon you've been wasting our bloody time,' snarled the Granger youth. 'You bloody Abos stick together, and if I find you've been lying to me, by God you'll regret it, Manuwa.'

'Boss know best,' retorted the tracker. 'But this place taboo. If stay now, spirit death will come.'

The two girls clung to one another as they strained to hear what was being said. Then there was the rattle of small stones in the narrow entrance tunnel and the ring of boots on stone as their pursuers milled around outside. Surely it would only be a matter of time before they were discovered? Maggie had visions of what would happen to them and she had to squeeze her eyes shut to blot out the terrible scenes.

'Better go down and make camp, boss,' said Manuwa. 'Track in morning. Reckon they gone through bush alonga river. Good tucker there. Plenty water.'

'It's a flamin' waste of bloody time,' stormed the eldest Granger. 'Come on. Let's get down before we break our bloody necks.'

'What if we don't fine 'em?'

'Who flamin' cares? We can always get another one from the nuns.' There was a shout of laughter and they continued joking as they clambered back down the steep hill, their voices becoming fainter until they died away.

Mia gave Maggie's shoulder a squeeze and edged away. 'Manuwa of my tribe,' she whispered. 'He know bad taboo bring white men alonga here.'

'What about me?' Maggie whispered, the image of that giant serpent clear in her mind.

'You alonga me, Maggie. Spirit keep safe.'

Maggie fell asleep thinking of Mia and their long journey away from Grangers Hill Station. The spirit of the Rainbow Serpent had indeed protected them on that occasion, and even now she could feel its comforting presence. For she remembered her time with Mia with fondness and the dark memories no longer had the power to wound.

Chapter Ten

Giles came out of his bedroom to find Olivia sitting in their lounge, a magazine discarded on her lap. 'Good morning,' he said as cheerfully as he could.

'Morning,' she replied. 'Got everything?'

He nodded and hitched the towel over his shoulder. He felt foolish standing there in a borrowed pair of swimming trunks and a shirt, all too aware of how white and thin his legs looked. He'd once been quite proud of his muscular physique; now, to his way of thinking he just looked pathetic. 'Better go,' he muttered. 'The others will be waiting.'

Olivia stood and kissed him softly on his cheek. 'Good luck,' she murmured.

Giles nodded and swiftly left the room. Running down the stairs he let himself out of the side door and walked purposefully down the street to the beach. It was early, the sky a pearl grey laced with streaks of blue, the sun still below the horizon. Nothing stirred and there was nobody around, for which he was grateful. He was still unsure of exactly what he thought he was doing. But he'd said he would swim this morning, and he had to begin to take a proper grasp of life if he was going to have any kind of future. This was his first step – but by God he was nervous.

'G'day, mate,' came the chorus as he reached the sand and dumped his towel beneath a palm tree.

Giles' grin was sickly as he nodded to the two amputees. 'I don't know about this,' he began.

'You'll be right, mate,' said Hopalong as he sat beneath the palm tree, unfastened the leather straps of his wooden peg leg and threw it aside. 'At least you can bloody walk into the water. We've gotta hitch down on our arses!'

Smokey nodded in encouragement as he unbuckled the tin

prosthesis and put it to one side. Grinning, Giles began to unbutton his shirt, and after only a momentary hesitation, stripped it off and dropped it beside the towel. He glanced over his shoulder. The beach was still deserted.

'Ready?' Smokey grinned up at him.

Giles nodded and the three of them began the short journey to the water's edge. He was aware of what a strange sight they must be, but somehow it no longer mattered. For in his concern for the other two, he'd almost forgotten his own disability.

Hopalong and Smokey crabbed into the water until they were afloat, then struck out for the rocks on the far side of the bay. Giles stood in the water up to his waist and watched them enviously. How he would have loved to join them, to power his way through the water with strong, deep strokes and feel the pull of muscle again.

He eyed the sea that rippled around his midriff, took a deep breath and plunged beneath it.

The water caressed him, its silky smoothness welcoming him as he kicked out and edged along the seabed. It felt strange being in this underwater world after so long, and the loss of his arm made balance awkward. His lungs felt as if they would burst and he emerged spluttering and coughing, shaking the water from his hair, breathing deeply of the cool morning air. He looked around him. The beach was still deserted, the sun just peeking over the horizon, and the other two men were almost on the other side of the bay, tiny black specks in a rainbow of splashing water.

By the time Smokey and Hopalong had swum back to him, Giles had learned to float in the water, and to propel himself with his legs. His teeth were chattering and he was covered in goose pimples, but he was determined to show the others what he could do.

'Good on yer, mate,' said Hopalong. 'See, we told ya it would be easy.'

'Time for tucker,' said an out-of-breath Smokey. 'You lost the race, you're buying,' he added to Hopalong.

The three of them made their strange progress back up the beach and Giles collapsed into the sand. He was exhausted, but it felt good after so many months of inactivity, and he had a roaring appetite. 'Same time tomorrow?' he asked.

'No worries, Olivia' said Maggie as she put the plate of breakfast on the table. 'He'll be right. The others will look after him.'

Olivia eyed the heaped plate and realised she had little appetite. 'I know,' she said, pushing the plate away. 'Even so I can't help but worry. Giles isn't as strong as he thinks he is.'

Maggie looked down at her and shook her head. 'Eat your tucker,' she ordered. 'He'll be right.'

Olivia watched her move away and serve the other diners. It was all very well for Maggie – she didn't understand, she thought darkly. Giles was her responsibility, and if anything happened to him she couldn't bear to think of the consequences. She should have gone down to the beach. Should have insisted upon swimming with him in case he got into trouble.

The dining-room door crashed back and the three men came in, calling for food. Giles pulled out a chair and sat down, his face radiant.

Olivia watched him as he told her about his swim, and she was forcibly reminded of the little boy he'd once been. For his enthusiasm had returned and there was a light in his eyes that had been missing for too long. An appetite for life as well as an enormous breakfast, she noted wryly as he took her plate and ploughed his way through it.

She reached across the table, her affection for him warm in her smile. 'Well done,' she murmured. 'I'm very proud of you, Giles.'

His gaze held her for a long moment before he returned to his breakfast. 'This is just the start, Ollie,' he said as he loaded his fork. 'When we get back to England, I'm going to see about getting back into law.' He looked at her again. 'I've wasted too much time feeling sorry for myself. Those two proved to me this morning that nothing is impossible, and it's time to get back into the real world.'

Her heart went out to him and she felt tears threaten. This was the old Giles. The Giles with plans for a future. 'That's wonderful,' she said softly, her eyes blurring as she reached for her cup of tea.

They were discussing plans to go down to the beach again that evening when a terrible scream tore through the hotel. The crash that followed had them all on their feet.

Maggie appeared, her face white with shock. 'Olivia,' she called. 'We need some help, here.'

Olivia shoved back her chair and raced into the kitchen. Lila was screaming, her plump hands tearing at her hair as her daughter howled. The noise was deafening, the heat from the ancient range almost unbearable. She took in the scene with a professional eye, ordered Lila to leave the room, and stepped swiftly over the litter of broken china to the Aboriginal girl in the corner.

The knife lay on the floor, bloodied to the hilt. The girl had her mouth wide open, the screams coming one after the other in crescendo as she swayed back and forth over her bloody arm.

'Stop that noise,' she ordered.

The girl's screams came to an abrupt halt at the authoritative tone, her eyes wide and terror filled as Olivia took her hand and examined the deep cut.

'Take your belt off,' she commanded Sam. 'And fetch me a clean tea towel, water and bandages.' Using the belt as a tourniquet, Olivia tightened it around the young girl's arm and gave it another twist. 'You'll need a doctor to stitch this,' she said as she cleaned the gaping wound. 'She's severed the artery.'

'You'll have to deal with it,' muttered Sam as he handed her the clean towels and bowl of water. 'We ain't gotta doc here.'

Olivia looked at him in horror. 'What?' She saw the nods of agreement and returned her attention to the girl who was starting to wail again. 'I'm not qualified to give anaesthetic,' she snapped, giving the belt another twist. 'She could bleed to death if something isn't done immediately.'

'You're all we got,' he said in his matter-of-fact way. 'So you'd better get on with it.'

Olivia gritted her teeth as she glared back at him. 'How?' she demanded. 'I've got no medical supplies.'

Sam dumped a cardboard box on the floor beside her. 'Should find everything you need in there,' he drawled.

She looked in despair at the rolls of bandage, the grubby bottles of pills that no doubt were well past their prime, and the hypodermic needles that probably hadn't ever seen the inside of a sterilizer. 'Take this and keep turning it,' she ordered. Scrabbling around in the box, she found a phial of morphine, a tobacco tin containing rusty needles and a twist of catgut, and a packet of cotton pads and dressings. There was iodine, aspirin, a half bottle of brandy and a hacksaw. She took this fearsome object out and held it up.

'Last owner had to use that once,' muttered Sam. 'Cane cutter mistook his leg for the cane. Had to chop it off.'

'Bloody hell,' she swore softly. 'You're living in the dark ages.' Gathering what she needed, she turned to look at the cluster of people milling around in the kitchen. 'Maggie, you stay. The rest of you get out.'

She squatted down and gently brushed back the tangle of red-brown hair from the frightened girl's face. 'We'll soon have you fixed up,' she soothed. 'Just try and sit still, there's a good girl.'

The heat in the kitchen was stifling, yet her years of experience meant her mind was clear, the order of priorities instinctive. 'Open the door and windows, and put these in boiling water,' she said to Maggie as she handed her the hypodermic, the scissors, a pair of tongs and two rolls of bandage. 'Then see if you can find me a darning needle and some cotton.'

103

Taking charge of the tourniquet again, she turned to Sam. 'Use bleach and scrub down that table. When you've done that, find me some freshly laundered towels.'

As they did as she asked, Olivia examined the wound. She had managed to stop the bleeding for now, and the girl had mercifully fainted so at least she wasn't screaming any more. 'Let's hope she stays out for a while,' she muttered to no-one in particular.

'I found a needle and cotton,' said Maggie as she returned laden with towels. 'You're not going to stitch her up with that, are you?'

Olivia eyed the reel of black cotton and the darning needle and nodded before dropping them in the boiling water. 'That table ready yet, Sam? Then you can help me get her up. Maggie, you put the towels down.'

Sam lifted the limp figure from the floor and gently deposited her on the table. Olivia tied back her hair and covered it with a clean tea cloth. She lit a candle, then scrubbed her hands and made the others do the same. Using the tongs, she carefully took the things from the boiling water and laid them in a row along the clean towel before holding the needle in the candle flame until it turned black.

She took a deep breath and slowly let it out. 'Let's do it,' she said.

Maggie felt a strange kind of pride in Olivia as she passed the scissors, threaded the needle and swabbed the wound. A pride that was tinged with envy, for she would never have dared do something like this and would probably have panicked. Olivia's hands were sure and steady, her pace unhurried but deliberate as time ticked away.

She watched as Olivia eased the tourniquet and breathed a sigh of relief. 'Looks like we've done it,' she said as she administered a shot of morphine before stepping away from the table to wash her hands. 'Better take her to a room upstairs so I can keep an eye on her,' she added.

Maggie and Sam exchanged glances. 'Reckon she'd be happier in her own place,' he muttered.

'Where is that exactly?' Olivia's tone was icy.

'Out back,' he replied.

'She'd be better off in a nice clean bed upstairs,' she retorted.

'We'd lose all our customers,' Maggie intervened. 'She wouldn't feel right, and neither would they.'

'Are you telling me she isn't allowed upstairs?' Olivia's voice held a dangerous calm.

Maggie swallowed. 'Not exactly,' she said finally. 'This is a small town. The lubras prefer to keep themselves to themselves.' She blushed as Olivia glared at her. 'They aren't banned from coming in here to drink or anything,' she blustered. 'They just prefer not to in case it causes trouble.'

Olivia looked down at the girl on the table. 'If there had been a doctor, would he have come out to see her?'

Maggie shrugged. 'Reckon so. But most of them prefer to see their own medicine men.'

Olivia raised an eyebrow as she felt the girl's pulse. 'I see,' she muttered.

Maggie wondered what was going through the other woman's mind, but hesitated to ask. 'The medicine men are real clever,' she said hurriedly. 'They know much more than any white doctor. You know, herbs and leaves and things.' Her voice tailed off. It was a sticky subject, and she knew the incident had not put Trinity in a good light.

Olivia paced back and forth as Giles poured her a drink in their lounge. 'I admit it was fairly pleasant,' she said. 'But it was still a compound.'

'Tell me about it,' offered Giles.

Olivia stopped by the verandah window and stared out over the roofs to the sea. 'It's down a narrow path and through a gate at the back of the hotel,' she said. 'It's quite large, and pleasantly shady, with a line of shacks all down one side.'

She fell silent, remembering the curious eyes watching the small cavalcade as they took the girl to her cabin. There had been naked children happily playing in the long grass while the men lounged in the shade of the verandahs. The gossiping women beneath the trees had seemed cheerful if their laughter was anything to go by.

'They have a laundry and a cookhouse,' she went on. 'And the shacks themselves are quite big. But their idea of hygiene makes me shudder.'

'At least they're cared for,' muttered Giles as he poured tonic into the gin. 'Surely that's better than being on the streets?'

Olivia nodded as she took the proffered glass. 'I suppose so. But they're still treated as second-class citizens, however one looks at it,' she persisted.

'Oh, dear,' he said with a gentle sigh as he sat down. 'You're not going to start one of your blasted crusades, are you?'

She looked down at him and remembering her childhood crusade to rescue every tramp in London by offering them her pocket money, suddenly saw the funny side of things. 'No,' she said. 'But the children need to be educated if they are to become anything but servants. The missionaries do their best, evidently, but it's just not enough.'

She eyed his wry smile. 'And they need better medical care. I made

Sam tell me the position here, and he finally admitted the nearest doctor was miles away and didn't appreciate being called out for a native.'

Giles took a long drink before replying. 'I get the feeling you've got a plan,' he said with weary acceptance. 'Might have known you couldn't sit still for long.'

She gave him a playful swipe around his ear. 'Yes,' she admitted. 'I do have a plan. But it will mean staying here for much longer than we first anticipated.'

He raised an eyebrow as he stroked his moustache. 'How much longer?'

'For as long as it takes to set up a medical centre. One that will cater for black and white.'

Irene Stanford didn't appreciate being thwarted. The inheritance she'd received when Eva left for England all those years ago had been generous, but she had hoped for a chance to get her hands on even more once Eva died. Clause fifteen had put an end to that – stating clearly that Irene's share of the inheritance had already been paid and there would be nothing else to come but the jewellery. Irene's hope of circumventing the clause had been dashed by her solicitor, who'd been adamant there was nothing she could do. Probate had been granted, the clause firmly in place, and after getting a second opinion, she realised she had to accept the fact Eva and Olivia had bested her.

She stood on the verandah of her little house in Cairns and stared out to sea. It was a pretty town, she acknowledged, sheltered by a horseshoe of mountains and edged by a sweep of yellow sand. There were a few hundred houses scattered around the surprisingly good main shopping area and palm trees dipped and swayed in the tropical breeze that blew off the sea, but on the whole it was just another seaside town with pretensions of grandeur.

It was frustrating to think there was no more money to come, but the trip to Cairns had not altogether been wasted, she thought with grim satisfaction. Mother's jewellery had been sold for a healthy sum and once the money was banked, she could afford to buy another property. Her smile was satisfied as she thought of William's ignorance. He had no idea of how wealthy she was. Had no idea she'd formed a series of companies so intertwined and varied that it would take an expert to discover the driving force behind them. From these companies, Irene managed a vast portfolio of shares and numerous rental properties down in Sydney. They were her safety net for when she'd had enough of living in the sticks, and that time was fast approaching.

106

She ran her hands over her slim hips and took in a deep breath. No wonder her son, Justin, had left for Sydney, and decided to make his future there. The outback was stifling despite the vast miles between the stations, and the constant pressure of living with a man who was neither exciting, nor particularly intelligent, was wearing Irene down. She used these trips to the coast to escape – to remind her there was another life outside Deloraine – even if it did take three days in a ute to get here.

She had friends in Cairns, a good hairdresser and manicurist, and a reasonable dressmaker. The pampering and shopping made her feel good, and it was pleasant to sit in one of the seaside restaurants with a glass of wine and good company.

Not that Cairns was up to much, she thought disdainfully. It was too parochial and set in its ways. A shabby seaside town that slumbered its way through the seasons and closed down entirely during the Wet. Sydney was the place for real shopping. For dinners with interesting men, dancing and theatres, a chance to catch up with Justin and his new girl, and all the things she missed so much being stuck out on Deloraine.

She left the verandah. Sydney and Justin would have to wait, she realised. And so would Arthur. There were more important things to do than meet her lover and spend hours in bed. She had plans, and until they were finalised, nothing must divert her. Grabbing her handbag, she left the wooden house.

Her car was a new, pale-green and white Holden. With whitewall tyres, rear fins and a tinted sun visor, it was top of the range and far too good to keep out at Deloraine. Irene loved the feeling of power as she raced down the main street and headed north – for there was nothing quite like pulling strings and making people dance to her tune.

Chapter Eleven

Olivia was restless. The heat was awful and sleep eluded her even though the day had been exhausting. She climbed back out of bed and pulled on shorts and a cotton shirt, and with her shoes in her hand, left the bedroom and made her way downstairs.

It was late and the hotel was in darkness as she slipped the lock on the side door and stepped out into the yard. Shoving her feet into the comfortable loafers, she took a deep breath of the sultry night air and looked up at the moon. It was glowing, full-faced and almost benevolent, and just for a moment she thought she could discern a smiling face. Grinning at her own stupidity, she shoved her hands into the pockets of her shorts and began to walk.

As always, her steps took her to the beach and she slowly ambled along the sand, her thoughts drifting in tune with the soft slap of the gentle waves. Eva had called her an 'ocean child', and when she was small she'd imagined she was a beautiful mermaid, stranded like the one in the fairy tale in this land of mortals. She grinned at the memory. How simple life was then. How easy to believe in magic and mermaids when you had fireflies dancing in the surrounding scrub and this wonderful beach as your playground.

She stopped walking and looked up at the sky. In London during the Blitz they would have called such a moon a 'bombers' moon', and the silence would have been rent by the thunder of hundreds of enemy planes – torn to shreds by the deadly whine of buzz bombs and the shattering boom of yet another part of the city going up in flames. But here, in northern Queensland, the silence was enhanced by the silky rustle of palm leaves, the saw of crickets and the sibilant hiss of waves on wet sand.

Olivia felt the magic of this place begin to work again as it always did, and she stared out to sea. The island was a silhouette between the night sky and the sparkling water, unchanged since she was the little girl looking out of the window. She turned, knowing where she was, where her footsteps would always lead her.

The house was in darkness, huddled with the others on the gentle rise above the sand. All was still, all silent, and this time there was no child at the window. The child was now a woman. A woman with questions that had so far not been answered. A woman that no longer believed in mermaids and fairies – for the magic had died – had been torn away by the revelation that nothing she had believed in was real.

Olivia tramped up the slope and stood for a long while in front of the house that had once been her home. It looked abandoned and rather sad, she thought. Just like me, really. I wonder if houses really do have a spirit in them – if they really do know when they weren't loved?

'Bloody silly nonsense,' she muttered. 'Your brains are addled, woman.' She hitched up her shorts and sat cross-legged in the sand, her shoulder resting against the white paling fence as she studied the house more intently. Despite her words, she couldn't help but feel the house was welcoming her back. And as she sat there in the still of a tropical Australian night, her memories came alive.

The house had seemed so much bigger then – with airy rooms leading off the hall and a kitchen running along the back. Her own room was at the front of the house, with a view of the sea and the endless sky. Mother's room was next to it, with Irene's across the hall. The sitting room was square and Olivia remembered the battered couch and chairs and the aspidistra in the ugly china pot that always stood in the corner. In winter there would be a fire in the hearth, and she remembered having to dress for school in front of it to keep warm, for the temperatures could drop swiftly during the night.

Olivia sat by the fence, her cheek resting on the paling as she trawled the familiar lines of this house that had once been home. The memories were like snapshots from an album – momentary glimpses of the past that were almost too fleeting to capture – yet real enough to make her shiver.

Olivia knew she wasn't supposed to be in Irene's room, but the door was open, Irene was out and the temptation had just been too much. She clambered up on to the dressing stool and found she had to kneel to see herself in the mirror. She patted her hair the way she'd seen Irene do it, and pulled a few faces before she got bored with this game and began to explore the clutter of interesting things on the dressing table.

There were earrings which pinched her ears and made her grimace. Necklaces which looked pretty against the blue cotton dress, and clips and brooches which sparkled in the sunlight pouring through the window. With great care she draped herself in the necklaces and hooked some of the brooches on her lace collar, then looked in the mirror to admire the effect. Deciding she needed something more, she reached for the box of powder she'd seen Irene dust over her shoulders before she went out during the evening.

Her chubby, baby hands were clumsy, the box too tightly fastened, and she gasped in horror when it slid from her grip and bounced across the floor, shedding the powder everywhere.

She knelt there for a long while, deep in thought, wondering if perhaps she should clean it up immediately, or do it later. Her gaze moved back to the make-up and the allure of lipstick and eyeshadow won her over. Irene wouldn't be back for ages. She'd clean up later.

The lipstick was bright red and felt sticky on her lips and she pouted just like Irene did when she eyed her reflection in the mirror. The black pencil made lovely lines on her brows, and the blue eyeshadow looked bonzer and matched her dress. It had been tricky to get it just right, but Olivia thought she looked marvellous.

'What the *hell* do you think you're doing?'

Olivia froze, her eyes wide with terror as she looked in the mirror at her older sister.

'You little bitch,' spat Irene as she looked at the painted face, the talcum powder on the floor and the mess on her dressing table. She strode into the room and ripped off the necklaces and earrings, catching her long red nails on Olivia's baby cheeks as she tore the brooches from the lace collar.

Then she yanked Olivia off the stool and gave her a resounding slap around the face. 'Get out,' she screamed. 'Get out and don't you dare come in here again.'

Olivia was shoved out of the room with such force she went sprawling on the hall floor. The shock of the fall coupled with the terror of Irene combined in a fearsome scream.

'What on earth's going on?' Eva appeared from the kitchen and scooped her up with floury hands.

'That brat has been in my things.' Irene stood in the doorway, her expression thunderous. 'Look at the mess. Just look at what she's done.'

'It's only a little powder and paint,' murmured Eva as she consoled Olivia. 'It'll clean up.'

'I might have known you'd take her side,' snapped Irene. 'Spoilt little bitch.' She turned a furious glare on Olivia. 'Shut up!' she screamed. 'You aren't hurt.'

Olivia cringed in Eva's arms. 'I sorry,' she sobbed. 'Not bitch.'

Eva kissed her and smoothed back her hair before setting her back on her feet. 'Go and get a biscuit, darling,' she said softly. 'Irene and I need to talk.'

Olivia fetched the biscuit and hovered just inside the kitchen door, listening to the furious row going on in Irene's room. She could hear Eva's harsh, lightly clipped retorts to Irene's sniping , but the words were incomprehensible. She gave a sigh and thought perhaps it would be better if she left home, then there would be no more fighting.

Emily and the pram had been a Christmas present and she loved Emily with a passion. She had a shiny, pretty face and eyes that closed when you put her to bed, and lovely curly blonde hair. Her dress was yellow with a bow around the waist. Frothy petticoats, lacy knickers and tiny white shoes completed the outfit. She could even say 'mama', just like a real baby – but then Emily was real to Olivia.

Emily was her friend, so she couldn't leave her behind with Irene, because her sister had made it plain she hated Emily by throwing her across the room the other day.

Olivia tucked Emily firmly between the tiny sheet and blanket and trundled the pram out through the kitchen and into the back garden. She stopped on the way to collect another biscuit in case they got hungry and was soon proudly pushing the pram along the sandy track which would take them into town. She would show Emily the shops, and perhaps they could catch the bus to Cairns just like she did with Mummy sometimes.

She and Emily had a lovely time. Lots of people stopped and talked to them and asked where they were going, and one kind lady even got her a piece of cake and a glass of lemonade and let her sit in the shade of a great big umbrella.

Her spirits fell as Irene came through the gate.

'Thank you for looking after her,' she said. 'Mother and I have been frantic with worry.'

'Looks like the little darling's been experimenting with your make-up, bless her. I tried to wash it off, but she wasn't having any.'

Irene's smile was bright. 'Little girls have got to start somewhere,' she said. 'Come on, Olivia. Time for home.'

Olivia slid from the chair and wiped the crumbs from her mouth. Irene didn't seem cross. In fact she looked quite nice in that red dress, with the sun glinting in her hair. Yet she was wary of the long red nails, and of the strange look in her sister's eyes as she collected Emily and pushed her out of the gate. The sting of that earlier slap was clearly remembered, and she didn't trust this smiling, nice Irene.

'Why do you always have to cause trouble?' hissed Irene as they walked down the street.

'I sorry,' Olivia mumbled. 'Emily want a walk.'

Irene's jaw hardened as she snatched up the pram and dragged Olivia across the road to the sand track.

Olivia watched in horror as Emily fell from the pram and was dashed against the concrete surrounding the telegraph pole. Tears welled and the sobs turned into wails as she struggled to break free from Irene's ferocious grip. 'Emily,' she wailed. 'Emily all broke.'

Irene picked up the doll by her feet and slammed it repeatedly against the telegraph pole until Emily's face was obliterated.

Olivia's horror silenced the wails as her darling Emily was murdered. She stood in fixed terror as Irene waved the precious doll in her face, making her see the insides of Emily's head and the awful pin that stabbed her beautiful blue eyes. Dumb with shock, Olivia stared up at Irene.

'That's what I'll do to you one day if you don't behave,' said Irene. 'Understand?'

Olivia nodded.

'And if you tell Mum anything about this, I'll do it tonight,' she threatened.

Olivia had no doubt she would. And that was the start of Irene's regime of terror that lasted almost up to the moment Olivia and Eva sailed for England.

Maggie was also restless. It was hot in the cabin and she tossed and turned until the sheets were mangled and damp with sweat. Without bothering to light the kerosene lamp, she climbed out of bed and padded across the floor to the door. The air was heavy with heat as she stood there in her nightshirt, and she lifted her hair from the back of her neck in an attempt to garner the faint relief of a mild breeze.

The silence was profound in that tropical night, and as she stood there in the glow of the full moon she breathed in the scent of warm earth and exotic flowers and watched the fireflies dance in the bushes. Their tiny, flickering pinpricks of light never ceased to enthral her, for they brought magic to the night – a magic linked to the childhood belief in fairies – a magic that even the most hardened of hearts couldn't fail to appreciate.

The click of a key turning and the soft complaint of rusting hinges made her start. Peering into the darkness cast by the hotel, she thought she saw something move. Then she heard the crunch of feet on the gravel and knew someone was leaving by the side door.

She edged back from the moon's glow and stood in the deeper shadows of her own doorway. The steps were too light to be Sam's, but who else would be out there in the middle of the night?

112

Maggie breathed a sigh of relief as Olivia emerged from the shadows and headed out of the yard. She obviously couldn't sleep either, and Maggie was tempted to join her on the moonlit stroll. Yet there was something in the other woman's demeanour that stilled her. For Olivia had the air of someone who needed only the solitary night as company.

Maggie watched her leave the yard and head for the beach. Her instincts had been right, for the beach was a place of contemplation – a beautiful, welcoming place, which brought some relief from the heat – especially on a night such as this.

She stood in the doorway for a while before turning back into the room. The sea had been a revelation after all the years in the dry, sepia world of the outback, and Maggie had spent hours on the beach at Manley during her years in Sydney. Now, after living here in Trinity, she knew she could never return to those thousands of dusty, dry miles that stretched endlessly across the centre of Australia.

For the sea held a fascination for her in the mysterious, changing facets of its nature. Calm, cool and welcoming in the heat of summer, it gave no hint of the mighty power that could be unleashed. When it was raging, thundering against the rocks, hissing over the sand, the rip tides boiling beneath the surface, Maggie would exult in the sheer drama of it all.

Having made a cup of tea, she sat at the table and flicked through the pages of a magazine she'd read a dozen times before. With the tea finished and the magazine pushed aside, she eyed the rumpled bed and knew she was still far from sleep. Olivia, or no Olivia, she needed to get out of here. Needed to walk, to feel the sand between her toes and the welcome coolness of the water.

She pulled on her swimsuit and topped it with shirt and shorts. Minutes later she left the shack and padded barefoot out of the yard and down the street. It had been some time since Olivia had taken the same path, and it was unlikely they would bump into one another. Yet Maggie didn't want her to think she'd followed her, and deliberately turned off the main road and followed the track between the beach houses.

Her bare feet made no sound on the sand as she passed the silent, dark houses. The scent of flowers was heady in the heat, the shadows cast long by the moon as she came to the end of the row. She wouldn't have chosen to come this way if Olivia had not gone for her walk – but in a way she was glad she had. For it was time to put the ghosts of yesterday behind her. Time to embrace this new life and forget what might have been.

She looked neither to the left nor right as she picked her way through the sharp-edged sea grass that grew beneath the palm trees. The sea was spread before her, glittering with thousands of diamonds of light beneath the full moon, laced with fringes of white foam as it splashed on the sand. Maggie stepped away from the shadows of the palm trees, her gaze fixed on the sight before her.

'So, you couldn't sleep either,' came the voice from the shadows.

'Bloody hell,' gasped Maggie. 'You frightened the bloody life out of me.' Her pulse was racing as Olivia moved into the light. Then she noticed the tracks of tears on the other woman's face before they were hastily rubbed away. 'Sorry,' she mumbled as she backed off. 'Didn't mean to intrude.'

Olivia stood up and brushed the sand from her legs. 'Good thing you did,' she said briskly. 'I'm sick of my own company.' She linked her arm through Maggie's. Let's walk.'

Maggie's gaze flitted over the houses as they ambled along the gentle dunes. 'Something's obviously upset you,' she said softly. 'Want to talk about it?'

'It won't change anything,' replied Olivia. 'The memories will still be there wherever I go – whatever I say.'

Maggie felt a chill of unease. 'Memories?' she asked. 'Memories of what?'

Olivia's smile was sickly as she faced Maggie. 'Don't let's talk about it now. The night's too beautiful.'

Maggie couldn't let the moment pass. 'Are these memories something to do with that house?'

Olivia stopped walking and eyed her for a long moment. 'It was my childhood home,' she said finally. 'Of course there are memories attached to it.'

Maggie stared at her, aware of how the colour must be bleached from her face. 'Of course,' she breathed. 'Hamilton. I should have known – should have realised.'

Olivia frowned. 'I made no secret of my name. Why should it come as such a shock?'

Maggie swallowed and shook her head in an attempt to clear the swirling thoughts and possibilities. 'That's why you went out to Deloraine,' she said, hardly aware she was voicing her thoughts.

'I went out to see my sister, Irene,' Olivia said flatly. 'Though what on earth it has to do with you, I can't imagine.'

Maggie's legs gave way and she sank on to the sand, her hands covering her face as the dark clouds swirled in her head. 'Your sister,' she breathed. 'Oh, my God.'

Olivia's arm went round her shoulders as she knelt beside her, and she could feel her warmth, her concern, the trembling in her hand. 'Maggie,' she said urgently. 'Maggie, what is it? For goodness' sake talk to me. You're frightening me.'

Maggie shook her head. 'It can't be,' she whispered. 'It's impossible.'

'What's impossible?' Olivia grasped her shoulders and forced her to look her in the face. 'What are you trying to tell me, Maggie?' she asked firmly.

Maggie shivered as she sat back on her heels and stared out to sea. The heat of the night could no longer touch her – for the only reality was the chill that struck mercilessly to her very core. 'You wouldn't believe me if I told you,' she muttered. 'You just would not believe it.'

'Try me.' Olivia's hands were still on her shoulders, her face grim in the pale moonlight.

Maggie swallowed as she rubbed her hands over her arms in an attempt to bring back the warmth. Her thoughts were in turmoil. 'I don't know where to start,' she said finally.

'Try the beginning.'

'I don't really know the beginning,' she said softly, her focus fixed on the tiny island out to sea. 'Only the bit I discovered a few years back.'

'It's as good a place as any,' encouraged Olivia. 'Go on, Maggie. Tell me.'

Maggie hugged her knees as she told Olivia about her escape with Mia, and the long weeks the two of them spent wandering in the outback before they arrived in the tiny settlement of Quilpie. 'Mia needed to get back to her tribe, and I needed to find work.' She sighed. 'We both cried when we had to say goodbye. It was hard, because we'd come to really like and depend on one another.'

'Did you ever see her again?'

Maggie shook her head. 'I don't even know if she's still alive,' she said softly. After a moment of silence, Maggie scrubbed her face with her hands and squared her shoulders. Her voice sounded strangely calm, even though her thoughts were in turmoil.

'Quilpie lies in the heart of Queensland's outback. It's about as far from the sea as you could get, and the men who work the vast sheep stations that sprawl across the blood-red earth are amongst the toughest. They live most of their lives on the back of a horse, or bent over a sheep in the enormous shearing sheds.'

Olivia remained silent as Maggie collected her thoughts.

'Quilpie boasted a hotel on each corner of the one crossroad in town. I lied about my age and experience and managed to blag my way into a job in one of them.'

Her smile was wan as she remembered the heat, the dust, the flies, the tough, rough men she saw every day. Quilpie hadn't only been a grazier's town, she remembered. For beneath that cinnamon earth lay riches beyond a man's dreams. Hidden from sight, waiting like precious eggs to be cracked open, some of the boulders littering the vast landscape held a wondrous secret. For once split, they revealed opal. This opal lured the diggers, the prospectors and fossickers, as well as the dealers and buyers. Quilpie was doing a roaring trade, despite the Depression.

'I had a room at the back of the hotel and forged a good relationship with the middle-aged owner and his wife. I worked in the bar sometimes, but mostly I waited table in the dining room or helped in the kitchen.'

'Must have been hard,' murmured Olivia. 'You were very young.'

Maggie shrugged. 'I enjoyed the rough and tumble, and although the fights could sometimes get out of hand they were soon sorted out over yet more beer.' She hugged her knees more closely and rested her chin on her arm. 'Matt Foley came into town almost a year after I arrived. I was sixteen when we sort of got married.'

'Sort of got married? That's like being "sort of pregnant". What do you mean?'

Olivia's eyes were wide with surprise, and Maggie noticed how she glanced at the bare finger of her left hand. 'I had no papers. They were still at the convent, and as I'd never had the nerve to go back and get them, I was stuck,' she sighed. 'We all make mistakes,' she said flatly. 'Mine was to fall for a curly haired, dark-eyed Irishman with a swagger in his walk and a laugh to make you tumble into bed.' She sighed. 'He was a gun-shearer, the nobility of the shearing shed who could lift a fleece faster than any man. There was stiff opposition that year from a bloke out at Eromanga, and he was determined to keep his reputation. He won, and in the heat of the moment proposed to me.'

She grinned. 'I jumped at the chance, of course, didn't have another thought in my silly head, despite Mrs Banks trying to warn me off – and the fact that no preacher would formally marry us because I had no papers.'

'So what happened?'

Maggie shrugged. 'We held our own ceremony – flew in the face of respectability – but of course it didn't work. I was too young – he was used to the freedom of being single, and of course eventually realised in truth he still was. The marriage was a sham, really – a game of pretend.' She blinked and tried to focus on the scenery. The hurt was still there, a reminder of youthful foolishness. 'We left

116

Quilpie with a horse, a covered wagon and two bedrolls. Over the next two years we travelled from one station to another, and I spent most of the time in the shearers' kitchen cooking enormous meals.'

She heard the bitterness in her voice and tried to temper it with a laugh. But even that sounded hollow. Although they couldn't be formally married, being with Matt was exciting at the start, and Maggie had enjoyed the sense of belonging. Had loved listening to his stories and watching the sparkle light up his eyes. And at night, when he held her, she almost purred with the pleasure of feeling his skin brush against hers as they made love beneath the stars. Yet the adventure of being free, of roaming endlessly across the empty land began to pall. She began to long for a permanent home, their own land and sheep. Children.

'Matt refused to discuss any plans for settling down,' she said finally. 'His dream was to become very rich, and I realised I was all a part of his plan to do just that. I worked hard in those bloody kitchens, but I never saw a penny of my wages.'

Olivia rested her hand lightly on Maggie's. Her touch was sympathetic, but she said nothing.

Maggie shifted in the sand. 'It was tough, but not nearly as tough as when I found out he'd been unfaithful in almost every town we passed through, and that most of my hard-earned money was gambled away.'

'As he's not around any more, I assume you left him?'

'It didn't quite happen like that,' she murmured. 'We were down near Dirranbandi. Work had almost dried up because the graziers were cutting back on stock and not hiring that many shearers. Matt had begun to get the reputation for fighting and drinking too hard, and although he never laid a finger on me, I was beginning to wonder how long it would be before he did.'

Maggie took a deep breath and stared ahead, not really focussing on the night sounds. 'Tensions were growing between us, and the lack of work was eating away our savings.' She fell silent. The sky was lightening. It would soon be dawn.

'I woke up one morning to find he'd gone. He'd taken his stock horse, his bedroll and the last of our savings.'

'Bastard.'

'Yeah. Too right he was a bastard,' agreed Maggie. 'But he was within his rights. At least he left the wagon, the old horse and most of the food and water.'

'So, what did you do?'

'I hitched up the wagon and drove out to the convent. It was only a few miles away, and I thought I might find out what happened to Dad.'

117

'And did you?'

'No. But I found out something far more interesting than that.' She turned and looked at Olivia, her gaze steady. 'It was that something that eventually brought me here to Trinity.'

'I didn't hear you come home last night,' said William as he buttered toast. 'Must have been very late.'

'It was,' Irene replied. 'I slept in the spare room so as not to disturb you.'

'Thoughtful of you,' he said as he poured them both a cup of coffee.

His sarcasm wasn't lost on her. She lit a cigarette and knowing how much he hated her smoking at mealtimes, deliberately blew smoke across the table. 'Not at all. It's cooler in there and your snoring keeps me awake.'

He eyed her for a moment then resumed his breakfast. 'I wish you'd warn me when you're going to disappear for days. I needed you here last night to discuss this year's stock sales.'

'That would have made riveting conversation, no doubt. I'm sure you managed,' she replied. The coffee was hot and strong, and chased away the cobwebs after a restless night. If only William would shut up and finish his breakfast, perhaps she could have a bit of peace before she went to the stables. There was still a lot to think about despite the journey north. Too many things that could still go wrong.

William put his knife down and wiped his mouth with the napkin. His eyes were cold, his expression grim. 'We need to talk, Irene.'

'I'm not in the mood, William,' she said as she stubbed out the half-smoked cigarette in the saucer.

'You never are,' he retorted. He threw the napkin on the table and leaned back in his chair, arms folded tightly to his chest. 'Why did you marry me, Irene?'

The question came as such a surprise she didn't know how to answer him. 'What on earth's the matter with you this morning?' She knew she sounded flustered, but so what? That was a hell of a question to ask anyone first thing in the bloody morning.

'I asked you a question, Irene. And I'd appreciate an answer.'

Irene's thoughts whirled. She'd married him because he was rich, respected and easily manipulated – but she couldn't tell him that. Neither could she tell him he had been her way out – her escape from Eva and Olivia and that stifling little house in Trinity. 'Because I loved you,' she replied.

'Ha!' He shoved the chair back from the table and stood up. With his hands in his pockets he stood there and looked down at her. 'You don't know the meaning of the word,' he said softly. 'The only person you've ever loved is yourself.'

'I love my son,' she shouted.

'*Your* son?' His face was ashen beneath the weathered tan. 'You seem to forget he's also my son.' He paused. 'Or is he?' He leaned across the table, his eyes hard with dislike. 'Is he my son, Irene?' he shouted.

Irene swallowed. This William was a stranger. He'd never raised his voice to her before, never questioned her fidelity or her honesty. 'Of course he's your son,' she hissed. 'How dare you suggest otherwise.'

He cocked his head and stared at her. 'You've had many lovers over the years. How could I be certain?'

Irene pushed back from the table and faced him. She was taller by several inches, but she still felt at a disadvantage. 'Because I say so,' she snapped.

He shook his head. 'Means nothing. You wouldn't know the truth if it bit you.'

'Justin is your son,' she said coldly. 'You only have to look at him to see that.'

He eyed her for a long moment before he glanced at the photograph on the dresser. He seemed satisfied, but was obviously not done with this argument. 'You say you loved me – so why did you take a lover only weeks after our wedding, Irene?'

She swallowed. William knew more than she'd thought, and she wondered just how comprehensive that knowledge was. 'If I don't get what I need at home, then of course I'll look for it elsewhere.' Her tone was hard, the need to hurt overwhelming. 'You're boring, William. Tedious beyond belief. Both in bed and out of it. I needed some fun for God's sake. A bit of life other than the endless rounds of cattle shows and stock bloody sales.'

'Then you will have no objections if I tell you to leave,' he said coldly.

'Leave?' The shock was numbing. 'What are you talking about? Deloraine is ours – yours and mine. I'm not going anywhere.'

'Deloraine is mine,' he said flatly. 'Lock, stock and barrel. It is in trust for Justin should he want it, if not, then for my brother's son. You can't touch it, Irene. It's about the one thing you can't steal from me.'

She frowned, her thoughts in turmoil. 'This is getting silly,' she said in an attempt to jolly him out of this dangerous mood. 'What on earth have you been doing over the past couple of days to get you all steamed up?'

119

'Coming to my senses,' he replied. 'Making plans that don't include you.'

'But . . .' She didn't know what to say. No-one had ever talked to her like this before and it felt strange and oddly unsettling. 'What plans?' She snorted in derision. 'Don't tell me you've got some woman tucked away.'

William was silent. His gaze slid to a distant spot over Irene's shoulder.

'That's it,' she breathed. 'You have the nerve to accuse me of all sorts of dreadful things and all the while you've been fucking another bloody woman.' Her voice had risen to a screech as she flew at him with her nails poised to gouge out his eyes.

He was strong, his hands like vices around her wrists as he held her from him.

Irene struggled for a while and gave up when she realised she was no match for him. 'Who is she?' she gasped, her temper white-hot and ready to boil over again.

'Someone I care for,' he replied. 'Someone who loves me, who doesn't find me boring, and who will never lie to me.' He let go of her wrists and pushed her away.

'And is this paragon of virtue planning to move in here?'

'In time. Yes.'

'Over my dead body,' snarled Irene. 'You'll have to get me out first, and believe me, William, that won't be easy.'

'I never doubted that,' he retorted.

'You'll pay for this, you bastard. I'll make sure you won't have a pot to piss in when I'm through with you.'

He winced. 'Your talent for being coarse is not attractive. Neither is your greed.'

'Greed has nothing to do with it. I'm entitled to at least half of everything – and you know it.'

He stood there, his face a mask of dislike. 'You'll get a fair settlement,' he said finally as he threw two documents on the table. 'That is the report from the private investigator I hired. The other is the divorce paper. Sign that and our solicitors can discuss terms.'

Irene snatched up the report and quickly scanned it. She felt the colour drain from her face as she realised William's knowledge of her affairs and business dealings was far more extensive than she ever could have imagined. She ignored the divorce petition and shoved it back across the table. 'I'm not signing anything,' she said.

'You will.' His stance was rigid, his face determined. 'There's enough evidence there to divorce you for adultery several times over.

The scandal will finish you. Read the petition – it's a way out, Irene. I should take it if I were you.'

She snatched up the divorce petition and read swiftly through it. Her hands were shaking as she put it back on the table. 'Why are you doing this?' she breathed.

'Because I've had enough,' he replied simply.

'I assume this woman you spent the night with in Brisbane isn't the same as the one you've really been screwing?'

He shook his head. 'The private investigator set it up. His statement and the photographs he took are enough for you to divorce me for adultery.'

Irene knew he'd covered all the angles. She was trapped. Yet she needed time to think, to plan her next move. Changing tack, she decided to play on his sympathy. 'But where shall I go?' she said, her voice catching. 'I'll have no home, no-one to help me with the horses. Nothing.' The tears were real enough, and she let them fall unheeded down her perfectly made-up face.

William drew a third document from the case on the chair. 'I'm sure Arthur will help you. After all, he's been very attentive.' He threw the document on the table. 'Those are the deeds to the property on the eastern borders of Deloraine. It's yours. The land, stables, house – everything. But only if you sign the divorce papers and we come to a final agreement over the settlement.' He took a deep breath. 'But I warn you, Irene, it won't be much. The money's tied up in the trusts – and your own wealth will be taken into account.'

There was plenty of fight left in her, but she decided now was not the time. The investigator's report hadn't proved as thorough as she'd first thought. A great many of her assets were still hidden, and with clever accounting she could dispose of most of the rest. William would be made to pay – she'd see to that. 'You seem to have thought of everything,' she said, her voice flat.

'I knew I needed to be thorough,' he replied. His voice was regretful, his eyes sad. 'I loved you, Irene. Thought we could achieve so much together. But all you've ever given me is lies and more lies and treated me like dirt.' He sighed. 'We'll both be happier, and if you were honest for once, you'd admit you've been planning to leave for a while.' His gaze was steady as he waved away her sharp interjection. 'Enough, Irene. No more lies.'

Irene watched as he plucked his hat from the peg by the door and turned to leave. 'Mother was right,' she snapped. 'Despite all your money, you are just a dirt farmer – and a lousy one at that.'

He turned in the doorway, the smile tinged with sadness. 'Eva was certainly right when she warned me that marrying you could be the

121

biggest mistake I would ever make,' he said. 'She told me what you were like. Said you were marrying me because you wanted to escape. Said you needed a man to help look after your horses. A man with money and land. A man so besotted he wouldn't see you for what you really were until it was too late.'

He shook his head, the smile still playing around his lips. 'I didn't appreciate her warning at the time, but I soon became all too aware of how right she was.' He sighed again. 'I wish she was still around. I would have liked to see her again.' He nodded and tipped the brim of his hat over his eyes. 'I'm going to Brisbane for the stock sales. Sign the papers and get out before I come back. You have two weeks.' His eyes were sad. 'Goodbye, Irene.'

Irene waited until she heard the screen door slam behind him before she slumped down in the chair and stared into space. Her own mother had betrayed her. Bitch, bitch, bitch. How dare she tell William all those things. How *dare* she! Served her right if she died in agony – she only wished she'd been around to see her squirm.

She pushed the heated thoughts to the back of her mind and pondered her future. William had outwitted her for once. The timing was wrong, for Arthur had yet to leave his wife, and now she wondered if perhaps he'd been stringing her along all these years. Then there was the small matter of Justin and Sarah's wedding. The scandal of a divorce now could ruin everything.

Irene's tears were bitter as she screwed up the deeds to the out-station and flung them against the wall. It was a dump. A shelter used by the droving boss during round-up. A shack in the middle of nowhere with few redeeming features, that would probably blow down in a strong wind. The land was good grazing, but the stables and corrals hadn't been fixed for years, and the thought of being exiled to this lonely outpost made her want to scream.

'You alonga finish, missus?'

Irene snapped out of her thoughts and eyed the lubra in the doorway. She and the rest of the servants had probably heard the entire argument, and no doubt were sniggering in the kitchen. Irene picked up the teapot and flung it across the room. 'Get out!' she screamed. 'Get out, get out, get out!'

Chapter Twelve

The church was full of friends, the scent of flowers heady in the English summer sun that streamed through the stained-glass windows. The music was soaring to the cantilevered rafters as Giles waited nervously for his bride.

Olivia looked wonderful in the flowing white gown, her beautiful face masked by drifts of almost ethereal lace. She came to stand beside him and they exchanged their vows. Then he reached for the veil, lifted it so he could at long last kiss his new wife.

Irene glared back at him. Her blood-red lips opened and she threw back her head as her victorious screech of laughter filled the church – and his head – chilling him to the bone.

Giles woke with a gasp of horror. He lay there in the soft, warm darkness, his pulse hammering, the sweat dewing his skin. The dream had seemed so real – so real he could have sworn he could still smell Irene's perfume. But why such a dream? He'd met the woman once, and as he'd taken an instant dislike to her, he'd given her very little thought since their return from Deloraine.

The travelling clock ticked away the minutes as he lay there. Finally, impatient with his thoughts and the discomfort of his bed, he tossed the sheet aside and padded naked to the double doors leading to the verandah. The hinges complained as he opened them just enough to see through. But there was little air, and certainly no breeze coming off the sea to cool him. He ruffled his hair as he paced the room. It was stifling. The room closing in on him like the prison cell in Italy.

His thoughts returned to those two weeks of incarceration when the agony was overwhelming as his arm festered in the filth and flies of the Turin gaol. The long journey north was by train, the POWs crammed in like sardines amongst the bewildered, frightened refugees. There had been nothing to drink and nothing to eat for two days, and the dead remained standing, for there was no room to fall. The stench of human waste, of fear and death still lingered – like Irene's perfume. He'd survived by turning within himself. Survived by blocking out the pain, the fear, the sheer horror of what was happening around him, and focussing on Olivia and home.

Giles closed his eyes and took a deep, trembling breath. He was safe – far from the train, the prisoner-of-war camp and the terror of his escape. The months of fear of capture – the fear of not reaching the coast and the little boat that would take them across the Channel, were behind him. He was on the other side of the world with the woman he loved. He was alive, with a good future ahead of him. There was no space in his life for those awful memories.

Turning from the window he snatched up the borrowed swimming trunks and struggled to pull them on. He wouldn't sleep again tonight, but a swim might chase away the nightmare and put him in a better frame of mind.

With a towel over his shoulders he padded out of the bedroom and into the connecting lounge area to collect his cigars and lighter. He stilled. Olivia's door was ajar and he could see the rumpled, empty bed.

'Olivia?' he called softly.

There was no reply and Giles looked at his watch. Five-thirty in the morning. There was only one place Olivia could possibly be. He picked up his smokes and lighter and headed out into the hall and down the stairs.

Giles stood on the gentle dune of sand that dipped towards the water and scanned the beach. There was no sign of Olivia, and he suspected she'd gone for a long walk. Olivia enjoyed walking and the exercise helped her to think. Giles found walking an utter bore unless it involved golf clubs – another pleasure denied him by his injury – and decided he preferred to perfect his swimming action rather than traipse all over the beach looking for Olivia, who probably didn't want to see him anyway.

He dropped the towel and splashed into the sea. The water was cool, the sky a canopy of stars that were slowly fading in the first streaks of dawn. Giles floated on his back, his thoughts meandering, touching on the darker elements of his life before being tugged elsewhere. This was not the place or the time for those thoughts, he acknowledged. This was the time for plans, for the future – a future, perhaps, which might include Olivia.

He had no idea how long he'd been in the water, but when he began to shiver he realised it was time to get out. With chattering teeth he ran up the beach and grabbed his towel. Rubbing it briskly over his torso, he dried off as best he could and with the towel over his shoulders, sat in the sand and lit a cheroot.

The smoke drifted as the crickets chirruped and the tiny waves lapped at the shore. It was so still, so silent, and Giles could now understand why this place brought Olivia so much peace. For there was something primal about the sea that touched his soul – that calmed and soothed the troubles away. Perhaps it was the rhythm of those soft waves, which seemed to echo the steady beat of his pulse? Or perhaps it was the return to the womb – that dark, watery cradle of his creation?

He grinned at his own foolishness. It was certainly a night for profound thoughts.

The sound drifted to him along the beach. As insubstantial as mist, it disappeared. Yet it had sounded like a voice.

He listened for a moment, but came to the conclusion it was probably a bird in one of the trees. Then he heard it again, and knew he hadn't been mistaken. Gathering his things, he began to walk towards the voices.

As he drew level with the beach houses he caught sight of the two women sitting in the sand. Their heads were together, their arms around one another – it sounded as if they were involved in an extremely intimate conversation.

Faltering, he eased into the twilight shadows of an overhanging palm tree. He felt intrusive, realising immediately that Olivia and Maggie would not wish to be interrupted. Turning back, he kept to the shadows and slipped through the alley between two houses.

His thoughts were racing as he hurried back to the hotel. What on earth did Maggie and Olivia have to talk about at this unearthly hour? And why the intimacy between them when they hardly knew one another? Olivia was reticent at the best of times, now it appeared she was pouring her heart out to a virtual stranger.

He shook his head. Women were a mystery.

Olivia had seen Giles approach and breathed a sigh of relief when he turned back and disappeared behind the houses. She had enough to contend with, without having to explain things to Giles. Not that she could explain, she thought, as the chill of foreboding chased away the last of the night's heat. For, how could she explain an intuitive dread? How to explain that sixth sense which came rarely, but with devastating insight that something was very wrong?

She shuddered as if icy fingers had run over her spine, but Maggie was too distraught to notice and Olivia kept her arm around the other woman's shoulders, holding her, trying her best to console her even though she had no real idea of where Maggie's story was leading.

She passed her a handkerchief once the sobs had turned to hiccups. 'Feel better now?' she asked.

Maggie nodded as she blew her nose and wiped away the last of her tears. 'A bit,' she admitted. 'I'm sorry, Olivia. I didn't mean to dump all this on you.' She lifted her chin, her eyes still swimming with unshed tears. 'But I couldn't help it. Not after you told me Irene was your sister.'

Olivia battled with the impulse to snatch Maggie up and take her back to the hotel. Battled with the urge to run away before anything more was revealed. Yet she remained silent. Running away was no longer an option.

'I still don't see the connection,' she murmured. 'You went to the convent to find out about your father, and suddenly you're here in Trinity getting in a state over the fact that Irene's my sister.' She sighed. 'I'm sorry, Maggie. But so far you haven't made much sense.'

'I was just eighteen when I went back to that convent,' said Maggie after a long moment of silence. 'I can still feel the chill of those marble floors, even now, and smell the incense they burned day and night.'

Maggie hesitated before pulling the wire cord that would ring the bell in the echoing hall. The inmates of this dreadful prison had not been allowed to use the front door except when they were rounded up and made to stand for hours in the quadrangle.

She blinked away the sharp images of her first day and grasped the iron pull. She was eighteen – a woman who had experienced a different kind of hell in the life outside these walls. She was no longer the little girl who could be cowed. No longer the child still confused and hurting from her father's departure and having to face the cruelty of the Reverend Mother.

The door opened and Sister Claire's face was wreathed in smiles. 'Maggie,' she exclaimed in her thick Irish brogue. 'Is it yourself? And after such a long time.'

Maggie grinned back with relief that Reverend Mother was nowhere in sight. 'How you goin', sister? You look well.'

The little nun pulled a face. 'Things are much the same,' she said. 'Only the heat seems to get worse.' She opened the door wider and stood aside. 'Come in, come in. I'll make us a cup of tea and we can catch up on all the news.'

Maggie followed her through the vast entrance hall until they came to the door that led to the kitchen. It was strangely quiet. 'Where are

126

the children?' she asked as Sister Claire filled the kettle and put it on the range.

'All gone, my dear,' she said sadly.

Maggie sat down with a thump. 'Gone? Gone where?'

'Some of the boys have been sent to a Catholic farm school in the Territories and the girls have gone to another place further south. Times are hard, my dear, and the church needs strong souls to carry on Our Lord's work.' She sat across the table from Maggie, her hands tucked inside the copious sleeves of her habit. 'But we shall soon have more children to bring life to this place. There are so many in need of our care in these terrible times.'

Maggie thought about this as she sat there in the silent kitchen. What Sister Claire meant was using children as fodder to keep the place going. Using their labour, destroying their youth and sending them out to work where they could be abused and tormented. So much for the protection of a loving church, she thought bitterly.

Yet Sister Claire had always been kind and she found herself telling her about the job in the pub and her two years of travelling with Matt. She didn't reveal she was alone again – it was too painful – and after all, she wasn't seeking sympathy.

'I came to see if there had been any word from Dad,' she said finally. 'And to pick up my papers. Matt and I couldn't have a proper marriage ceremony without my birth certificate, and it makes it diffi-cult when it comes to getting a proper job.'

Sister Claire's eyes misted over and she remained silent for some moments before she pushed back her chair and walked to the range. Her back was turned to Maggie when she spoke. 'There's only one letter for you. It came almost three years ago. Reverend Mother has it in her office.' She paused. 'I'll be after fetching it for you.'

'And my birth certificate? Is that in there as well?'

Sister Claire kept her back to Maggie, her head dipped, her stance rigid. 'The records are in confusion,' she said finally. 'What with all the coming and going, we seem to have mislaid a great many over the years.'

Maggie pushed away from the table and went to stand by the nun. She put her hand on her shoulder and forced her to turn around. 'Without those papers I don't exist,' she said quietly. 'I can't get properly married. Can't apply for a job, and can't get the dole. What is it you're hiding from me, Sister Claire?'

The little nun shook her head, the high spots of colour on her cheeks burning with the same feverish intensity as her eyes. 'You'll have to talk to Reverend Mother,' she said, the words tripping one over the other in her haste to have done with the conversation. 'I have no authority to go through the files.'

127

'But I only left four years ago,' Maggie persisted as the niggle of doubt wormed its way into her thoughts. Sister Claire was definitely hiding something. 'You know how vital those papers are – how the hell could you lose them?'

She saw the little woman flinch and realised she was shouting. With a muttered apology, she tamped down on her frustration and anger by clenching her fists and turning away.

'I'm sorry, my dear.' The gentle hand on her shoulder was trembling. 'Come with me. It's better if Reverend Mother explains.'

Maggie took a deep breath and followed the little nun out of the room. The squirm of doubt had grown. She was suddenly a little girl again, waiting for the summons to Mother's office. She felt her pulse begin to race, and she smeared her sweating palms down her cotton dress as they walked back through the hall to the highly polished oak door.

Sister Claire tapped lightly on the wood and entered, closing the door behind her. Moments later she was signalling for Maggie to join her.

The room was the same. It was as if Maggie had never left. The carpet glowed with warm colours against the polished floor she'd spent so many hours scrubbing. The desk was just as broad, just as bare, the walls decorated only by a crucifix. The tall, elegant windows she'd washed more times than she could count still glittered in the sun behind the lacy curtains. The Reverend Mother's grey eyes were just as mean, her grey face just as pinched.

'Margaret Finlay. I can't say it's a pleasure to see you again after your disgraceful behaviour.'

Maggie gritted her teeth and glared back. 'The feeling's mutual,' she said coldly. 'I had hoped I'd never have to come here again, but you have something that belongs to me, and I want it back.'

The eyes were flint, the dislike clear in every inch of that bony face. 'You came here with nothing. You left with nothing. It is as it should be.'

'There is a letter from my father,' said Maggie firmly. 'And my birth certificate. Give them back and I'll never bother you again.'

The Reverend Mother eyed her for a long moment, her thoughts inscrutable behind the grey mask of contempt. She finally pulled out a drawer and tossed the letter on to the desk before leaning back in her chair, arms folded in the depths of her black habit.

'The birth certificate,' demanded Maggie as she picked up the letter.

'Still arrogant, I see,' snapped the old nun. 'What right do you have to come in here making your demands?'

128

'The right to what is mine. Hand it over.' Maggie was breathing hard and she wondered if the old bitch could hear the thud of her heart drumming against her ribs. For the sound of it filled her head and pulsed in every fibre of her being.

The elderly nun rose majestically from her chair. She was thin to the point of emaciation, the black habit emphasising the narrowness of her girth as she slowly made her way to a row of shelves. Long, bony fingers tapped along the lines of boxed files, came to a halt and plucked one from the rest. She carried it in grim silence to the desk and sat down. 'How old are you now?'

'Eighteen,' she replied. 'Old enough to marry and to go to work – but only if I have that certificate.'

The eyes drifted over her before returning to the file on the desk. 'Your arrogance will be your downfall,' she said as she opened the file. The gaze that once again drifted to Maggie's face was bright with a new kind of malevolence. 'But then that is hardly a surprise to those of us who know your background.'

Maggie gritted her teeth and refused to rise to the bait. She would not allow this vicious old cow the satisfaction of knowing just how accurately each barb found its target.

The fingers plucked through the papers, lifting out one and then another. The box file was slammed shut and put to one side. 'Your father left these in our safekeeping with strict instructions they were not to be handed to you until after his death.' The grey eyes bored into Maggie. 'As you are eighteen and he's not been heard from for over three years, one assumes he's dead.'

Maggie reached for the slip of paper.

The Reverend Mother flicked it out of reach. 'This is your birth certificate,' she said. 'And this,' she picked up the second piece of paper from the desk and waved it in Maggie's face, her eyes gleaming with spite. 'This is your adoption certificate.'

Sam had fired up the generator and was switching on the lights and preparing the dining room when Giles came clattering through the side door demanding a stiff whisky. 'Bit early, mate. Sun's barely up.'

'I don't care,' muttered Giles through chattering teeth. 'I need a drink.'

Sam eyed him for a moment before going into the bar and pouring him a double. Returning to the hatch, he placed it on the counter. 'You right, mate?' The Englishman looked green around the gills and was shivering fit to bust.

'Been swimming,' muttered Giles. 'Got chilled.'

Sam raised his chin and his eyebrows, but said nothing. If Giles wanted to take a swim in the middle of the bloody night, who was he to complain if he got cold and needed a drink to warm him up?

'I'd better get dressed,' mumbled Giles as he drained the whisky and collected his towel. 'I hope breakfast won't be long. Got a real appetite this morning.'

'So do I,' growled Sam. 'There's no flamin' sign of Maggie, despite her promising to come in today, and Lila's refused to come into work until her daughter gets better.'

'She's on the beach with Olivia,' said Giles as he turned away and headed for the stairs.

'What the bloody hell's she doing on the flamin' beach at this time of the flamin' morning?'

'Who knows?' said Giles. He grinned as he turned on the bottom step. 'But it looked to me as if they could be there for some time. They were deep in conversation.'

'I've got a hotel to run,' snapped Sam as he slammed through the hatch. 'Bloody women,' he muttered under his breath as he went storming through the side door and out into the yard. 'As if they don't have all flamin' day to yarn, they gotta do it all bloody night as well.'

Olivia knew her face was ashen, for she'd felt the colour drain as Maggie talked. 'Adopted?' she breathed. 'You were adopted?'

Maggie nodded. 'Turns out I was left at that convent when I was barely a week old. The Finlays adopted me soon after.' She scooped up a handful of sand and let it sift through her fingers as she stared out to sea. 'And I never knew. Mum and Dad never said a thing, never even hinted I wasn't their own.'

She turned to Olivia, the pain stark in her face. 'Why, Olivia? Why did they let me go on thinking I was theirs?'

Olivia swallowed the hard lump in her throat. This was crazy – the whole scenario like something out of a bad dream. 'Perhaps they loved you so much they were afraid of losing you,' she said finally. 'Perhaps they didn't want you to find your real parents, because they were frightened you would stop loving them.'

Maggie nodded as she sifted another handful of sand. 'Maybe,' she murmured. 'But surely it was better to say something, than for me to find out in such a horrible way?'

Maggie would never realise how deeply Olivia understood her pain. Would never know how much the story was affecting her. 'I'm sure they would have told you in time,' she said gently. 'It's just that circumstances got in the way.'

'You're right,' she sniffed. 'And I know they loved me – even poor old Dad. He just couldn't cope after Mum died, and he was only doing what he thought was for the best.' She gave a snort of laughter. 'He took me back to the place he'd found me. How was he to know what a hell it was?'

Olivia swallowed again. The question was burning to be asked – but did she want to hear the reply? Could she take on board the implications of the answer if it proved as she suspected? She looked away from Maggie and realised she was jumping to conclusions. So many years had passed since Maggie's unfortunate birth – of course there was no connection. She was being ridiculous, her judgement impaired by her own circumstances.

Sam stomped down the sandy lane, and was in the process of cutting through the alley between the beach houses when he heard the last part of the women's conversation. It pulled him up short.

His bad mood was swept away as he realised he must not risk being seen. Must not let them know he'd overheard part of what was obviously a very serious conversation. Yet he was intrigued, for this intimate exchange had echoes of one he'd had not so long ago – and he needed to know more if he was to put the pieces of the puzzle together.

The sun was rising fast now, chasing away the shadows, bringing the first swarm of flies to flit and dance around his sweating face. Sam flattened his back against the wall of the house and unashamedly listened in.

'Why did you leave it for so long before coming here?' asked Olivia. 'People move on, change houses, change their names, even. It was one hell of a task after all these years.'

Maggie looked at her face and wondered mildly why it appeared so strained. She shrugged. 'Things weren't as easy back then as they are now,' she said with a calmness that belied the inner turmoil. 'I had no money, no work, and the only transport I had was an ageing horse and wagon. Dirranbandi is hundreds of miles south of here.'

'You could have written,' said Olivia.

Maggie nodded. 'I thought about it. Even sat down and drafted a letter out, but I never sent it.' She fell silent, her thoughts churning. 'I thought the personal approach would be better,' she said finally. 'A letter can be ignored, thrown away. I would stand a better chance if we met face to face.' She took a deep breath. 'Besides, I wanted to see this woman. Needed to face her and find out what made her give me away like that.'

She fell silent again as she remembered the urgent need to travel north to find this so-called mother who'd left her to the mercy of that bitch Reverend Mother.

131

'Believe me, if it had been possible I would have walked all the bloody way. I wanted answers. But most of all I wanted to tell her just what kind of life she'd abandoned me to. I wanted to hear her apologise.'

Olivia remained silent, but Maggie thought she could see the pain in her eyes, the questions she wanted to ask, the fear of the answers. Maggie took a deep breath and let it out slowly. She didn't want to hurt Olivia, but she deserved to know the truth. Perhaps, once she'd told her everything, she could truly start again. For once aired, the anguish would no longer be secret – would no longer have the power to wound.

'I managed to get work on some of the sheep and cattle stations as I headed east to the coast. I cooked – it was about all I was good at – that and housework.' She laughed. 'Good grounding for Sam's hotel, though.'

'We all pick up skills through life that come surprisingly handy at times,' murmured Olivia.

'Like yesterday, with your nursing.'

'Mmmm.' Olivia was staring out to sea, watching the sun creep slowly above the horizon.

Maggie dug her hands in her pockets as she paced back and forth in the sand. She was too restless to sit, too on edge to appreciate the glorious sunrise. 'I was in Sydney when the war broke out. Work wasn't a problem then, and I got a job in a clothing factory. We started out making suits and dresses, and then got a contract for making army uniforms. The pay was good, the company lively and I settled down for the duration.'

She kicked at the sand with her toes. 'I liked Sydney. It was always busy and bustling, and then of course there was the sea. I couldn't get enough of it, and used to spend hours cycling to one or another of the beaches.' She grinned down at Olivia. 'Bit like you really.'

Olivia smiled back, but Maggie could see it was forced, for it didn't quite reach her eyes. Where there should have been warmth was a sense of separation – a guarded distance as if she was afraid of what she might hear. She swallowed. Her revelations would strike Olivia hard – but surely the truth was better than a lifetime of lies and secrets?

'The war ended and I'd saved a fair amount of money, so I caught the train and came up north. It was easy to find the town, and the house, because the address was on my birth certificate. All I needed now was for my mother to be still there. It was a long shot, but I had to give it a go.'

'And was she?'

Maggie stilled and stared out to sea. 'She was there all right,' she said softly.

The house looked as if it had been freshly painted, and it gleamed cheerfully in its red and white. Maggie unfastened the gate and closed it behind her. Her heart was hammering against her ribs and her hands were sweaty as she walked up the rickety stone path to the front verandah and knocked on the screen door.

She stepped back as the woman came down the short hallway to the door. She was of the right age, but was she the woman she was looking for? Maggie took in the slender frame in the expensive dress that to Maggie's expert eye had been purchased in Sydney. She noticed how the blonde hair had been styled in lustrous waves like Betty Grable's, and how the make-up was perfectly applied. This was a woman more at home in the city than on the beach, and Maggie wondered why she chose to live here in Trinity.

'Yes?' The smile was pleasant, but Maggie noticed the long red fingernails tapping with impatience on the doorframe.

'My name is Maggie Finlay.' Maggie's voice was rough with emotion and she tried to clear her throat.

The light-brown eyes were wary and the fingernails drummed just that little harder on the doorframe. 'I don't believe we've met.' The cold-eyed woman blocked the way into the house. 'What do you want exactly?'

Maggie rustled around in her handbag that always had too many things stuffed in it, and pulled out her birth certificate. She took a deep breath, and was almost stifled by the rapidity of her heartbeat. 'I'm your daughter,' she rasped.

The colour drained behind the mask of make-up and the long nails ceased tapping on the frame. 'Is this some kind of sick joke?' she snapped. 'I have no daughter.'

Maggie was not to be put off. 'Then how do you explain this?' She thrust the birth certificate in the other woman's face.

The eyes narrowed as they quickly scanned the worn document and the hand reached out to rip it from Maggie's fingers. 'You've made a mistake,' she snapped. 'I'm not your mother.'

Maggie stuffed the precious document back in her bag. 'I think you are,' she retorted. 'I've asked around and it's too much of a coincidence for there to be two women who lived in the same house and have the same name.'

There was a long silence in which Maggie felt the chill of the woman's scrutiny as it trawled over her.

'What exactly do you hope to gain by coming here with your

133

revolting insinuations?' The voice had a steely edge, and the mouth thinned to an unattractive red slash in the pale face.

'I want the truth,' replied Maggie with honest simplicity. 'I want you to admit you're my mother, and I want to know why you left me in that God-awful place where I was abused and mistreated. I also want to know who my father was.'

The woman snorted as she reached for the slender red box of Craven A cigarettes in her pocket. She took her time to light one, and then blew a stream of smoke to the roof of the verandah. 'The convent obviously didn't teach you any manners,' she said finally.

Maggie leaped on the words. 'So you admit it, then?'

The woman stared at her for a long, still moment before she nodded. 'It was the best place for you in the circumstances.'

Maggie's heart was thudding so painfully she wondered if she would fall down in a faint on this woman's doorstep. 'Why?' she persisted. 'You're obviously rich. Why couldn't you have brought me up?'

The red lips slithered one over the other as the light-brown eyes glistened. 'Because I didn't want to,' she replied. 'Because I was glad to be rid of you.'

The words tore through Maggie and she had to clutch the wall to stop from falling. Black clouds swirled, blotting out the sunlight, making it hard to focus on the woman in the doorway.

'You said you wanted the truth,' came the sibilant voice through the haze of anguish. 'You said you wanted answers.' Her perfume was cloying as she leaned towards Maggie. 'But I think you're beginning to realise the truth isn't very pleasant. Want me to go on?'

Maggie stared at her wordlessly. She felt like a butterfly caught in the sticky web of some exotic spider.

The voice was soft and venomous as the spite spilled between those red lips. 'I didn't want you – never wanted you. You were a mistake. An abortion would have been preferable.'

Maggie couldn't move, couldn't speak. She could only stare in fascination into those light, golden eyes and wonder at this woman's cruelty. She wanted to scream a denial. Wanted to lash out and inflict the same hurt she was experiencing. Wanted to run as far as she could from this spiteful, vindictive woman who could never possibly call herself a mother. Yet she remained on that doorstep as if turned to stone.

'I was walking back from a dance,' said the pitiless voice. 'I was alone, because my friends all lived in the opposite direction. We lived in Melbourne then – not here, in this dump.'

Maggie watched as she smoothed back a pale gold wave of hair

134

with a steady hand, patting it in place with those long, polished talons. The bitch was actually enjoying herself, she realised in awe.

'I didn't know there was an escaped lunatic on the run from Cairns. Didn't know the police had been hunting for him for weeks, or that he'd made his way south.' Her eyes grew cunning as she leaned forward and Maggie could feel her warm spittle against her face. 'He came out of nowhere and grabbed me. Dragged me into the bushes and raped me.' She stood back again, her top lip curled in disdain. 'You are the result.'

The trembling began in Maggie's toes and travelled all the way up until she found it almost impossible to speak. 'Thanks,' she said finally, her voice gruff with emotion. 'Thanks for letting me see what you really are behind all that powder and paint. I don't have to fantasise any more.'

Maggie turned and walked down the path. Leaving the gate unlatched and creaking in the breeze, she walked away. It would be the last time, she vowed, that she would talk to Irene Stanford.

Olivia saw the pain in Maggie's eyes and reached out to console her. She knew all about Irene's ability to cower, to almost hypnotise her victim into acquiescence. 'Oh, Maggie, I'm so very sorry,' she whispered. 'I didn't know. I had no idea of any of this.'

Maggie stood stiffly in Olivia's embrace. 'Why should you?' she said. 'I'm just so sorry I've landed you with it all.'

'But you stayed on, Maggie.' Olivia tucked Maggie's hair behind her ears and cupped her face. 'You're braver than I. The first sign of hostility and I ran away.'

Maggie shrugged. 'She doesn't come down to the house very much,' she muttered. 'I've only seen her a couple of times since. We don't speak, and certainly never acknowledge one another.'

'Do you think that story about the rape is true?'

Maggie squinted into the sun. 'Who knows? Who cares? Irene's the only one with the answers, and she's such a vindictive bitch, how could I believe anything she said after that?'

'If only Jessie was still around,' murmured Olivia.

'Who's Jessie?'

'Someone who would have had all the answers and would have told us the truth,' said Olivia with a sigh. 'But it's too late. She died some time ago, and I suspect the truth died with her.'

Maggie's smile was tremulous as she gave Olivia a hug. 'It doesn't really matter,' she said. 'We've found each other – that's the important thing.' With a giggle, she swiped away the last tear from her cheek. 'How does it feel to be an aunt, Olivia? Not too crook, I hope?'

Olivia licked dry lips and forced herself to remain composed. Yet the breath was trapped in her throat and all she could do was shake her head.

Sam eased away from the house and quietly made his way back along the alley and up the sandy lane. His thoughts were whirling, his pulse racing so fast he was finding it hard to breathe.

Slamming through the side door he ignored the yells from the dining room, the smell of burning toast and the screeches of the fighting kitchen maids. He reached for the telephone. He needed some advice – and quick.

Chapter Thirteen

Irene put down the receiver and stood deep in thought. Things were going from bad to worse. In fact, she realised, they had started to deteriorate when that little tart, Maggie, had turned up out of the blue.

She lit a cigarette and tried to put her thoughts into some kind of order. Her sleep had been disturbed by strange dreams, and the awful heat had made it impossible to remain in bed. Now, in the light of that telephone call, she knew there would be many sleepless nights to follow.

She began to pace the shadowy corridor. Her gaze flickered over the valuable oil paintings that lined the walls, and the china ornaments William's grandmother had collected over the years. Her feet were silent on the Persian runner that glowed with warm colour despite its age. She was tempted to snatch the lot and find a buyer down in Sydney, but knew she'd never get away with it. The Stanford collection was well documented and William had catalogued everything, the provenance safely tucked away somewhere she'd yet to discover – and without that she didn't have a hope in hell.

She stubbed out her cigarette in an exquisite Meissen dish, turned on her heel and wandered back the way she'd come. Deloraine homestead had begun life as a two-roomed wooden shack in the middle of nowhere. It was still isolated by at least two days' drive to the nearest neighbour, but as the years went on and children were born, the succeeding generations of Stanfords added on to the building. Now it was a labyrinthine collection of corridors and rooms, which eventually led to the wrap-around verandah. Tall, narrow, double doors led to this verandah, where, in the summer, when escape to the coast was impossible because of the stock round-ups, the inhabitants slept on iron bedsteads.

Irene eventually came to the bedroom she'd shared with William for more years than she cared to remember. She stood in the doorway, hands deep in her pockets as she looked around. William's closet was open as usual, the shirts and trousers spilling out. His spare riding boots were stuffed beneath the Queen Anne boudoir chair, and his hairbrush had been thrown onto the bed. It had taken a good deal of money to get the four-poster all the way out here, and the drapes had been hand-made down in Sydney. Yet the place had an air of neglect – a dusty, forlorn look about it, and Irene realised for the first time it was indicative of her marriage.

Impatient with her meandering thoughts, she pushed open the double doors and stepped onto the verandah. Screened in to keep the flies at bay, it was cooled by ceiling fans and a collection of tropical plants. Cane screens divided the whole into sections to give privacy to those sleeping out. Tables and chairs were placed in cosy groups and a gas refrigerator hummed in the corner, cooling the drinks. The beds had been made up some time ago, for the heat was rising and it was already too hot to sleep indoors.

She slumped down on a bed and leaned back against the wooden wall as she stared through the foliage out to the yard. The men were drafting off the bullocks and the dust was rising in a great sepia cloud as the Queensland Blues barked and the men cracked their stockwhips. Grey gallahs were circling, blue and yellow parakeets were squabbling, and the sulphur-crested cockatoos were lording it high in the gum trees. At night, all would be still but for the chirruping crickets and the grazing grey wallabies that ventured into the grassy compound surrounding the homestead. Bats would fly from their roosts, silhouetted against the moon, and the cane toads would trumpet their bass calls.

Irene sighed. Some of the men had already left to begin repairs on the manager's house, and she had made a start on the packing. It was strange to think this could be the last time she'd sit here. Strange to realise that now it was denied her, Deloraine meant far more than she'd ever suspected.

She reached for her cigarettes, found the packet was empty and crushed it before throwing it hard against the fly screen. An empty packet. An empty life. Things weren't supposed to turn out like this, she thought bitterly. Yet fate seemed determined to vanquish any of her plans – to keep her on the sidelines, and isolate her from the things she most desired.

'It's not fair,' she breathed. 'Why the hell should it always be me that's punished?'

Pushing away from the wall, she stood and tucked the checked shirt into the waistband of her moleskins and took a deep breath. Life seemed to have the habit of thwarting her, regardless of any plans she might have, but at least this way she'd be free of William. Free to come and go as she pleased. Free to begin again. It would just take time and patience – and that was the hardest part, for Irene acknowledged her tolerance level was minimal.

She left the verandah and stepped back into the bedroom. Dragging two large cases from the top of the wardrobe, she began emptying drawers and cupboards. The maids had been instructed in the art of packing her precious china, silver and crystal, and there were already crates and boxes stacked on the back verandah. The tack would go with the horses once the new stables were finished.

Her mind was working furiously as she automatically folded her clothes and packed them neatly in the cases. Shoes and boots were stacked in their boxes and would go in the crate with the linen. She would buy new furniture and kitchen utensils in Cairns and charge them to William's account. He couldn't be allowed to get away without paying for something.

With her clothes packed, she stripped the expensive bed of its linen, took down the drapes and carried the bundle all out to the kitchen to be laundered. They could be packed with the rest of the linen – they had cost too much to be left behind. The bed could stay – it would only remind her of William, and that was the last thing she needed.

She wandered from room to room and collected the silver photograph frames, the bronze horses and her riding trophies. Then she gathered up the photo albums and returned to the denuded bedroom, where she spread them out on the bed.

Most of the albums were very old, relics of a different era that had been left behind when Eva and Olivia sailed for England. The faces meant nothing to her and she stacked these albums on one side to be thrown out. The newer albums were covered in tooled leather, the shiny paper protecting each page still crisp and smooth to the touch. Irene stretched out on her stomach, her ankles crossed like a child as she slowly turned the pages.

Here were Mother and Father, smiling happily as they stood in front of that pretentious house in Melbourne. Father was handsome, she realised, with his beard and moustache and wide, brown eyes. He was tall and strongly built, his hand square and capable as it rested on Mother's shoulder. Mother was tiny beside him, and she remembered Eva telling her that Frederick could encircle her waist with his fingers when they'd first married.

Irene stared at the photograph. Eva's apparent frailty was deceptive, for there had been few occasions that Irene could remember when Eva had shown any sign of being overwhelmed by circumstances. She ran the house and the servants with a no-nonsense approach, survived Father's long absences by keeping herself busy with committees and ladies' circles, and had become a driving force for numerous charities. Tiny she might have been, but beneath that veneer of feminine frailty lay a core of steel. Her glare had been enough to stop anyone in their tracks if Eva disapproved of their behaviour, and her utter belief that she was right in everything made her difficult to argue with.

Irene pushed the album aside and rolled on to her back. Things had begun to go wrong shortly after her seventeenth birthday. Father was on the point of leaving for yet another surveying trip, and as June turned into July, Irene realised she was in deep trouble.

It was harsh, that winter of 1914. The wind was icy, the rain torrential as it swept in from the Bass Straits and tore up the Yarra. The news of war in Europe merely emphasised the bleakness, and the men were already leaving to enlist, spurred on by a national euphoria that sometimes verged on the hysterical.

Irene felt the wind buffet her as she tucked her chin in the fur collar of her coat and held on to her hat. At least the rain had stopped, but the warmth of her lover's bed was long forgotten as she struggled to keep her balance on the slippery pavement, and watch for a passing taxi. Her thick tweed skirt was long and tight, making it impossible to run, and the narrow heels of her leather boots kept catching the roughly laid cobbles.

If she wasn't careful she'd twist her ankle and fall, she thought grimly as a passing motor car drove through a puddle and splashed a fine spray on to the path in front of her. And yet that might be a good thing – a fall would solve all her problems.

She hurried on as the rain returned and began to slash the wind, her thoughts flitting from one possibility to another as her boot heels rapped out a tattoo on the cobbles and her long skirt and dainty hat became sodden. The imposing house finally came into view, and she hurried up the short flight of white steps to the colonnaded front door. She was about to slot the key in the latch when Jessie snatched the door open.

'Get in out of the rain, you silly girl,' the woman scolded. 'It'll be the death of you one day, running about in all weathers without a decent coat.'

'Do stop fussing, Jessie,' retorted Irene as she let the woman divest her of the soaking coat. 'We can't all sit about doing nothing just because of a bit of rain.'

'Hmph. Strikes me there's no 'arm in keeping dry and warm.' Jessie draped the coat over her arm, her scrutiny making Irene feel

140

uncomfortable. 'What's so important you gotta be runnin' about out there?'

'None of your business,' snapped Irene.

'It is when I gotta nurse you back from the pneumonia,' Jessie mumbled. 'Remember last year?'

Irene ignored her. The illness last year had seemed to last for ever, and although Jessie and Mother had nursed her through it, Jessie was after all only doing the job Mother paid her for.

She turned to admire her reflection in the hall mirror as she carefully pulled out the ornate hatpins. Her colour was high, stirred by the cold and the wind, and there was a sparkle in her eyes that made her look very well. She smiled, noting how her small, even teeth gleamed in the gaslight. Sex in the afternoon was certainly to be recommended, she thought.

'Pretty is as pretty does,' said Jessie who was fond of coming out with these strange adages. 'Looks as if you swallowed the cage along with the canary. Reckon you've been up to some kind of mischief, miss.'

Irene shot her a glance before returning to her scrutiny. Jessie was easy to cajole out of these suspicions – it just took a kind word, a hug – but she wasn't in the mood. Let her think what she wanted, she thought as she eyed the ruined hat. It was none of her damn business anyway.

With a sigh of regret for the once lovely hat, she drew off her gloves and handed them over with the hat to the waiting Jessie. She patted her hair. It was drawn from her face and swept back into a tumble of curls that had the same lustre as her favourite horse, the fires of red and copper burning brightly amongst the brown. With a tweak here and there and a fluff of the frills on her high-necked blouse she was soon satisfied with her appearance.

Jessie was still hovering and it was beginning to annoy her. 'Has tea been served?' she asked with telling sharpness.

Jessie nodded. 'You know it has,' she said grimly. 'Same time every afternoon. Lost your watch, have ya? Or just too busy to notice the time?'

Irene saw the gleam of suspicion in the other woman's eyes and decided she would ignore any insinuations. Jessie was rough and common, God only knew why Mother employed her. 'I'll take tea,' she said imperiously. 'Have the maid draw me a bath, and make sure there's a fire in my bedroom so I don't freeze when I'm dressing for dinner.'

Jessie glared before bearing away the sodden clothing to the kitchen, where it would be dried before the range.

141

Irene adjusted the blouse at the waistband of her skirt. It was getting tight, but her afternoon's exertions had given her a raging appetite.

Eva was waiting for her – alone for once – yet her expression was grim. She sat in the low chair by the blazing fire, her back ramrod straight. Her dark hair was brushed in lustrous waves from her face and loosely coiled at her nape. Pearl drops dangled from her earlobes and the fire sparkled in the diamonds on her fingers. As usual, her attire was immaculate, from the highly polished ankle boots to the rust-coloured skirt and pristine white lace blouse. She was every inch the matriarch.

'Where have you been?' she asked as Irene helped herself to tea and sandwiches.

'I've already had this conversation with Jessie,' she said firmly.

Eva waited as Irene sat in the opposite chair and placed her cup and saucer on the delicate side table. 'Rudeness doesn't suit you,' she said quietly. 'You're such a pretty girl, with so many things to be grateful for, why do you persist in being so nasty to everyone?'

Irene ate the sandwiches and drank some of the tea. At last she was beginning to warm up. 'I've been visiting friends,' she said brightly. 'Surely that isn't a crime?'

Eva stood and looked down at her daughter. 'What friends?'

Irene shrugged, careful not to make eye contact with her mother. 'Just friends,' she muttered. 'You don't know them.'

Eva's gaze was firm. 'I pride myself in knowing all of your friends,' she said finally. 'So why be so secretive?'

Irene drank tea and helped herself to another sandwich and a piece of cake. She was ravenous, and these ladylike morsels hardly took the edge off her hunger. 'I'm not being secretive at all, Mother,' she replied. 'They are new friends I met at the riding stables. If you like, I could invite them to tea next week?' She looked squarely at her mother, defying her to argue.

Eva held the gaze, her expression thoughtful and yet with a hint of something that might have been construed as sorrow. 'You've been with him,' she said.

It was a statement, not a question, and Irene realised there was no point in denying it. The subject was not new and she was weary of having to explain herself. 'What if I have?' she said as her chin lifted.

'He's married, Irene. That's why.'

'Not for long,' retorted Irene as she leaned forward in the chair and held her hands out to the warmth of the fire. 'He's getting a divorce.'

The sharp intake of breath was swiftly muffled. Eva cleared her throat. 'He has a wife and four little girls,' she said coldly. 'Why suffer the ignominy of divorce when he obviously can obtain everything he needs without one?'

Irene felt the colour flood her face and she looked away. 'It's not like that,' she muttered.

Eva's steely fingers grasped her chin, forcing her to look up into her eyes. 'Of course it is,' she said. 'What else would a man of his age want with a girl like you? Don't take me for a fool, Irene. I know you too well – and I know his sort too. He'll use you for as long as he wants and at the slightest hint of trouble he'll shun you.'

Irene twisted from those cruel fingers and stood. She was taller than her mother by several inches, yet she felt at a disadvantage in that fearsome glare. 'He's not like that,' she insisted. 'We love each other.'

Eva sat down again, her hands plucking at the cameo brooch at her neck. 'Oh, Irene,' she said with a deep sigh. 'You're so young. There's plenty of time to fall in love with the right man.' She looked up at her daughter, her eyes strangely bright. 'If your father should hear of this he would be destroyed. Don't see him again, Irene. I beg you.'

'I love him, Mother. Passionately and for ever. I'm going to see him as much as I can before he leaves, and when he returns we'll be married.'

The eyes were sharp in the little face, the high cheekbones angular in the shadows cast by the fire. 'You're not pregnant, are you?'

The words hit Irene like the blast of icy wind. She reddened and clenched her fists. 'Don't be ridiculous,' she shouted. 'Of course I'm not.'

Eva rose again from the chair, her expression clear and understanding. 'That's it,' she breathed. 'You're expecting his baby.' She reached out and grasped Irene's arm. 'Does he know?'

Irene wrenched away from her mother's grip. 'Give me some credit,' she stormed. 'I'm not some shop girl or kitchen maid. How dare you accuse me of such a thing.'

'They can 'ear you all over the 'ouse,' said Jessie as she closed the door behind her.

'Get out,' screamed Irene. 'This is a private conversation.'

'Not when 'alf the 'ouse can 'ear it,' said Jessie as she folded her arms and stood squarely in the centre of the room.

'Jessie stays,' snapped Eva.

'Why? She's only a nosey housekeeper. A servant!'

The slap was sharp and unexpected on Irene's cheek. 'Jessie helped to bring you up, you ungrateful girl. She loves you as much as I do and I will not have you being so insulting. She stays.'

Irene was shocked into silence. The rage, the shame, the sheer

143

terror of her secret being discovered were all swept away in that one, swift act of retribution. She put her hand to her cheek. Eva had never slapped her before and Irene could still feel the sting of those striking fingers. Yet she was aware she must get her emotions under control. Aware she would have to appear calm and firm in her denials if she was to make them believe her.

'I'm not expecting,' she said stubbornly. Her pulse was racing, the heat driving up through her body and into her head, making it swim.

Eva put her arm around Irene's waist. 'I've suspected for some time,' she said softly. 'Our bedrooms are next door to one another. I've heard you in the mornings.'

Irene stared back at her. She hadn't realised the walls were so thin. Hadn't realised every sound had been transmitted during those awful, bilious attacks that seemed to assault her every morning. She felt the fight and defiance leave her as she sagged against Eva. It would almost be a relief to confess, to share the terror of what was happening to her.

'Yes,' she whispered. 'I am pregnant.' She looked at her mother. 'But everything will be all right. He'll come back to Melbourne after the trip, leave his wife and we'll set up home together.' She grasped Eva's hands in an attempt to emphasise the truth of her words. 'We've made plans, Mama. So many plans,' she added breathlessly.

'Won't 'appen, luv,' said Jessie as she plumped down on the couch. 'What's 'e want with another mouth to feed? He's 'ad 'is fun, and believe me, gel, once that's over, he's gorn.'

'The scandal of this could destroy him and his wife,' said Eva. 'His reputation will be ruined, and he'll lose your father's esteem. And he'll need that if he's to attain his ambitions, Irene. That's why he won't stand by you.'

She paused for a moment, her eyes bleak. 'It will also destroy your reputation and shatter your father's trust if this gets out.' She put her hand on Irene's shoulder. 'How could you be so foolish?' she asked softly. 'Silly, silly girl to think he meant anything he said in the heat of the moment.'

With dread, Irene began to realise they could be right. She thought back over the past four months and suddenly saw the affair for what it was. Shabby, secretive and rather seedy. She had approached the subject of running away together and he'd been evasive. Had tried to make him promise to leave his wife, but he'd always found some excuse. He never took her out to dinner, or to the playhouse, never took her dancing. They met only in the decaying rooms above the feed merchants in Flinders Street that were leased by a bachelor acquaintance. But surely, after all they had been to one another, he

144

wouldn't abandon her – not now – not when she loved him so passionately?

'I'm not making any plans until I've spoken to him,' she said finally.

She caught the look that passed between the two women and stamped her foot. 'This is my baby and my life,' she screamed. 'I'll do what I want.'

She was in the throes of storming out of the room when Jessie caught her arm and pulled her back. 'You know full well it ain't gonna 'appen, miss,' she said firmly. 'Let me and yer ma sort this out proper, like.'

Irene was sobbing as she looked from one woman to the other. They were bitter tears. For in her heart she knew they were probably right and that he wouldn't stand by her. 'What can I do?' It was a plaintive wail.

Eva patted the seat beside her. 'Come,' she said. 'Sit down, Irene, and blow your nose. I know you're frightened and feel very alone at the moment, but if we use all our resources, I'm sure that between the three of us, we can come up with a plan.'

There was the most God-awful row going on in the kitchen to which everyone in the dining room was unashamedly listening. It made for an interesting start to the day – a change from the usual slumberous morning ritual – and there were knowing grins exchanged as the entertainment carried on full flow. Not that many of them understood the babble of native gobbledygook that was being screeched at full blast by at least three women to the accompaniment of crashing pots and shattering china – but one of the shearers very helpfully offered to translate so they could at least get the gist of what the argument was about.

Giles was eating breakfast, so fascinated by what was going on around him, he hardly noticed the toast was cold and like leather and the bacon so crisp it was on the point of cremation. The original argument was over who had the right to fry the eggs in the new pan Sam had brought back from Cairns – things had rapidly deteriorated into a slanging match which involved name-calling and accusations of heinous crimes such as sleeping with another woman's husband, and stealing someone's grog.

Giles grinned as he finished breakfast and poured out a cup of tea. Someone had put the milk in the urn along with the tea and sugar and the whole mess was almost undrinkable. Sam would be so glad to have Maggie back in charge after this shambles, Giles wouldn't be at all surprised if she didn't get a raise in her wages. She was certainly worth it – even if the entertainment this morning had been enjoyable.

Everyone's attention was snatched from the argument by the slamming of the side door. They watched as Sam strode into the hall, and there was a deathly hush in the dining room as they waited for his explosive roar that would bring the row to an abrupt halt.

It didn't happen. Instead, ashen-faced, he ignored everything and reached for the telephone.

Giles, not usually nosey, wished he could hear what was being said so earnestly into the receiver. He saw Sam turn his back to the dining room and almost hunch over the telephone as if determined to keep the call private. Not that there was much chance of anyone overhearing a word with all that screeching going on in the kitchen.

He left the lukewarm tea and wiped his mouth on the napkin, his thoughts whirling. Could this urgent call have anything to do with Maggie or Olivia? Sam had stormed out of the hotel looking for Maggie and had been gone quite a while. Deciding it was none of his business, but loath to miss the drama, he lit a cheroot and leaned back in his chair. As a spectator sport, this was almost better than watching Arsenal playing at Wembley in the cup final.

Sam was still talking on the telephone when Maggie and Olivia entered the hall. Giles was about to signal a greeting when he saw the two young women hug before going their separate ways. Maggie disappeared into the kitchen, and Olivia wearily climbed the stairs.

'There'll be fireworks now, I reckon,' said Hopalong with a nudge of his elbow. 'Maggie won't stand for it.'

'Shut up!' Maggie's voice echoed around the hotel in the ensuing silence. 'Put that down and clear up this flamin' mess. One more word out of any of you and I'll bloody well take this broom to your backsides.'

There was a deathly hush in the dining room, with every eye turned towards the kitchen as Maggie emerged and stood in the doorway, hands on hips, face red with fury. 'The entertainment's over,' she shouted. 'Get on with your tucker or clear off.'

Chairs were scraped back, tea was gulped and plates swiftly emptied. The mass exodus left Giles still sitting at the table with a broad grin on his face. 'Well done,' he said. 'You'd have gone down a treat as a Sergeant Major.'

Her shoulders lost their rigidity and she folded her arms. 'Someone has to take charge,' she said. 'That lot of bludgers don't know their arse from their elbows most of the time.' She blushed, perhaps realising what she'd said might offend him, and turned back towards Sam, who had finished his telephone call and was standing in the hall, arms folded, a deadly twinkle in his eyes.

'Reckon you could be right there, Giles, mate,' he drawled. 'Proper little harridan when she gets going. Fair frightened the flamin' life outta me.'

146

Maggie swiped at him, but missed as he ducked away. 'I'll do more than frighten you if you don't get in that flamin' kitchen and help clear up the mess,' she said with dark, comical menace.

Sam was grinning broadly as he winked at Giles and meekly followed Maggie into the kitchen.

Giles left the dining room and ran up the stairs. It was odd Olivia hadn't joined him for breakfast, he mused. She must be hungry after being out so early this morning. He opened the door into the connecting lounge, his cheerful mood dying as he looked into her bedroom. Olivia had an open suitcase on the bed and was packing.

She shot him a glance over her shoulder as she threw her clothes into the case. 'We're leaving,' she said.

'Why?' Giles closed the door behind him and went to stand beside her.

'Because,' she replied.

He reached out and stilled her hand, forcing her to look at him. 'That isn't an answer,' he said softly. 'What happened down on the beach this morning, Ollie?'

'Nothing,' she said with an uncharacteristic shortness.

Giles took a deep breath and expelled it slowly. Why did women always say there was nothing wrong when it was patently obvious there was? His mother was a past master at it and would send his poor father demented. 'You were gone far too long for it to have been nothing,' he said firmly. 'I saw you with Maggie. You were crying.'

She turned from him, her hair coming loose from the plait and masking her face. 'That was Maggie,' she said as she resumed her packing. 'I was merely in the right place at the right time when she needed to get something off her chest. I don't know why you have to make such a fuss, Giles. It's unimportant.'

He edged around her, closed the case and sat on it. Ignoring her protests, he put his arm around her waist and drew her close. 'You're lying,' he said softly, the accusation tempered by a teasing light in his eyes. 'Come on, Ollie. I know you too well, remember? You always were a lousy liar.'

She dipped her chin as she gave a wan smile. 'I never could fool you, could I?'

'Not in a million, trillion years,' he said, echoing their childhood declaration. He was tempted to kiss that smooth cheek, to run his hand through that lovely hair and pull her closer – but he knew that if he did that he was lost. Olivia needed to talk, needed to let go of whatever it was that troubled her. 'Why are we leaving?' he asked again.

'I need to get away from here,' she replied. 'Need time to think.'

There were so many questions he wanted to ask, but knew it was better to remain silent. Olivia hated silences. She would tell him soon enough if he was patient.

She remained within the crook of his arm, her head dipped, her fingers plucking at the hem of her skirt. 'Maggie and I had a long talk,' she began. 'She told me things that were so personal, I don't want to repeat them.'

'Fair enough,' he said as he eased from the top of the case to a more comfortable position on the bed. He pulled Olivia down beside him and kept his arm around her waist. 'But if they were personal to Maggie, how on earth would they affect you?'

'Because of Irene.'

He was totally confused now and thought it best just to keep his mouth shut and let Olivia tell him in her own way. No doubt it would eventually become clear, but for the life of him he couldn't see what on earth Irene had to do with all this.

Olivia's voice was halting as she began a sketchy outline of Maggie's life before she arrived in Trinity.

Giles listened and as the story progressed, he surmised there were probably far more profound confidences between the lines, but respected Maggie's privacy. It was a heart-rending tale nonetheless, and he could only imagine what had been left out.

Olivia's voice faded and she sat for a long while, head bowed, fingers clenched on her lap. 'It turns out,' she said, her voice thick with emotion. 'That Irene is Maggie's mother.'

The silence stretched as Giles tried to assimilate this shocking news. He expelled his breath in a low whistle. 'By golly,' he said.

Olivia looked at him, a smile teasing the corners of her mouth. 'Never let it be said you are guilty of overreacting,' she teased.

'I don't understand why you're so upset about it all,' he blustered. 'You and Irene might detest one another, but Maggie has obviously become a friend. I would have thought you were both delighted to find you were related to one another.'

'We are,' she replied. 'Poor Maggie's had it rough, and I'm glad she can at last claim someone as family.' She dipped her head again. 'But it's not as simple as that, Giles.'

He was confused again. 'Don't like suddenly finding you're an aunt – eh?' he teased. 'Or is it the fact you and your niece are probably about the same age?'

'If only that was all,' she said with a sigh. 'I would hate to hurt Maggie, but there are other factors involved, Giles. If we don't leave, Maggie may soon regret taking me into her confidence.'

148

Chapter Fourteen

Maggie ignored the angry glares being shot between the kitchen lubras and orchestrated the clean-up. There was food and broken crockery scattered on the floor and the congealing remains of egg and bacon stuck to the wall where someone had obviously thrown it.

'Leave you alone for five minutes and look what happens,' she hissed as she tipped the dustpan full of broken crockery into the dustbin.

'You said you were coming in,' muttered Sam. 'How was I to know you were going walkabout?'

She slung the dustpan aside and filled a bucket with hot, soapy water. 'Take this,' she ordered one of the snivelling girls. 'And make sure you mop in the bloody corners.' She watched the girl make a half-hearted attempt at swirling a lot of water around and snatched back the mop. 'Like this,' she snapped. 'You know how, Maisie – so don't go crook on me.'

The amber eyes were round, the full bottom lip trembling as the girl took the mop and began to wash the floor. Maisie was a past master at the histrionics, but Maggie could not be swayed. She'd seen this carry-on many times and was not impressed.

She finally nodded her approval and ordered the other girl to scrub the range while she rescued the bags of sugar and sacks of flour that had been knocked over in the fight. Sam was stacking the remains of the china and counting the knives. 'So where were you when this took off?' she asked.

'Out,' he replied, his head bent as he counted plates.

Maggie lifted an eyebrow. 'Out?' she snapped. 'Out where?'

Sam slammed the drawer on the knives and leaned against the dresser. 'I needed some fresh air before I started the day,' he said blithely. 'No harm in that, is there?'

He was lying. Sam never went anywhere at that time of the morning

149

unless it involved a fishing line or a horse. 'Must have been an important phone call if you could ignore the racket going on in here,' she
murmured. 'But I suppose you're not going to tell me the truth about
that either?'

She looked at him squarely and was gratified to see the colour rise
in his face and the way his gaze slid away from her. At least he had
the decency to acknowledge he'd been fibbing, she thought.

Sam rolled up his sleeves and washed out the dirty water from the
bucket and refilled it. 'Clean that up,' he said quietly to the younger
girl as he pointed to the mess on the wall. 'Then you can go.'

'No, she can't,' said Maggie. 'There's still the dining room to clear
and the washing up to be done. They can both stay on and do it, and
perhaps it will teach them not to fight in my bloody kitchen again.'

It was Sam's turn to raise a questioning brow. 'Your kitchen?' he
said.

'Yeah, mine all the time I'm manager here,' she said firmly as she
finished tidying up the flour and sugar and returned the tins of jam to
the cold store. The kitchen was at last beginning to look more ordered
and her temper had cooled.

'As manager you should have been here,' he said gruffly.

'As the bloody owner, so should you,' she retorted.

They stood in the kitchen as the maids scurried back and forth from
the dining room. They looked at one another for a long moment and
then simultaneously broke into laughter. 'Fair go, Maggie. How was
I to know World War Three was about to break out?'

'You're right,' she admitted. 'But asking Maisie and Gloria to work
together was always risky. They've been after the same man for
years, and now Gloria's finally got him. It's a miracle either of them
is still alive.'

'I didn't know,' he spluttered, the laughter still twinkling in his
eyes.

'You wouldn't,' she returned. 'You're hardly ever here.'

He folded his arms and leaned once more against the dresser, his
long legs and big feet threatening to trip the scurrying maids as they
loaded the drainer with dirty plates and cutlery. 'Reckon I asked for
that,' he said softly. 'Sorry, Maggs. Won't happen again.'

'I'll believe that when it happens,' she muttered.

'Reckon it's safe to leave these two while we sit and have a cuppa?
Throat's drier than a goanna's backside.'

'You have a lovely way of putting things,' she said dryly. Then she
grinned. 'I know just what you mean, though. I could do with a
cuppa. It's been a long night.'

Sam made a fresh pot of tea and they took it into the dining room.

The girls had cleared the tables and replaced the cloths, and had even swept under the chairs. The clearing of the air had obviously boosted their enthusiasm for work. Long may it last, thought Maggie as she sank into a chair and kicked off her shoes.

She sipped her tea and began to relax. It had come as a nasty shock to see how quickly things could deteriorate, and she still puzzled over why Sam hadn't been around to stop it. The suspicion grew as she sat there and watched him roll a smoke.

'You gotta woman on the go?' she asked with studied nonchalance.

'Not so you'd notice,' he said around the cigarette as he lit up.

'So where were you this morning? And why didn't you put a stop to all that nonsense instead of making a phone call?'

He shrugged. 'It was already out of hand when I got in. I didn't think another few minutes would matter.' He blew smoke to the ceiling and avoided eye contact. 'Our guests seemed to like the entertainment, anyhows, so no worries.'

Maggie regarded him in silence and finally gave up. Whatever he'd been doing was actually none of her business, and she believed him when he said he'd no woman on the go. But it was intriguing nevertheless and she decided to keep a closer eye on him.

'Sorry I wasn't around. Olivia and I got talking and I lost track of time,' she said.

He nodded and screwed up his eyes against the smoke as it trickled from his mouth. 'I saw you both come in. Must have gone out early, I didn't see you leave.'

Maggie realised he was probing, but two could play at that game, and she wasn't yet ready to share her wonderful news. She had to get used to the idea that Olivia was her aunt – get used to the feeling of belonging again. She nodded to his question. 'It was so hot neither of us could sleep,' she said. 'Reckon there's a storm brewing.'

Sam stretched out his long legs and crossed them at the ankle as he leaned back in the chair. 'Feels like it right enough,' he agreed. 'There's no air, and the heat's rising on the hour.' He stared at the passing shadows of pedestrians on the other side of the frosted-glass windows. 'Reckon we could be in for a beaut unless it moves on.'

'Where exactly do you plan on going?' Giles asked.

'I hadn't really thought,' she admitted. She stared out of the window, the only sound in the room coming from the squeaking ceiling fan, which stirred the humid air and did nothing to relieve the awful heat.

'You're running away again, Ollie,' he said softly. 'Don't you think

151

you'd be better off staying here and facing things? Poor Maggie will be devastated if you leave so soon after she's found you.'

'I ...' Olivia began. 'We ...'

'What were you going to do? Sneak out while she was busy in the kitchen?' Giles sat on the bed and watched as Olivia paced the room. The tension in her was obvious, from the rigidity of her shoulders, to the tight wrap of her arms around her waist.

'You make me out as a terrible coward,' she stammered. 'Of course I wasn't.'

'So, why the rush? We don't need to be anywhere, unless there's something else you're not telling me, and I think you owe it to Maggie to at least try and explain why you want to leave.'

Olivia reddened. 'I can't,' she said. 'There are things I need to do before I face Maggie again.'

Giles noted her heightened colour and the gleam of entrapment in her eyes. He ran a finger over his moustache. Olivia was frightened of something, but what the hell it was, he had no idea. 'I think you'd better explain,' he said quietly.

Olivia stopped pacing and stood in front of the window. Her narrow shoulders were tense again, the thin shirt damp with sweat. 'It's complicated,' she said.

Giles let out a long sigh. 'I don't care,' he said with an edge of frustration. 'You've been secretive ever since your mother died. I still have no idea why we're even here in Australia, now you're compounding the mystery by being perverse.' He glared at her back, his voice harsh with command. 'Come on, Olivia. Spit it out.'

She turned and looked at him, her dark-brown eyes wide with surprise. 'I'm not one of your service minions,' she said sharply. 'There's no need to shout.'

He glared back at her. This was worse than pulling hens' teeth. 'Then for God's sake talk to me,' he rasped. 'Nothing you can tell me will come as a shock – so get on with it, woman.'

'Depends on what you consider shocking,' she said quietly.

She struggled to smile and Giles saw the glint of a teardrop on her eyelashes. He yearned to sweep her up and embrace her. Longed to kiss away the tear and tell her it was all right if she didn't want to share her secrets with him. Yet he knew she needed to unburden herself, needed to voice the demons and let go before she could move on. So he remained silent.

Olivia stood once more with her back to him as she stared out of the dusty window. Her voice was low, so low that at times Giles had to struggle to make sense of what she was saying.

When her words finally faltered, and she finished her story, he could hardly take it all in. The silence stretched as the air thickened with heat and humidity. His thoughts raced as the ceiling fan battled above his head to stir some kind of life into this oppressive little room.

'It's all rather a mess, isn't it?' she said into the silence.

Giles sighed. That had to be the understatement of the year. He stood and put his hand on her waist. 'Yes,' he agreed. 'But does it really matter? You and Maggie have found one another – surely it's enough?'

Her eyes were dark, the long black lashes sweeping almost to her brow as she looked into his face. 'I need to find the missing pieces of the puzzle, Giles,' she said. 'With Jessie gone it will probably prove impossible, but I have to try.' She paused. 'Will you help me?'

'If I can,' he murmured. 'But only if you promise not to suddenly change your mind when the going gets rough and try to run off again.'

She nodded. 'You're right,' she murmured. 'Maggie doesn't need to know any of this until we are sure of our facts. I should just enjoy her company and get to know her properly.' She looked back at him. 'Running away isn't the answer, is it?'

He pulled her close and breathed in the light perfume she'd dabbed behind her ears. 'Never was,' he murmured into her hair. 'The Olivia I know has never run from anything, and although I can understand your reluctance to stay here after what you've told me, it isn't in your nature to back off from a challenge.'

She rested her forehead against his shoulder and sighed. The tension left her and she leaned against him.

He closed his eyes, aware of the tremor running through him – aware of her scent and the way she fitted so neatly against him. He kissed the top of her head. 'Whatever the outcome, we can face this together,' he murmured.

Irene had taken William at his word and drafted the men from their normal work on Deloraine to what she needed doing on the other homestead. She had inspected the stables and after a great deal of reorganisation and bullying, finally pronounced them suitable. The old manager's homestead would now have a new roof and stone chimney, and the shutters and windows would be repaired along with the verandah.

She'd then kept the men off Deloraine to build an extension on the back and to fit a proper bathroom. Hot water would come directly from the bore, and the cooling tank she'd ordered from Cairns would be fitted while she was away in Sydney.

The city always made her feel so alive, she thought as she stood at the hotel window and looked out over the harbour. The sheer exuberance of the people lifted her spirits. It was a young city, a vibrant, energetic, ambitious city that made her wish she was at least twenty years younger and just starting out again – like Justin.

The memories of yesterday and the meeting with her son clouded her mood. Justin had shown no surprise when she told him about the divorce, and she suspected William had beaten her to it. She had hoped for sympathy and understanding, but Justin had given her neither, merely the cool admission that it was bound to happen some-time, and that he was relieved she had agreed to his father's demands and not caused a fuss. They had eaten lunch in silence, and his casual kiss on her cheek as he left had made her feel more isolated than ever.

She picked up her handbag, refusing to let the memory of yester-day cloud her good mood. Justin would come round when he wanted something – he always did. She left the suite of rooms and hurried downstairs. She was meeting Arthur for lunch, and because his invi-tation had come as such a surprise after their last conversation, she didn't want to be late.

Arthur was already waiting for her. He rose from the leather chair in the lobby and kissed her cheek. 'You look well,' he said in the deep, rumbling voice that still held the rounded tones of his English heritage despite the many years in Australia.

Irene smiled. Arthur would always be the perfect English gentle-man. He was still handsome, despite having celebrated his sixty-fifth birthday recently. His hair was thick and white, swept back from a deep brow. The nose was long and straight, the eyes a penetrating blue. He wore an expensively cut suit and blue shirt, which Irene guessed were straight from Savile Row in London, and enhanced his colouring and trim figure. A gold signet ring glinted on his little finger, as did the gold watch on his wrist.

She linked her arm through his, glad he'd relented and looking forward to a few hours of pleasure in her suite. 'You promised me lunch,' she said.

Arthur looked over his shoulder at the crowded dining room. 'Not here,' he murmured. 'I've arranged for us to eat in my suite.'

She looked at him in surprise. Arthur never booked a suite for himself, far too indiscreet for a married man. 'You've taken a suite? Why didn't you tell me?'

'Thought it best in the circumstances,' he rumbled.

Irene found she was being led to the elevator. Unwilling to cause a scene in such a public place where she was well known, she remained tight-lipped until they were alone again.

She watch him close the door, saw the tension in his jaw, and realised this was not to be the pleasant tête-à-tête she had imagined. She sat down on the comfortable couch and waited to see which way Arthur was going to jump.

Arthur poured them both a healthy slug of gin to which a dash of tonic was added along with ice and a slice of lemon. He handed her the glass and instead of sitting beside her as he usually did, chose to remain standing. 'Lunch won't be long,' he said.

Bugger lunch, thought Irene. What the hell's he up to? She forced a smile. 'You're being very mysterious, Arthur,' she said, her smile warm, her tone teasing. 'You don't usually bother to wait for drinks and lunch when we come upstairs – far too busy getting my clothes off.'

He took a sip of his drink and then placed the crystal glass on a side table. 'I meant what I said the last time we spoke, Irene. It's over between us.'

'Don't be silly,' she retorted, her smile faltering. 'We're good together, and after all, we have so many business interests tied up, we couldn't possibly just . . .'

'Irene, stop it.' His voice was commanding and she fell silent. 'We've gone as far as we can with this affair, and now your husband's set a private detective to follow me around I cannot afford the scandal. I've arranged with my lawyers for our business dealings to be terminated, so you don't have to fret on that score.'

'Terminated?' she breathed.

'Terminated,' he said flatly. 'The company has been liquidated, the assets divided between us.' He smiled as he smoothed down his dark-blue silk tie. 'You'll find you've done rather well out of our partnership, Irene – I've been very fair.'

Irene slammed the glass down on the side table. 'You said you'd wait until we could discuss this,' she snapped.

'There really wasn't anything to discuss,' he said with quiet firmness. 'Our assets are split fifty-fifty, and I've taken care of the lawyers' fees. We've both made a huge profit, so be satisfied with that.'

She looked at him and thought how smug he was. How untouchable behind that urbane veneer. 'All this is because William and I are getting a divorce, isn't it?' she demanded.

'Partly,' he replied. The blue eyes she had once found so attractive now looked cold.

She glared at him, the temper rising. 'So I'm good enough to fuck when I'm someone else's wife, but a bit of a liability if I'm divorced?'

He winced at her vulgarity, just as William had done. 'You will always be a liability, Irene,' he said, his expression grim. He spread his hands and shrugged. 'We had fun together, and a profitable few years of business dealing. Now it is time to move on.'

Irene remained seated, her hands tightly locked together on her lap. 'And if I don't want to move on?' Her voice was low, edged with bitterness and the knowledge she couldn't win against this man. 'I'm sure your wife would be most interested in our "business partnership". I wonder what she'd do if she knew the truth?'

He shrugged. 'Treat the news with the same amount of disinterest as she has done before. It's over Irene. My business affairs are wound up here. I'm returning to London.'

She was about to reply when they were interrupted by room service.

Arthur took the trolley and after tipping the waiter, closed the door. 'Do you have time for some lunch?' he asked as if unaware of the shattering effect he'd had on her. 'I've ordered lobster, I know it's your favourite.'

Irene stood and snatched up her handbag. She would have liked to have tipped that trolley and its contents all over the floor. Was sorely tempted to hit him over the head with that bottle of champagne he was opening. Yet she did neither. Instead, maintaining what little dignity she had, she crossed the room and opened the door.

'I hope it chokes you,' she spat as she slammed the door behind her and marched down the corridor.

Four hours later she was only a little less angry. It wasn't the fact that he'd dumped her unceremoniously after so many years, but that he'd had the gall to make decisions about their business enterprises. She had gone through the papers his lawyer had delivered shortly after her exit from his suite, and had found that indeed he'd been very fair. She was wealthier than she could ever have dreamed, but it was on paper, unfortunately, so her circumstances remained the same. She would still have to live in that poky little homestead on the edge of Deloraine until the assets were liquidated.

She had a long, leisurely, scented bath and carefully made up her face, willing herself to remain calm. Justin was bringing Sarah and her family over for drinks, and, as they hadn't met before, Irene wanted to make a good impression. None of them must guess she was less than in command of herself – but Irene knew from past experience it wouldn't take much for her temper to boil over.

The knock on the door heralded their arrival. They were early, dammit. Irene pushed away from the dressing table and eyed her reflection in the pier glass. She nodded with satisfaction. The tightly fitted cream shantung suit showed off her figure and enhanced her colouring. Her nails and hair had been done that morning, and the pearls in her ears and around her neck glowed in the sunlight that streamed through the window. She patted her hair and went to open the door.

Sarah was small and too thin by half. Her hair was brown, her eyes insipid behind the thick glasses. The dress she was wearing was obviously expensive, but on Sarah it just looked drab and uninteresting. Irene kissed her cheek and welcomed her as warmly as if she found it a pleasure to see her again. One had to be seen to be enthusiastic, for after all, the girl was the heiress to a large fortune.

'Mum, this is Bob and Isabel.' Justin made the introductions and they shook hands.

Irene felt rather more at ease. Isabel was sheathed in a silk dress, with pearls at her neck and around her wrist. Bob was handsome, tall and to Irene's experienced eye, had probably had more women than she'd had hot dinners. It could turn out to be a most interesting drinks party.

'And this,' said Justin, as he reached behind Bob and tugged a child forward. 'Is Sally.'

Irene felt the smile freeze as the child shook her hand with too much enthusiasm. The child's eyes were black and oddly shaped. Her face was flat and round, the thick, straight hair as dark as jet. And now Irene could see her clearly, she realised she wasn't really a child. 'Hello,' she said as brightly as she could. 'And how old are you?'

'She's fifteen,' said Bob with a proud gleam in his eye. He put his arm around his daughter's waist. 'Getting a big girl now, aren't you, Sal?'

Irene swallowed and murmured something inane before swiftly turning away. How dare Justin not warn her, she silently fumed. He must have known, must have realised this would change everything.

She began to pour drinks. The hotel had provided sandwiches and sausage rolls and small things on salt biscuits, and she handed them around, her smile fixed, her conversation light and inconsequential. Yet, as the talk flowed around her, she found herself watching Sally – wondering why Bob and Isabel paraded her about like this and did not put her in a home.

The girl was clumsy and kept knocking into things. She seemed to have the mind of a child of five, bouncing about on the chair, demanding attention in that deep, rough voice, her words almost unintelligible. Irene couldn't quite disguise the shudder of disgust as Sally shoved cake and sandwiches in her mouth and carried on talking.

It was as if Bob could read her mind. 'We couldn't let her go into a home,' he muttered as he helped himself to a refill. 'She's our daughter, and we love her.'

Irene was ill at ease in the knowledge her disgust had been so clear to this attractive man. 'You must find it very difficult,' she said as she topped up his drink with ice. 'Socially, I mean.'

He shrugged. 'Our friends have known Sal since she was born. We've never had a problem.'

Irene's face was stiff from the effort of maintaining a smile. 'You are to be commended,' she said.

Their conversation was interrupted by a screech followed by a terrible, shattering clatter. Sally had upended one of the side tables and was now sitting amongst the debris of broken china and spilled food, her mouth wide as she screamed. Half-eaten food was smeared down her dress and in her hair, the mess compounded by a runny nose and tears. Irene thought she would throw up.

'We'd better get her home,' said Bob. 'She gets overexcited when she meets new people.' He helped his wife clear the mess, and with Sally squirming in his arms, turned once more to Irene. 'I hope we'll see you again before the wedding? Izzy and I are in the city for a couple of weeks yet.'

She nodded and shook his hand, impatient for them to leave.

They said goodbye, leaving Sarah on the couch with Justin. The two of them were deep in conversation, making plans for the future. 'It'll all be so lovely, Mrs Stanford,' she sighed. 'And once we're settled, we can think about starting a family. I thought two boys and two girls would be nice, don't you?'

Irene gritted her teeth. The day had been a disaster and her nerves were so tight she could almost feel them twang. Here they were, sitting in the middle of a God-awful mess created by her idiot sister and all she could think about was bringing more just like her into the world. 'Is idiocy inbred in your family?' she asked with icy demand.

'Mother! How dare you?' Justin shouted.

Irene looked at him. He was taller than his father, and towered over her, yet she was unafraid of him. 'I don't want any morons born into this family,' she said coldly. 'Better to ask these questions now before it's too late.'

Sarah's myopic eyes blinked behind the glasses and she got to her feet. 'Justin?' she said softly.

'It's no use whining to him,' snapped Irene who was now thoroughly out of control. 'If there's the slightest chance of you dropping something like that, then the wedding's off.'

Justine put his arms around Sarah and held her close as the tears began to run down her face and soak his shirt. He glared at Irene over Sarah's head. 'That was unforgivable,' he breathed. 'Apologise, now.'

Irene tossed her head. 'I will not,' she snapped. 'I have every right to ask, considering you're foolish enough to want to marry this weak, ugly little mouse with a half-wit sister. I don't care how wealthy she is – nothing can make up for mental instability.'

Justin steered Sarah across the room and opened the door. He glared in silence back at Irene and slammed the door behind them.

Irene stood there in the silence, the debris of the drinks party all around her, the anger ebbing away in the cold light of realism. She'd done it again. She'd spoken out of turn and alienated someone she loved.

The crystal decanter was still half full of sherry, and she threw it hard against the wall where it smashed into a million pieces. Panting, she watched the sherry trickle down the paint and seep into the carpet. She'd had every right to ask – every right to express her doubts, her fears. If her son was too stupid to realise what he was getting into then it was his lookout.

She lit a cigarette and reached for the telephone. Sydney had suddenly palled. She would fly home tonight and continue with her plans for moving out of Deloraine. Justin was old enough to make his own mistakes, and if he and his father were so clever they didn't need her – then they could clear up any ensuing mess themselves.

Chapter Fifteen

The heat was intense, the humidity so high it wrapped itself around everything like a hot, damp blanket. It drained energy and sapped the spirit, and the pace of life slowed to a crawl. Every breath of air was welcomed as the inhabitants of Trinity looked to the skies for some sign that rain would fall, or that wind would come off the sea and blow the threatening storm away.

Yet the clouds were gathering, layer upon layer in tiers of grey and black that gave the impression they were solid enough to be sliced through with a knife. Lightning shimmered in this looming mass, great sheets of if flickering on and off like a faulty bulb. And now and again the forks of electricity snapped and crackled in the breathless atmosphere, searching for somewhere to strike.

The beach houses were deserted as the graziers returned to their isolated properties. With the lightning and the threatening storm there was a very real risk of fire. Shearers, ringers and jackaroos packed up their swags and returned to the hot, dusty world of these properties, knowing that every hand would be needed if such a disaster struck. The hotel emptied as the week drew to a close, and Trinity soon took on a deserted air.

Despite the heat, the ominous clouds and the draining humidity, Olivia was pleased she'd stayed. With the hotel being so deserted it had given her and Maggie a chance to talk, and to get to know one another. It had also given her the chance to catch up on her letters to England and to begin making plans for the future – plans she kept to herself until she was ready to share them.

Another week was drawing to a close and still the storm hadn't broken. Olivia shook hands with Bob Kealeigh and walked down the neat path and through the gate. The satisfactory conclusion to their business made her smile and she turned and waved to him before hurrying back to the hotel.

Sam had made iced coffee and they were seated on the verandah in the hope of catching the slightest breeze. 'Here she is,' he said. 'The mystery lady. Where've you been disappearing to, Olivia?' His eyes twinkled with mischief. 'Reckon there must be some bloke on the go.'

She grinned and took her place at the table. The coffee was loaded with ice cream and dark, sweet rum, and was utterly delicious. She picked up a spoon and scooped some of this wonderful concoction into her mouth.

'So,' said Giles in his usual fashion. 'Are you going to tell us what you've been up to – or are you determined to fuel the gossip?'

She laughed. 'I didn't realise my comings and goings were that interesting,' she said.

Maggie grinned. 'This is a small town,' she said. 'Everything's interesting, especially now there are so few people to talk about.'

Olivia drank some more, then leaned back in the cane chair and lifted her hair from her neck. 'God, it's hot,' she groaned. 'I'd forgotten about these dry storms.'

'Olivia!' It was a chorus from the other three.

She held up her hands. 'I give in. Come on. Come and see what I've been doing.'

They followed her back down the street, and Olivia found it hard to stop smiling. 'There,' she said as they came to a halt. 'What do you think?'

The other three stood on the dusty road, their surprise and puzzlement clear, and Olivia hugged her secret close, waiting for the right moment to enlighten them.

The shack had once been the home of the widow, Mrs Parker. Now it was abandoned and had been left to moulder for almost ten years. The grass was thigh high behind the rotting picket fence and the weeds had taken over flowerbeds and paths. There was no glass in the windows, the fly screens had disintegrated and the stone chimney looked as if it might come crashing down any minute.

'It's Ma Parker's old place,' muttered Sam. 'Should have been pulled down years ago.'

'Good grief, Olivia,' spluttered Giles. 'Please don't tell me you've bought this wreck.'

Olivia grinned. 'It has great potential,' she said firmly.

'For what?' breathed Sam. 'Firewood?'

She decided not to enlighten him yet. 'I agree it would probably be best to tear it down and start again, but that's half the fun, surely?'

Maggie's eyes were round with astonishment. 'Why didn't you tell me you were planning to stay in Trinity?' she asked. 'I'd have found you something much better than this dump.'

'It's not for me – not really,' she admitted.

The silence was profound as they looked at her in confusion. She giggled and reached in to her handbag. 'Here are the deeds to Trinity's new community health centre,' she said.

'Health hazard, more like,' muttered Giles.

'Bloody hell, she's serious,' breathed Sam.

Olivia turned to Maggie. 'I took the liberty of making you joint freeholder,' she said. 'I hope you don't mind.'

'Mind!' Maggie's face was wreathed in smiles. 'Of course I don't mind. But I haven't got the sort of money that will turn this place into anything, let alone a health centre.'

Olivia put her arm around her shoulder and squeezed. 'The finances are down to me, Maggie. You don't need to worry about anything but looking after the place should I want to go back to England for a while.'

'But why me?' Maggie breathed.

'Because although you're my niece, you're the nearest I ever had to a sister and I wanted to share my good fortune with you.'

Maggie's tears threatened and she sniffed them back. 'It's too much, Olivia. This must have knocked you back a fair bit, and I'd feel like a bludger not contributing to the cost.'

'Nonesense,' she said firmly. 'You're the only relative I have worth admitting to, and my mother left me a sizeable inheritance. I don't see why you shouldn't share it.'

'But I don't know anything about nursing – I'd be useless.'

Olivia gave her a peck on the cheek and passed her a handkerchief. 'You don't need to. I've written to some nursing friends of mine back in England. They are young, single and sick of rationing and living and working in a bombed-out London. Coming out here will be an adventure hard to resist. Believe me.'

She looked around her at the astonished faces. 'You see, Trinity lacks a great many things, but young women and a decent medical centre are top of the list. Once we've got this place up and running, who knows where it will lead?'

'A population explosion once the blokes out on the stations hear about an influx of sheilas,' said Sam dryly.

They all laughed. 'Then perhaps we'd better get a good maternity unit going, and a crèche as well as a nursery school,' said Olivia.

Maggie put her arms around Olivia's waist and gave her a hug. 'You're a dinkum sheila and no mistake,' she said.

It was the most heart-warming compliment Olivia could hope to receive and she too was close to tears as they walked arm in arm back towards the hotel.

*

162

The two weeks were almost up. William would be returning in a matter of hours, and although her furniture and packing cases had already been carted over to the other house, she still had to organise the removal of her horses. The oppressive heat had grown steadily worse as the days wore on and by the look of the black thunderheads they were in for one hell of a storm.

Irene stood in the centre of the lounge, hands in the pockets of her moleskins, and took a final look at what had once been her home. The place looked bare now she'd taken her trophies and ornaments – soulless without the feminine touches of cushions and frills and soft rugs.

Her gaze drifted over to the table and the broad, brown envelope she'd placed there for William. The papers had been signed, reluctantly, but she'd realised she really had no other option. William held all the cards, and after the debacle in Sydney, she needed to maintain at least a modicum of dignity.

She gave a deep sigh as she drifted from room to room. The life had gone out of the house once Justin had left – had gone out of their marriage, too, she realised. For their son had become the focus, the lynchpin of their relationship, and as they immersed themselves in his upbringing, and the day-to-day running of Deloraine, it had been all too easy to drift apart.

His leaving had emphasised the rift between her and William – had made them face the unpalatable truth that they were almost strangers who just happened to share the same house. Some couples still had love to bind them, which could be rekindled once the children left home, but Irene was a realist. She and William had never been in love, and any passion they might have shared had long gone.

Emerging out of the front door, Irene stood on the verandah and looked at the sky. The clouds were piled one upon another in shades of deepening grey. A weak sun struggled in this thick blanket of menace, casting a strange sepia light over the earth. It was as if the silver grass was poised for the slightest breath of air. As if the drooping gum trees were wilting with their need for enlivening rain. The dogs lay panting in the kennels as the cattle shifted restlessly in the pens. Horses and men moved slowly in the sludge of reflected heat as if their legs were weighted. The silence was ominous.

Irene slammed the screen door behind her and strode across the yard to the stables. Jimmy had already trucked three of her horses over this morning, the fourth was proving difficult. She stood and watched him coax the mare into the horsebox and finally bolt the door. There was no doubt about it, she thought, as she tacked up Pluperfect. She would miss Jimmy. He was good with horses and a godsend when it came to the heavier duties around the stables.

Pluperfect was also playing up. Tossing his head and dancing on his toes, he drew back his top lip and snapped at Irene's fingers as she forced the bit into his mouth and tightened the bridle. His ears flattened and his nostrils distended as Jimmy fired up the old truck and Irene had to use all her strength to keep him under control.

With the horsebox chugging away amidst a cloud of dust, Irene took one last look at Deloraine and gave Pluperfect his head.

The ride swept away the cobwebs of another restless night, and despite the heat and humidity, Irene felt refreshed in spirit as they approached the second homestead. She slowed Pluperfect into a trot and regarded this outpost of exile she'd been forced to accept.

The homestead was square, with a new sloping corrugated-iron roof that swept down over the narrow, front verandah. The slabs of wood that made up the walls had been painted along with the window frames, the front door and fly screens. The chimney had been repaired and looked sturdy enough, the ironstone bricks mellow in the strange light of this storm-laden day.

Irene rode Pluperfect into the clearing that had been made around the house. The only shade for the homestead came from a drooping pepper tree that was alive with the hum of bees. Yet, on the far side of the clearing, gum trees surrounded the new corrals where the rusting troughs had been replaced, so at least the horses had some shelter. The pastures behind the newly erected stable block were green, watered by underground streams that criss-crossed Deloraine, making this particular station one to be envied. Even in the severest drought, Deloraine had never run dry.

Irene rode towards the stables and realised Jimmy was about to leave. 'How about coming over here to work?' she offered.

He took off his hat and mopped the sweat from his dark brow. 'Reckon the boss wouldn't like it, missus,' he said.

'I'll pay you the same wages,' she said hastily. 'And sort out a place for you to sleep.'

'Sorry, missus,' he mumbled as he squashed the disreputable hat back over his halo of tangled brown hair. 'Gotta get back.'

Irene pursed her lips and watched as the Aboriginal clambered back into the truck and set off. Without a man on the place she would find the going rough, but obviously William had already had a word with his men and she wouldn't get help there. The maids had also refused her offer of work, and so had the cook. It had been too many years since she'd done her own housework and cooking, let alone the laundry – and she had no intentions of starting again now. She would have to go into Trinity and post a notice for a stable lad and a couple of girls to help in the house, which was a damn nuisance, because

164

she'd been avoiding Trinity – now it looked as if she had no option. Her gaze followed the trail of dust until it disappeared. The silence closed in along with the heat. From where she stood she could see no sign of civilisation – no sign that refuted the knowledge she was alone in this vast emptiness. It was going to be tough out here – solitary too, and before she could give in to the flood of emotion that was welling inside her, she turned away.

Having settled Pluperfect in his stable, she checked the bolts on the doors, the feed bags and water buckets, and finally headed for the house. She supposed she should think of a name for this corner of Deloraine, but she didn't really care. She wasn't planning on staying here for ever.

The wooden floors had been scraped and freshly varnished and the scent of polish greeted her as she opened the front door. The maids had done a good job, she realised, as she went from room to room inspecting their work. The bedroom overlooked the porch and was sheltered from the sun. It looked homely enough, with her pictures on the walls, the rugs on the floor and her favourite little Queen Anne chair in the corner. The new bed had been made up, the linen crisp and inviting as the ceiling fan whirred.

She wandered across the narrow hall into the sitting room. The stone fireplace looked quite imposing now it had a beam of pine set into it as a mantel. Her glass and china was put away in the delicate cabinets she'd inherited from Eva, and her trophies and bronzes were displayed on shelves that ran along one wall. The couch and chair had seen better days and she had contemplated buying new, but had decided they were comfortable enough to keep for a while longer. It wasn't as if she was planning to socialise – so what the hell did it matter?

The kitchen and bathroom were at the back of the house, each room square and serviceable – the only luxury that of hot water which was piped directly from an underground bore. A generator gave her electricity and its soft hum was her only companion.

Irene stripped off her clothes as she ran the bath, and after a long soak she wrapped herself in a towelling robe and padded back into the kitchen.

The range had yet to be lit, and because it was already stifling, she didn't bother. The larder was full of tins, the Deloraine cook had left her bread and milk and butter on the slab of marble, and there were the remains of a joint of mutton in the meat safe. Pouring a gin and tonic, she took her sandwich and padded out to the front verandah.

The sky was black, the moon playing hide and seek amongst scudding clouds. There were few stars and the night had brought no relief from the heat. She sat on one of the two chairs she'd brought over

165

from the homestead and listened to the silence. The very essence of this primal land seemed to call her, to wrap her in its cloak of ancient mystery and sweep her into the endless darkness.

The loneliness closed in as the full impact of what she'd lost began to take hold. And for only the second time in her life she experienced the agony of being abandoned. The tears came unheeded, rolling down her face to splash on her hands as she was reminded of that first time.

The shabby little room above the feed store in Flinders Street looked even more drab than she remembered as Irene waited for him to arrive. She paced the dusty floor, stopping now and again to pull the sagging net curtain aside to peer anxiously down into the street. He was late, and if he didn't come soon she would have to leave. Jessie was already suspicious and had made a point of telling her she must be home within the hour. Irene knew that if she was late, Jessie would tell Eva of her suspicions – and another row was the last thing Irene needed.

The sound of his feet on the stairs made her start, and she brushed her coat and patted her hair. She had taken a great deal of care over her appearance today, and despite the sleepless nights and the morning sickness, she knew she had never looked lovelier. Yet, would that be enough to prove her mother and Jessie wrong in their estimation of him? She hoped so, for it was her only weapon.

He burst through the door, his handsome face glowing with the cold. 'Sorry I'm late,' he said as he embraced her. 'But I had some errands to run for your father, and couldn't get here any sooner.'

She melted into his embrace, the touch of his lips warming her and making her tremble with longing. She clung to him, wanting the moment to go on, needing his warmth and his strength to imbue her with courage for what she had to tell him.

As they finally drew apart she reached up a gloved hand and touched his hair. It was the colour of burnished copper, with strands of gold that gleamed in the poor light from the window. His eyes were the deepest brown, flecked with amber beneath the tawny, winged brows. The nose was straight above the thick moustache and cleft chin, the mouth sensuous and made for laughter. He was handsome, his youthful exuberance belying his thirty-eight years.

He kissed her nose and her brow. 'I've missed you,' he murmured. 'We have so little time before I have to leave. Where have you been these past few days?'

She wanted to tell him, but first she had to know the truth. 'Do you love me?' she asked, the doubts creeping unbidden into her voice.

He frowned and pulled her closer. 'Silly girl,' he muttered as he ran his lips over her face and down her neck.

166

She pulled away. If he carried on like that she would be lost, and she needed straight answers to her questions. 'Well, do you?' she demanded.

He ran his hands through his hair, making it flop into his eyes. 'Of course,' he said as he reached for her again. 'Come on, Rene, don't let's waste time by talking. Time together is precious enough without all this nonsense.'

Irene placed her hand firmly on his chest and held him at bay. 'You said you'd leave your wife for me,' she said. 'Is that true?'

His feet shifted and he looked ill at ease suddenly. 'It's difficult at the moment,' he said. 'The girls are still so young, and Helen doesn't have the best of health. It's hard enough for her when I'm away for so many months at a time.' He looked down at her. 'You haven't said where you've been these past few days.'

'Running errands,' she snapped. 'And don't try and change the subject.'

His eyebrow lifted. 'Oh, dear,' he said with a sigh. 'We're not going to have another tantrum, are we?'

Irene shook her head. She didn't want to upset him, and certainly didn't want to lose him by behaving like one of his children. 'But we do need to talk,' she said. 'I have something important to tell you, and you must listen.'

His gaze was immediately wary and he folded his arms across his broad chest. 'I'm expected back at your father's office,' he said. 'Make it quick.'

Irene swallowed. She could feel the rapid tattoo of her pulse and the squirm of terror rising inside. All her future plans hinged on this one moment. 'I'm expecting a baby,' she said breathlessly.

The dark eyes were piercing as the colour was swept from the handsome face. 'I hope not,' was all he said.

Irene was trembling. She'd had no idea how he'd react, but this didn't even approach her wildest dread. She ran her tongue over her dry lips. 'It was confirmed yesterday,' she whispered. 'I hoped you'd be pleased.'

'Whose is it?' His voice was hard, so unlike the soft, lover's voice that usually sent shivers down her spine.

'Yours,' she said, the hurt clear in her tone, the shock of his question resounding in her head.

'And how can I be sure of that?' he returned. 'I was not the first, Irene, and I doubt I'll be the last.'

'You bastard,' she shrieked as she whipped out her hand to slap his face.

He caught her wrists, held her tightly and glared down at her.

167

'How could you be so stupid?' he snapped. 'I thought you knew how to take care of things.'

Irene swallowed. When he'd broached the subject at the onset of their affair she hadn't understood what he could mean, and unwilling to appear gauche and unsophisticated, she'd lied. Yet, as time had gone on and she began to believe they really could have a future together, she'd realised the only way of truly wresting him from his wife was to have his child.

'I did . . . I do . . . ' she stammered. 'I don't know how it could have happened.' She looked up at him. 'I'm frightened,' she admitted. 'Mother is threatening to send me away and she absolutely refuses to believe you'll stand by me.' The tears were hot on her cheeks as she leaned against him. 'But you won't desert me, will you? Not after all the things you said? The promises you made?'

He gently pushed her away and ran his hands through his hair again. 'What can I do, Irene?' His voice was soft, cracked with emotion. 'I'm at least twenty years older than you, with a sick wife and four young children. This was only meant to be a bit of fun – I thought you understood that? I thought I'd made it very plain right from the outset. If I stand by you the scandal will ruin my entire family – ruin everything I've worked so hard for all these years.'

'And what about my reputation?' she snapped, the fear making her sharp.

He went and stood at the window, his hands on either side of the glass, his head resting on the frame as he looked down into the street. 'There's a woman I've heard about. Lives down at the port. I'll make enquiries.'

Irene frowned. 'Woman? What woman?'

'A woman who will solve your little problem,' he muttered. 'For a price.'

Irene shivered as the full impact of his words finally made sense. 'But I love you,' she gasped. 'This is our baby you're plotting to murder.' She ran to him and grasped him around the waist as she leaned against his broad back. 'Please don't do this. Tell me you meant all those things you said when we were making love, and that we'll be together always. Tell me you want this child and that you'll stand by us no matter what.'

'They were just words said in the heat of the moment,' he murmured. 'Dreams voiced that I thought neither of us really expected to come true, but were pleasant to while away an afternoon.' He turned from the window, the anguish clear in his face as he put his arms around her. 'I'm sorry,' he whispered. 'So very sorry.'

Stunned by his rejection, the full horror of her predicament became

168

crystal clear. The chill of foreboding swept through her as she felt the pressure of his kiss on her forehead. Then he was gone. She heard the slam of the door and the pounding of his feet on the wooden stairs, followed by silence.

Her wail of anguish rose and swirled to the ceiling as she sank to the floor. 'But you said you loved me,' she sobbed. 'You said we'd be together always. I did this for you,' she howled.

There were only the silent dust motes to hear her as they drifted softly on the frail beams of light radiating through the grimy window.

Irene sat on the verandah in the sultry night and stared into the darkness. It was as if she could still hear those sobs. Could still feel the stab of anguish when she finally realised all her plans for entrapping him had gone astray and that he wanted no part of her or the child she carried. His ambition had been too strong for her – her fear of what her father would do if he discovered the truth, a sure-fire way of keeping her silent.

She blinked and lifted the glass to her lips, barely tasting the strong gin and tonic as the memories came back to haunt her.

An envelope had arrived two days later. It contained a name and address of a woman down in Port Phillip – and forty pounds in single, grubby notes. The note with this Judas gift demanded she use the money for the purpose it had been given, and that he didn't wish to see or hear from her again. If she decided to go against his wishes, then he would deny all knowledge of her, or the child.

Eva had found Irene in tears and had demanded to read the letter. To give her credit, Eva had not said 'I told you so,' but had held her as she sobbed. That night she and Jessie had tucked her into bed and stayed with her until she slept, just as they had done when she was a child.

It was to be the last time she would sleep in that house in Melbourne. The last few hours of any intimacy between her and Eva, for the rift when it came had been irreparable.

Irene came down the stairs the following morning to discover the hall cluttered with suitcases and hat boxes. She finally found Eva and Jessie in the drawing room, deep in argument.

'I ain't leaving you 'ere,' said Jessie, arms akimbo, face red with anger.

'You'll do as you're told,' retorted Eva, her tone brooking any argument.

'It ain't right,' muttered Jessie. 'You're 'er mother, should be you going with 'er, not me.'

Irene had heard enough. She stepped into the room. 'Nobody's going anywhere until I know what's happening here,' she said

169

firmly. 'What are my cases doing in the hall?' she demanded.

Eva turned from Jessie and clasped her hands in front of her. 'You and Jessie are going north,' she said. 'I've made arrangements for you to catch the evening train.'

Irene shot a glance at Jessie, whose colour was still high, expression bordering on the belligerent. 'I don't want to go with Jessie. Why can't you take me?'

'Believe me, miss, I don't want to be going all that way on me own with you, neither. But yer ma won't 'ave none of it.' The arms were folded tightly beneath the pendulous bosom.

Eva took a deep breath. 'Your father is leaving at noon for this expedition into the Northern Territories,' she said, the tight grip on her emotions making her voice unsteady. 'I must remain here until he returns.'

'You could leave a forwarding address,' said Irene stubbornly.

'No, I couldn't,' retorted Eva. 'You will do as you are told for once, Irene. I have enough to worry about without you behaving like a spoilt brat.'

Irene weighed up her options. She certainly couldn't stay in Melbourne. The woman down in the port was not an option either – far too dangerous. But the thought of travelling in Jessie's company for longer than a day or two was not her idea of a good time.

'How far north are we going?' she asked finally.

'Cairns,' replied Eva.

Irene's eyes widened in horror. 'It's the other end of the country,' she gasped. 'It will take days to get there, and where will we stay?'

'I've arranged for some money to be transferred to a bank up there and Jessie will buy a house where you will stay until the child is born. I will come as soon as I've had word your father is safe.'

'But that could be months,' protested Irene.

'Let's hope not,' replied Eva firmly. 'Either way, you will present yourself as a young widow.' She sighed. 'Unfortunately, in this time of war that will be only too believable. You and Jessie can work out a suitable story during your journey, and once decided you must stick to it if you want to avoid any scandal.'

'Will we come back here when it's all over?'

Eva shrugged. 'It will depend entirely on how you comport yourself after the child is born. There must be no more scandal.'

'I'll put it up for adoption,' said Irene firmly. 'What do I want with a baby?'

Eva's gaze was unwavering as she looked into Irene's face. 'Perhaps you should have thought about that earlier,' she said flatly.

*

170

The journey north seemed endless as they changed from one train to another. Irene ignored Jessie for most of the time and stared out of the window as they rattled through desolate plains that shimmered in the heat. Born and raised in a city, Irene couldn't compare the stations they passed through with any other she had seen – for they weren't really stations, just sidings with water for the engine – the only sign of life a man on a horse waiting for a lift to the next dusty outpost.

She frowned as they passed isolated homesteads surrounded by scrub and silver grass where sheep and cattle grazed beneath a vast sky, and wondered what kind of people could bear to scratch a living in such isolation. It must take a special man or woman to withstand life out here, she decided – but it was not for her. There was too much space – too much sky.

Yet her father loved this desolation, this emptiness, and despite his declarations to the contrary, was obviously impatient to leave Melbourne after only a short break between his surveying assignments. Life in the city had no hold on him, and although he professed to love his wife and daughter, it seemed to Irene he loved freedom more. What strange creatures men are, she mused.

After a week of travelling they began to chug through green hills and the verdant cane fields that lay at the foot of hazy, blue mountains. A sweet aroma permeated the air, increasing as they approached the tall grey chimneys at El Arish, and Irene asked one of the other passengers what it could be.

'It's the refineries,' came the answer. 'The sugar's processed here and then the distilleries turn it into rum.'

Irene turned her attention back to the window. It was another world up here in the tropical north of Australia, where palm trees grew higher than houses, and lush green plants with searing pink and orange flowers spilled over dark rocks where waterfalls tumbled into rivers and lakes. Exotic birds flew amongst this green, their colours rainbow bright against the mysterious dark foliage and she exclaimed with delight. Perhaps her enforced exile wouldn't be so bad after all.

They moved into a small hotel in Cairns, and Jessie began to hunt for a temporary home for them both. Three weeks later they had settled into the small wooden house perched on the dunes that overlooked the sea at Trinity. It was further north than they had first planned, but it was the only house Jessie and Irene could agree upon.

Irene's pregnancy advanced as the heat and humidity rose and the summer took hold. The wet season arrived, flooding the dirt streets, drumming on the tin roofs and masking the horizon. The sea changed from turquoise to slate, whipped into foamy peaks by the hot winds that came from the Torres Straits. These squalls of wind and rain lasted only for an hour or so, and soon the sun was beating down again, the earth steaming beneath a clear sky.

Irene began to hate the child she was carrying. It squirmed and kicked and made her feel sick, and she couldn't wait to be rid of it. She avoided mirrors, for she looked fat and ungainly, and none of her pretty clothes fitted her any more. She also began to despise Trinity and the poky little house she'd been forced to share with Jessie. She missed her friends in Melbourne, missed her mother and her horses. There was nothing to do, nothing to take her mind off her predicament and she was sick of pretending to be widowed and could barely dredge up the energy to appear enthusiastic about this damn baby.

The social life consisted of earnest, dowdy women sitting about knitting for the boys fighting in Europe, or feverish fund-raising which involved selling home-made jam. Irene soon came to realise she had nothing in common with these unsophisticated country women, and used the excuse of her 'widowhood' to avoid their company.

Jessie fussed around her, making tempting meals in the stifling kitchen, and knitting tiny jackets and bootees for the coming child. Irene gave up telling her she would have the kid adopted the minute it was born – her words fell on deaf ears – Jessie was adamant she would change her mind.

Irene wrote long letters home, surprised at how keenly she missed her mother. The news from Melbourne was worrying, for the expedition had run into trouble, and there had been no word and no sighting of the intrepid explorers for some months. Her father and her lover were deemed missing, and Irene's frustration grew as each week passed. She was so far from civilisation – so divorced from the reality of life at home – so reliant on news from others, and although she could have done nothing tangible, she knew she could have rested easier if she was back in Melbourne.

Eva's own despair could be read between the lines of her letters, and for the first time in her life, Irene thought she could understand what she must be going through. It was an unfamiliar bond, but one that could never be spoken of, for her liaison with her father's right-hand man was taboo.

Irene's own despair was tempered by the long letters she wrote to him, knowing they might never reach him, but hoping nevertheless that one day he might read them. She was on the point of giving up any hope of a future with him when she received news from a friend, of his wife's death. She renewed her efforts, writing long into the night, the ink blurred from her tears as week followed week and the hated child grew inside her. She had to keep faith in him. Had to believe he would survive the expedition and eventually return to Melbourne.

The post had to be collected from the little post office in the town, and Irene volunteered to fetch it each day. She didn't want to risk Jessie opening the wrong letter, or asking awkward questions. Yet the risk was minimal, she acknowledged, as she sifted through the mail. There had been no word from him since he'd sent the money for the abortion. How she wished she'd been brave enough to go through with it, instead of suffering this awful exile. If only he could write back. If only he could acknowledge the bond between them. With his wife dead and his children motherless there were no barriers between them. If he survived this expedition, then surely he would change his mind?

Her hand stilled as she turned an envelope over and saw the unfamiliar writing. The black ink and looping script had a look of authority about them. With a racing pulse she sat down on a low wall that overlooked the sea. The letter didn't feel very thick, but that didn't matter. He'd replied – at last he'd replied.

She tore it open and devoured the words on the single sheet of paper.

Miss Hamilton,
I regret the decision you have made despite my client's advice. You no doubt have your reasons, but my client has instructed me to inform you that he wants no part in your scheming. As you are aware, my client is not at present able to correspond directly with you, but before leaving on this latest expedition, he instructed me to return any letters you may send to him, with the warning that any further contact will be treated as harassment.

He vigorously denies any intimate relationship with you, and is not prepared to acknowledge any child you may have as his own. If you persist in this slander, he will have no other recourse but to take this matter to the courts. Please consider this letter as the final contact between yourself and my client.

His signature was a scrawl at the bottom of the page and Irene crushed the letter in her fist and stared out to sea. The words were cruel, but if he thought a solicitor's letter would end things between them, then he was very much mistaken. His circumstances had changed since he left Melbourne – he was free.

Irene sat on the sea wall and stared unseeing out to the horizon. If he and Father survived, then he would return home to find he was widowed and in charge of his four children. He would be lonely.

All the time there was no news of the expedition there was still hope, she realised. But if her plan was to work, it meant keeping this damn baby. She smiled for the first time in many weeks. It would be a small price to pay when the rewards were so great. He was wealthy and handsome and now, because of his wife's timely passing, unshackled by marriage – he would have no excuses this time.

Her thoughts raced and the impatience grew. If only this kid would get born she could go back to the south and begin her campaign of befriending his children. Jessie could look after it, she decided. She'd done nothing but plan and knit and think up silly names ever since they'd come here. The guise of widow would have to remain, though, and the thought was irksome – but if it meant getting what she wanted without any scandal attached to her, she was prepared to put up with the deceit.

The thought that her lover, or her father, might not survive despite all her plotting was so impossible, she dismissed it. And any objections her parents might make were also cast aside. It was none of their business.

Irene rubbed her back in an attempt to ease the niggling pain that had been there all morning. She struggled up from her seat on the wall and took a deep breath as she eyed the long, sandy track she had yet to walk before she could reach the house. It was probably the heat making her feel so awful, she decided.

The sun glared on the white sand with blinding intensity as she began the walk she had once deemed so easy. The added burden of the baby was making it difficult to walk very fast and the deep, drawing pain in her back had intensified. She stopped for a moment to mop the sweat from her face and catch her breath. It couldn't be the baby, surely? There were still two weeks to go.

Jessie was waiting at the door as always and for once, Irene was pleased to see her. 'It's coming,' she gasped as she almost fell into Jessie's arms.

'Thought so, you've been off colour lately.' Jessie steered her into the bedroom and helped her undress. 'Lie down, ducks, while I get everything ready.' Jessie bustled out of the room.

Irene collapsed onto the cool, crisp sheets and closed her eyes. A thrill of excitement shot through her as the pains became more frequent. It would soon be over and life could begin again. She would regain her figure and her looks, go shopping for new clothes and enter the social whirl of Melbourne. But best of all she could escape this prison and return from exile.

'Right, deary,' encouraged Jessie some time later. 'You gotta push, luv. No good moaning and thrashing about. This baby wants to be born and you ain't helpin'.'

Irene grasped the sheets and arched her back. She was soaked with sweat and ravaged with pain. No-one had told her it would be like this. 'Get this *thing* out of me,' she screamed. 'Get it *out!*'

Chapter Sixteen

Despite the awful, draining humidity, Giles had never felt physically better. He swam twice a day now, and was no longer embarrassed about his missing arm. His appetite for life had returned, and after seeing how well Hopalong and Smokey were doing at their sawmill, he realised that being an amputee didn't mean the end of a fruitful life. Yet his spirits were low as he and Olivia walked the sand and watched the lightning flicker in the distance.

Olivia seemed to sense his mood. She stopped walking and put her hand on his arm 'What is it, Giles? What's worrying you?'

He stared out over the black sea as he tried to put his thoughts into words. 'Just feeling somewhat restless,' he said, before he chuckled. 'Feeling a bit out of things, if you want to know the truth. What with the medical centre and Maggie and everything.'

She looked up at him, her eyes puzzled. 'But why? The community health centre is a project we can all take a hand in. I thought you were keen on the idea?' She folded her arms around her waist, the pale moonlight catching the planes of her face.

'I am,' he said. 'But . . .'

'What?' Olivia's voice was sharp with impatience. 'Come on, Giles. You've been throwing a blue all day. Spit it out.'

He couldn't help but grin. 'You're becoming more Australian by the day,' he said. 'Throwing a blue, indeed.'

Olivia cocked her head and grinned back. 'Fair go, mate,' she drawled. 'You can take the cobber out of Australia, but you can't get Australia out of the cobber.'

'Good grief,' retorted Giles in an admirable imitation of Eva. 'You could cut that accent with a knife.' He looked down at her, the teasing lilt to his voice at once more serious. 'You've changed so much since we came here, Ollie, and I've come to realise I hardly know you at all.'

'I haven't changed, not really,' she said with a shake of her head. 'But my priorities have.' She sighed as she sat down on the sand and hugged her knees. 'I came here to find the truth,' she said softly. 'And what I found was something so unexpected, it has turned my original quest on its head.' She smiled. 'This place and the people in it have become more important to me than trying to find the pieces of a long-forgotten puzzle.'

'Are you not the least bit curious?' Giles sat down beside her.

'Of course I am. But the fire in Brisbane back in 1929 wiped out all records – so it looks as if I'll have to accept I will never know what those papers in Eva's bureau were hiding.'

Giles fumbled with his lighter and finally managed to draw smoke from his cheroot. He had to ask, but was afraid of her answer. 'Will you be staying here?'

She rested her chin on her knees and stared into the darkness. 'For a while,' she murmured. 'Maggie and I are only just getting to know one another and there's a lot to do before we can have the medical centre up and running.'

'But once you do,' he persisted. 'Will you be coming back to England?'

She remained silent for so long, Giles wondered if she'd heard the question, or was merely trying to avoid it.

'Maybe,' she said finally. 'I don't know.' She stood up and brushed sand from her trousers. 'There's not much to go back to, to be honest, Giles. Just a big empty old house and a job in a Victorian hospital that probably should have been condemned years ago.' She took a deep breath and slowly let it out. 'I feel at home here,' she said. 'Wimbledon's like another life – so distant it's almost as if it had never existed.'

Giles swallowed. It was as if all his precious memories of their childhood had been swept away in her careless words. He struggled to his feet and brushed away the sand from his clothes. 'And what about me? Where do I fit into this brave new world?'

She regarded him calmly. 'Wherever you want to fit,' she said.

The tension between them was matched only by the electricity in the storm-laden air.

'As a friend? A surrogate brother? Or something else?' He took a deep breath. 'What if I said I wanted to be with you always?'

Olivia dipped her chin and her hair fell in a curtain of silk between them. Her thoughts were whirling, for his words had come as a shock. 'Always is a long time,' she murmured.

He reached out and tipped up her chin with his fingers until she was

176

forced to look him in the eye. 'Olivia Hamilton,' he said firmly. 'I have loved you since you were a skinny little girl with plaits and scabby knees. There is nowhere I would rather be than with you, and I don't care if we end up in Timbuktu as long as we're together. If this is where you plan to stay, then so do I.' He paused. 'That's if you want me by your side, of course. As a husband.'

'That's quite a declaration,' she said breathlessly. Olivia looked into his eyes and saw the longing there, the bleak honesty that was so much a part of him – and realised with a jolt that Giles loved her deeply in a way she had never suspected so her next few words must be carefully chosen.

She felt the tremble in his fingers as he cupped her chin and the answering tremor in her own body. 'You are my dearest friend,' she began with the softest regret. 'My soul mate, the one person I have ever really trusted. But I never ...'

She saw the hurt in his eyes as his fingers released their tenuous tilt on her chin, and wanted so much to be able to tell him she loved him in the way he wanted. Yet his declaration had changed everything and all her previous perceptions of him had been swept away. She didn't know at this very minute how to ease his pain – only that it wouldn't be fair to lie to him, to give him hope. 'Giles,' she began.

He put his finger to her lips, the anguish clear in his eyes. 'Shh,' he whispered. 'Don't say any more. I realise this has come as a shock, but with so much happening, I was afraid of losing you. It was always going to be risky, but I had to tell you, don't you see?'

She nodded, her emotions in too much turmoil to allow her to speak.

His lips lingered momentarily on her brow and then he turned and walked away.

He made a solitary figure on that empty beach, and Olivia was tempted to run after him. Yet she remained there in the silence of the sultry night with only the sea for company. Giles couldn't see it now, but she was being cruel to be kind. It wouldn't have been fair to lie to him, to make him think she regretted turning him down. The deep affection she held for him was not enough to lay the foundations of marriage, and hopefully he would realise that one day. Yet the thought of hurting him, of losing his friendship, was almost too much and she shoved her hands in her pockets and walked in the opposite direction. She needed time alone to think.

Giles climbed the stairs to their suite of rooms and closed the door behind him. The hotel was in darkness and there was thankfully no sign of either Sam or Maggie. He threw himself into the chair and his shoulders slumped as the agony swept over him and he replayed the little scene on the beach.

He had seen the doubt in her eyes, the puzzlement, the searching for words that didn't have the power to wound. Her affection was obvious, otherwise she would have rejected him immediately, but she wasn't in love with him – had never been in love with him, he could see that now.

He reached for the bottle of whisky and filled a glass. 'Here's to all hopeless cases,' he said sourly as he saluted the empty room. Downing the drink in one, he poured another. He'd been a fool to speak out. A fool to risk what they had just because he wanted more. It was that realisation which had made him silence her before she could reply – for he'd known what that answer would be and couldn't bear to hear it.

The second whisky slipped down as easily as the first and he poured another. He sat in the dark, listening to the night sounds, feeling the tension in the air as the storm marshalled its forces for the coming onslaught. The heat had brought him to this moment of madness. The heat, the dust, the flies – but most of all, it had been the realisation that Olivia meant to stay in this strange, alien country – had begun to put down roots by buying that ridiculous ruin – had taken the first irrevocable step towards a future that would not include him.

He ripped off his shirt and trousers and threw himself onto the bed and stared at the ceiling. Despite the fan rattling overhead, it was so hot he could scarcely breathe, and yet he dared not open the windows or screens because of the mosquitoes. What kind of country was this where everything that crawled and flew and slithered could do you harm? What kind of country that lurched from drought to flood with no halfway measures?

He shifted restlessly against sheets that were already damp with his sweat. Trinity might be a paradise on earth, but in Eden there was always a serpent – and the heatwave was all a part of that. He missed England and the cool, green summers. Missed the gold and amber and copper of the autumn leaves and the icy blast of the winter wind which brought the snow. He missed oak beams and a raging fire in the inglenook of his local pub, warm beer and the sound of familiar accents, and the invigorating tramp over the coastal golf links where the wind was salty and stung his face.

Giles drained his whisky and closed his eyes. He was feeling sorry for himself, but at least he now knew where he stood in the scheme of things. His bitterness made him spiteful. Olivia had used their friendship to bring him out here and she obviously no longer needed him.

178

He realised how tense he was and eased his shoulders. He wasn't being fair to Olivia, for after all, he'd been willing enough to come all this way. But, being a realist, he knew the time had come for them to go their separate ways. His gamble had not paid off and, like Olivia, he needed to get on with his life – needed to return home to England, and immerse himself in law books so he could forget her.

The whisky had made him maudlin as well as sleepy, he realised. As he drifted towards oblivion his last thought was of Olivia in the moonlight. The tears slowly rolled unheeded down his cheek. He hadn't even had the chance to kiss her.

Olivia had been walking for what seemed like hours. She finally turned and made her way back to the hotel. The heat was heavy with menace and her thin shirt was sticking to her back as she quietly entered through the side door and made her way upstairs.

The hotel looked strange with all the downstairs windows boarded up, and she hoped it would be enough. Sam was obviously worried by the approaching storm, and Giles had suggested she should leave. But she couldn't do that. Her skills might come in handy if anyone was injured, and besides, if Maggie wasn't leaving, neither was she.

Their rooms were in darkness and Olivia could hear Giles snoring. She went into her bedroom and stripped off her clothes. It would have been nice to have a bath, but it was too late. She plumped down on the bed and lay there in anticipation of feeling at least a little cooler beneath the fan. It didn't help at all, merely stirred the humidity around the room.

Unable to sleep, she climbed back off the bed and stood at the window. Giles' declaration shouldn't have come as such a shock, she'd realised during her walk. Maggie had told her he was in love with her, so why did she feel so at odds with herself? She loved him, there was no denying it; but in love – romantic love? Never. He'd been around forever it seemed and perhaps she'd been guilty of taking him for granted. Now she could see the signs, for in hindsight, she'd realised how much of a sacrifice it must have been for him to come all this way so soon after his rehabilitation.

If only he'd waited, she thought. Waited for what? The niggling doubts crowded in. Waited for the storm to blow over? Waited until they got back to England? She shook her head in frustration. The thoughts were going round and round in her head, and although she hated to see him hurt, she'd told him the truth. Waiting wouldn't have changed anything.

Olivia stared out at the hazy moon and the thickening clouds. There was no substitute for a deep friendship – but she knew she needed

179

passion and excitement when it came to loving a man, and she just didn't feel that way about Giles.

She gave a deep, sad sigh as she stood there in the darkness, her thoughts jumbled and confused. They had spent little time apart – except for the war years and then they'd both been too busy to think of anything but the task in hand. Of course she'd been worried about the number of missions he was flying. Of course she was devastated when he'd turned up on her ward looking so ill they were frightened he wouldn't make it through the night. She would have felt the same about any friend.

Olivia lit a rare cigarette and blew smoke through the screens where it drifted on the sluggish air. It was impossible to make any sensible judgements when it was so hot, she thought crossly. If only this damn storm would break and give them all a breathing space, she might be able to sort this mess out and find a way of easing his hurt.

'She's coming your way, mate, and she's a beaut, so batten down the hatches. Over.'

Sam flicked a switch on the two-way radio. 'How fast? Over.'

'Like a bloody train,' came the reply from the weather station at Cape York. 'Stacked like Rita Hayworth, and twice as dangerous.'

Sam grinned at the images this conjured up. 'When can we expect her? Over.'

'We're talking cyclone, here, mate. Sometime tomorrow, I reckon. She's finished with Thursday Island and is heading towards us here at the Cape.' The crackling intensified. 'Gotta go, mate. Good luck.'

Sam broke the connection and sat back. He and Maggie had done all they could about protecting the hotel. The windows had been boarded over, the bar cleared of all the glass, the furniture stacked away and the shutters nailed tight. The Aboriginals had more sense, they'd gone walkabout a couple of days back and probably wouldn't be seen again until everything was over. His horse would have to take its chances with everything else, and had been turned out into the paddock.

He sighed as he leaned back in the chair and surveyed his room. It looked bare now he'd packed up his things and stored them beneath the hotel. Life in this tropical paradise had its compensations, but this wouldn't be the first storm he'd lived through and he doubted it would be the last. Yet he was glad he had someone with medical knowledge on the place – they might need Olivia if things got out of hand.

He pushed away from the two-way radio and ran his fingers through his hair. He was on edge, infused with the same electricity that seemed to be charging the air. He knew he wouldn't sleep tonight and felt the

180

need for company – Maggie's company. With a grin of pleasure he realised he missed her when she wasn't around, and enjoyed their sparring when she was. Maggie had managed to break through the veneer of aloneness he'd erected, and he found he didn't mind at all.

Peering through the side window, he saw her light was still blazing across the yard. Before he could change his mind, he grabbed a couple of beers on his way through the bar, and was soon knocking at her door.

'I can't sleep either,' said Maggie as she let him in. 'The tension in the air is almost unbearable. I wish the damn thing would break.'

Sam followed her into the room and opened the bottles of beer. 'Got a message on the two-way from Cape York. She should be with us by this time tomorrow.'

Maggie accepted the bottle of beer and took a healthy slug. 'Why are storms always female?'

'Because they're dangerous,' he retorted with a glint of humour in his eyes.

She turned away from him, her face masked by the sweep of her hair. 'We will be all right, won't we?' Her voice betrayed the inner fear despite the squared shoulders and rigid spine, and he could see the droplets of perspiration on her back and shoulders.

'You never know with a cyclone,' he said. He bit his lip. He hadn't meant to tell her just how serious this particular storm might be. 'It could blow itself out, or twist off somewheres and miss us completely,' he added hastily.

'Cyclone?' she hissed, her face drained of colour, her eyes dark with fear as she whipped around to face him.

He tried to make light of it. 'It's just another name for a storm,' he said.

'Yeah,' she grimaced. 'Like tornado, hurricane, typhoon – they're all nasty, especially if they come off the sea.' She drank the beer straight from the bottle. 'Bloody hell, Sam,' she gasped as she wiped her mouth on the back of her hand. 'Why didn't you warn us it could be that bad?'

He realised this was no time for silly jokes, or for making light of something that could prove deadly. 'Sorry, Maggs,' he said. 'I just didn't want you going crook on me.'

Her eyes were rounded. 'I'd'a done more than go crook on you,' she spluttered. 'I'd'a got the hell out while I could.'

'Exactly,' he said as he dug his hands in his pockets.

She eyed him thoughtfully for a long while before taking another drink. 'We still could,' she said. 'Make a run for it, I mean, before it hits.'

181

He shook his head, 'Everything I own's tied up in this place. I can't just leave it, Maggs.

She looked around the cabin and slowly nodded. 'Yeah,' she said. 'I know what you mean.' She thought for a moment. 'What about Giles and Olivia? Have you warned them?'

'I told Giles this morning we could be in for a serious blast, but apart from Olivia's safety he didn't seem too concerned. Said he'd survived the Luftwaffe, so he could survive a bit of wind.' He scuffed his boot on the floor. 'Don't reckon he understood exactly. The Poms don't have cyclones.'

'What about Olivia?'

'She said she would stay. Insisted on it, thank God. We might need her medical skills if this thing does hit.'

Maggie seemed to have lost her thirst. She put the bottle down and folded her arms tightly around her waist. Her face was pale, her eyes darkly shadowed. 'I've never been in a cyclone,' she said, her voice unable to diguise the fear. 'What will it be like?'

Sam decided she should be told the truth – he owed her that much. 'It will be noisy,' he said evenly. 'It will shake the houses and lash the trees and sound like a thousand banshees tearing down on us.'

Her fingers covered her mouth as she blinked like a wide-eyed possum.

Sam thought she had never looked so beautiful, so vulnerable. He opened his arms and she stepped into his embrace. He held her close, his chin resting on her head. 'No worries, Maggs. We'll be snug in the hotel and stay there until it blows over. You'll be right, mate.'

She lifted her chin and looked up into his face. 'Is that a promise?' she whispered.

Sam felt as if he was drowning in her eyes. He could feel her warmth, her slenderness against his chest. Could feel the electricity in the air that had nothing to do with the approaching storm. Her lips parted and after only an instant of hesitation, he kissed her.

His breath seemed caught in his chest as her lips moved beneath his, and all the pent-up emotion he'd been so long in denying, spilled over. He never wanted this kiss to end. He needed to hold her, to posses and protect her. With his heart hammering against his ribs he ran his hands over her slender frame, pressing her closer – so close she was crushed against him – so close their breath was intermingled.

Her fingers were working feverishly at the buttons on his shirt as he slipped her dress down over her shoulders. Her skin was like silk, warm and fragrant, and slightly slick with heat, the pulse in her neck so tempting to kiss – to devour – to make his own.

He wrestled with his shirt as Maggie stepped out of her dress. A tide of electric need shot between them as they both hesitated – eyes held, breath held in a moment of pure, aching pleasure – a moment of desire yet to be fulfilled, but the more pleasurable because they knew where it would lead.

And then she was in his arms again. Naked flesh on flesh as she moulded herself to him – her hunger every bit as great as his. He buried his hands in her hair and she arched her neck, exposing her vulnerability. She ran her fingers down his back, her nails sending a shiver of pleasure right through him.

Sam picked her up and carried her to the bed and as they discovered each other during that long, hot night, all thoughts of cyclones were dismissed.

Chapter Seventeen

Olivia stood on the beach, her face lifted to the darkening sky as she revelled in the cooling breeze. The rain had yet to come, but she could smell it in the air – could see it in the ominous, swirling cloud that was beginning to obscure the island out to sea.

A lone curlew cried mournfully as it swooped over the empty water and headed for inland shelter. The palm trees were swaying, their fronds dipping low to the sand, as the sea glowered, sliding pewter waves one over the other until they broke in a slap against the rocks. She could feel the pent-up fury – the lull that always came before a storm – and it excited her. For this was pure energy. A force of nature that would not be denied.

'There you are. I've been looking for you.'

Olivia turned and smiled as Maggie came to stand beside her. 'I just wanted a last look before it's too late,' she said.

'Could all be gone this time tomorrow,' replied Maggie with a surprising lack of regret.

Olivia eyed her and noticed the glow in Maggie's face, the light in her eyes. 'What have you been up to, Maggie? You look positively radiant.'

Maggie actually blushed as she dipped her chin. 'Is it that obvious?'

Olivia laughed and gave her a hug as she realised what it was that had made Maggie so beautiful on this ominous day. 'You and Sam have finally sorted yourselves out,' she declared. 'Good on you.'

Maggie hugged her back. 'I'm so happy, Olivia. I couldn't care less if a thousand storms hit us today.' She did a little dance in the sand, her hair and skirt flying, arms stretched out as if to encompass the quickening wind. She came to a breathless stop and pointed up the beach. 'Look,' she gasped. 'The pelicans are finally leaving.'

Olivia watched the lumbering birds waddle along the sand until their wings caught the wind and they soared above the churning water.

With almost effortless grace the flock turned and headed inland. How elegant they were in flight. How at one with the sea and the sky, their great white wings gleaming in the half-light.

Olivia and Maggie watched the pelicans until they were out of sight. The other birds had gone some days before, and Olivia realised there was a strange silence deep beneath the gathering moan of the wind and the crash of the surf.

'We'd better get back,' shouted Maggie above the noise. 'Sam's already thrown a blue this morning, and Giles looks as if he's half dead with a hangover.'

Olivia nodded, her gaze fixed on the horizon. The island had finally disappeared and the thick blanket of menace was approaching fast. Palm tree fronds set up a clatter like gravel rattled in a tin can, waves swelled and smashed against the hard, dry sand and the wind had begun to increase in strength.

With hair flying, they linked arms and struggled to keep their footing as they tramped back up the dunes to the road. The wind was at their backs, pushing in ever-increasing gusts. It whipped the soft, light sand of the dunes into whirling eddies that stung their bare arms and legs and threatened to blind and disorientate them. Yet the kindred spirit they had found was so strong, they knew that together, they would come through.

The Trinity Hotel was the oldest and sturdiest building in town. It had already withstood several bad storms and two floods, so it was the natural choice for the locals when it came to shelter.

Sam had brought down the two-way radio so they could keep in contact with the outside world, and had set up matresses and blankets in the square hall between the ladies' lounge and the kitchen. It was the centre of the building, with no windows, and could be closed off by the sliding doors he'd installed after the last storm.

He looked around the enclosed space. The few who had stayed in town numbered less than thirty. Most of them were midde-aged, but there were two young couples with small children and several pensioners. It was their calm acceptance that impressed him, for they knew what they were in for, and what was expected of them, and had prepared for a long wait until they could return to their homes. Baskets of food were set on the floor alongside blankets, pillows and the contents of their medical chests. Fresh water was stored in a variety of metal containers and there was milk for the babies.

'Thanks for your help,' he said as Hopalong and Smokey came to shake his hand and say goodbye. 'But you'd be better off staying here.'

185

'Nah, mate. She'll be right.' Smokey tipped his hat back and tugged at his ear. 'Gotta get back to the sawmill and make sure the machinery's tied down tight.'

Sam watched the two of them limp out of the side door and hoped they'd make it in time. It was a fair way inland to the sawmill, and that old ute was unreliable at the best of times. Yet he could understand their need to protect their homes and their livelihoods.

He moved restlessly between the mattresses, hoping he'd remembered everything. The Calor gas tanks had been detached and padded up before being stored away at the back of the hotel. A line of buckets and a stack of toilet rolls had been placed in the narrow corridor between the hall and the side door, and were enclosed by some ancient bamboo screens he'd found in the storeroom.

The generator would be kept going, for they would need light, and he'd unearthed four primus stoves from his camping equipment for heating water in case the generator broke down or was damaged. All breakables had been packed away, the windows and doors boarded up all but the side door, which he would do once Maggie and Olivia showed up.

He glanced at his watch and wondered where the hell Maggie was. She'd been gone far too long and by the sound of it the wind was picking up.

Giles was suffering. The whisky had been a mistake and now he was paying for his overindulgence with a monstrous headache. All sense of balance seemed to have deserted him and dark spots swam before his eyes as he attempted to make himself useful.

Running his tongue over dry lips he grimaced. Even his teeth hurt this morning. He knew he looked as bad as he felt, for the bathroom mirror had told him so earlier. His breath was sour, and his throat was scratchy despite all the coffee he'd thrown down it, but he had only himself to blame, he realised. He'd behaved like a petulant schoolboy last night, and he deserved everything he got.

He looked around the gathering. There was still no sign of Olivia and he was beginning to fret. Surely she hadn't gone down to the beach this morning? It would be sheer madness. He cocked his head and listened. Above the soft murmur of the Trinity residents, he could hear the whine and moan of the wind as it swirled along the main street and whistled up the side alley, and he could already feel it buffeting the hotel.

Where the hell was she? He needed to talk to her, to reassure her after last night. His bags were packed and waiting upstairs and, once the storm had passed, he would be on his way. He didn't belong here, he knew that now. His home was in England, his roots, his future – a future without Olivia by his side. It was the hardest decision he would ever have to make – but make it he must, otherwise neither of them would have a life.

'Can you see old man Gallagher?' Sam scratched his head as he stood beside Giles and looked around the room.

Giles emerged from his gloomy thoughts. 'Who? What does he look like?'

'Old,' said Sam. 'And sour. Bad-tempered, skinny old bludger with a mean streak and body odour that knocks you sideways. I'm surprised he isn't here.'

Giles looked around at the people settling themselves on the mattresses. There were several old men, but they seemed to be with their elderly wives or younger offspring. 'Can't say I recognise anyone who fits such a description.'

'Me neither,' said Sam with an exasperated sigh. He ran his fingers through his hair, making it stand on end. 'Silly old bugger. I told him to get here early – even promised him a free breakfast.'

'Why did you do that?' Giles was puzzled. No-one else had been offered a free breakfast.

'Because he's a tight-fisted old bludger, who needs to be bribed to get him to do anything – even if it is for his own bloody good. It was the only way I could think of getting him here.'

'Perhaps he prefers to stay in his own home and ride it out,' suggested Giles.

'Hmph,' snorted Sam. 'That old pile of timber threatens to fall down when anyone breathes on it. I'll have to go and fetch him.'

Giles stayed him by grabbing his arm. 'I'll go,' he said firmly. 'Tell me where he lives.'

'Can't ask you to do that, mate,' said Sam. 'Old man Gallagher's my responsibility.'

'So's this place,' said Giles. 'And all the people who trust you to keep them safe. Especially Maggie and Olivia. At least let me do something, old chap. I feel so bloody useless, just standing about getting in the way.'

Sam's blue eyes were thoughtful. 'You sure, mate? It's a bastard out there already, and it ain't gunna get any better.'

'Yes,' said Giles with rising impatience. 'I might only have one arm, but I'm not totally useless.'

Sam grinned. 'Reckon there's time. But you'll have your work cut out to get him here in a hurry. I can already hear the rain.'

Giles listened as Sam gave him instructions, then headed for the side door. He would fetch Gallagher, then start looking for Olivia and

Maggie. His spirits rose. At last he felt he was actually doing something worthwhile. It was quite like old times.

The door was snatched from his hand and slammed back against the wall as the wind almost knocked him off his feet. The force of it battered him, making him stagger, and with his head down he battled against it.

He collided with something soft. The relief was immense as he grabbed Olivia and Maggie and pulled them inside. 'Where have you been?' he yelled.

Olivia's voice was whipped away as she yelled back.

Giles shook his head. He could hear nothing but the wind. 'I'll be back,' he mouthed as he wrestled with the door and forced it shut. He leaned against it, and felt the chill of the first drops of driving rain. Pulling his collar to his chin, he bent almost double as he fought his way through the gathering maelstrom. At least Olivia was safe.

'You'd better get back here before she hits,' said William at the other end of the two-way radio link.

'I'm not leaving the horses,' Irene said.

'They'll be right,' retorted William. 'Get over here, Irene. I don't want to be responsible for anything happening to you if this storm turns out as bad as they predict.'

'Shame you didn't think about that earlier,' she snapped. 'You didn't seem to care about my welfare when you booted me out and left me to fend for myself with no help – not even from Jimmy.'

'This is different,' he replied, his voice edgy with impatience.

'You're damn right it is,' she hissed and pulled the plug on the connection. She sat back and eyed the ugly great radio and felt like kicking it. Yet she resisted the temptation. It was her only link to the outside world – she might need it.

Lighting a cigarette she stood and peered out of the window. The sky was dark over to the east and the heat was beginning to wane. They were in for a beaut, and the thought of being here alone was not pleasant. Perhaps she should swallow her pride and go to Deloraine? The house was sturdy and she wouldn't be alone there. Yet she dismissed the idea almost immediately. Pluperfect and the other horses couldn't be left, and she'd be damned if she would give William the satisfaction of seeing her in need of his help.

Slamming out of the door, Irene crossed the yard and headed for the stables. She had lined each stall with quilts and blankets and had checked them several times already that morning – but it wouldn't hurt to do it again. The decision to keep the horses stabled had been a difficult one, for they could be crushed should the building collapse.

Yet if she let them free in the paddock, they could be blown to kingdom come or battered to death with flying debris. Neither option was appealing, but she had gone with her first instinct.

The animals were lathered in sweat, ears flat, eyes rolling as the deep rumble of thunder echoed across the empty miles. They stamped and snorted, their flanks twitching as they swayed back and forth in their stalls. Irene tried to soothe them with soft words, but soon realised nothing would calm their fears until the storm was over.

Pluperfect was strangely calm, and Irene stroked his nose, aware of the pent-up fury that could be unleashed as swiftly as the approaching storm. His withers were twitching and a light foam of sweat stained his black neck. Yet his ears were pricked, and unlike the others, he remained still.

'You be good, my precious boy,' she murmured as she pushed him back and bolted the top of the stable door. She stood there and listened for a moment. Pluperfect snorted and stamped, but she knew it was only because he hated being enclosed. She ran her hand over the sturdy wood, relieved the stables had been rebuilt, for if Pluperfect decided he really didn't like it in there, it would take a very strong stall to hold him.

She turned from the stable yard, her boot heels ringing on the cobbles. The thunder grumbled in the distance and the false night was illuminated by a streak of lightning that seared a path through the sky before hitting a remote hillside.

Looking towards the coast, Irene saw the rapidly approaching bank of cloud, the long black fingers of rain and wind spiralling down towards Trinity. The little town was obviously taking a battering. As the first breath of cooling wind ruffled her hair she scented rain in the electric atmosphere. She had done everything she could to protect herself and her horses. Now she just had to sit it out and hope to God they all survived.

Olivia collected everyone's medical supplies and put them together in a large box under the stairs. She raided the linen cupboard for sheets and towels and added them to the stash. As she worked with almost mechanical efficiency, her thoughts were centred on Giles.

Sam had told her where he'd gone and at first she'd been furious with him for putting Giles in danger, then she'd realised he'd needed to feel useful – needed to be a man again, fully in charge of his destiny and still capable of the acts of bravery he'd shown during the war.

Olivia finished storing away the precious medical supplies and helped herself to a cup of coffee from the enormous urn Maggie had set up on the floor, well away from the mattresses. It was hot and strong and very nearly soothed her, yet she couldn't help remembering their conversation the night before and the unsatisfactory conclusion. If only she had said something profound or sensible, perhaps Giles wouldn't have felt the need to be the hero. If only she could have told him how much he meant to her, he would still be here in the relative safety of this Victorian hotel.

She finished the coffee and listened to the gathering force outside. The wind was howling now, buffeting the building, tearing around it like a dervish, plucking at anything that hadn't been nailed down. The rain thundered on the roof and lashed the boarded windows, and somewhere upstairs she could hear the banging of a loosened screen.

'He'll be right,' said Sam as he put his arm around her shoulders.

Olivia shrugged him off. 'You don't know that,' she snapped. 'How can you know that?'

Sam shrugged. 'He's not a fool,' he said. 'He'll go to ground with old man Gallagher.'

Olivia's nerves were shot as she thought of Giles struggling against the elements. 'He should be here,' she shouted above the banshee roar of the wind and the thunder of the rain.

Sam grabbed her shoulders in his large hands and made her look at him. 'He's his own man,' he said flatly. 'Giles wanted to go, insisted upon it. Give him some slack, Olivia.'

She eyed him with furious intensity and realised there was nothing she could do about Giles anyway. He was on his own, just as he had been during the war – but she prayed he'd come back safe, and wouldn't do anything too foolish to put himself into danger.

'Sit down over there and calm down,' yelled Sam as something crashed to the floor upstairs. 'I might need you later on and you'll be no bloody use if you're hysterical.'

Olivia plumped down on a mattress, and eyed him crossly as he turned and walked away. How dare he accuse her of being hysterical? She was a nursing sister who'd driven an ambulance around bombed-out London, for goodness sake. What was a bit of wind compared to doodlebugs and the blood-chilling wail of the air-raid sirens?

'Don't mind him, luv,' said the young woman beside her. 'He's as crook as we all are – just his nerves talking.'

Olivia found she'd been holding her breath. She let it out a long sigh and then smiled. The young couple were cosied up on the next mattress, their small boy playing at their sides. 'I reckon we should all take a lesson from him,' she shouted in the girl's ear.

The little boy was about eighteen months old. He was absorbed in a pile of wooden bricks, his chubby hands curled around each one as he studiously tried to pile them high. Olivia placed two bricks for him and the child looked at her with solemn eyes. She smiled and was rewarded with a cheeky grin that revealed two darling dimples in these chubby cheeks.

Olivia felt the tug of longing as she picked him up and put him on her lap. She had always adored babies, but this was the first time she'd experienced such a surge of need. The first time she'd really noticed how lovely they smelled and how soft they were. She glanced across at the young couple, noticed how his arm was protectively around his wife, how they fitted so well together. Another surge of something akin to jealousy tore through her and she looked away. Her time would come.

The thick blanket of black cloud crept ever closer to the shore as Hurricane Mary built up her fury. She had started life as a tropical storm – a high, light wind over the warm tropical waters east of New Guinea. The combination of low pressure, light wind and warm water had intensified the dangerous weather conditions, and now the tropical storm had taken on a new menace. With winds of over seventy-five miles per hour Hurricane Mary was almost a thousand miles wide and bearing down, fully fledged, on the northern coast of Australia.

The sea was the colour of slate beneath the rolling, black swirl of cloud. It rose in oily, spiteful waves, which thundered up the sand and boomed against the rocks with a great explosion of surf before it drew back with a hiss of menace. Palm trees thrashed as the wind slammed across the beach and spun the sand into a thousand whirling dervishes. Rain hammered on corrugated-iron roofs as the wind plucked at loose planks and tore verandah posts from the beach houses. Gum trees swayed, bending almost to the point of breaking as their leaves were ripped away by the coils of dark, deadly spirals that devoured everything in its path.

Hurricane Mary had only just begun to flex her muscles – there was much more to come.

Giles staggered up the neglected garden path and sought shelter in the lee of the ramshackle house. He was out of breath and soaked to the skin, but the sheer exhilaration of fighting the elements, of reaching his destination without mishap, made him want to laugh.

He flattened himself against the wall as the wind picked up an empty oil drum and threw it down the path, where it crashed into the fence. A sheet of corrugated iron was ripped from the roof and he ducked as it flew like a discus across the front yard and slammed into the house on the other side of the street. Leaning back against the wall of the delapidated house, he tried to catch his breath as he surveyed his surroundings.

The rain was hammering on the tin roofs, bouncing off the impacted earth, running in swiftly flowing rivulets down the street, banking up in the gutters and deep potholes where it spread into miniature lakes. It was a grey curtain falling over the town and visibility in the false twilight was almost down to zero. Giles found he was shivering from the cold and from the excitement of the moment. He felt bruised and battered as he clung to the side of the house, but elated, nevertheless.

The windows of Gallagher's place had been taped, just like the ones in London during the Blitz, and he could see the old boy peering at him through the murky glass.

'Let me in,' he yelled above the scream of the wind. 'Open the bloody door.'

He heard the faint scrape of a bolt being drawn and put his shoulder to the door. Slamming it behind him, he flinched as he was assailed by the most dreadful stench. 'We've got to leave now,' he shouted.

The eyes were gimlet in the leathery face, the mouth turned down and mean, the nose a broad, reddened hook. 'I ain't going.' The voice was a rasp, the tone determined.

'You can't stay here,' yelled Giles as he grabbed a greasy coat from a chair and thrust it into the old man's arms. 'It's not safe.'

'I been here all me bloody life,' came the sour response as the old man sat down in the empty chair and dropped the coat on the floor. 'Ain't fallen down yet.'

Giles's eyes were watering as he looked at him in despair. Stinking or not, if he'd had two arms, he'd have scooped him up and carried him out of here – the old chap couldn't have weighed more than six or seven stones – but in his present circumstances, that was not an option.

'I haven't got time to argue with you,' he yelled above the roar and hammer of the storm. 'We've got to go. Now.' He grabbed Gallagher's arm and tugged him from the chair.

He was surprisingly strong and managed to wrest from Giles' grip. 'Get yer 'ands off me, yer bludger,' he shouted. 'I ain't lettin' no pommy bastard tell me what to do.'

The wind shook the foundations and buffeted the walls. The rain beat hammer blows on the iron roof so it was almost impossible to think, let alone hear anything. Giles ran his hand through his hair as he looked out of the window. He could see nothing, for the rain had drawn a dark curtain over Trinity, but he could hear things being tossed about and the crash and splinter of collisions – and could only guess at the chaos outside.

192

He turned from the window and glared down at Gallagher and wished he could leave him here. But that was no longer an option, and his sense of duty wouldn't have let him leave anyway. He and this stinking old fool were stuck with one another.

Deciding he wouldn't stand for any more insults, he bore down on Gallagher and grabbed him by the scruff of his filthy neck. Shoving the table against the wall, he pushed Gallagher beneath it. It was the only piece of sturdy furniture in the place, and he'd been in enough air raids to know it might save them from flying, falling debris if the house did fall down around their ears.

'Stay there,' he ordered.

Gallagher's ratty face peered out from the gloom as he watched Giles run around the shack grabbing what he could. 'You got no bloody right coming in here touching my things,' he yelled.

Giles wished he didn't have to. He had an armful of blankets and old clothes which stank to high heaven and were probably infested with fleas. He threw them at Gallagher and then wrestled with the filthy, stained mattress and propped it against the table. It was all he could do, and he hoped it was enough.

Taking a deep breath, Giles crawled into the small space and huddled beside Gallagher. The old man's aversion to soap and water manifested itself in a ripe, putrid wave as he raised his arms and shifted to a more comfortable position. It was like sharing a cell with a rotting corpse.

The utility bounced and swayed as Smokey rammed his tin foot hard on the accelerator. The wind was strong enough to force the ageing vehicle off course and he was having the devil's own job to keep it on the track.

'Pull over,' shouted Hopalong, who was clinging to the door in an effort not to be thrown through the windscreen.

'Not bloody likely,' yelled Smokey. 'We're nearly there.'

Hurricane Mary gathered all her strength and tore down the track in a fury of swirling earth and debris. She scooped up the utility and flung it aside before carving a ragged, angry path through the surrounding trees.

Both men screamed as they were tossed skyward. Earth and sky became one in the dizzying, blinding, disorientating whirlwind of pain and terror. Heads thudded against roof and door. Limbs jarred against handbrake and steering wheel. Ribs cracked and glass shattered as the utility rolled determinedly on.

The tree was tall and thousands of years old. It had withstood just about everything the elements could throw at it despite the cavities

193

within its vast trunk that had been bored by generations of termites. But the wind and rain had finally loosened the great, twisting roots – had finally weakened the hollow trunk.

The utility rolled out of control down the embankment and smashed with a tortured screech of metal against the ancient bark.

A judder ran through the giant trunk. For a breathless moment in that maelstrom of fury it held tall and straight. Then slowly, inexorably, it began to tilt.

Smokey was reluctant to open his eyes. The rain was like needles on his face, the wind tearing at his clothes, threatening to carry him off. He hurt all over, but that was all right, for he wasn't being thrown about any more – in fact he was lying on something soft.

Memory returned and his eyes snapped open. He'd been thrown clear, but where was his mate? 'Hopalong,' he yelled. 'Where are you?'

'I'm stuck.' The voice sounded so small in the howling wind. 'Get me outta here.'

Smokey grimaced with pain as he crawled through the mud towards the ute. There was something very wrong with his left arm and the rain was blinding him. But he had to reach Hopalong before it was too late. He could smell petrol.

He reached for the utility door. The broken bones in his arm ground against one another and he collapsed back in the mud with a cry of agony.

'Smokey! Smokey, I can smell petrol. Get me out, get me out!'

'Coming, mate,' gasped Smokey as he dragged himself up again and reached for the door. There was little likelihood of the ute blowing up with all the rain, but there was no guarantee.

The door was buckled and Smoky sweated as he wrestled with the handle. Now he understood how frustrating Giles must find life with only one arm. The door finally swung back and the wind snatched it from him, knocking him back in the mud again. He smeared rain and mud from his eyes and realised his hand was trembling. Pulse hammering, fear gnawing away at him, he almost bit through his bottom lip in an attempt to vanquish the pain in his arm.

He reached for his mate – then realised they were in bigger trouble than he'd thought.

Hopalong was trapped upside down, his wooden leg jammed between the pedals and crushed metal. There was a lot of blood and he could see the glimmer of bone through the gash in his good leg. Hopalong's face was ashen, his eyes unfocussed as he hung there.

'Hold on, mate,' Smokey rasped. 'I've gotta get yer leg off first.'

Hopalong screamed as Smokey jarred his dislocated shoulder and pushed against his broken thigh.

194

Smokey's fingers were numb with cold and slick with rain and blood as he struggled to untie the straps that bound the wooden leg to Hopalong's stump. He was about to unbuckle the last strap when he heard the ominous tearing creak overhead. Looking up, he saw the giant tree loom with menacing determination to crush them both.

Hopalong screamed as Smokey grabbed him around the waist and pulled as hard as he could.

The tree screamed as its roots were torn from the mud and its branches were snapped in its headlong rush down to earth.

Smokey screamed as he fought to drag his mate from certain death.

The tree thundered down onto the utility with crushing finality. The only scream still to be heard was the scream of the wind.

Chapter Eighteen

＇

Irene huddled beneath the heavy kitchen table and pulled the eiderdown more firmly around her shoulders. The wind was battering the little house as if determined to rip it from the ground and fling it skyward. She felt she was at the centre of this insane vortex, and as the house shuddered around her she could almost sense it was holding its breath – waiting for the moment the roof would be torn away.

The screaming assault never faltered as darkness descended. Hurricane Mary whipped around the house, jostling the stone chimney, tugging at the roof and pressing with all her might against the walls. Rain lashed against the windows and drove through even the smallest of fissures between the slab walls. It punched against the roof in a monotonous pummel until Irene's head rang with the noise.

Then, without warning it was gone.

She lifted her head and listened. The silence was heavy with menace and just as terrifying as the storm had been. She shivered as she crawled from her hiding place, for within that terrible silence, she could hear the horses screaming.

Stumbling out of the door she almost fell through the gaping hole in the verandah where the planks had been ripped away along with the railings. She grabbed the doorjamb to get her balance and looked down in horror at the murky water lapping the top step.

It was only then she realised the little house was in the centre of a vast lake. Instead of rich, red earth the muddy sheet of water was feeding off several runs of fast-moving streams and spreading into the paddocks. The ground was so hard, so dry, it could not absorb the rain and it had become the perfect conduit for these new rivers.

Irene, aware she was trembling, licked her lips. She couldn't swim – had never even tried to learn despite the years of living in Trinity – for she feared water – feared its power. Yet it was imperative she reached the horses, for she could still hear their awful screaming and the crash and thud of their hoofs as they tried to kick their way out of their prison.

She hesitated, steeling herself for the coming ordeal as she tried to gauge how deep the water might be. Her teeth were chattering as she shoved her feet into boots and eyed the sky. A perfect circle of summer blue was directly overhead, but surrounding this glimpse of normality were the swirling black clouds of the storm past and the storm yet to come. She was in the very eye of the hurricane.

How much time had she already wasted? How much longer did she have before the darkness closed in again? She couldn't allow herself to think about the consequences of getting caught in the fresh onslaught. It had been her stupidity that had imprisoned the horses – it was up to her to rescue them.

She stepped down into the water and yelped as it reached almost to her waist. It was not only freezing, it threatened to knock her off balance. Fear kept her on her feet – it gave her strength she'd never known – a determination and courage she'd never before realised she possessed. With her arms stretched out to maintain her balance, she forced one foot in front of the other and waded through the surging tide of destruction.

A slender tree swirled past, its spiny fingers clawing at her hair and her clothes, threatening to drag her under as it slowly rotated in the tide. She grappled for what seemed like minutes to be free of it. Her nails were torn, her hair ripped from her skull as she battled to stay alive. A rolling oil drum banged into her, making her stumble wildly before it floated away. The bloated carcass of a kangaroo had become entangled in the tree along with that of a possum, and their dead eyes seemed to be staring at her. She screamed with frustration and fear as she tore at the branches to free herself.

Finally the tree let her go.

Panting with fear and the exertion, she staggered up the gentle slope towards the stable yard through increasingly shallow water. The sky was darkening again; she had only minutes to free the horses and return to the house.

Her hands were clumsy as she drew back the bolts and quickly stepped aside. The mares charged in panic out of their stalls, eyes wild, manes flying. Their hoofs slipped on the wet cobbles as they careered around the yard. They bucked and kicked as they scented the air, nostrils flaring, ears flat. Then they were off – galloping out of the yard, heading for the higher ground in the distance.

Pluperfect had kicked a gaping hole in the door and was screaming his hatred and fear as Irene hurried to set him free. She fumbled with the bolt as he slammed his hoof against the door. He seemed intent

197

upon injuring himself, and she could already see blood staining the puddles on the cobbles.

'Stop it,' she shouted. 'Pluperfect, calm down, boy. I'm here, I'm here.'

He kicked again, harder this time, making the stable shudder and splinter. His screams of fear and rage were terrible to hear and Irene felt sick with remorse. If only she'd let them run free in the first place, she thought as she fought with the bolt and tried to loosen it in between the jarring, crashing thunder of Pluperfect's hoofs. How could she have been so stupid after all the years of experience to think he would have been safer here in a place he hated with a vengeance? She was just incredibly lucky the whole damn stable hadn't collapsed and crushed all of them.

The bolt finally slid back and, before Irene could react, Pluperfect barged straight into her. He reared up, the flashing hoofs pawing the air, the whites of his eyes glinting with malice in the fast-gathering gloom.

Irene threw up her arms to protect her face as she stumbled back.

Pluperfect's front hoofs hit the ground with a shuddering crash before he reared again.

Irene's boots slipped on the greasy, wet cobbles. Arms windmilling in an effort to keep her balance, she staggered beneath those flailing hoofs.

Pluperfect was well and truly spooked. He'd hated being in that stable – hated the scream of the wind and the thunder of the rain on the tin roof – now he was past recognising the woman who'd loved him with passion – and saw only the whirling arms – another enemy – another terrifying thing to attack. With a scream of terror he lashed out.

Irene, still off balance, saw the blow coming and could do nothing about it.

Pluperfect's aim was sure as his hoof caught the side of Irene's head. He snorted as she fell, then reared again, his front hoofs flashing in the remains of the light as they swept down on the sprawled, kicking legs.

With another snort of satisfaction he danced on his toes and raced about the yard. His ears pricked as the rumble of thunder heralded the return of the storm. Gathering the remains of his strength, he set off after the other horses. At last he was free.

'Sounds like it's over,' Giles muttered as he lifted his head from the shelter of his arms. 'Come on, old chap. Let's get you to the hotel.'

'Will I still get me breakfast?' The eyes were alight with cunning.

'Only if you get a move on,' said Giles with an uncharacteristic sharpness. He was worn out and at the very edge of his patience with the old goat. The sound of the storm was still in his head despite the errie silence, and all this old fool could think about was a free meal.

Gallagher crawled out from beneath the table and shrugged into the disreputable coat. 'I gotta collect some things first,' he muttered.

Giles looked out of the window at the carnage in the street. There was a circle of blue overhead, but he was mistaken to think the hurricane was over. 'There isn't time,' he said as he grabbed Gallagher's arm and dragged him to the door. 'We're in the eye.'

Gallagher looked at him with contempt. 'What's a Pom know about hurricanes?' he sneered. 'In fact, what's a Pom doing all the way out here anyways?'

Giles was wrestling with the door. 'Trying to save your skinny, ungrateful arse,' he retorted. He tried again, but no matter how hard he pushed, he could not open the door. There had to be something blocking it.

Ignoring the old man he peered out of the window. His spirits sank. The hulk of an ancient tractor was jammed in the narrow alley, effectively holding them prisoner. He eyed the window, his mind working fast. It was their only way to escape.

'I ain't climbing out of no window,' snapped Gallagher. 'And if you break it, you'll pay to have it mended.'

Giles gritted his teeth. The ungrateful old sod should be left to stew in his own filth, although Giles knew he would never leave him here alone – it wasn't in his nature to do so. He tugged at the window, putting all his force into it. But the window was glued tightly by years of dirt and mould and decay. Giles finally lost his temper, picked up a saucepan and slammed it against the glass and rotten wood. It splintered with a satisfactory explosion and he knocked out the remaining wooden struts and slithers of glass.

He swung his leg over the sill and held out his hand. 'Come on. It's easy.'

Gallagher shook his head. 'I'm too old to be climbing through windows,' he whined.

Giles climbed back into the shack, grabbed Gallagher by the hand and hauled him to the window. With one arm around his skinny waist, he found a strength he hadn't realised he possessed and hoisted him from the floor before dragging him through.

Their feet sank in thick mud, the murky water swirling around their ankles.

'I'll catch me death,' whined Gallagher.

Giles glared down at him. 'One more word out of you, and so help me, I'll knock the rest of your rotten teeth down your throat.'

Gallagher brushed his coat and glowered back – but had obviously realised Giles meant what he said, for thankfully, he remained silent.

Giles grabbed his arm and forced him into a shuffling run. The storm was closing in fast, the respite merely a few moments of false calm before the assault began all over again – they had very little time to get back to the hotel at the other end of town.

The side street had taken on the appearance of a war zone. Roofs were missing, there were gaping holes in walls and fences had been torn up and scattered. Windows were smashed, screens and shutters left to bang in the remaining gusts of the wind. A sheet of corrugated iron had embedded itself in the wall of a house and a fishing boat was sitting in the middle of the road.

The water was swirling around his ankles as Giles steered the old man around a fallen telegraph pole, and now the wind had dropped to a more gentle pace, he could hear the thunder of the sea as it crashed against the rocks.

'I gotta rest,' Gallagher wheezed.

Giles eyed him with concern. He was clutching his chest and fighting for breath. His skin was grey and shiny with sweat, and there was a bluish tinge around his mouth. Giles looked up towards the end of the street. They still had a long way to go, and the circle of blue was moving rapidly away, the darkness returning. He would have to find somewhere for them to shelter.

'You're not dying on me now,' he muttered as he put his arm around Gallagher's waist and half carried the old man across the street.

The house didn't look too badly damaged apart from the ravaged garden. The roof was intact as far as he could see and the chimney looked as if it could withstand anything. He propped Gallagher against the woodpile and turned the handle.

The door opened on well-oiled hinges, and Giles muttered a prayer of thanks for the Australian habit of never locking anything. He grabbed hold of a sagging Gallagher and struggled into the hall, kicking the door shut behind him.

Giles hauled his burden along the narrow passage and deposited Gallagher gently on the kitchen floor. It was a small house, like every other in this tiny settlement, but it had been built to last. He ran from room to room collecting pillows and blankets. Whoever owned this place certainly took pride in it, he thought, as he clutched his booty and returned to the kitchen. Everywhere smelled of polish and the pillows and blankets were freshly laundered.

200

Gallagher groaned and brought his knees to his chest. 'Me pills,' he gasped. 'I need me pills.'

Giles put a pillow beneath his head and, with a grimace, delved into the greasy pockets of the disgusting coat. He pulled out a small bottle, read the label and put a single tablet under the old man's tongue. 'Don't chew it,' he warned. 'Just let it dissolve.'

'Pommy bastard,' groaned Gallagher. 'Think I don't know that?'

Giles didn't even bother to reply. The wind was picking up again and he could already feel it buffeting the house. He shoved the table over Gallagher, covered him in a blanket and crawled in beside him. 'Here we go again,' he muttered.

The wind howled as it tore up the street and thumped the house in a series of jarring blows. The rain pelted the windows and the roof, the din echoing around the little house and in his head.

There was no warning. Just the shattering crash of glass and timber and the resounding explosion as the chimney took the full brunt of a falling tree. Hurricane Mary swept in to the remains of the little house and tore it to pieces.

Sam hugged Maggie and kissed the top of her head. Aware of the curious, knowing looks of the assembled locals, he knew their secret was out. Yet he didn't mind one bit. Maggie had brought him such joy, such peace of mind – a feeling of having come home at last – that he wanted the world to know he loved her. He smiled as he pressed his face into her hair. The old, solitary, moody Sam was gone forever.

The wind had dropped and the rain ceased to batter the hotel. Everyone turned their eyes skyward as they listened to the ensuing silence. It was ominous – as if the world was holding its breath.

'We're in the eye, I reckon,' he muttered. 'Better check for damage. Will you be right?'

Maggie's face was glowing as she nodded. 'Don't be too long,' she murmured.

He kissed her softly on the mouth and they both giggled as a shout went up and they were applauded with whistles and whoops. 'Yeah, all right,' he said with a sheepish grin as he stood up. 'Show's over.'

'Good on yer, mate,' shouted one of the men.

'About bloody time,' yelled another.

Sam could feel the heat in his face as he left the crowded hall and began his tour of the building. He wasn't used to being the centre of attention, but somehow it gave him a spring to his step, and as he walked around his property he felt ten feet tall.

The boarded-up windows were still intact, the stables were still standing, and apart from the water lying in great pools in the yard, the hotel had survived the first onslaught.

Upstairs was the worst, he realised as he stood amongst the debris on the landing. The carpets were sodden where the rain had blown in through shattered windows. The boarding had been ripped away on the northern side of the hotel. Wallpaper hung in tatters and the ancient couch and chairs he'd left up here had been blown across the room and were heaped up in a soggy mass in one corner.

He took his torch and examined the ceiling. There were no bulges or cracks, so the roof must have held. Yet he could hear the splash of water running down the outside of the building and guessed there was a lot of guttering missing. He turned away and quickly went from room to room checking on the boards they'd nailed across the shutters. Any repairs would have to wait until the storm had passed over them – no point in doing anything now, even if there was time.

Giles' and Olivia's set of rooms were the last to be inspected, and Sam paused as he checked the window catches and peered out at the ravaged main street. Iron roofs had been peeled back like wrappers on a chocolate bar, palm trees had become embedded in the remains of houses or lay drunkenly across verandahs. There was a ute upended in the front window of the general store, festooned in rolls of fabric and lavatory paper. Cartons and cans and oil drums littered the pavement and newspapers clung wetly to the hitching posts. Water raced down the street in an endless stream and he could hear the sea crashing in the distance.

If it rained much more they would be flooded, and it would be 1929 all over again, he realised. The water had reached the first floor then, and it was a week before it was low enough to begin mopping up. The landlord and his customers had had to resort to sitting on the roof to avoid being drowned, and they'd been stuck there for over a day before they could be rescued.

Not that they minded all that much, he remembered with a grin – they'd taken two barrels of beer up on to the roof with them and the shenanigans of getting them down were now part of Trinity's folklore.

Sam frowned as he thought of the work ahead of them. It wasn't how he'd planned to begin his new life with Maggie – but he had the feeling it wouldn't matter, and that between them, they would come through this.

He took one last look at the mayhem. There was no sign of Giles, and he hoped for Olivia's sake he'd found somewhere safe to shelter. He didn't want to have to face her with bad news – he was feeling guilty enough already – and if anything did happen to Giles, then it would be his fault for letting him go out there.

Sam checked the latch one last time, and as he turned from the window, he caught sight of the suitcases. Olivia had said nothing about leaving, and Maggie certainly wasn't aware of any such plans.

He stood there for a moment, barely aware of the rising wind and the first splatters of rain on the screens as his thoughts raced. Olivia had unfinished business here – so why would she leave? And what about Maggie? She would be devastated to lose her so soon after they had discovered one another.

He couldn't let that happen, he decided as he closed the door firmly behind him and made his way down the stairs. He had to find a way to keep Olivia here. For he was on the brink of discovering the solution to the mystery of what he suspected had brought her to Trinity in the first place.

'Get hot drinks down everyone,' said Olivia. 'And advise them to go to the lavatory now before the storm comes back.'

Maggie saluted. She had a wide grin and her eyes were sparkling. 'Yes, matron,' she said.

Olivia grinned back and flicked a tea towel at her. 'Get on with it,' she said with mock severity.

She watched Maggie pour the last of the tea and organise some of the other women to hand it around. Olivia was impressed at how calm she was – how seemingly unafraid and unaffected by the horrendous noise and devastation the hurricane had brought. But then of course she and Sam had finally acknowledged their feelings for one another, and that must overrule everything.

Disliking the surge of jealousy that tore through her, she put down the rolls of bandage and walked out of the claustrophobic hall into the ladies' lounge. It was at times like these she realised how alone she was, and although the air was fresher in here, her shoulders remained tight, her nerves stretched to the very limit. If only Giles hadn't gone off. If only he'd taken the chance to get back here during the lull. Something must have happened to stop him.

She wrapped her arms around her waist and tried not to dwell on the possibilities. Giles was not a man to shirk what he saw as duty. Not a man to hesitate in a moment of crisis – he was no doubt safe somewhere, holed up with Gallagher until the storm had blown itself out. 'Damn you,' she muttered. 'Why do you always have to be the bloody hero?'

Olivia stood there in silent contemplation, realising her anger was aimed at herself, not at Giles. She should have stopped him from walking away the night before. Should have made him listen to her. Then perhaps, just perhaps, he wouldn't be hurting quite so much, or so determined to show her how tough he was.

203

The thoughts whirled and she suddenly became impatient with herself. She was doing no-one any good by standing here feeling sorry for herself and worrying about Giles. It was time to pull herself together and get on.

Yet she was loath to return to that crowded hall, and knew there was nothing she could do to help, for thankfully there had been no casualties. Leaning her forehead on the cool glass of the window she tried to see through the boards that had been nailed across it.

The sheer noise of the hurricane had chilled her just as the thunder of enemy bombers over London had done – and by the look of it, the ensuing chaos was just as random. The street was desolate. Water glimmered in a swirling sheet around the shattered buildings and felled trees, and the eerie silence was ominous. There was no sign of life – no sign of Giles.

Irene blinked as the first drops of icy rain splashed on her eyelids. She looked up at the lowering sky and, for a second, wondered what she was doing lying in the stable yard in the rain. She caught sight of the empty stall and memory returned with brutal clarity.

She tried to sit up. A wave of agony tore through her and with a scream she fell back onto the wet cobbles. Lying there, her body seemed to pulse with the sheer force of pain and she found it hurt to even breathe.

The rain was harder now, the sky darkening as the clear patch of blue moved away. She could hear the moan of the wind and feel it begin to pluck at the hem of her coat. If she stayed here she would die.

Fear overruled the torture and she tried to move again. But this time, her body wouldn't obey her. No matter how hard she concentrated, she was incapable of moving even a finger. She lay there in petrified silence as the wind whistled around her. There was something warm and sticky running down her face and the pain in her head was overriding everything. She could barely see, barely think, but instinct told her she was in great danger if she tried to move again.

She lay there breathless, trying to cope with the pain as the rain became needle sharp on her exposed flesh. It was easy to surmise what had happened. Pluperfect had kicked her in the head. Then she'd hit it on the cobbles when she fell. Trying to sit up had probably done further damage. Now there was blood seeping into the runnels of water. But why couldn't she feel anything from the neck down? What had happened to her?

Irene painfully swivelled her eyes until she could see the homestead and the sheet of water surrounding this tenuous refuge. She was alone.

204

The stable doors were banging now – a monotonous tattoo that seemed to get inside her head and underline the agonising throb of pain that delved so deeply there. The stalls were her only option – her only sanctuary – but how to reach them when she couldn't move?

Sweat mingled with blood and rain as she lay on the cobbles – try as she might she could not move. The overwhelming agony in her head took her energy, her will, even the instinctive need for survival. But it could not erase the terror of dying out here all alone.

The wind seemed determined to pluck her from her island, however, fate had been kind after all, she realised through the fog of agony. She had fallen in the tenuous lee of the stable wall, and although the wind vented its fury on the stable doors by swinging and banging them, it could not reach her with all its force. The rain beat down, blinding her, chilling her, enhancing every pulse of agony that seemed to grow more intense as she waited for death and blessed oblivion.

She closed her eyes and as the wind howled and the doors banged and the water crept nearer and nearer, she fell in and out of consciousness. In the lucid moments when the agony returned, she remembered Pluperfect's vicious attack after her fall, and after snatching a glance at her legs, she realised the appalling truth. The blood was flowing fast and had already soaked her moleskins. Her feet were at a strange angle and she thought she could see several glimmers of jagged bone through the shredded trousers. Both her legs had been trampled almost to a pulp.

The stark awareness of her situation kept her conscious and more determined than ever to survive. Yet, as she lay there on the soaking cobbles, the panic rose. The water was edging towards her. If the storm didn't pass soon, she would drown. And she'd always had a fear of drowning – it was why she'd never learned to swim, why her nightmares were always about water.

Inch by inch the water rose as rivers became bankers and streams became torrents – all feeding the empty miles of parched flood plains. Inch by inch the island of cobbles was covered and the water began to lap at the stable wall.

Chapter Nineteen

Olivia stretched out on the mattress, but found she couldn't sleep. The memories of many nights spent huddled in air-raid shelters were too strong. It was as if she was back in the Blitz, for like the Londoners, these stalwart people of Trinity were coping in their own way. Some were trying to sleep; some were murmuring quietly to one another; others were weeping. There were no hysterics, no screams, and it was as if they felt humbled in the presence of such power, for everyone talked in whispers.

The hurricane had battered the hotel throughout the night, and although it was still dark in the enclosed hallway, her watch showed it was in fact seven in the morning. Olivia sat up and stretched. She felt she ought to be doing something, but so far they had come through unscathed. Restless and ill at ease with the thought that Giles was still out there, she stood up and paced between the mattresses.

Then suddenly it was over. The silence seemed to fill her head just as the screaming venom of the storm had done. She stood there listening as the others stopped talking, or woke from troubled sleep. A deep sigh ran through them and like sleepwalkers they rose from their mattresses and stood in bewildered silence as if uncertain of what to do next.

'It's over,' breathed Maggie as she gave Olivia a hug. 'We're safe.'

Olivia nodded, but her thoughts were with Giles.

'Better take a look outside,' muttered Sam as he unbolted the door and flung it open.

Along with the others, Olivia and Maggie emerged into a silent, still world of grey devastation. The destructive hurricane had littered Trinity with palm fronds and fallen trees. Sand had been spun in the vortex and now stuck to everything like pebbledash. Sheets of corrugated iron were embedded in the thick mud of the yard, palm trees were beheaded, fences ripped away and vehicles tossed like toys into buildings, their underbellies exposed like beached turtles.

206

A rusty, slow-moving river ran down the main street, and puddles reflected the lowering sky. Water poured from the guttering at the side of the hotel, but the stable was standing, and so was Maggie's cottage. But only just, for the roof had been peeled back as if by a giant can opener.

Olivia had experienced the shock of emerging into an alien world after the bombing raids in London, and she'd thought she could no longer be affected, but she was wrong, for Trinity no longer resembled the peaceful corner of paradise she loved – it was desolate and ravaged – a war zone.

'Gunna take a fair bit of cleaning up,' muttered Sam.

Olivia watched as he splashed through the water to the paddock. His horse was trembling as it stood quietly at the fence. Sam stroked the drooping neck and led him out for a walk around the yard. He seemed uninjured, and she could see the relief on Sam's face.

'Better check my place,' said Maggie. 'Want to come with me?'

Olivia shook her head. 'I have to find Giles,' she said.

Maggie kissed her cheek and gave her a quick hug. 'He'll be right, you'll see,' she said firmly.

Olivia eyed the flattened buildings and the obliteration of everything familiar and prayed she was right. She turned back into the hotel to fetch the medical bag, got directions from Sam, then headed out of the yard and into the street.

The others had already collected their belongings and were traipsing through the water and past the wreckage of their little town to see what damage had been done to their homes. Like refugees they moved in silence, their haunted eyes the only clue to their thoughts.

Olivia came to a stunned halt as she surveyed the main street. Littered with trees and palm fronds and assorted flotsam and jetsam, it resembled nothing familiar. Some of the buildings had collapsed, leaving gaping holes along the boardwalks, and the disappearance of so many trees had altered the skyline.

She thought fleetingly of the little house on the beach and wondered if it had survived – but there was no time to find out, for she had to find Giles.

Splashing through the water, Olivia climbed over fallen trees and around upturned boats and trucks. She looked away from the corpses of dead animals and the tattered remains of once beautiful birds – aware of the silence, the stillness, the finality of it all. The sky was pewter, still heavy-laden with the promise of more rain, but the air was keener now the awful heat had been banished.

Olivia slowly made her way around the obstacles, climbing over fallen trees, avoiding jagged iron and loops of razor wire that had become enmeshed in the debris, until she reached what had once been Gallagher's shack.

The little wooden building had collapsed, the chimney standing like a sentinel over the remains. 'Giles!' Her voice was shrill and strangely loud in the glowering silence. 'Giles,' she called again as she clambered around the rusting hulk of an ancient tractor and began to lift away the piles of shattered timber.

'Answer me, damn it,' she yelled as fear took hold and there was no reply.

Irene opened her eyes. Something had changed, and for a moment she couldn't think what it was. Then she realised the wind had stopped and the rain was softer on the tin roof. She blinked as drops fell on her face, and looked up at the sky. It was grey, still heavy-laden with rain.

The cobbles beneath her were stained with her blood, but the sturdy walls had withstood the violent attack, and had sheltered her from the worst of the onslaught, although the water was lapping at her, tripping over the cobbles and soaking her with its chilly fingers. At least the damn door had stopped banging, she thought in a fog of pain. One particularly heavy gust had blown it off its hinges and ripped it away, and for a while she'd thought she would follow it.

She lay helplessly on the cobbles, the fear and pain making her sleepy. Yet she knew that to sleep would be the worst thing she could do, for she'd lost so much blood, she would simply slip into a coma. She had to stay awake. Had to keep alert until help arrived. It could be hours before William was able to get to her – that's if he came at all.

The tears were warm on her face as memories came unbidden and she realised she had lost everything and everyone she had ever loved. Her mother had died, the breach never healed. Her son no longer needed her now he had Sarah, and William was planning a new life with someone else. As for the terrible thing she'd done all those years ago – it still haunted her.

The knowledge she had been responsible for so much unhappiness didn't ease her own heartache, merely enhanced the overwhelming sadness for things that might have been. For she was truly alone.

If I get through this, she vowed silently, I'll try and make up for what I've done. Yet her inner voice told her it was too late.

Sam let the horse back out in the paddock where he kicked up his heels and raced around as if relishing his escape from the driving wind. The Aboriginal quarters had been obliterated, Sam realised as he stood with his hands in his pockets and surveyed the mess. The only sign anyone had ever lived here were the blackened circles of their campfires.

'It won't take long to build again,' said Maggie as she came to stand beside him.

He put his arm around her. 'Ever the optimist,' he said, his slow smile chasing away the gloom as he looked down at her. 'How's your place?'

Maggie shrugged. 'The rain got in where the roof was lifted at one corner, but it'll be right.'

He took her hand, still amazed that this wonderful little woman could be so undaunted by what had happened over the past twenty-four hours. 'Come on,' he said. 'Let's get out of here and see what the old place looks like.'

They walked hand in hand out of the paddock and into the main street. Picking their way around the debris, they headed for the beach, and stood in horrified fascination at the sight that greeted them.

An impenetrable forest of seaweed floated and swayed in the grey sea, and lay in thick tangles that were piled high for several feet beyond the waterline. Graceful palm trees that had once swayed and rustled along the coastal path were no longer there, and the brightly coloured shrubs and trees that had been so much a part of Trinity had been cut down by the axe of the wind. But it was the sand that had really changed the face of this seaside town. Whipped into a frenzy by the wind, it now rose in vast dunes that smothered the remains of the beach houses. It climbed as high as the roofs, smothered the yards and verandahs and trampled everything in its path.

Sam looked down at Maggie and squeezed her hand. 'It's gone,' he said softly. 'It can't hurt you any more.'

Maggie lifted her chin and turned away. 'It's a bloody silly place to have a house, anyways,' she said gruffly. 'Come on. Better get back and start clearing up.'

Sam nodded. 'Gotta make a couple of calls on the two-way,' he said. 'Make sure Hopalong and Smokey got back all right, and that Ma's okay.'

Maggie smiled and dipped her chin. 'I can't imagine you with a ma,' she said.

'Tough old sheila, my Ma,' he said proudly. 'The best mother-in-law in the world. But not one to cross, believe me. Could stop a stampeding bull at fifty paces with one of her glares.'

The hotel felt strangely quiet after having so many people overnight, and Sam helped Maggie stack up the mattresses before he got on the radio. 'G'day, Ma,' he said as he pedalled furiously to maintain contact. 'How's it up there? Over.'

209

'She'll be right. Got a bit of water in, but no real harm done. What about you?'

'Nothing a bit of clearing up won't fix,' he replied. He looked over his shoulder. Maggie had gone into the bar and was busy cleaning up where the rain had come under the door. 'Ma,' he said. 'I need a favour.'

'You're asking for help.'

It was a statement, not a question, and not for the first time, Sam marvelled at the old girl's astuteness. 'Reckon I am,' he replied. 'That thing we talked about the other day – it's getting complicated.'

'Never was straightforward,' she replied gruffly. 'What do you want me to do, Samuel? I'm stuck up here, and you're down there.'

'I'll drive up,' he said.

'Fair go, Samuel,' she replied. 'Reckon it'll take a while to clear up first. The roads are impassable this far north.'

Sam grinned. Ma had always refused to call him anything but Samuel, and it made him feel like a little boy again. 'I'll come the minute the road's open,' he told her. 'And I won't be alone.'

There was silence at the other end, which went on for so long, Sam wondered if the connection had been broken. 'It'll be good to meet Maggie at last,' said the old woman at the other end of the line.

'How did you know it was Maggie?' Sam stared in amazement at the ugly great box.

'I might be old,' she said with asperity. 'But I'm not senile. You and Maggie were made for each other by the sound of it. But of course, just like a man, it took ages for you to see that.'

Sam laughed, told her a little more about the reason for his visit and promised to travel north as soon as he could before signing off. He'd been very careful of what he said, but luckily Ma was astute enough to read between the lines. The main problem with the two-way was that everyone listened in. Now the whole of northern Queensland would know about him and Maggie, and would no doubt carry on gossiping about it for hours.

Still, he supposed with a grin, it would give them something else to think about when they were mopping up after the hurricane.

He changed the radio frequency and started to call Hopalong. 'Are you there, mate? Sam calling. Over.'

The atmospherics hummed and white noise filled the headset. 'Hopalong, Smokey? This is Sam. How's it back there? Did you get home okay?'

A faint voice drifted past the background chatter of other radios. It sounded like Smokey, but it was too distant to be sure – and definitely far off his usual frequency. Sam frowned and adjusted the settings.

'That you, Smokey? Can't hear you, mate. What frequency you on?'

'. . . ute. Tree . . . Hopalong bad, mate.'

Sam was fully alert as he adjusted the dials and strained to hear what Smokey was saying. He had to be using the two-way in the ute, it was the only explanation – which meant they hadn't made it home – which meant they were in trouble. 'Where are you, mate?'

'East Barron . . . Blown into . . . Ute smashed.'

'Hold on, mate. Is that Barron Falls? Over. Do you read? Baron Falls?'

'Yeah.'

White noise swamped the weak voice and Sam desperately tried to find a clearer channel. 'Smokey,' he yelled. 'How bad you blokes hurt? Answer me, mate.'

There was nothing but atmospherics. Sam stopped pedalling and thrust away from the radio. 'Maggie,' he yelled.

'I'm here, no need to shout.' She nodded at a pile of blankets, flasks of tea and several rolls of bandages. 'Thought we might need these,' she added.

He grabbed her and held her close. 'Good girl,' he breathed. 'We gotta find Olivia. There ain't time to fetch the doc, and I reckon he'll be flat out after the hurricane anyway.'

'Olivia's gone to look for Giles.' She glanced at the clock on the wall. 'Something must have happened, they should have been back ages ago.'

'Come on.' Sam snatched up the blankets, bandages and flasks of tea, and they raced out of the hotel and clambered into the utility. 'Thank goodness I put it in the shed for once,' he muttered as he started the engine and ground the gears.

Giles lay in the darkness and dredged up a weak smile. He would have recognised that voice anywhere. 'Olivia,' he called. The effort was too much and he rested his cheek back on the shattered rubble. His cry had sounded so feeble, and, buried as he was beneath so much debris, he wondered if she'd even heard him.

The silence and the darkness of their tomb closed in. Giles listened and heard her call once more, but his reply was even weaker than before and he lay there trying to work enough saliva into his mouth to call again.

As he did this, he attempted to get his bearings. His torso seemed unharmed and the blood had stopped running down his forehead, so the cut couldn't have been serious. But below the waist it was a different story. He was almost alight with pain, and he could only guess at what could be pressing so determinedly on him, effectively pinning him and the old man to the floor.

211

He tried to ignore the agony and concentrate on Gallagher. He could hear him breathing, but it was shallow and inconsistent. He touched the other man's hand, and realised he was very cold.

Gallagher moaned and shifted beneath him, and Giles cried out in pain. 'Don't,' he gasped. 'Keep still.'

'Hello? Is someone down there?'

It was an unfamiliar voice, and Giles was momentarily confused. He'd thought he'd heard Olivia. 'Help,' he responded. 'Help us.'

The unfamiliar voice called out again, louder this time. 'Olivia. Over here. They're trapped.'

'Who's trapped?' Olivia called back.

Giles tensed. She was coming. Olivia was coming.

'Dunno,' replied the unfamiliar voice. 'But there's someone down there.'

Giles lay there and fought the waves of nausea and dark clouds, which threatened to overwhelm him. He concentrated on the sounds overhead. They were lifting things up and throwing them aside, and discussing what they should do about the tree that had carved a path through the little house and was now at the very heart of this pile of ruins.

'Wait,' said Olivia. 'Let me listen.'

'Ollie,' he groaned. 'Ollie.'

'Giles,' she yelled. 'Giles, is that you?'

'Ollie,' it was almost a sigh, for Giles was fast losing consciousness.

'Get help,' Olivia ordered. 'You and I will have to clear as much as we can, Joe. But we won't be able to do much until someone's shifted this damn tree.'

Her very presence seemed to give him strength and Giles dragged himself back to consciousness and listened to the sounds above ground. Sheets of iron and chunks of wood were being dragged away, the shattered chimney stones hurled aside. Olivia and Joe were obviously working alone, and Giles wondered how long it would take before he could breathe fresh air again.

The roar of an engine and the squeal of tyres shattered the silence. 'Outta the way.'

Giles sighed with relief. It was Sam, and by the sound of it, at least half the male population of Trinity. He listened as they gathered and inspected the damage and planned a strategy.

He could see nothing, but could picture the scene – could imagine Sam's frown as he tried to think of a way of getting to him and Gallagher – could almost see him pushing his hat back and rubbing his forehead as he spoke. 'Reckon we'll have to cut that tree up before we pull it off,' he said. 'If we don't the whole bloody thing will just cave in.'

Giles listened to the ring of axes and the steady sawing of wood as the men worked in silence. Their quiet desperation was almost tangible, and it echoed his own as he heard branches crack and the tramp of boots overhead. One false move and he and Gallagher would die down here.

'Clear this lot and chuck it over there,' ordered Sam. 'Olivia, get outta the bloody way, woman.'

'I need to get to them,' she said firmly. 'How long is this going to take?'

'It's a big tree,' he replied. 'But it won't take long if you keep out of the bloody way.'

'Get on with it then and stop talking,' she snapped.

Giles grinned despite the agony in his lower half. Trust Olivia to give as good as she got.

He was tense as he waited for the moment when the main body of the tree would be lifted away. Gallagher's breathing hadn't improved, and despite their bodies sharing what little warmth they had, the old man was freezing.

All work stopped and the silence closed in.

'Right oh,' shouted Sam. 'Get in line, and on my say so, lift the bugger.' There was a scuffle of boots and some muttering. 'One, two, three, lift.'

Giles closed his eyes and tried to regulate his pulse. He was scared – almost as scared as when his plane spun out of control and he'd had to parachute out. He could hear the tearing of buried tree limbs being dragged from the pile of rubble. Could hear the slither and crash of things falling around him. Could hear the soft oaths as the men took the full weight and began to drag the tree away – and felt the draught of cool air as his prison shifted and rocked and dust filtered down into his eyes and nose.

Olivia called for silence in the ensuing gabble of talk and speculation. 'Giles? Can you hear me?' she shouted.

'Yes,' it was almost a whisper. Giles turned his face towards the glimmer of daylight overhead, and reached out his hand.

'I can see his hand,' she shouted. 'Go steady. He's not that deep.'

Giles heard the slither of iron and the tinkle of broken glass. Could hear the rasp of wood and nails and the clatter of chimney stones as they worked above him in grim silence. Waves of nausea assailed him and he had to force himself to concentrate on that tiny glimmer of light. Olivia was so near, so very near.

Inch by laborious inch the pinprick of light became brighter. Now he could see the sky – it was grey and he felt a stab of disappointment – it should have been blue.

Then Olivia wriggled through the hole and dropped down beside him. Her tone was sharp, but it had more to do with fear than anger. 'What on earth are you doing down here?'

'Trying to get out,' he rasped. She was covered in mud, her face was filthy and her hair was as wild as a bird's nest, but Giles thought she had never looked lovelier.

'Smart arse,' she hissed as she took his wrist and felt his pulse.

'Bossy boots,' he retorted, yet his voice sounded terribly weak and pain shot into his head as he tried to lift himself from the rubble.

'Keep still,' she said softy as she placed her hand on his chest and smoothed back the hair from his forehead. 'Where does it hurt?' she asked.

Giles closed his eyes as Olivia ran her cool fingers over his head and checked his arm and his torso. 'Everywhere,' he groaned. 'But you've got to see to Gallagher first. Think he's had a heart attack.'

'Someone get me a torch,' Olivia called up through the hole. 'And see if you can get any more of this rubble cleared. But be careful. I want them out in one piece, not crushed.'

A torch was handed down and Olivia crawled around Giles and began to examine Gallagher. 'Pulse is thready and he's very cold. What makes you think he's had a heart attack?'

Giles was almost bankrupt of strength, but it was important Olivia knew about the pills. 'Pills in his pocket,' he muttered. 'Put under tongue.'

He must have passed out, because the next time he opened his eyes it was to feel the prick of a hypodermic in his arm.

'Lie still,' Olivia murmured. 'I've given you a shot of morphine to help with the pain. We're going to move you now.'

Giles looked away from her, afraid she would see the naked adoration in his eyes and regret her soft approach. He lay there swooning with the effects of the morphine, almost coccooned in a swirl of well-being as it began to take hold.

He was only vaguely aware of Olivia strapping his legs in splints. Only partially alert enough to feel the agonising jolt as he was lifted onto something hard and flat and hoisted into the open air. When he opened his eyes again he found he was lying on the flatbed of the ute, covered in a blanket. Olivia was still directing proceedings and sounding more like a headmistress by the minute. Giles smiled. God, he loved her.

Gallagher was deposited next to him. His glare was still belligerent despite the laboured breathing. 'Will I still get me free breakfast?' he rasped to Olivia, who'd climbed in next to him.

Sam shot the bolts on the back. Squatting between the two men he loomed over Gallagher. 'You should be bloody grateful you're still alive, you old bludger,' he said crossly. 'Instead of thinking of your belly, why don't you thank this bloke here for saving your worthless, bloody life?'

Gallagher glowered as Sam told him how the kitchen table had probably saved their lives, and how his own place had also been flattened. 'If it wasn't for Giles, you'd be crows' meat,' he finished.

Gallagher looked across at Giles, the rheumy eyes thoughtful. 'Reckon you ain't so bad,' he said gruffly. 'Not for a Pommy bastard, anyway.'

Chapter Twenty

Olivia pulled the blanket up to Gallagher's chin and patted his hand. 'Rest, and try to sleep,' she said softly.

'Where's me tucker?' he muttered.

'I'll see what I can do, but as you can imagine, things are a bit chaotic in the hotel at the moment.' She eyed him thoughtfully. 'If you're hungry, then there probably isn't much wrong with you, so I suggest you shut up whingeing and let me get on.'

She turned and bent over Giles. He was ashen, the deep shadows around his eyes making him appear very vulnerable. At least the morphine had kicked in – he would be out of it for a while yet.

'How is he?' asked Maggie as she brought a bowl of soup for Gallagher and helped him to sit up.

'He'll be fine,' she said. 'It's Giles I'm worried about. The tree landed across his hips, and I'm fairly certain he's fractured his acetabulum as well as both femurs.'

Maggie raised an eyebrow, and Olivia smiled. 'His hip socket and thigh bones,' she explained. 'I just hope I'm wrong about the hip, as they take for ever to heal and could affect his mobility later on.'

'Sam's radioed through to the flying doctor, but it could be some time before he gets here,' said Maggie, who was spooning soup into Gallagher's mouth. 'There's been so many injuries the poor man must be flat out.'

'Olivia.' Sam was hovering in the doorway. 'We have to go.'

Olivia nodded. Sam had been like a cat on hot bricks every since they'd come back to the hotel. She collected the hastily put together medical bag and after tucking Giles more firmly beneath the blanket, turned to Maggie.

'Keep an eye on his temperature, and if he gets too hot, keep him cool with damp cloths. He can't have any more medication for at least four hours.' She measured out the dosage and laid the syringe carefully on the side table. 'Just in case,' she said.

'You don't expect me to give him an injection, do you?' Maggie's brown eyes were wide with horror.

'I hope I'm not away that long,' she replied. 'But if I am, then yes.' She put her hand on Maggie's shoulder. 'Use the spare syringe and practise on an orange – worked for me.'

'Come *on*, woman.' Sam shouted. 'We're wasting time.'

Olivia and Maggie exchanged grins and Olivia followed him out of the room. Minutes later they were edging around the debris in the street and heading north-west to Barron Falls.

William had known instinctively something was wrong. He'd tried getting through to Irene on the two-way, and although he'd guessed she would check on the horses the minute the storm had receded, he'd become concerned at her lengthy absence.

He drove at speed over the waterlogged terrain, the utility bouncing and jolting as it splashed through the puddles and streams. The silly bitch should have come back to the homestead like he'd suggested. But that was Irene all over, too darn stubborn for her own bloody good.

His face was grim as he steered around the potholes and the fallen trees. Deloraine's luck had held. Apart from a few downed trees and a collapsed barn, they had come out of it fairly unscathed. Fence posts had been ripped up and a few roofs would need mending, but the stock was safe and the repairs could be done swiftly once the water went down.

The manager's old house was a different matter, he admitted silently. It was exposed, the surrounding countryside dipping away from it in endless empty miles that were ripe for a hurricane to race across.

He gripped the steering wheel. If anything had happened to her he would never forgive himself. Twenty-two years of marriage had to count for something, and although he no longer loved her, he still felt responsible. And although he knew old habits died hard and that Irene had never been one to take orders, he should have gone with his first instinct and driven over earlier and forced her to come back with him.

The little homestead looked so lonely now the trees had been ripped away, and as William slewed the utility to a screeching halt he knew his worst fears had been realised. For the door was open, the verandah swept away and no sign of Irene, even when he called out.

He splashed through the water and hauled himself up into the house. Walking swiftly from room to room he noted the damage

217

wasn't too bad – but Irene definitely wasn't here, and that worried him.

He jumped back down to the ground and headed for the stable block. The water was receding fast, the iron-hard earth soaking it up like a sponge through the cracks. He could see the horses cropping in a far paddock, and a pile of old rags or something pressed hard against the stable wall. But still no Irene. His mouth dried as his pulse raced. 'Irene?' he called. 'Irene, where are you?'

There was no reply.

He stepped on to the cobbles and was about to search the stalls when he realised the bundle of rags was his wife. He gasped in horror as he knelt beside her. Irene was sprawled and obviously helpless, her clothes soaked in blood. She looked so pale, so vulnerable, yet, as she looked back at him he could see the defiant spark of determination in her eyes. Irene was certainly a survivor, he acknowledged, but for how long?

'I'll have to get help,' he said as he knelt on the cobbles and held her hand.

Irene opened her mouth, but no sound came. Her eyes widened in fear as she struggled to speak. The confusion and terror were plain in her ashen face.

'Don't try and speak,' he said kindly. 'And don't move. That's a bad head injury.'

Her hand was limp in his, but he could feel her terror as her gaze sought his and held it. 'I have to leave for a while, Irene,' he insisted quietly. 'You're too badly injured to take you back to Deloraine in the ute. I'll have to get one of the boys to bring the plane over.'

Her breath was a sigh and for a moment William thought she'd mercifully passed out. Then her eyelids flickered open and he saw the fear again. 'I won't be long,' he whispered. 'I promise.'

She tried to speak again, the tears rolling from the corners of her eyes, glittering on her wan face.

He had no idea what she was trying to tell him and was lost for words. He covered up his awkwardness by patting her hand. 'Shh. Don't try and talk. Rest. I'll be back before you know it.'

Irene's eyelids fluttered again. She had passed out.

William looked down at his wife as he covered her in a horse blanket. He had never seen her so helpless before, and in those quiet few moments he realised this was the real Irene. The Irene who battled so manfully to prove she was tough, when inside she was hurting. The Irene who just needed to be loved and cherished, but didn't know how to make it happen.

The sadness was heavy on his shoulders as he splashed back through the water to the homestead and radioed through to his stock manager. Then, with the plane on the way, he radioed to the hospital at Cairns, warning them of their arrival. Returning to the stables, he tucked the blanket more firmly around her. He would have held her and shared his body warmth, but was afraid to touch any part of her in case he hurt her further – afraid that one jolt could sever her spinal cord and kill her.

Her eyes opened again, the tears trembling on her lashes as she tried to communicate something to him. But no intelligent sound came from her mouth, only an anguished moan.

'Won't be long now,' he murmured. 'Don't try and talk or move. Just rest.' He searched the horizon for some sign of the station plane. Irene was critically injured. Her breathing was shallow and her skin was hot. If help didn't come soon she would die. He took her hand, and, resting on the cobbles next to his wife, he waited for the plane.

The main road was almost impassable, and Sam eventually gave up and steered the ute out into the country. It was flatter here, with less damage and they could go that bit faster.

'Where is this Barron Falls?' asked Olivia as she grabbed hold of anything that might stop her from being thrown about.

'West,' he replied shortly, all his concentration on the ground ahead. 'Up on the tablelands. Big tree country up there – could take a fair while to find them.'

Olivia remained silent as she clung to the door. The situation had emphasised the desperate need for a medical centre, and the sooner she got on with it, the better. At least the hurricane had done her one favour, she thought grimly. It had flattened the old house, so all they had to do now was clear the site and rebuild.

Sam brought the ute to a screeching halt. 'Bugger. This is it. We'll have to walk.'

Olivia looked around her. They were on a steep incline and surrounded by fallen trees. The only indication that this was a track lay in the flattened earth she could just see beneath the snapped branches and exposed roots of what must have once been a magnificent rainforest.

She grabbed her medical bag and climbed down. 'How do we know which way to go?' she asked.

'Follow the track,' said Sam. 'It eventually leads to the sawmill, so they'd have been travelling this way to get home.' He took an axe from the back of the ute, and slung a length of rope over his shoulder. 'Might need these,' he muttered as he led the way.

Olivia needed all her energy and concentration to pick her way through and around the chaotic mess the hurricane had left behind. It

219

had almost certainly ripped through here with tremendous force, and she dreaded to think of what they might find when they came across the two amputees.

They had been walking for some time when Olivia, head down, watching where she trod, walked straight into Sam. He caught her in his arms. 'Whoa, there, mate.'

Flustered by the sheer maleness of him, she drew back from his embrace and smeared the sweat from her face. 'Why did you stop?'

He pointed. 'Through there. Look.'

Olivia followed his pointing finger. A ragged path had been torn through the undergrowth and she could see the imprint of tyres in the mud. She looked further down this path and realised it came to a halt beneath a giant tree that had been felled by the wind. The glimmer of something white peeked between the gnarled branches.

'Oh, my God,' she breathed. 'If they're under that I'm surprised either of them is alive.'

'Smokey was alive enough to make the call,' muttered Sam as he led the way towards the tree.

Olivia followed him, her mouth dry, her pulse racing. She had no idea what they might find beneath that tree, and she was afraid her nursing skills would not be enough.

The tree had fallen sideways on to the utility and effectively sliced it in two. Its great trunk rested across the mangled metal, the rotten timber having exploded to reveal the soft underbelly that had once been home to generations of termites. From one of the snapped branches that lay in the midst of the shattered windscreen there swayed a wooden stump complete with leather strap.

Without a word Olivia and Sam clambered around the truck in search of the two men.

'Sam? That you, mate?'

They stilled. 'Smokey?'

'About bloody time,' groaned Smokey. 'Over here.'

Olivia pointed and began to wriggle beneath the fallen trunk. She had seen the flash of a check shirt as Smokey moved.

The two men were lying on top of one another in an almost impenetrable tangle of fallen branches and trapped scrub. Olivia crawled as close as she could, but her path was soon blocked. With growing frustration she tried to clear a way through, but it was impossible.

'How bad do you think you're hurt?' she called.

'Dunno,' groaned Smokey. 'Ribs hurt like buggery, and me arm feels like it's bust. Hopalong passed out a while back – ain't heard nothing from him for ages, but he's still breathing.'

'Can you move at all?'

'Not with this old bastard lying on me,' he drawled.

Olivia knew she could do nothing for either of them until she'd cleared a path. She crawled back to Sam and explained the situation.

'They're quite fortunate, actually,' she said as she smeared the sweat from her eyes and tucked her hair behind her ears. 'They've landed on their back in an indentation in the earth which looks like heavy duty tyre tracks.'

'Logging trucks are up and down this track every day,' Sam explained.

'Lucky for them it was so well used,' she said as her pulse slowed and breathing returned to normal. 'The tracks would have cushioned their fall, and probably protected them slightly from the full force of the crashing branches.'

Sam swung the axe. 'I'll chop, you haul.' He eyed her thoughtfully. 'Are you up for this, Olivia?'

'Too right,' she replied. 'Get on with it. We're wasting time and soon we won't have any daylight.'

The ring of the axe echoed in the eerie stillness as inch by inch they cleared a path through the mangled maze of tree branches, ferns and sharp tropical leaves that cut flesh as keenly as any knife.

'Mind how you go with that flaming axe,' drawled Smokey.

'If you don't put a sock in it, I'll flaming go home,' muttered Sam.

They kept up this barrage of verbal abuse as the axe swung and Olivia tied the rope to the severed branches and hauled them out of the way. She was sweating and trembling with exhaustion as she fought to keep up with Sam, and ignore the stinging, biting insects that hovered around her in clouds. The mosquitoes were having a field day in the damp humidity of this tropical rainforest.

The light was beginning to fade when they finally reached the two men. They had two hours at the most before darkness fell. They would have to be quick.

'I'll see to Hopalong first,' she explained to Smokey. 'Then we'll move him off you.'

Smokey nodded. 'How is he?'

'I won't know until I've examined him,' she replied. She felt Hopalong's pulse. It was very faint. His skin was icy to the touch and there was a tinge of blue around his mouth. She ran her hands swiftly over him and realised he'd broken his arm and probably a couple of ribs. There was a nasty gash in his side, but it was no longer bleeding, which was a good sign. Yet it was his amputated leg that bothered her the most. It was at a strange angle to his hip, and almost raw where it had been torn from the strapping.

221

'What happened to his leg?' she asked as she cleaned the ragged flesh on the stump and swiftly bandaged it up.

'Had to pull him out quick,' rasped Smokey. 'Didn't get the buckle undone in time.'

Olivia looked across at the wooden appendage swaying in the light breeze. Smokey's actions had no doubt saved his mate, but had probably dislocated Hopalong's hip joint.

'I'm going to give him something to help with the pain, then Sam and I will get him off you,' she said as she filled a hypodermic.

'About bloody time,' Smokey grumbled without malice. 'The bludger weighs a flaming ton and a half.' He gave a snort of wry laughter. 'Always said he should go on a flaming diet.'

Olivia and Sam carefully lifted Hopalong and carried him back to the utility. Covering him with a blanket, they turned to head back for Smokey.

'No worries, mate,' he said as he staggered up the track towards them. 'Busted me tin leg, but I can still flaming walk.' His face was grey and as he stumbled and almost fell; Sam caught him, picked him up and carried him.

'Don't you tell the blokes in the pub about this,' Smokey muttered against Sam's chest. 'Never flaming live it down.'

The hospital in Cairns had thankfully been spared the worst of the storm. Every nurse and doctor had been called in and the accident and emergency department was under siege. Volunteers were doing the best they could, but there seemed no let-up in the flood of people needing help. The three operating theatres were working flat out, and the flying doctor's plane had already made four landings on the airstrip. Cairns's single ambulance couldn't keep up with the demand, and now there were utility trucks, lorries and cars parked haphazardly out front as more casualties were brought in.

William paced the corridor unable to settle or think straight. Irene's injuries must be worse than he'd thought for it to take so long. He finally came to a halt and stood, unseeing in front of the window. Night had fallen but a stream of light fell across the front entrance from the hospital building. He emerged from his gloomy thoughts as a utility truck screeched to a halt outside. No doubt another casualty of the storm. The hospital had never been so busy.

He tensed as a man and woman climbed out and went to the back of the utility. That was Sam from Trinity, and the woman beside him looked very familiar. He peered out of the window as she stepped into the stream of light. It was Olivia. Galvanised into action, he raced down the corridor.

Olivia was walking beside a stretcher, the man lying there obvi-

222

ously badly injured. Sam was pushing a wheelchair, its incumbent grumbling and muttering. Olivia looked exhausted and filthy and was covered in scratches and bites. William waited until her two charges had been whisked away by the nurses before he approached her.

'Olivia. Are you right?'

'William?' She seemed puzzled to find him there. 'I'm fine except for the mosquito bites. What are you doing here?' she asked.

'It's Irene,' he replied after nodding a greeting to Sam. 'She's bad, Olivia. I don't know if she'll pull through.' He heard the tremor in his voice and knew he was close to tears.

'Where is she?'

'Operating room two,' he said as he took off his hat and ran his shirtsleeve over his forehead. 'Been in there for hours.'

'I'll be here a while,' she said distractedly. The waiting area was in complete chaos. 'Looks like they need all the help they can get.' She flashed him a weary smile. 'Let me know when she comes out of theatre and I'll try and pop in to see her.'

'She'd like that, I'm sure,' he said eagerly.

Olivia frowned. 'We really don't have anything to say to one another,' she said with a sigh. 'But of course I'll come and see her. She is my sister, after all.'

'I'm sorry your reunion didn't go too well. What were those papers, by the way? Perhaps I can help?'

'I doubt it, but thanks anyway,' said Olivia. She pushed back her hair and sighed as she watched the harried nurses trying to cope with the influx of patients. 'Look, I'm sorry, William. I'm tired and filthy and this is neither the time, nor place, to go over old wounds.'

William realised he would get no further with Olivia tonight. She was preoccupied and needed elsewhere. 'Just promise me you'll find time to see her,' he said.

Olivia nodded before turning away to talk to Sam. 'I'll stay here until the panic's died down. You go back to Trinity and make sure Giles is all right.'

'Flying doctor will probably have been by now,' said Sam through a vast yawn. 'If it's serious enough you'll probably see him yourself.'

William watched her walk away. Within minutes of talking to a harassed doctor, she was greeted with relief and sent to look at her first patient. 'Reckon I'll be getting back to Irene,' he mumbled.

'See you later, mate.' Sam loped out of the hospital and climbed into the ute.

William returned to pacing the corridor outside the operating room. It was to be another hour before the doctor emerged through the swing doors.

223

He took off his mask, his eyes weary, colour wan in the harsh electric light. 'Your wife's in a bad way, Bill,' he said sadly. 'Sorry, mate, but her brain's been damaged. She's alive, but only just, and if she does pull through, she'll never leave her bed.'

William had to sit down. 'Brain damage?' he gasped. 'I knew it was serious when she couldn't talk, but surely there must be something you can do to repair the damage?'

The doctor shook his head. 'This is a country hospital. She's in too bad a way to fly her down to Sydney, and even if we did, I doubt they could do more for her.' He gave a weary sigh and dry-scrubbed his face with his hands. 'Sorry to load you with this, Bill, but at least her legs will heal in time.'

'Fat lot of good they'll be if she can't walk,' William snarled.

The surgeon's hand gripped his shoulder. 'We'll just have to wait and see. But I warn you, it's touch and go.'

'Jeez,' he breathed. 'Will she pull through, do you think?'

The doctor's hand was suddenly heavy on his shoulder. 'I'm sorry, Bill. She's very weak after losing all that blood. We aren't out of the woods yet.'

William sank his chin to his chest and tried to digest the awful news. The guilt was overwhelming. If only he'd insisted upon her returning to Deloraine. If only he'd waited until after the hurricane to send her packing. If only – what a sad, useless phrase that was, he realised, for nothing could be changed.

He knew the doctor was impatient to return to theatre, 'How soon will we know if she'll pull through?' he asked.

'The next twenty-four hours are the most critical. After that – it's up to Irene.' His face was sad. 'But she'll never walk again, Bill, and probably never talk either. You must be prepared for the worst.'

'Then it would probably be better if she didn't make it through,' William sighed. Irene would prefer death to a living hell of silence and immobility.

The doctor shrugged. 'It never ceases to amaze me how even the sickest person clings to life, Bill. Irene's strong. She may surprise you.' He looked at his watch. 'Gotta go, mate. Busy night.'

William watched him stride down the corridor and push through a door. He sat there, numb with shock, the thoughts whirling in his head. The future he'd planned with Martha had been ripped to shreds by the hurricane. If Irene did survive the next few hours, she would need round-the-clock care – and as it was his fault she'd been injured in the first place, it was up to him to see she had the best care he could provide – and a proper home to return to. He would have to begin making arrangements to adapt Deloraine.

224

Chapter Twenty-One

Giles knew he'd been lucky. The flying doctor had taken him up to Cairns for treatment, but the X-rays revealed only a dislocated hip joint and a hairline fracture in his leg. Getting the hip back into position had been a momentary agony that was soon eased with medication, and once his leg had been put in plaster, he felt he was taking up a hospital bed on false pretences.

'Don't be silly,' said Olivia on one of her evening visits. 'Your hip must still be painful and you need to rest it a while before walking on it – the plaster cast will only add further stress to the weakened area.'

Giles took her hand. 'Talking of rest,' he said quietly. 'You've been on the go for over two weeks. You look completely shattered.'

'I can go on a bit longer,' she said as she smothered a yawn. 'The worst is over.'

'You're supposed to be on holiday,' he reminded her.

'This trip was never meant to be a holiday,' she said as she smoothed back her hair beneath the neat little white cap. 'And I've achieved nothing, really. Now, with Irene incapable of little more than eye contact, I doubt I'll ever get to the bottom of the mystery.'

Giles lit a cheroot and reached for the ashtray on the bedside chest. 'Mystery is right,' he mumbled. 'Never did tell me what all that was about.' He eyed her keenly. She did look tired. Her eyes were shadowed with weariness and her mouth drooped. 'Want to tell me about it?'

Olivia tucked the sheet more firmly beneath the mattress, plucked the cheroot from his fingers and stubbed it out. 'No point,' she said. 'Irene's the only one with the answers, and she's barely alive.' She stood and kissed him softly on the cheek. 'I've got to go, Giles. Night shift, you know. But I'll try and pop in tomorrow morning before I go to bed.'

Giles stayed her by catching her wrist. 'I realise I spoke out of turn,

Ollie, but I never wanted to lose our friendship.' He saw the flicker of something in her eyes and her expression softened.

'You'll never lose that,' she said with infinite sweetness. 'I do love you, Giles, but not in the way you want. I'm sorry. I really wish things could have been different.'

Giles leaned back into the pillows and his smile was sad. 'At least we both know where we stand with one another now,' he said.

Olivia kissed his forehead and stepped away. With mock severity, she wagged a finger at him. 'Standing is the last thing you can do,' she said. 'If I catch you trying to walk before the injuries heal, you'll have me to answer to.'

He couldn't help but grin. 'Bossy as always,' he teased.

She grinned back. Then, with a glance at the watch pinned to her apron, she backed away. 'Must go. Terribly late already and matron will have my guts for garters.'

She blew him a kiss and he watched her leave the ward. Watched her greet the handsome young doctor and laugh at something he said. Saw the animation enliven her face and the spring in her step as they walked away and out of sight. He'd seen that doctor many times during the two weeks he'd been here, and had heard the rumours. He seemed to be hanging around whenever Olivia was on the ward, and Giles had noticed how keen he was to engage her in conversation. The feeling appeared to be mutual.

A wave of jealousy and frustration rushed through him as he wondered if they shared cosy meals during their time off, or perhaps went dancing or to the cinema. He'd heard Cairns was quite lively.

The thought of her in another man's arms was too much and the frustration of being in this blasted bed made him edgy. Yet he knew something like this was inevitable, for Olivia was distancing herself from him – taking charge of her life – following her own destiny – a destiny that didn't include him. Friendship was all she could offer him, and, although he treasured that, it wasn't enough. She had settled back in Australia as if she'd never left, and what with the plans for the medical centre and the ties with Maggie, he doubted she would ever return to England.

He leaned back against the pillows and closed his eyes. His cases were packed and stowed away in the cupboard at the end of the ward. There was no need to return to Trinity. The airport had reopened and once he'd been discharged, he would see about a flight down to Sydney. From there he would book a passage for home. It was time to set Olivia free. Time to take charge of his life and move on.

During the two weeks following the storm, Maggie and Sam spent

226

every waking minute getting the hotel repaired and ready for business again. The roof and several of the shutters and screens had needed mending, and the guttering replaced. Water damage upstairs had meant stripping off wallpaper and dumping carpets, but the floors had been waxed and looked better than ever, and a fresh coat of paint on the walls had brightened the whole place up.

Now the hotel was finally back to what passed as normal, and the town was beginning to appear less like a war zone. The clearing up had revealed the true extent of the damage, but the rebuilding had begun almost immediately, and once the water had receded, life could settle down to its usual, leisurely pace.

The time had simply flown, and in the first flush of their newly found love, the long days and passionate nights seemed to invigorate both of them. It was late Sunday night, and they were sharing the comfort of the big old chair in the lounge when the crash of a door brought Sam to his feet, causing the discarded teacups to rattle on the table.

'I hope you got one of those for me. Throat's as dry as a duck's arse.'

'Smokey!' Maggie leaped from the chair and threw her arms around him. 'You didn't tell us you were coming back. How did you get here?'

He blushed and his shock of fair hair fell into his eyes as Maggie kissed him. 'Got a lift,' he muttered. 'The road's been cleared and it didn't take long at all.' He hitched his plastered arm to a more comfortable position in the sling.

Maggie was about to ask who had come from Cairns at this time of night, when she noticed Smokey's companion. 'Aren't you going to introduce us?' she teased.

Smokey reddened further as he took the girl's hand and drew her forward. 'This is Ann,' he said. 'She's taking a few days off now the hospital's a bit quieter, and as I'm still the walking wounded, she thought she'd keep an eye on me.'

'G'day.' Maggie smiled and the two women shook hands. Ann was small and pleasantly rounded, with an open face and smiling eyes that looked at Smokey in adoration. Maggie liked her instantly.

'Dark horse,' muttered Sam as he slapped him on the back. 'This calls for a beer.'

'Better do something to eat,' said Maggie. 'You must be starving, Smokey, if you're on the mend.'

With the pile of sandwiches rapidly diminishing, they sat in the lounge drinking beer and catching up on the gossip. Ann was a nurse, so she was well up on the latest.

227

'How's Olivia doing?' asked Maggie when there was a lull in the conversation. 'I've tried reaching her on the phone, but that Matron sounds a right old dragon, and refuses to pass on any messages.'

Ann smiled. 'She's that all right,' she agreed. 'Olivia's still working flat out, even though the worst is over.' Her eyes gleamed with fun. 'There are rumours about her and one of our interns. And the bets are on as to whether or not it will come to anything. But the smart money's on a wedding before next summer.'

'Poor old Giles,' sighed Maggie. 'Looks like he's lost out.'

Ann shrugged. 'He's a realist, I reckon. And he's definitely getting better. Caught him flirting with one of the sisters the other night.'

Maggie pulled a face. 'Certainly doesn't appear to be letting the grass grow under his feet,' she murmured. 'But I have a feeling he's putting up a front.'

'Fair go, luv,' interjected Sam. 'The bloke's got to have a life, and a little bit of flirting never hurt.'

Maggie raised an eyebrow. Trust Sam to stick up for Giles. But then, what else could she expect, they were both men. 'What about Irene Hamilton?' she asked, changing the subject.

Ann's expression was sad. 'Still hanging on, but the prognosis isn't good. Her injuries have left her completely helpless, without the ability to communicate or do anything for herself. Her poor husband has barely left her side since she's been admitted.'

Smokey opened another bottle of beer. 'Hopalong won't be getting out of that place for a while, but the old bastard's on the mend.' He grinned. 'He's getting a new leg, specially fitted, and all shiny tin, so we'll have to have a formal cremation of the old one and think up a new name for him.'

Maggie digested all the news and wondered how Giles was coping with the rumours about Olivia and the handsome doctor. Poor Giles, she thought. He's been through so much and after coming all this way to see Olivia snatched away by someone else simply wasn't fair. But Olivia had to make up her own mind, and it wouldn't be good for either of them if she stayed with Giles through pity, or a false sense of loyalty. As for Irene – she was sorry for the woman, but that was as far as it went. It was William she pitied, for if Irene did survive, his life would be hell.

She sat back as the conversation flowed around her, and noticed how Ann and Smokey couldn't keep their eyes and hands off one another. Her sadness for Giles was swept away in the pleasure of seeing Smokey so obviously in love and she found she couldn't stop smiling. 'How long will you be staying?' she asked in a lull during the conversation.

'That's what we came to talk to you about,' said Smokey. 'Reckon I owe you one, mate. So me and Ann thought we'd take over this place for a week so you and Maggs can take a bit of a holiday.'

'Don't owe me bugger all,' muttered Sam, the colour rising in his face. 'Only did what anyone would have done. Besides, I'd have to be out of me mind to let you loose in this place for a whole week. You'd drink all me profits.' His eyes twinkled with mirth.

'Fair go, mate,' retorted Smokey. 'I've helped you before, and with Ann keeping an eye on me, I reckon I won't be drinking too much for a while.' He blushed as Ann smiled at him. 'Need to save me money and get the sawmill up and running again for when Hopalong comes back.'

'What do you reckon, Maggie?' Sam's eyes were still warm with laughter. 'Should we risk our livelihoods to this young reprobate?'

Maggie laughed. 'Why not? Ann seems sensible enough, and Smokey appears to be a reformed character.'

'You sure about this, mate? It's a fair old responsibility, and you're obviously still crook.'

'The busted ribs are mending, and me arm's right. Ann and me can cope. Reckon we could do with some time together away from the hospital,' he drawled. 'We'll manage, no worries.'

Sam slapped his thigh. 'That's settled then. We'll leave tomorrow and head down to Cairns and see Hopalong. If the hospital can spare her, we'll take Olivia along for the ride.' He grinned at Maggie. 'Thought we could visit Ma up in Port Douglas. She's been wanting to meet you, and this will be the ideal opportunity.'

Maggie giggled. It would be lovely to see Olivia again, but visiting Sam's mother-in-law wasn't exactly her idea of a romantic holiday. Yet it would be interesting to meet her – interesting to find out more about this intriguing man she'd fallen in love with.

'What do you mean, he's discharged himself?' Olivia glanced at the neatly made bed. There was no sign of Giles ever having been there.

'He was most insistent, and as the doctor was quite happy with his progress, there didn't seem much point in making him wait another day.' The ward sister was a homely looking woman, with tired eyes. 'I'm sorry, Olivia, but he did leave you a note.'

'Thanks,' she muttered as she took the letter. Turning away, she hurried out of the ward and into the garden. It had been a long night and she was aching to sleep when she'd called in to see Giles, but his defection had swept away the weariness and her fingers trembled as she tore open the envelope.

229

My Dearest Olivia,

By the time you receive this, I will be on my way back to England. I have decided to return home and begin taking charge of my life again. You will think me cowardly for leaving this way, but I think it is for the best, as neither of us likes saying goodbye. I had always hoped that one day you would be able to love me as I love you – I know now that is not possible, so I take my leave of you and wish you all the luck for the future. The memories of our times together will always be precious, and I thank you for your friendship and loyalty, which I will always treasure.

Write to me when you can, I shall be returning to Wimbledon.
Yours always,
Giles

Olivia's tears were warm on her face as she stood there in the early light of a new day. The world suddenly felt lonelier without Giles – less friendly and altogether rather frightening. He had been her rock and her best friend ever since she was ten – now she could picture his sad departure and feel the awful loss his absence had created. Giles could not be allowed to leave like this.

With the letter still clasped in her hand, she hurried through to reception. 'What time did he leave? Do you know where he was heading?'

The woman pursed her lips. 'He ordered a taxi at six this morning and went straight to the airport.' She looked at her watch. 'Eight-thirty. He said his flight was leaving at six-thirty, so he must be well on his way by now, but I have no idea where he was heading.'

Crushed, Olivia turned away and bumped straight into Dr David Watson. 'Sorry,' she muttered. 'Can't stop.'

'Whoa, there, Olivia. You've obviously been crying. What's the matter?' David held her arm, his expression puzzled.

She looked up into his handsome face and knew she didn't love him. He was a mild flirtation, a pleasant interval between the long hours and the hectic hospital schedule. It had been fun, but nothing more. She'd known about the rumours and had ignored them. In hindsight, they were probably the reason for Giles leaving so suddenly, and the guilt was unbearable. How could she have been so thoughtless?

Sam couldn't help but smile, and his face ached as he drove the utility along the cleared highway to Cairns. Maggie was sitting beside him, chattering nineteen to the dozen, happier than he'd ever seen her. He felt so good he thought he would burst, and couldn't

230

wait to introduce her to Ma, who would no doubt love her almost as much as he did.

He steered the utility through the early morning traffic and turned off for the hospital. They would find Olivia first, see Hopalong and then head for Port Douglas. Ma was certainly in for a surprise.

'Stop the ute,' shouted Maggie. 'There's Olivia.'

Sam slammed his foot on the brake and brought the utility to a screeching halt beside Olivia, who'd just climbed down from the local bus.

She didn't seem at all surprised to see them, merely distracted. 'Oh,' she said once she realised who was in the utility. 'What are you doing here?'

'Coming to collect you,' said Maggie gaily as she opened the door. Sam saw her expression change and heard her voice sharpen. 'But something's wrong, Olivia. What is it?'

She climbed in next to Maggie and stared sadly out of the window. Sam thought he could see the tracks of tears on her face, and looked across at Maggie. They exchanged worried glances.

'What's happened, Olivia? Come on, luv. Spit it out.'

'Giles has gone, Maggie. I tried to find out where, but no-one could tell me at the airport.'

Sam looked at Maggie and raised an eyebrow. He hadn't expected Giles to up-sticks and clear off – he'd thought the bloke had more go in him. 'There can't have been many flights this morning,' he drawled. 'Surely they could have told you something?'

Olivia's eyes were bleak as she looked at him. 'Two flights left,' she said. 'Both of them less than an hour long, heading south. There are hundreds of connecting flights from Townsville and Rockhampton. He could have taken any one of them.'

Maggie put her arm around Olivia as Sam eased off the handbrake and continued to drive towards the hospital. 'Reckon we came along just at the right time,' she said with brittle jollity. 'Sam and I are off to Port Douglas, and we thought you could do with a change of scenery.'

Olivia looked out of the window. 'Why didn't he give me the chance to say goodbye, Maggie? Have I hurt him so badly he couldn't bear to face me?'

Maggie squeezed her shoulder. 'You know blokes,' she said in a conspiratorial whisper. 'They avoid trouble like the plague. He probably thought he was doing the right thing.'

'Fair go, Maggie,' interrupted Sam. 'A clean break is often the best way.'

'See what I mean?' Maggie grinned. 'Come on. Let's get you packed and then we'll be off.'

231

'I'm not in the mood for a holiday,' said Olivia. 'You and Sam want to be alone, and I'd just be in the way.' She sighed as Sam drew the utility to a halt in the car park. 'Besides, there's still work to be done here, and it might help to keep busy.'

She seemed so calm, so distant and so very sad that even Sam realised what a blow it had been to discover Giles had gone. He revised his opinion of her. For this cool Englishwoman could be rattled. She wasn't as in control as he'd thought. 'I reckon you should come with us. You're too tired to be much use to anyone, and you've done enough. We'll visit Hopalong while you hand in your notice, then we'll meet out here in about an hour.'

Olivia's smile was wan. 'Is he always this masterful?' she asked Maggie with an ironic tilt to her brow.

She nodded. 'Only when he really wants something,' she giggled. 'Most of the time I get my own way.'

Sam would have argued the point fiercely, but realised the girls were teasing him, so kept quiet. Women were a strange bunch, he thought as he watched a group of chattering nurses crossing the road. No matter how well blokes thought they knew them, they always managed to outwit them and come up trumps.

Olivia turned to face Maggie. 'We ought to make time to see William and Irene before we leave,' she said. 'Irene's not expected to live much longer, and poor old William needs some moral support.'

'We?' Maggie's eyes rounded. 'What would I want to see her for?'

Olivia shrugged. 'Regardless of what she's done in the past, she's helpless and dying. I thought you might want to make your peace with her before it's too late.'

'I thought she was in a coma?' Maggie's tone was flat.

'Not really, it's the drugs keeping her out of it most of the time. She evidently has her lucid moments.'

'I don't think there's much point, do you? She can't talk, and there's nothing I want to say to her.'

'What harm can it do to just go and see her?' Olivia's voice was coaxing.

'That's what I thought before,' Maggie said with flat calm. 'Look where it got me then.' She stared out of the window.

Olivia sighed. 'Your choice,' she murmured. 'But if you change your mind, she's in the private wing, room five. I'll be there in about an hour.'

Olivia turned down the offer of the post of ward sister, said her good-byes and packed up the few bits and pieces she'd collected during the two weeks. She had made some good friends and would miss them.

Would miss the familiar bustle of a busy hospital, and the camaraderie of feeling part of a well-trained team.

Yet the sadness of the last few weeks was becoming too much of a burden. She had forced Giles to leave like a thief in the night. How could she have been so blind to his feelings? How on earth had she not realised he'd loved her so deeply and probably had done since he was just a kid?

Then there was Irene. The sister who'd hated her all her life, but who was her closest relative. Irene's life was ebbing away, and it saddened her, for she could still remember the vibrant, beautiful young woman she had once been. Could still visualise her energy and lust for life. She had loved and lost and put all her energies into her horses – how bizarre it should have been one of them that would end her life.

Olivia left her bag in reception and walked through into the private wing. This visit to room five was more for William than Irene, she admitted. The poor man was bewildered and guilt-ridden by what had happened, and when he'd confided his lost hopes for a future with Martha, she could almost feel his anguish. Guilt was a powerful emotion and it could crucify those burdened by it – William was just such a victim.

She smiled as she saw Maggie nervously pacing the corridor. 'I'm glad you came. It won't be so bad, you'll see,' she murmured as she opened the door.

Irene was awake, but the world was hazy, dulled by the drugs that dripped through the tangle of tubes and into her arm. She swivelled her gaze – the only part of her she still had under control. William was still there, sitting in a chair by the window, engrossed in a newspaper.

At the sound of the opening door, Irene felt a shock of anguish. Her eyes widened as Olivia and Maggie stepped into the room.

'Good to see you awake at last,' said Olivia with the enforced cheerfulness that probably had become second nature during her years of nursing.

Irene saw her eyeing the tented sheets over her legs. Saw the stab of pity and wanted to scream in defiance. She didn't want her here. Didn't want either of them to see her in such a pitiful state. Yet she had no means to convey her anguish. No way of communicating the sheer agony of being viewed as a cripple by these two enemies.

'How are you feeling today?' Olivia was standing beside the bed. The other one over by the door. At least she had the grace to look awkward and clearly uncomfortable with the situation.

Irene stared back, painfully aware she was dribbling. Why didn't William see? Why hadn't he cleaned her up as he'd done before?

'She's a lot better,' said William as he hurriedly cast the newspaper aside and stood to shake hands. 'The doctor's pleased with her progress, and she's aware of everything around her.' His weary face was lined, the eyes haggard as he attempted to inject some hope into the situation.

Irene saw him frown as he was introduced to Maggie. Noticed how his gaze darted between the two young women, his expression puzzled. She caught Olivia watching her, and wondered if she could see the anguish, the vulnerability she felt. To be faced by both of them at such a time was almost unbearable, and the vow she'd made during the storm to heal the breach was forgotten. She would never forgive either of them – for she despised their pity.

'I thought it best if we both came,' explained Olivia. 'You see, I know who she is.'

Irene's pulse was racing, the machines on either side of the bed hummed and beeped and the noise of them seemed to fill her head. She knew. Olivia knew the truth. Her eyes widened in horror as spittle ran from her slack lips.

'Why should it come as such a surprise, Irene?' Olivia's tone was cold. 'We were bound to find one another eventually.'

'No.' The word resounded in Irene's head as she rolled her eyes and battled with the lack of air in her lungs. Olivia didn't understand. How could she? Was she here only to taunt her – to gloat over her misfortune and get her own back for all the times Irene had bullied and manipulated her? If so, she wanted her gone – wanted both of them gone, and out of what was left of her wretched life.

Irene felt the hot, Judas tears on her cheek, but was incapable of wiping them away.

'It's no good turning on the waterworks,' snapped Maggie. 'You did what you did, now you want to get it off your conscience before you die. Well, it's too late. The damage was done long ago, and if you expect me to forgive you, you'll have a long wait.'

'Don't talk to my wife like that,' snapped William with rare sharpness. 'I don't know what the hell all this is about, but I won't have her upset.'

'I can see this visit was a mistake,' said Olivia as she looked across at Maggie and saw the anger in her. 'You're still too emotionally raw to deal with all this, and Irene's obviously in no fit state to defend herself.'

She looked back at Irene, the loathsome pity clear in her eyes. 'I regret we were never close. I regret any pain this visit might have

234

caused you, but I just wanted to try and bring some kind of peace to this divided family.' She dipped her head. 'I've failed, obviously,' she murmured. 'The hurt you've inflicted over the years has been too great.'

Irene thought her heart would explode. There was a terrible tightness in her chest and a buzzing in her head. The machines were going haywire and the room was swimming around her. She so wanted them both to understand why she did what she did. So needed to explain how at every turn her love had been spurned. How fate had dealt the cards and she'd had a losing hand. She hadn't meant for her life to turn out like this. Hadn't meant to be the cause of such unhappiness. If only . . .

The darkness closed in, and swept her down into the blissful void where thought and pain and loss didn't matter.

Olivia pressed the alarm bell by the bed. 'We need the doctor,' she explained to William. 'Her pulse is racing, her heart is obviously under a great deal of strain, and I don't like her colour.'

'I knew we shouldn't have come,' said Maggie anxiously. 'Now look what we've done.' The anger ebbed swiftly and a look of pain shadowed her face. 'She will be all right, won't she?'

'She'll never be all right,' hissed William as he took Irene's limp hand between his palms and tried to rub some warmth into the chilled skin.

The doctor rushed in, followed swiftly by three nurses, who chivvied them out of the room. They stood like castaways in the corridor, helpless to do anything but wait.

'What was all that about?' William demanded. 'I thought you came to wish her well. To say goodbye. Not cause this sort of trouble.'

He looked from Olivia to Maggie, who'd turned her back on him and was standing at a window, staring out, her arms tightly folded around her waist. 'And who the hell is she, Olivia?' he hissed. 'What's going on here?'

Olivia sighed and went to stand by Maggie, one hand on her shoulder. 'This is Irene's daughter,' she said gently.

William stared at them both in astonishment. Then, having digested this bombshell, he rammed his hands into his pockets and stared at the tips of his scuffed boots. 'If I'm honest with myself,' he muttered, 'it isn't really a surprise, but I still find it hard to believe she could deceive me all these years with something so important.' He paused, his gaze thoughtful as he looked at the two young women. 'But I know Irene very well, and she was always good at hiding things from me. Yet there's something else going on here. Something far more serious that's been eating away at her for the last year or so.'

Olivia eyed him coldly. 'I think disowning one's daughter is serious enough, don't you, William? Not only did she put her up for adoption when she was only hours old, she denied all knowledge of her last year when Maggie came to find her.' She sighed. 'I'm sorry, William. I know this isn't the best of times to tell you something like this, but it's better you know the truth.'

William nodded and his eyes were sad and bewildered as he looked towards the closed door where the medical staff were working on Irene. 'She had so much,' he breathed. 'And she threw it all away.' He looked back at Olivia and Maggie. 'Why would anyone do that?'

Olivia shrugged. 'Irene was always her own worst enemy. She liked to manipulate and play on people's emotions. Enjoyed the power of pulling strings and watching people dance to her tune. Jealousy ruled her, and she couldn't bear anyone else getting the attention. I think that had a lot to do with the way she treated me as a kid. She wanted Mum to herself. Yet, underneath all that spite, I have the feeling she was desperately lonely.'

The doctor emerged from Irene's room, his expression solemn. 'You can go back in now, William. She's medicated and will sleep for a while. But her vital signs are not good. You should prepare yourself for the worst.'

Olivia rested a consoling hand on William's arm. 'I'm sorry,' she murmured.

'She needs me,' he muttered. 'I must go to her.'

Olivia was in the process of turning away when he caught her wrist. 'Thank you for coming, and for telling me about Maggie. But Irene is still my wife, and if it's any consolation, I will stay with her until the end. She'll need the reassurance of knowing she isn't alone any more – that she was loved.'

Olivia and Maggie left the hospital and found Sam leaning against the utility in the car park. They were both grateful for his silence as they dumped Olivia's bag in the back and clambered in.

Olivia stared out of the window, barely noticing the scenery. The weariness that almost overwhelmed her had only a little to do with the lack of sleep and the long hours on the wards. It was the knowledge that she too had thrown away her chance of making things better between herself and Irene. It was strange to feel so sad when there had been nothing but enmity between them. Strange to realise how alone she would be once Irene had died.

She sat there as Maggie and Sam murmured to one another and felt the isolation of an outsider. The singular, invisible barriers that now surrounded her had set her apart, and she realised the world could be a lonely place for someone who had no-one to call their own. Was this how Giles felt? Was this what drove him to flee back to England? She knew it must be, and silently vowed to write him a letter so it would be waiting for him when he reached Wimbledon. For although they could never be lovers, their friendship was too precious to discard.

'Are you okay?' Maggie's hand was on her arm, her eyes concerned.

'Not really,' Olivia admitted.

Maggie nodded. 'I know what you mean. I feel sorry for her, even after what she's done. That must be a terrible way to die – not being able to speak or move – to be absolutely helpless. I'm sorry I lost it back there.'

'It was understandable,' muttered Olivia. 'Irene always had the ability to stir up the emotions.'

Maggie blinked away the tears. 'It's ridiculous,' she said impatiently. 'I dislike her intensely, but seeing her like that – knowing she's dying . . .'

'Time we all had something to eat,' said Sam as he pulled in at a roadhouse some minutes later. 'A good slug of coffee and a fry-up will put us all in a better frame of mind.'

Olivia clambered down and breathed in the hot, humid air. Despite her surprising sorrow at Irene's passing, she was already impatient with the gloomy thoughts that had beset her over the past few hours. Irene had chosen her own path in life, and Olivia couldn't pretend to feel more than pity for her.

As for Giles – she came to the conclusion that his sudden departure had been just what she needed. It had forced her to realise how deep their friendship had been, and how much she had depended upon him. Had forced her to look at her life and take stock. This wasn't the end, she realised, only a new beginning, and it was good to be alive.

She took in her surroundings with pleasure. The birds had returned three days after the hurricane and now the bush was alive with their songs. The sky was blue and clear, the sea sparkling with a million diamonds of light. 'You're right,' she said as she linked arms with Maggie and Sam. 'I'm starving.'

The enormous breakfast was washed down with cup after cup of coffee, and the three of them returned to the utility pleasantly sated.

'Shouldn't take more than a few hours to get up to Port Douglas,' drawled Sam. 'Enjoy the view, girls. It's the best in the world.'

Olivia leaned back against the cracked leather upholstery and looked out of the window as Sam drove along the winding, twisting coastal road. Tall grasses swayed in the warm wind and the scent of flowers drifted up to them as they passed by the shallow tumbles of ebony rocks that spilled down to the beach.

237

The sea was turquoise beneath the cloudless sky, and where the tide had ebbed, it was lying in jewelled pools on sand the colour of palest coral. Tiny, deserted bays fringed the coastline, each sheltered by drifts of sand and rock and the sturdy grasses and shrubs that clung to life on the very edge of the road. This truly was paradise.

Olivia hadn't really known what to expect, for when she'd been a child they had not had a car, and therefore hadn't had the chance to explore further than Cairns. She was pleasantly surprised to find Port Douglas was just a sleepy settlement where the few houses were perched on rolling hills that swept down to the sea, only their roofs visible amongst the lush, verdant tropical surroundings.

Bright flowers peeked from beneath the canopy of palm trees and birds of every hue darted overhead. The town itself consisted of a single road lined with wooden buildings that were shaded by deep verandahs and elegant palms. The beach was sandy, the water blue and enticing.

'Here we are,' said Sam as he pulled in and switched off the engine. 'Ma's little corner of paradise. It would take a crowbar to get her out of here, and I can't say I blame her.'

Olivia eyed the wooden bungalow with pleasure. She could fully understand Sam's relative's reluctance to move. It was perfect. The little house was similar to most in Australia. Constructed from timber, it was set on a gentle slope with views out to sea. The garden was neat behind the picket fence and the bougainvillea smothered the porch and clambered up the stone chimney to the corrugated-iron roof. Palm trees and ferns gave shade to the windows, and the flyscreens and the door had recently been painted bright scarlet in contrast to the white walls.

'Won't she mind having so many visitors at once?' Olivia eyed the house and saw the net curtain tweak at one of the windows. She was feeling nervous all of a sudden, and as it was an unusual emotion, she couldn't analyse it.

Sam laughed. 'The more the merrier,' he said. 'Ma knows we're coming. I radioed through last night. She's probably been cooking up a storm ever since.'

Olivia followed the other two up the neat path and admired the flowers. There were so many exotic varieties she couldn't possibly have named them, but the roses were familiar and smelled wonderful.

She stood back as the door opened and a bustling little woman emerged. Sam's mother-in-law had to be in her late 70's, but as she flung her arms around Sam's waist and berated him for being late, Olivia realised she had the vibrancy of a much younger woman.

The grey hair had been neatly set in waves around a pleasant, homely face that was devoid of make-up. The skin was lined from too many years in the sun and reminded Olivia of a russet apple, yet that didn't detract from the sharply intelligent blue eyes. Dressed in sprigged cotton, the sturdy little woman was the epitome of what everyone expected a grandmother to be – yet her sense of fun, of the ridiculous, could be seen in the outrageous earrings, which swung back and forth as she talked and laughed and was introduced to Maggie.

'I see you're admiring my parrots,' she said brightly as her gaze turned to Olivia and her fingers tweaked the earrings. 'These are my favourites, but I've got lots more.' She cocked her head, her eyes bright with interest. 'You must be Olivia,' she said as she held out her hand.

Olivia nodded and was a little disconcerted by the penetrating gaze that was fixed upon her. This elderly woman reminded her of someone, but for the life of her she couldn't think who it could be. She shook the proffered hand, and smiled. 'Good to meet you at last. I hope you don't mind so many of us turning up at once?'

'Glad you did,' she replied firmly. 'Got enough food indoors to feed a flaming army, so you'd better be hungry.' She pushed the door open and waved them through. 'Come in, come in. No point in standing outside. I expect you could do with a cuppa.'

Olivia followed the others into the narrow hall. The linoleum shone and the walls were colourful with row upon row of family photographs. She would have liked to stop and look at them, but they were being chivvied along and it would appear rude.

The sitting room was over-furnished, but highly polished, the scent of beeswax, almost, but not quite, stifling the aroma of cats. The curtains had been drawn to keep out the sun and it took her a moment to adjust to the dim light after the brightness outside.

Both armchairs were occupied by sleeping cats. The small table under the window was covered in a lace cloth and laid out for tea with what she guessed was the best china. A sideboard and low dresser took up most of the room and were cluttered with ornaments and photographs. The carpet was a nightmare of orange and brown, which clashed horribly with the pink flowery curtains, but in a strange kind of way it didn't matter. For there was a sense of home here, a feeling of peace and settled contentment.

'Shove the cats off and sit down. I'll make the tea.'

Olivia eyed the fat tabby with the baleful yellow glare and decided to let sleeping cats alone. She perched on the edge of a wooden chair by the overladen table and grinned at Maggie. 'Isn't she lovely?'

Maggie grinned back and squeezed Sam's hand. 'Too right.'

239

Sam kissed the top of her head and perched on the arm of the chair. 'Ma's a one-off. Bonzer lady.'

'What do we call her, Sam? She isn't our relative, and it seems disrespectful to call her Ma all the time.'

The old woman came through from the kitchen at the back of the house. She was carrying a teapot which she'd covered in a knitted cosy. Placing it carefully on the table beside Olivia, she stood back and folded her hands. She looked from Sam to Maggie and then down at Olivia. 'I don't mind you calling me Ma,' she said finally. 'After all, that's what I am, and I'm proud of the name.'

Olivia wasn't quite sure about all this. She didn't want to offend this lovely old lady, but the English reticence was too firmly entrenched to show such disrespect to one so senior. The years of being brought up by Eva had indeed left their mark.

The old woman's parrot earrings swung as she laughed and, after shoving the recalcitrant cat off the chair, she sat down. 'You can call me whatever you like, my dear,' she said. 'But I've never been one to stand on ceremony. Your mother would have told you that, I'm sure.'

Olivia stilled. 'My mother? What . . .? How would my mother . . .?'

The plump hand reached out and grasped her fingers. 'You don't remember me at all, do you, luv?'

Olivia's mouth was dry and her pulse was racing as she shook her head.

'The last time we met you were a little girl about to leave on a great big ship for England. You knew me as Jessie.'

Chapter Twenty-Two

Olivia stared, almost speechless with shock. Yet, as she looked at the elderly woman before her, she could see now why she'd reminded her so strongly of someone. It was the eyes, the tilt of the head, and the bustling nature of the little woman, which had stirred up the memories. Age had withered her, but the very essence of Jessie was still there and she wondered how she hadn't realised immediately.

She swallowed, aware of how rude her staring must appear. 'But Irene said you were dead,' she breathed.

Jessie patted her hand and got up again to pour tea. 'She would,' she said flatly.

'But why?' Olivia handed around the cups distractedly. 'What's it to do with Irene if I wanted to see you?'

Jessie loaded up a plate with cake and sandwiches and freshly baked scones and handed it to Sam. 'She had a lot to lose,' she replied enigmatically.

Olivia caught the knowing look that passed between them, and wondered just how much Sam was involved. 'You knew the connection between Jessie and the family, didn't you, Sam?' she demanded. 'Getting us up here was all a ruse, wasn't it?'

'Now, don't go blaming Samuel,' Jessie said mildly as she piled plates and handed them around. 'He was just trying to help.'

Olivia pushed the plate aside. She'd lost her appetite for everything but straight answers. 'Help? In what way?'

Jessie sipped her tea and replaced the cup in the saucer. 'Samuel tells me Maggie already knows about Irene being her mother, and I'm sorry I wasn't able to help her through what must have been an awful time. Irene is not the easiest person to deal with, and I imagine poor Maggie was put through the wringer.'

'You don't know the half of it,' muttered Maggie, her expression bitter. 'And as for you,' she said to Sam. 'Why the hell didn't you say something? Just how long have you known about Jessie's link to me and Olivia?'

Sam tried to put his arm around her shoulder and was shrugged away. 'Aw, don't be like that, Maggs. I thought it would be a nice surprise, and what with the storm and everything . . .' His voice tailed off and he looked at Jessie for help.

Jessie lightly pinched Maggie's cheek. 'You're here now, that's all that matters, darling. And you have no idea how glad that makes me.' She smiled, the tears evident in her eyes. 'It's definitely time for Samuel to settle down again, and although I will always miss my darling daughter, I just know she'd have approved of you. I just know.' She sniffed, the earrings swinging. 'I know there are questions you need to ask, and we will talk later, but for now, let's try and keep a clear head about all this.'

She turned back to Olivia. 'And what about you? Aren't there things you wanted to talk to me about? Things that have worried you enough to bring you to the other side of the world?'

'How did you know that?' Olivia leaned back in the chair and stared at her.

'I didn't,' she said with almost detached calm. 'But after Irene's visit I put two and two together, and your very presence here has proved me right.'

'Irene came up to see you? When was this?'

'About a month ago. Shortly after you went to see her, I imagine.'

Olivia tried to digest this piece of news and all the old bitterness rose again. 'So, not content with lying about your death, Irene came up here to make sure you kept quiet?' She looked into the sad, gentle face and decided this was probably not the time to heap on the misery by telling her of Irene's expected demise. 'I'm sorry if this has caused you trouble, Jessie. I never meant it to.'

Jessie patted her knee. 'No worries, darling,' she said comfortably. 'Irene's behaviour is water off a duck's back,' she said with a sigh. 'She was obviously rattled, and thought she was being clever with her veiled threats. But I know her too well and realised almost immediately what must have happened.' She sipped her tea. 'It was a strange conversation. The sort where nothing much is said but the meaning is very clear nevertheless.'

'Tell me what happened that day, Jessie.' She shot a look at Maggie who was nestled in the crook of Sam's comforting arm, but the inner tension could be seen in the line of her shoulders and in the look of her eyes. 'And don't be afraid of hurting our feelings – Maggie and I are tough. We can take it.'

The bright gaze drifted between Maggie and Olivia, and Jessie placed her cup and saucer on the table. 'Tough you might be,' she said finally. 'But sometimes it's better not to interfere in things beyond our control.'

'I've come a long way, Jessie. I think I've earned the right to know the truth after all these years.'

'Very well,' sighed Jessie. 'I'll tell you what happened.'

Jessie had been cleaning the front windows when the flashy pale-green and white Holden pulled up outside. With whitewall tyres, rear fins and a tinted sun visor, it was top of the range, and Jessie knew her youngest grandson had lusted after such a car ever since he'd seen one in a showroom down in Melbourne.

Intrigued, she remained hidden by the lace curtains. It was probably some city visitor trying to find their way around town. Then she caught her breath as the elegant woman stepped from the car and approached her gate. What on earth was Irene doing all this way north? She hadn't visited for years – something had to be wrong.

Jessie dithered and hesitated as the sharp rap echoed around the house. Irene meant trouble, and Jessie had known her too many years to expect any change in her. Yet Jessie was not a woman who made a habit of avoiding the unpleasant, so she relented and went to open the door. 'You'd better come in,' she said flatly.

'Try not to be too pleased I've come all this way to visit.' Irene was obviously doing her best to swallow the sarcasm, but was unsuccessful.

'Shut the door after you. You're letting in the flies.' Jessie realised she was being ungracious, but that was how Irene affected her and she was too old to change. She heard the screen door slam behind Irene as she led the way down the hall and into her lounge.

'Better sit down,' she said as she grabbed the marmalade cat and sank into a chair with it on her lap. She saw the curl of distaste on Irene's lips as she silently debated whether to move the tabby or not, and the fastidious way she smoothed her skirts before she perched on the very edge of the most uncomfortable chair in the room.

'What do you want, Irene?' she asked finally.

'Why should I want anything?' Irene's tone was almost careless as she stripped off her gloves and looked around in disgust at the room. 'I see you haven't changed the decor in years.'

Jessie ignored the insult. 'Be a first if you didn't want something,' she snorted. 'So why are you here?'

Irene brushed cat hairs from her skirt. 'I have some sad news,' she said with studied solemnity. 'Mother is dead.'

Jessie eyed her thoughtfully. 'I'm sorry to hear that,' she said. 'Eva was a fine woman.'

Irene was obviously growing impatient – Jessie could see it in the way she fidgeted and fiddled with those ridiculous white gloves. 'Did you write to one another over the years?' she asked.

Jessie realised where this could be leading and was careful in her reply. 'For a while,' she replied with a shrug. 'Nothing regular.'

'But you haven't been in touch recently?' Irene persisted.

Jessie wasn't going to make this easy for Irene – not after all she'd put her through in the past. 'Why? What's it to you?'

'No reason,' replied Irene with haste.

Irene never did anything without reason – she was lying – but then why should I be surprised, thought Jessie? Irene wouldn't know the truth if it bit her. 'Heard from Olivia lately?' she asked, knowing it would take Irene off balance and put the conversation back under her control.

'We don't keep in touch,' she said shortly.

'Pity,' Jessie muttered. 'Families should stick together.' Her scrutiny was searing as she continued. 'But then you never were struck on family togetherness, were you, Irene?'

Irene was obviously itching to give full rein to her legendary temper and Jessie wondered how long it would take for that icy veneer to crack. The younger woman looked down at her manicured nails, so red against the white of her skirt.

'Olivia has her own life,' she began. She raised her chin and the two women eyed one another with mutual dislike. 'And now she's inherited Mother's entire estate, she can well afford to go back to England and live in comfortable ignorance. I can't say I'm not bitter. Mother left me nothing but a few bits of old jewellery, but what's done is done.'

'Eva made provision for you when she left for England,' retorted Jessie. 'You had the choice of taking your share of the inheritance then or later. You chose to have it then, and can't expect any more.'

'My inheritance is none of your damn business,' Irene hissed. 'How dare Mother discuss it with you.'

Jessie shrugged. 'You brought the subject up in the first place,' she said gruffly.

Irene glared at her. 'Olivia and I have never got on, but the future is what must concern us now,' she said. She paused and licked her lips. 'I would hate to see lives disrupted by tittle-tattle or gossip – or well-meaning interference on certain people's part.' The smile was stiff and false, the chill hardening her eyes. 'Do I make myself clear?'

Jessie had already guessed why Irene had come to see her, now it was confirmed. Olivia had come to Australia and was probably still here, and asking questions. No wonder Irene was rattled.

244

'I understand perfectly,' she said with studied calm. She stood and dumped the cat back into the chair. 'Your veiled threats don't frighten me, Irene. I'm an old woman and I've seen too many things to be cowed by the likes of you.'

They glared at one another in silence before Jessie spoke again. 'But for once I am in agreement with you. Olivia should be left to live her life without any interference from either of us.'

Irene towered over her as she stood and glared at her. Then she pushed past Jessie and left the house. She stood for a moment on the garden path and breathed deeply before climbing back into her car.

'I watched that fancy Holden roar down the street and disappear around the corner,' said Jessie as she emerged from the memories. 'I stood there for a long while, deep in thought, before turning away and coming back in here.'

She smiled at Olivia and Maggie, wishing she hadn't spoiled their visit – wishing they didn't look so pale and disturbed – yet they had demanded the truth, and it was their right, after all. She poured Samuel more tea. He was the only one enjoying the sumptuous meal she'd prepared.

'This room doesn't get much sun, and I'm grateful for that. It's why I always keep the curtains closed. I'm getting too old to handle the eternal heat, the flies and the stinging, biting things we have up here – yet the idea of returning to England has never been an option. I've been away too long and my roots are firmly entrenched right here in northern Queensland.'

'Mum made the transition easily enough,' said Olivia. 'And she was out here for years.'

'Eva had family to return to and the comfortable cushion of money and connections to sustain her,' Jessie said with mild acceptance. 'I realised there was nothing back in England compared to the opportunities I had here.'

She sat back in the chair and eyed the array of photographs. They were amongst her most precious possessions and she would never part from them. 'I have six children, ten grandchildren and three great-grandchildren, with another one expected any day now,' she said proudly. 'There have been tragedies, of course. Like when my step-daughter Stella, and her little Paul were killed by that terrible fire and poor Samuel was almost beside himself with grief.'

She looked at her son-in-law and smiled. He had finally healed and was so very different to the man who'd come to her in almost inconsolable grief on his return from the war. She suspected the healing was due to Maggie, and she was delighted they had found one another.

'I am at an age where sorrow and death are no longer strangers, and despite everything, this country has been good to me, and to my family. Australia gave me a second chance.'

Her gaze trawled the photographs and settled on the face of her second husband. 'I met Joshua Reynolds shortly after coming north from Melbourne. He was a widower with a young daughter Stella. Eva lent us the money so we could move here to Port Douglas, and raise a family. We had a home and work and altogether a better, more comfortable life than any I might have had in England.'

'Mum spoke of you often,' said Olivia. 'And I can remember you coming to Trinity for visits. But I never realised you still wrote to one another.'

Jessie sighed and rearranged the photographs, pulling the sepia print to the fore. 'We were as different as chalk and cheese,' she said fondly. 'Eva was a real lady, and I was privileged to become her friend.' She picked up the photograph and gave it to Olivia. 'They make a handsome couple, don't they – Eva and Freddy?'

She waited for the photograph to be handed around and then replaced it on the dresser. 'Eva missed him terribly when he went away for months on his surveying trips. She would confide in me, knowing I would never tell anyone just how deeply she felt about those absences. Yet she was like a young bride when he eventually came back home – excited and full of plans, the house coming to life again.'

'Must have made it even harder when he had to leave for yet another trip,' said Olivia.

Jessie nodded. 'She seemed to shrink, physically, but her energy levels rose and she threw herself into charitable works until he returned. She worried me during those frenetic periods, for she seemed too driven.'

'Irene must have changed things,' murmured Olivia. 'I remember Mum telling me how she had so longed for a baby.'

'There were miscarriages and disappointments, but Irene was her joy.' She smiled. 'Mine too. I looked on her as as my own, and both of us invested so much love in that precious child – dreamed so many dreams.'

Jessie fell silent, the sadness making her feel old. 'In hindsight, I realise we spoiled her. Made her what she is today.'

Her gaze fell on the photographs of Irene, and she bit her lip. She had once loved her with the same passion as Eva, yet it was all too easy to equate that golden-haired child with the malicious woman

246

she'd encountered before the hurricane. For the eyes were determined as they stared out of the photographs, the poses markedly self-possessed for one so young.

Jessie clicked her tongue with impatience. 'Irene and I lived in Trinity for a while, during the Great war. We had the most awful rows. Irene was manipulative, even as a child, and I can still remember the tantrums, the jealousies, the almost wanton need to be the centre of attention that finally destroyed the relationship between Irene and her mother.'

'Was that when she was expecting me?' asked Maggie.

Jessie looked at the slender, pretty young woman sitting so closely to her beloved son-in-law and felt a surge of love. 'Yes,' she said softly.

'What happened between Irene and Mother to cause such a rift?' asked Olivia. 'It must have been very serious.'

'It was,' muttered Jessie. She eyed Olivia for a long moment and knew where this conversation was heading. Olivia had not asked the question she'd expected. The young woman was probing, questioning, leading this conversation into darker shadows. And Jessie knew she would not be satisfied until she had all the answers.

Jessie opened a dresser drawer and took out the bundle of letters. Her spirits were low as she looked at the familiar handwriting. She missed Eva, and wished she were here to help. Missed the flow of news that had trickled steadily across the world over the years. For her letters had brought the woman who wrote them much closer. Had once again rolled back the years and strengthened the unlikely ties that bound them.

She fumbled with the envelope, gave up on it and put it in her lap. 'I've left my reading glasses in the bedroom,' she explained. 'But I don't need them. I know this letter by heart. It was Eva's last, written almost a year and a half ago.'

'So you knew she was dead when Irene came to see you?' Olivia had tears in her lovely brown eyes. 'What did she say in the letter, Jessie?'

'She expressed her love for you, her gratitude for my friendship, and her deep regrets that the breach with Irene would never be healed. She also questioned certain decisions she'd made many years before, and the consequences of any action taken to destroy all traces of the truth. She begged me for guidance. Her conscience would not let her rest.'

'Why? What had she done? Did she collude with Irene over my adoption? Is that what made her feel guilty?' Maggie had thrust herself forward in the chair, her face pale, her eyes dark with anguish.

'No, my darling. She had nothing whatsoever to do with what

247

happened to you. In fact she tried her utmost to find you. But Irene was saying nothing and there were no records to be found. When Eva left for England with Olivia, she had to finally accept there was nothing more she could do but hope you were safe and happy.'

Maggie burst into tears and Sam held her. Olivia blinked away her own tears and tightly bunched her hands in her lap.

Jessie looked down at the faded handwriting and sighed. There had been no response to her urgent reply, only a letter passed on through a London solicitor, which contained the deeds for her little house and a cheque for a thousand pounds. Eva had thought of her right to the end, ensuring she was comfortable in her old age.

The fat ginger tomcat stalked across the room and wound himself around her ankles. His purr was a deep rumble, a reminder he needed feeding. Jessie stroked him absent-mindedly. 'Wait on, Blue,' she murmured. 'I'm busy.'

'So what was on her mind?' Olivia was tense and very still as she sat at the table and Jessie could see she was battling to keep her emotions under control.

'Your mother knew she was dying when she wrote this letter,' she said softly. 'I wrote back at once, but it was too late. I've since wondered if Eva gave in to her conscience – or whether time had simply run out, leaving fate to decide the outcome.'

She looked back at Olivia. 'After Irene's visit I realised you had to be here in Australia and asking questions. It was then I rang through to Samuel for advice. I knew you couldn't be far from Trinity.'

Her smile was soft, the regret a deep ache that would not be denied. 'Your presence here, and the questions you have, proves to me that Eva couldn't destroy the truth.'

The silence stretched and the tension in the room was almost tangible. 'You found the papers, didn't you?'

Olivia nodded. 'They were the reason for this journey home,' she muttered.

She stood and pulled the thin cotton curtains aside and leaned against the window frame as she stared out at the surrounding tropical rainforest. Coming so soon after the terrible scenes in Irene's hospital room and the long hours on the wards, she wondered if she was truly ready for what was to come. Closing her eyes, she thought of Priscilla, her childhood companion, the one person who had known her better than anyone. What would her imaginary friend's advice have been for a moment like this?

Olivia took a deep breath. The time for childish things was past – she had to see through the glass darkly and face the demons alone. Priscilla couldn't help her any more. She turned back to face the

248

others and looked at Maggie. She could understand all too well how this must be affecting her, and wished wholeheartedly she didn't need to take this conversation to its inevitable conclusion. Yet it was time for the truth. She and Jessie owed her that at least.

'I cannot begin to describe the horror I experienced when I found those documents. Or the heartache.' She fell silent, remembering those dark days of tears and pain, and the realisation that Eva had lied to her. 'Yet, as the months have gone on, I've realised they made sense of so many things that up until then, had remained a mystery.' She held Maggie's gaze and tried to convey her love and support silently. 'Then I came home to Trinity and discovered you were also a part of the equation. That threw me totally.'

Maggie felt as if she'd been slapped. 'Thanks,' she retorted. 'I thought we were friends?'

'We are,' said Olivia as she grasped Maggie's hand in earnest entreaty. 'Please don't ever doubt that.'

She looked deeply into Olivia's eyes and wanted to believe her, and yet a part of her couldn't. Hurt and isolation had made her wary – had ensured her mistrust of anyone. Even her love for Sam was tempered by the fear that one day he might leave her – and the inbuilt safety mechanism was still firmly in place to protect the soft, inner core that could so easily be damaged.

Maggie lifted her chin, aware the earlier tears had shown her as weak. Above all, she decided, she must maintain the outward show of cheerful acceptance and rough good humour they all expected from her. 'We'll be right,' she said with forced brightness. 'Reckon there's not much more that can shock me after the sort of life I've had.'

Olivia returned to her place at the window, her arms folded tightly around her waist.

'You sound so very bitter,' said Jessie, her face drawn with anxiety.

Maggie gave a cough of derision. 'Not really surprising when you consider what I've been through.'

The silence was profound, and Maggie felt the comforting warmth of Sam's arm around her shoulders. She leaned against him and, as she began to retell her story, she felt the anger and bitterness pour out. She held nothing back, despite the knowledge that this elderly woman was being hurt by her revelations, for Jessie must have been part of the betrayal – an important influence on Irene's decision to be rid of her illegitimate child.

'So, now you know it all,' she said finally. She looked at Jessie, her emotions raw. 'I can understand why Irene didn't want me,' she said. 'I was a mistake. A shameful result of some misguided affair that would damage her reputation and ruin her life. But you say Eva tried to find me all those years ago. Why didn't you tell her where I was? You must have known about the orphanage. It would have been so easy to trace me from there.'

'I didn't know,' said Jessie flatly. 'Irene told me nothing of what had happened to you.'

Maggie pushed away from Sam and stood, the anger running through her in hot waves. 'You must have known,' she shouted. 'She was living with you at the time. You said so.'

Jessie nodded, seemingly unfazed by Maggie's outburst. 'True enough,' she said. 'But I suspect you already have some idea of how resourceful and sly Irene can be, and I was certainly no match for her.'

She looked down at the cat on her knee and absently stroked the ginger fur. 'I realise you probably don't believe me, but I had no idea of what she'd done until it was too late.'

'But Olivia found those documents,' Maggie persisted. 'Eva must have discovered the truth eventually.'

'No,' said Olivia with unaccustomed sharpness.

'What do you mean?' Maggie crossed the room and stood in front of Olivia, forcing her to look her in the eye. 'Why else would those bits of paper bring you all the way back here if they didn't reveal my existence?'

Maggie saw the look that passed between Olivia and Jessie. It was fleeting, but Maggie could have sworn it was a silent plea for help. 'Come on, Olivia,' she said roughly. 'You say you're my friend. So prove it. Tell me the bloody truth and stop this nonsense once and for all.'

Olivia took a deep breath. 'Those papers were nothing to do with you,' she said clearly into the silence. 'I didn't know anything about you until that night we spent on the beach together.' She took Maggie's hands. 'They were simply the proof that everything I had ever taken for granted was a lie,' she said softly.

Chapter Twenty-Three

'Those bits of paper you found are only a part of the truth,' said Jessie, breaking the tension. 'To understand why they existed at all, you need to hear the full story.'

Maggie slumped back into the chair and Sam pulled her closely into his embrace as if to protect her from anything Jessie might divulge. Olivia returned to her seat by the table, her face white and anxious.

Jessie realised they were hurt and confused, and could only hope the truth might make some amends for the decisions she and Eva had made all those years ago. She ran her fingers lightly through the cat's ginger fur and felt the reassuring rumble of his purring. If only Eva were here, she thought sadly. She was so much better at expressing herself, so much more capable of finding the right words.

Jessie looked at the photographs on the dresser, her gaze searching for and finding Eva. The tiny figure in the elegant white gown gave no hint of the ferocious tenacity and strength of character she possessed, but it could be seen in the dark eyes and strong chin. The thick, wavy hair and delicate cheekbones spoke of femininity, but Eva's will had been stronger than any man's, her thinking beyond the constrictions of the society in which she lived. Not for her the silent acquiescence of her generation of women who rarely thought for themselves and were happy to remain in their husband's shadow.

She was a woman before her time, Jessie realised. A woman who'd had to learn to be independent. A woman who met each crisis in her life and dealt with it as best she could and to hell with what society made of her. But the scandal of what had happened with Irene had nearly broken her. She'd had no alternative but to return to England.

As she sat there in the expectant hush she thought she could feel the strength of Eva's presence, and as she began to talk, it was as if Eva was telling her what to say.

*

251

Eva paced the floor, her thoughts flitting from one thing to another as she felt the silence of the great Melbourne house closing in. It was so lonely without Irene and Jessie, and the worry over Freddy's whereabouts was giving her sleepless, restless nights.

Not that she wasn't concerned for Irene's welfare – she was – but at least she knew she was safe and well and being looked after properly. Which was more than could be said for Freddy. He was out in that terrible wilderness where a man could lie injured and undiscovered for months, and the images of what could have happened to him were so haunting she couldn't bear thinking about them.

She stopped walking and stood at the long windows that overlooked the garden. The wide plot stretched behind the house in a swathe of verdant green bordered by a riotous mixture of flowers and delicately blossomed trees. It was raining as usual, the temperature cool for summer, reminding her of England. The scent of the roses emphasised the memory, and she experienced an almost overwhelming desire to return home – to see her parents and sisters again, and feel the security that only family could bring in times of trouble.

Eva let the muslin curtain drop. 'Stuff and nonsense,' she muttered. 'Father would say "I told you so" and Mama would agree with him.' They had been against her coming to this raw colonial outpost – against her marrying Frederick despite his family connections. To admit she wasn't happy was admitting defeat – and that was not Eva's way.

She sat down in her favourite chair by the window and picked up a book. Moments later she set it aside. It was impossible to concentrate with so much on her mind.

Staring through the sheath of muslin, she put her hands gently on the burgeoning mound of her unborn child. Freddy had already left on his latest surveying expedition when she discovered she was to be a mother again, and she was almost relieved she hadn't told him her news, for there had been disappointments before. Yet the promise of new life might have sped him home sooner – might have made him less willing to take risks.

She sighed and her thoughts wandered naturally to Irene, who was due to have her own baby any time now. How she wished she could be there in Queensland. Mothers and daughters should be together at such moments – should be enforcing the ties that bound them, bringing them closer.

Eva sighed. She had never really been close to Irene, she realised. Had never really known her at all, for if she had, would the girl have had such an unsuitable affair? Would she now be planning to give her baby away with as little thought as she might have for throwing away an old dress? Her hands stilled and she frowned as her own unborn

252

child moved inside her. Was it a sin to love too much? An error of judgement to allow one's precious child to become the focus of all one did and said? Was it a mother's lot to bear the children and sit by as they broke her heart?

Her eyes misted with tears. Irene had been such a beautiful child, but these past two years had revealed a wanton, spoilt young woman who was a stranger to the truth unless it suited her. Yet the times they lived in meant her punishment was harsh, Eva admitted. To have to make the terrible sacrifice of giving her baby away so there was some hope for a decent future was something Eva doubted she could do. But then, she silently admitted, I desperately wanted my babies. They were planned and eagerly awaited – their loss mourned deeply – how could I ever understand what Irene's going through?

The light tap on the door interrupted her thoughts, and Eva smoothed her skirts and patted her hair. 'Come.'

Eliza was the new housemaid and still a little rough around the edges, but she was learning, Eva noticed, as the girl sketched a curtsy. 'It's the Governor, Mrs Hamilton. I wasn't sure if you was receiving this afternoon.'

Eva felt the chill of foreboding. 'Show him in, Eliza.'

The Governor was a large man in every sense of the word. Over six feet tall, with broad shoulders and a hearty voice, Maurice Wilson seemed to fill the room. 'Dear lady,' he boomed as he towered over her and kissed the air above her fingers.

'Governor Wilson,' she said with an inclination of her head. 'May I offer you some refreshment?'

He shook his leonine head, his expression grim. 'Thank you, but no, dear lady. This is not really a social call.'

Eva nodded to Eliza, who left the room and closed the door behind her. She felt faint, but was damned if she was going to make a fool of herself in front of this appalling man. Charming he might be, but Maurice Wilson, Governor of Melbourne, was all too obviously of the lower classes. A man who'd made good in this relatively new colony, regardless of his suspect background.

She sat down with as much dignity as she could muster under the circumstances. 'You have news of my husband.' It was a statement, the tone firm despite the rising fear.

Maurice Wilson nodded and sat down on the couch beside her. 'A runner came in from the last search party two nights ago,' he said, his face solemn.

Eva's fingers were tightly clasped on her lap, and she could feel the throb of her pulse in her neck. 'Two nights ago? Why wasn't I informed immediately?'

253

'I thought it best to wait until we had something definite to tell you,' he said ponderously.

'He's dead, isn't he?' Eva's tone was flat, her expression a mask of control which hid the inner anguish.

'They found him in a dry riverbed. Judging by his injuries, the tracker can only surmise he was thrown from his horse and tried to make his way to water. As you probably know, the drought in the Northern Territories has been particularly bad. He didn't stand a chance. I'm sorry.'

Poor Freddy, she thought as the image of him crawling across that harsh, red desert in search of water came to haunt her. Poor, darling Freddy. If only you had been as other men and stayed at home. She dipped her chin, her eyes blinded with unshed tears. But that wasn't his way. She'd loved him for his sense of adventure. Admired him for the courage and unflagging enthusiasm for this tough, merciless land. Freddy had died as he'd lived – in the heart of the country he loved. 'What of the others?' she asked.

Maurice Wilson patted her clasped hands. 'Only one survivor, dear lady, and he's too sick to make any sense as yet. The search party found him several miles away from your husband, so it appears the expedition became separated.' He paused, his fingers stroking the back of her hand. 'Is there someone I can call to be with you? I understand your daughter is visiting friends in the north.'

Eva shook her head and eased her fingers from his grasp. She didn't want him touching her. Needed to be alone. Needed him gone.

'They are bringing him back to Melbourne, and I've taken the liberty of arranging the funeral. I hope you don't mind?'

She looked at him, her mind numb with grief. 'How soon?' she asked.

'In three days,' he replied.

Eva sat in silence, her thoughts frozen.

'Are you sure I can't contact anyone for you, Eva?' Maurice's voice was unusually restrained, but, thankfully, he didn't attempt to touch her again. 'I could send a wire up to your daughter?'

Eva stood, her emotions rigorously under control. 'I will contact my daughter,' she said firmly. 'But there is something you can do for me. I wish to see the survivor.'

He hesitated. 'I really don't . . .'

She held up her hand to silence him. 'I wish to see him today, Governor. He's the only one who can tell me about my poor husband's last days. Will you make the arrangements?'

'As you wish,' he sighed. 'But don't expect too much from him. He's very ill.'

Eva held out her hand. 'Thank you for coming, Governor. I know it couldn't have been easy.'

His vast hand smothered her fingers. 'I will let you know the details of the funeral arrangements,' he said solemnly. 'And if there is anything else I can do, you need only ask. Frederick was a good man and much admired at Government House.'

Eva waited until he'd closed the door behind him, then she slumped back down on the couch and gave in to her grief.

Jessie returned to the present and tipped the cat from her lap. 'I'm going to make another pot of tea,' she said firmly. 'All this talking is thirsty work.'

She refused Samuel's offer of help and gathered up the tea things before hurrying into the tiny kitchen at the back of the house. Setting the kettle on the hob, she fed the cats. She needed these few quiet moments to think. Needed to get things in the right order. It had all happened so long ago, and although the memories were clear, the timing was crucial if she wasn't to make a hash of it.

Filling the teapot, she washed and dried the cups and carried everything back into the other room. She didn't like the heavy silence that greeted her, or the strained smiles, and was forcibly reminded of the day Eva had arrived in Trinity.

The tea was hot and strong and went some way to reviving her flagging spirits. The sooner everything was out in the open, the better, she decided. The strain was beginning to tell and she was getting too old for all this. Too old to be digging up painful memories – too old to carry the burden of the secret the three of them had shared for so many years.

'Mother told me about the funeral,' said Olivia into the silence. 'She found it overwhelming and was glad when it was over.'

Jessie nodded. 'The Governor pulled out all the stops,' she said. 'The nearest thing to a state funeral he could provide. The streets were crowded, the cortège endless, with black horses and black plumes and a glass hearse. There were speeches and dignitaries and an enormous lunch provided at Government House. Eva was exhausted by it all and would have preferred to say her goodbyes to Frederick in private without all the razzamatazz.'

'All the more difficult because of her condition,' said Olivia.

Jessie saw something in her eyes that made her uneasy. She decided to answer the question as asked and ignore further implications. 'It certainly didn't help,' she said gruffly. 'But Eva was a tough little woman. Nothing got her down for long.'

Olivia looked at her hard, but remained silent. Jessie finished her tea and tried to settle back in the chair. She peered through the gap in the curtains as she attempted to put her thoughts in order. It was growing dark, she realised with surprise. The day had flown – but it was far from over.

'Did Eva ever find out what happened on that expedition?' asked Maggie. 'Did she get to speak to the survivor?'

Jessie looked at Maggie and nodded. 'Yes. But the short conversation posed more questions than answered them.'

'He couldn't tell her much, then?'

Jessie's expression was grim. 'He knew a lot more than he was letting on. But, considering the sort of man he was, it shouldn't have come as a surprise.'

'Why, what happened?'

Jessie stared out of the window. She could remember Eva telling her in great detail of that meeting. Could remember every word of their conversation.

Eva entered the hushed hospital ward and sat down on the hard wooden chair beside the iron bedstead. She looked at the man lying there and wondered how they had reached this crossroads in their lives. They had all started out with such hope, and now, here she was, a widow.

His eyelids fluttered and he turned to look at her. 'I'm sorry,' he murmured. 'So sorry, Eva.'

Eva hitched her handbag closer, her gloved hands tight on the handle. 'What happened?' she demanded.

He moved his legs beneath the sheets and winced. 'We got separated. Fred said he knew where there was water. Wouldn't listen to me, and went off on his own.'

'You were the guide, his right-hand man. You should have gone with him,' she retorted.

'I had three other sick men to look after. Fred was quite capable of making his own way and his own decisions.'

Eva glared at him. 'How is it you are the only survivor?'

'I knew of an old Aboriginal watering hole. It was a gamble, of course, there was no guarantee it hadn't dried up, but I had to try.' His smile was weary and didn't quite reach his eyes as he turned to look at her. 'I was lucky, that's all.'

Eva looked at him. She knew the kind of man he was – a philanderer, a liar – and far too ambitious. Despite his injuries, she couldn't bring herself to like him – or believe him. The words were too glib, as if they'd been rehearsed, and there was something in the way his eyes shifted away from her that said he wasn't telling her everything.

256

'You seem to have a charmed life,' she said coldly. 'Out of sixteen men, you are the only one to have come out of the Territories alive.

Their gazes held and the silence stretched. He was the first to look away.

'But because you survived, and because I know you for the man you really are, your luck has just run out,' said Eva. 'Not only have I lost my husband because of you – I have also lost a daughter, and probably a grandchild.'

He turned his head, the fire of his hair gleaming in the stream of light coming through the windows. All pretence was gone from his eyes, which had an arctic gleam to them. 'Your husband was a fool and your daughter a slut,' he said nastily. 'You should look to yourself before you cast blame.'

Eva felt the blood rush to her face and she strengthened the grip on her handbag. Deciding not to rise to his taunts, she changed the subject. 'What are your plans for the future?'

A gleam of something unpleasant lit his eyes. 'My wife is dead. I have four daughters to raise and the ability to earn enough will be hampered for a long time by the injuries I've incurred during your husband's last expedition.'

Eva understood him completely, and had come prepared. She twisted the gold clasp and opened the handbag, pulling out a banker's note. 'This should support you and your daughters for some time,' she said as she held the money order out. 'But it comes with the proviso that you leave this part of Australia, and never attempt to contact me or my daughter again.'

His eyes widened as he saw the amount she was prepared to pay him.

'This is not negotiable, and there will be no more,' she said firmly. 'If you should be tempted to blackmail me, then I will bring into question your part in this fatal expedition.' She leaned closer to him so her words couldn't be overheard. 'I believe you abandoned my husband,' she murmured. 'I believe you wanted only to save your own skin. God only knows what happened out there between you and Freddy, but I have a good imagination as well as a keen intelligence. Cross me again, and you'll find I'm a dangerous adversary.'

Eva threw the money order onto the sheet and stood up. 'I regret the day we met, Bluey MacDonald. Goodbye.'

'Bluey MacDonald,' breathed Maggie. 'My father.'

Jessie looked down at her fingers. 'I'm sorry, Maggie. It can't be easy to learn about him like this.'

Maggie's face was ashen. 'Do you know where he is now?'

Jessie shook her head. There had been rumours of him resettling on the western coast. Whispers that he'd used Eva's money to find himself a rich wife. But Maggie didn't need further evidence of her father's failings – it was bad enough to know he was a wrong 'un.

'That just about puts the tin lid on it,' snapped Maggie. 'My mother's spiteful and my father's a weasel.' She looked up into Sam's face. 'Still want to marry me?' she asked. 'Now you know what kind of people I come from?'

Sam kissed the top of her head and drew her back into his embrace. 'I'm not marrying them,' he said softly. 'I'm marrying you – and don't you dare go crook on me now, Maggs. I've already ordered a new suit.'

She grinned and buried her face against his arm. 'This settles it then,' she giggled. 'God forbid you waste a new suit.'

Jessie felt the relief flood through her. Fate had brought Bluey MacDonald and Frederick Hamilton together on that long trek across the Nullarbor. His influence had eventually destroyed Eva's family. Yet Maggie and Samuel would move on from this day because their love was strong enough to withstand anything – and Bluey MacDonald's part in this family's unfortunate history would remain in the background where it belonged.

Olivia cleared her throat. 'Did you hear from him again?' she asked.

Jessie saw how pale she was, how tense and still, as if she knew this was not the end to the tale. She busied herself by pouring tea, and taking a sip. It was sour and tepid and did nothing to ease her thirst. Ignoring the question, but knowing it would have to be answered at some point, she returned to the events that affected Eva during those terrible days.

'Eva had to move out of the house shortly after the funeral,' Jessie began. 'The house belonged to the government and the new surveyor and his family were due to arrive within weeks. Eva packed up everything and put most of it in storage. Then, despite her doctor's advice, began the long journey north to be with me and Irene.'

Eva arrived in Trinity on 10 March 1915. The tiny house had been scrubbed and polished until everything gleamed, and Jessie was eagerly waiting by the window for the first sight of the carriage.

'Remember, Jessie,' said Irene as she came to stand beside her. 'You're to leave the talking to me.'

Jessie folded her arms and glared back at her. 'She has a right to know the truth,' she said stubbornly.

The fair curls bounced as Irene shook her head. 'And I'll tell her,' she snapped. 'But when I choose to. One word from you and I'll make your life hell. Is that understood?'

Jessie bit her lip. She had never lied to Eva, and didn't approve of what Irene was planning to do. 'You haven't exactly made it easy anyway,' she retorted. 'Now you're asking me to go along with something that is impossible to forgive.' She shook her head. 'Eva isn't stupid, Irene. She'll know I'm hiding something from her.'

Jessie's arm was grasped in tight, hurtful fingers. 'Then you'd better make sure you play the part,' she hissed. 'You'll do as you're told.' She twisted Jessie's arm. 'Or I'll tell her you've been bringing Joshua Reynolds in here and sleeping with him in the next room to mine. I'll tell her he's made a pass at me, and make sure he'll never work in that school again.'

Jessie's eyes were watering. Irene was hurting her arm. 'That's a wicked lie,' she gasped. 'Joshua's never been in the house – and as for making a pass at you ...' The words failed her.

'You and I both know he hasn't the brains to do such a thing, but Mother doesn't. I'm sure she and the school board can be persuaded otherwise.'

The jingle of harness echoed up the sandy lane. Jessie returned Irene's glare, then looked away. The girl could be very persuasive, and at the end of the day, Jessie was only a servant – it would be her word against Irene's. She was in a no-win situation.

'She's coming,' she said through a constricted throat. 'Hadn't you better go out and meet her?'

Irene smiled and patted her hair. 'Why don't we both go?' she suggested. She could afford to be generous now she'd got her own way. 'I'm sure Mother would like to see us both after such a long absence.'

Jessie stood in the shadows of the porch as Irene ran down the path to greet the carriage. She watched as Eva struggled down the steps and embraced her daughter, and noticed how drawn and ill she looked. Eva had been hit hard by Frederick's death and the long journey coming so soon after had obviously been too much.

Walking up the path with her arm around Irene's waist, Eva smiled. 'Jessie,' she murmured as she reached out a hand. 'It's so good to see you again. I've missed you.'

The two women embraced and Jessie was shocked by Eva's frailty. There was nothing of her. She drew back and forced a smile. This homecoming would not be pleasant for Eva, and Jessie realised it was up to her to remain strong – for she would be needed now more than ever. 'Good to see you too,' she said with forced brightness. 'Come on in out of this awful sun and I'll make you a cup of tea.'

259

Eva laughed. 'Jessie and her cups of tea,' she joked to Irene. 'The panacea for all ills and disasters – the answer to everything.' Her step was more sprightly as she went into the house and admired the burnished copper, the freshly washed curtains and shining linoleum. 'You've made it all very homely, Jessie,' she said as she took the pins from her hat and mopped her brow with a scrap of handkerchief.

'I done me best,' said Jessie, as she organised the coachman's unloading of the bags. 'But the dust is just as bad up here as it is in Melbourne, and of course the sand is impossible – gets everywhere.'

Eva smiled at her and Jessie saw the weariness shadowing her eyes, the deep sadness etched around her mouth. 'You've always been a good home-maker, Jessie.' She clasped her hand. 'Speaking of which, I understand there's to be a wedding soon? When do I get to meet Mr Reynolds?' she asked.

Jessie blushed. 'It's a school day, so Joshua's in Cairns with Stella. I've asked them over for Sunday lunch, if that's all right?'

'Of course. This is your home, Jessie,' said Eva firmly. 'I will be delighted to meet Joshua and his little girl after hearing so much about them in your letters.'

Jessie settled Eva in the lounge with Irene. The bags had been carried into the third small bedroom and she paid off the driver before hurrying into the tiny kitchen at the back of the house. She made the tea, her hands clumsy as the tension mounted. Irene and Eva were talking, catching up on the news, commiserating over Freddy's death and the horrors of the pompous funeral. The house was small, and although neither woman raised their voice, their words easily carried. Jessie could hear everything.

'How are you, my dear? I got Jessie's wire to say everything went smoothly.'

'I'm well, thank you, Mother,' replied Irene. 'But I shall be glad when I get my figure back. None of my pretty clothes fit me any more.'

'And the baby? The little girl? Was it very hard to give her up?'

There was a long silence, and Jessie hovered in the kitchen doorway.

'I've changed my mind,' said Irene. 'For now, anyway.'

Jessie realised she'd been holding her breath and let it out in a long sigh. Yet the tension was almost unbearable, and she found she was clinging to the door handle as if her life depended upon it.

'But that's wonderful, darling. I knew you couldn't just give her away. Babies are so precious, and once they are a part of our lives it is impossible not to love them.'

'Oh, I don't love it,' said Irene.

260

'You don't love her?' Eva's tone was incredulous. 'Why keep her then?'

'I've got my reasons,' replied Irene.

'Which are?' Eva's tone matched Irene's coolness.

'It's pretty enough and doesn't cry too much,' she retorted. 'And once Bluey sees it he's bound to change his mind and marry me.'

Jessie closed her eyes and took a shallow, trembling breath.

'What's he got to do with all this?' demanded Eva.

'He's its father,' retorted Irene. 'He has everything to do with it.'

'You can't use a child to blackmail a man into marrying you, Irene. Have you no pride, no sense of decency or shame?'

'Pride's a pretty poor commodity when you're an unmarried mother,' snapped Irene. 'As for decency. Hmph. It's his child as well as mine – and now he's widowed, he can't deny either of us. He's coming up here next week to visit, and I can guarantee we'll be going back to Melbourne as husband and wife,' she finished triumphantly.

'And what if your plans fail? What then?' Eva's tone was chill, the words clipped.

'I'll have it adopted,' said Irene.

'You really are a bitch, aren't you?' Eva spat. 'A spoilt, selfish little bitch. How dare you use a child like that.'

'Why not? It might as well serve some purpose. It's too young to know any different if it stays with me or goes somewhere else.'

Jessie leaned against the doorpost. The tears were hot and blinding, but she refused to let them fall. That poor, darling, nameless little baby would be better off anywhere than with that harpy, she thought with bitterness. But at least Eva was fighting for her. At least there was a voice to speak out on her innocent behalf.

Eva was silent for a long while. 'You mind is obviously made up, Irene,' she said eventually. 'She is your child, unfortunately, and as you seem hell-bent on this course of action, there is little I can do. But I'll tell you this. I will never forgive you for this wanton abuse of motherhood. That baby is an innocent victim whatever the outcome.'

There was a rustle of skirts as Eva rose from her chair and headed for the hall. 'Jessie?' she called. 'I know you're listening. What do you have to say about all this?'

Jessie smeared the tears from her eyes and took a deep breath. Eva didn't know the half of it, but Irene was watching her and she knew she had to remain silent. 'I don't like it, Mrs Hamilton. I don't like it a bit,' she said gruffly.

'Me neither,' retorted Eva. 'But it seems we have little choice but

261

to go through this charade.' She took Jessie's arm. 'Come, let me see this child. Does she have a name?'

Maggie stared at Jessie in horror. 'Why didn't you do something to stop her?' she demanded. 'You let that bitch use me like a pawn in some terrible game of chess. I was a baby, for God's sake. A tiny baby!'

Jessie could understand her rage – knew how it felt. 'Maggie,' she began as she reached out to her.

'Don't touch me,' snarled Maggie. 'I despise you.'

'Fair go, Maggie,' gasped Sam. 'You can't talk to Ma like that. She only did what she was told.'

Maggie stood, the anguish and fury boiling over and out of control. 'So did the SS!' she shouted. 'They were carrying out orders too, and millions died.'

The slap was sharp and echoed in the silence. Maggie gasped, her hand flying to her cheek where Olivia's fingers had scorched a stinging trail.

'Calm down,' Olivia said firmly. 'You're getting hysterical and it's not helping any of us.'

Maggie was stiff with resentment as Olivia pulled her close and held her tightly. 'It's all right for you,' she snapped. 'You weren't used and left on the bloody scrap heap. What the hell do you know about anything with your happy childhood and your loving mother?'

Olivia drew back, the hurt evident in her eyes. 'I'm not going to apologise for that,' she said with studied calm. 'I was lucky, and I can't begin to imagine how it must have been for you.' Her expression softened. 'But there's no need to take it out on Jessie. She was a pawn in this awful game, just as much as you.'

'Maggie. Please listen to me.' Jessie's voice was tearful. 'You don't understand.'

Maggie looked down at the little woman and felt nothing but disgust. 'I understand all too well,' she said coldly. 'And I'm not staying here to listen to any more of this.'

'Yes, you will.' Jessie's voice was commanding as she hauled herself out of the chair and blocked Maggie's departure. 'Sit down, Maggie.'

Maggie hesitated, the shock of Jessie's vehement outburst making her suddenly unsure of what to do. She looked at Olivia, whose face was pale and taut with some inner pain. Looked at Sam, who was obviously confused and saddened by what was happening. 'Why should I?' she demanded with truculent bravado.

'Because I say so,' retorted Jessie, with arms folded and shoulders square. 'This is my chance to put things right, and I will not be silenced any more.'

Maggie returned to her chair, and experienced a surge of warmth as Sam forgave her outburst and held her close. She took a deep breath. Perhaps it didn't matter that she'd been used as a means to an end, she thought through her pain. It was now that mattered, and the bright, hopeful future she would have with Sam. Yet the knowledge of Jessie's revelations would remain with her always, and she would have to bury it deep if it wasn't to destroy her.

'Strikes me you've said enough already,' she muttered. 'Irene's plotting obviously didn't work, otherwise I wouldn't have ended up in that orphanage.'

Jessie shook her head. 'I'm so sorry, Maggie. I haven't expressed myself very well at all, and now I've simply made things worse.'

Maggie stilled. 'How could they be worse?' she asked.

Jessie sat back down, her chin dipping to her chest. It was as if she was bereft of the spirit that had brought her this far, and she seemed to shrink and grow even older. 'It didn't happen like that at all,' she said softly.

Eva could bear it no longer. The baby's crying was breaking her heart. She climbed from her sickbed, bent over the cradle and picked her up. 'Poor little mite's wet and hungry,' she murmured. 'She shouldn't be left to cry for so long.'

Irene shrugged as she studied her reflection in the mirror. 'So feed it,' she said as she smoothed her hands over her hips and admired her restored figure.

'She isn't thriving,' said Eva. 'You should be feeding her yourself. There's no substitute for a mother's milk.'

Irene curled her lip. 'It's bad enough being trussed up like a turkey without stinking of milk as well.' She pinched her cheeks to bring more colour to her face and tweaked a curl into order. 'Get Jessie to clean her up, there's plenty of milk in the kitchen. And hurry. He'll be here soon.'

Eva eyed her daughter and wondered how such coldness was possible. She carried the baby into the kitchen, and while Jessie warmed the milk, she changed the sodden napkin. The baby gurgled and kicked her chubby legs. She was such a sweet little thing, with big brown eyes and a head of rich brown curls. How could anyone fail to love her?

Jessie handed her the bottle in silence, their eyes meeting across the table in mutual despair as Eva fed the child. If only Irene would take an interest in her, Eva thought, she might come to realise the enormity of what she was planning.

'I told you to leave her to Jessie,' said Irene as she came into the kitchen. 'I need you to help me get ready.'

'She's nearly finished,' said Eva softly as the baby's lashes feathered the chubby cheek and the eyes drooped in sleep.

'Now, Mother.'

Eva noticed the high spots of colour on Irene's cheeks and the glint of determination in her eyes. Irene was so used to being the centre of attention she obviously couldn't bear taking second place. Even to her own child.

Eva gently handed the sleepy baby to Jessie. 'You appear to be dressed,' she said to Irene. 'What's so urgent?'

'My hair,' snapped Irene. 'I need you to do something about the way it falls at the back.' She turned to Jessie. 'When it's finished puking, dress it in those new things Mother brought up from Melbourne.'

Eva could see nothing wrong with Irene's hair, but followed her into the bedroom anyway. For the baby's sake, she wished she hadn't set eyes on Bluey MacDonald, or given him the money. The day would not turn out well if her judgement of him was accurate, and she feared for the little one's future. Yet she maintained a silence, for Irene must learn for herself what kind of man she'd got entangled with.

Lunch was eaten in silence, the tension growing as the hours ticked by and still there was no sign of their visitor. Jessie cleared the plates and brought coffee into the parlour as Irene began to pace.

Eva longed to shed the stiff, formal dress and return to her bed, but she sat with a book in her lap, watching her daughter tear herself apart. She finally gave up on the book. She couldn't concentrate enough to read, and found she was listening out for the baby. She was restless and uneasy and wished for anything to break the awful silence, and lift the heavy air of despair that seemed to be affecting all of them. She glanced up at the ornate clock on the mantel. It was getting late.

'He's been delayed,' snapped Irene. 'He'll be here. He promised.'

'Irene,' began Eva. 'Don't you think . . .?'

'What?' Irene whirled from her station at the window.

Eva looked at her daughter and saw the stark realisation in her face that he wasn't coming. Her heart went out to her. 'Darling,' she murmured. 'I'm so sorry.'

There was a rap at the front door and Irene swiftly turned. 'He's here,' she said triumphantly. 'I told you he would come.' She hurried out of the room and bumped into Jessie, who'd emerged from the kitchen, the baby in her arms. 'Give it to me,' she demanded.

Eva's hands trembled as she watched from the doorway. Irene grabbed the baby and draped the fleecy shawl more attractively over her arm. She made a lovely picture, with her high colour and the dark, curly-headed baby in her embrace – but if that really was Bluey at the door, he had more nerve than she gave him credit for.

Irene opened the door with a flourish.

'Mrs Hamilton? Got a wire for you. Sign here.'

Irene took a step back. 'No,' she breathed.

Eva took the telegram, signed for it and closed the door firmly in the gawping face. She took the baby and handed her back to Jessie before steering Irene into the parlour. Sitting her down, she looked at the brown slip of paper. It was from a Melbourne solicitor.

'What does he say?' asked Irene. Her face was white, her tone clipped and anxious.

'Client denies all involvement. Court order issued this day against Irene Hamilton approaching client or his family again. Further suit will be made if Irene Hamilton persists in her claim for paternity. This is final warning.'

Eva's hand was trembling as she crushed the telegraph. Bluey had decided to keep the money and not risk Eva's wrath. 'He's not worth it, Irene. You and the baby are better off without him.' She threw the telegraph into the empty fireplace. 'Of all the spineless, bare-faced liars,' she hissed. 'I hope he rots.'

Irene stared at the grate and the curl of brown paper. Her expression was inscrutable.

Eva crossed the room and perched on the arm of the chair. 'Don't worry, darling. You still have me and Jessie and the baby. We're made of sterner stuff than that weakling. We don't need him.'

Irene shrugged off Eva's hand and stood. 'You have no idea, have you, Mother?' she said coldly. She walked to the mirror above the fireplace and eyed her reflection before turning back to face Eva. 'I needed him to rescue me from the disgrace. Needed him to escape life with you and Jessie and that damn baby. Have you any notion of what it has been like for me stuck up here in the backwoods, with no friends, no parties, nothing to do all day but get fat?'

Eva stared at her in horror. 'But . . .' she began.

'But nothing,' snapped Irene. 'I'm sick of doing things your way. Sick of being stuck in this house with a screaming brat. From now on I'm going to live my life as I please.'

'What about the baby? Surely you don't mean to go through with the adoption?'

'Why not?' Her expression was set, her eyes cold. 'It's of no use to me any more, and certainly won't fit in with my plans for the future.'

Eva licked her dry lips. 'And they are?' she asked.

'To get some life,' she retorted. 'To have fun. Then, when I'm ready, I'll find a rich man and marry him.'

Eva looked across at Jessie. She held out her arms. Jessie carefully passed the baby over and Eva looked down at the sleeping child, her heart so full she was incapable of speech. This tiny scrap hadn't asked to be born. She hadn't asked for anything but what was her right. Eva could not and would not allow Irene to give her away.

'I will keep the child,' she said, her voice rough with emotion. 'And as you have omitted to even name her, I will call her Olivia.'

'That's impossible,' breathed Olivia. 'I can't be Irene's daughter. Maggie's got the birth certificate to prove she was. And what about the child she was expecting at the time? What happened to it?'

'Eva miscarried shortly after arriving in Trinity,' said Jessie flatly. She looked back at Olivia. 'You found those papers,' she said. 'You discovered Eva had adopted you. It was the reason for you coming all this way. You needed answers. Needed to find the truth.'

'Yes,' she said flatly. She sighed and looked down at her hand. 'According to the papers I found, Eva adopted me when I was six. But none of this makes sense, Jessie. Why would she wait six years?'

'And what about me?' demanded Maggie. 'Are you telling me my birth certificate is a lie as well?' She shook her head vehemently. 'That won't wash, Jessie. Irene as good as admitted I was her daughter.'

Jessie bit her lip. The time had come to put things right, to cast aside any lingering doubts. She rose from her chair and, holding out her hands, led the two young women to the gilded mirror above the mantel. 'What do you see?' she asked softly.

The silence was complete as Olivia and Maggie stared at their reflections and saw for the first time what Jessie had known all along.

Irene had given birth to twins.

266

Chapter Twenty-Four

Maggie stared at their reflections as she fought to control her breathing. It was as if her heart was trying to batter its way through her chest – as if the sea was in her head, churning, pounding, crashing against her eardrums until all other sound was stifled. An almost overwhelming surge of elation swept through her, but was swiftly followed by a rush of horror as the full extent of Irene's betrayal was laid bare.

'No,' she muttered as she shook her head and tried to ignore the reflections in the mirror. 'No. It's not possible. Not even Irene would have done such a thing.'

Olivia's grip at her waist was firm, belying the tremor Maggie could feel coursing through her body. 'Look in the mirror, Maggie,' she said with soft wonder. 'Can't you see?'

Maggie's hand was trembling as she attempted to swipe away the tears that ran down her face. 'I don't want to see,' she rasped. 'It's not true.'

Olivia drew her close. 'It is, Maggie,' she insisted. 'Look.'

With a reluctance born from a fear of what might be revealed, Maggie forced herself to look in the mirror. Through the blurring of tears she searched for and found the elusive similarities that neither of them had noticed before, yet would forever bind her to Olivia.

The echoes of one another were so delicately etched that it was almost like looking into the face of someone vaguely remembered from the past – not really a stranger – more a fleeting acquaintance. Maggie realised with mounting horror that, on such close scrutiny, she was, in truth, a pale substitute for the dark-haired, brown-eyed beauty that stood beside her. Her own light-brown hair held bright darts of auburn fire, and her eyes were flecked with gold, making them appear more hazel in the light of the lamp Jessie had just lit. Yet the shape of their eyes and the arch of their brows were reflected, as

267

were the contours of their faces and the way they held their heads. Narrow shoulders were aligned, the slender torsos a mirror image despite the differences in their clothing.

She pulled roughly away from Olivia and hugged her waist. The suspicions crowded in and the other woman's touch was suddenly repugnant. 'Did you know about this?' she demanded. She could hear the false calm overlaying the rising fury that threatened to spew from her in a hot tide of vitriol. Yet she knew that if she was to get the answers she needed, she had to keep control.

Olivia's eyes flickered towards Jessie before they settled once more on Maggie's face. 'Not really,' she began.

'Not good enough,' snapped Maggie. 'Come on, Olivia, spit it out. Tell the bloody truth.'

Olivia folded her arms around her waist and Maggie saw the tremble of her breath as she composed herself. A dart of concern was swiftly dismissed. Why should she be the only one affected by all this, when Olivia was obviously part of the plot to keep her in the dark?

'Nothing made any sense until today,' Olivia began. Her voice wasn't quite steady and she refused to look Maggie in the eye. 'There were so many questions I had no answers to, and although I could see certain similarities between us, there were several explanations, none of which seemed to make sense.'

'Such as?' Maggie hugged her waist, her tone measured, the rage and hurt burning just beneath the surface of her control.

Olivia's brow puckered as she stood there for a moment deep in thought. 'Why did Eva wait until I was six before she adopted me? Why not adopt me as a baby? As much as I hated the idea, being Irene's daughter seemed the only logical explanation. It explained why Irene resented me. Why she was always such a bitch, so jealous of the love Eva and I shared. It also went part of the way to explain why Eva kept everything so secret. Why she waited all those years before making me legally her daughter.'

Maggie shivered, despite the remnants of the day's heat in the room.

'Eva adopted me one week after Irene and William were engaged. In hindsight, this was no doubt an attempt to keep Irene's dirty little secrets firmly out of sight.'

The bitterness was copper in Maggie's throat. 'Dirty secret or not, you could at least have talked to me about it – given me some kind of warning,' she snapped.

Olivia's dark eyes filled with tears, and Maggie could see she was struggling to remain composed. 'How could I, Maggie? I had no proof, and they were, after all, only suspicions. Irene told me Jessie was out of the picture, and there seemed no likelihood of ever discovering the truth. I thought it best to keep my suspicions to myself rather than upset you even further.' She dipped her chin, her voice soft and full of regret. 'I'm sorry, Maggie. I was wrong.'

'I trusted you,' hissed Maggie. 'I told you things I've never even told Sam. Yet you didn't see fit to tell me about this.' She took a deep breath, fighting to remain calm and focussed – but it was getting harder and she knew it wouldn't take much more to break her.

Olivia reached out, but Maggie twisted away. She didn't want to be touched. Didn't want to acknowledge the pity she could see in Olivia's eyes. 'Why me?' she demanded of Jessie. 'How come Irene chose to give me away and not her?'

Jessie had seemed to shrink, the vitality drained from her face as she sat in the chair and twisted a handkerchief through her trembling fingers. 'There wasn't a maternal bone in yer mother's body,' she muttered. 'She was shocked to the core when she found out she was expecting twins – as far as she was concerned, one was bad enough, but two was an imposition. The only reason she didn't 'and you both over to the nuns was 'cause she thought she could use one of you to trap yer father into marriage and respectability.'

'Why me?' Maggie's voice was cold and determined as she repeated her question.

'It could have been either of you,' replied Jessie, her hands fluttering on her lap. 'It was done on a whim.'

The bitterness filled her throat. 'A whim?' she shouted. 'I was given away on a bloody whim?'

'It was the wrong word to use,' said Jessie hastily. 'I'm sorry Maggie. I never was much good at explaining things.'

'You're doing fine so far,' snarled Maggie. 'Get on with it.'

Jessie licked her lips. She was clearly nervous. 'You were a restless baby, always 'ungry and looking for attention. That particular morning, Olivia was asleep, but you was crying and wouldn't be soothed. Irene picked you up and put you in the pram, saying she would take you out for some fresh air. She was gone for a long time and I was just beginning to get really worried when she come back.' A solitary tear tracked a path down the wan cheek. 'The pram was empty,' she whispered. 'The only trace of you was a tear-stained pillow and a single white bootee.'

'So you rushed out and tried to find me?' The heavy sarcasm filled the silence, and Maggie knew she looked and sounded ugly but was past caring. The whole bloody lot of them could rot as far as she was concerned.

'Irene and I 'ad the most God-awful row. She refused to tell me a

269

damn thing, and when I went into town no-one had seen nor 'eard anything. I 'ad no leads, not so much as a hint of what might have happened to you. Irene refused to tell me anything, and I began to wonder if she'd just abandoned you, or done you some kind of 'arm. The next hours were the worst in me life. I borrowed an 'orse and traipsed back and forth for miles, covering the town and the paddocks, every ditch and sand dune, every acre of the rainforest – but there was no sign of you – and eventually I 'ad to give up.'

Maggie's resentment and rage cleared enough for her to realise there was no point in blaming Jessie. Irene had been thorough, and poor Jessie would have been no match for such a devious mind. 'Thanks for trying,' she muttered. 'At least someone cared what happened to me.'

'I care,' said Olivia softly.

'Do you?' Maggie rounded on her, the rage finally spilling over. 'Why? We're strangers. Two women from opposite sides of the bloody world with absolutely nothing in common but a bitch of a mother and a complete bastard for a father. You were the chosen one. The good kid that never cried. We're better off without one another, and the sooner you go back to your nice, comfortable little life in England the better.'

'Maggie, please ...' Olivia reached out to her, eyes pleading for understanding.

'Don't touch me.' Maggie's voice was a hiss.

They stood facing one another. The only sound in the room was of their rapid breathing. 'Why?' Olivia broke the silence – her voice arctic. 'Afraid you might have to accept who and what we are? Afraid the truth is more painful than all the lies we've been fed over the years? I'm hurting too, you know – you aren't the only one that's been damaged by all this. None of it was my doing, Maggie – just as it wasn't yours. So don't shut me out. We need one another more than ever before.'

The thunder of the sea was even louder in Maggie's head now. The rejection, and the agony of knowing she'd been judged worthless lay heavy and cold, stifling the heat of rage, and dulling her senses. Unloved and unwanted by either parent, the pattern of her life had been clearly set from birth, through childhood and into that disastrous sham of a marriage. The thirty-two years could be summed up in a single word. Abandoned.

Olivia felt an ache in her heart as she saw the tragic expression on Maggie's face. Tragic, not through any self-pity, but because of the dull acceptance she saw there. Tragic because Maggie had no idea of how much she was loved by those who really mattered – and seemed on the brink of rejecting her one true chance of fulfilment. She stepped forward, wanting to reach out to her. Needing to reassure and comfort, but wary of alienating her further.

'I'll look after her,' muttered Sam, his expression a mixture of grim determination and sadness as he gently put his arm around Maggie's shoulders. 'Come on, luv. Let's get some fresh air.'

Olivia watched as Maggie let him lead her out of the room, and wondered if she would ever find that bright spark of life again that had made Maggie the person she was, the person they all loved.

'Reckon you'll be going back to England now you've got what you come for,' said Jessie sadly.

Olivia dragged her thoughts into order. 'I'm not going anywhere until I know Maggie's all right,' she muttered as she pulled aside the curtain and peered out into the darkness. She could just make out the glimmer of Sam's white shirt and the red glow of two cigarette ends.

'Don't reckon she's going to forgive that easy,' muttered Jessie as she hauled herself out of her chair and began to clear away the debris of the uneaten tea. 'That girl's hurtin' and there's no tellin' what all this will do to 'er. Gawd alone knows what's going through 'er mind at this minute.'

'She's hurt and angry and confused,' said Olivia flatly. 'I'm the obvious target for all that, and I hold no illusions about us getting any closer until she's come to terms with everything.'

'And what about you, Olivia? How are you?' The aged face was deeply lined, the eyes concerned.

'Lonely.' The word slipped out and there was no taking it back, yet it described her feelings exactly. She felt bereft, adrift on an endless sea with no rudder and no sail. For Maggie wasn't the only one who'd lost everything. She took a deep breath. 'I mean . . .'

'I know what you mean,' interrupted Jessie, her head nodding, the parrot earrings swinging. 'Your fondest memories have been made ugly. Your love and trust for Eva damaged by what I've told you today. But you'll come to understand why Eva never told you. She loved you as if you were her own – you know that, don't you?'

Olivia nodded. She was unable to speak.

'Then don't see it as a betrayal. See it as a gift of love. She was only shieldin' you from an ugly truth, and would never have wanted to 'urt either of you.' The soft, gnarled hand gripped her arm.

'And Maggie? Will she ever forgive me for being the chosen one – for having all the things she should have had?'

Jessie's eyes were bright. 'Eventually, I reckon. But it'll take time.' She gave a short cough of laughter. 'She 'as more than her fair share

271

of yer mother's attributes than either of you will be willin' to admit – but strength of purpose and tenacity are not bad things to inherit if they're used correctly, and Maggie ain't the sort to be vindictive.'

Olivia pulled her cardigan over her shoulders. She needed air and time to think. Leaving the tiny house, she stepped out into the garden. There was no sight of Maggie or Sam and she took a deep, appreciative breath of the flower-filled air as she leaned against the picket fence and stared out at the encroaching rainforest. The night was cool after the heat of the day, the stars so bright and clear she felt she could almost reach out and pluck them from the sky. The moon sailed benignly across the vast velvet backdrop of night, its reflection mirrored in the calm ocean, and Olivia wondered if Giles could see the same moon above London.

She stared into the night, serenaded by the carpentry of crickets and the deep bass of cane toads. The loneliness deepened as she realised how much Giles would have loved this place. Deepened further as she silently admitted she had made a terrible mistake in letting him go.

Irene's funeral was ten days after their return to Trinity, and despite Olivia's misgivings, Maggie had been determined to attend. Sam drove them down to Cairns, he and Olivia obviously affected by the shroud of silence Maggie had deliberately wrapped around herself since their return home. It was her protection, her refuge, and the only person she'd permitted to breach that wall of resistance was Sam. She wasn't ready to face Olivia – the resentment and hurt were still too raw.

Maggie's heels echoed on the stone floor of the wooden church as she walked up the aisle and took her place on the hard bench. The air was cloying, filled with the heady, over-sweet scent of lilies. White candles flickered in the hot breeze that drifted in through the open door and the sun poured through the stained-glass windows on to the assembled mourners. Yet Maggie barely noticed, for her attention was fixed upon the coffin.

As the service droned on she didn't pay attention to the words or the hymns. She stood when others stood. Sat when others sat. Bent her head as if in prayer. Yet all she could see was the coffin. All she could think about was the woman inside it. The anger was cold now, the former heat of hurt and pain buried deep, replaced by icy acceptance. Irene had cheated her again. Cheated her by dying. Now she couldn't be faced. Couldn't be questioned and accused, and made to acknowledge the selfish cruelty of what she'd done to her own flesh and blood.

Maggie watched as the coffin was lifted by the pallbearers and carried out into the baking heat of the churchyard. Still shrouded in her aloneness, Maggie followed the cortège to the graveside. She knew one of the bearers was her half-brother, but didn't have the energy or the will to wonder if he mourned his mother's passing. For after all, why should she care? They were strangers, and after today they would probably never see one another again and he would remain ignorant of their conjoined heritage.

The words of interment and the slow lowering of the coffin into the deep, rich black soil were followed by the thud of earth on the coffin lid and the single red rose from William.

Maggie stood by the gaping hole, only vaguely aware of the others drifting away. She picked up a handful of soil and let it trickle from her fingers onto the polished oak. Then she brushed her hands together and turned away. Irene had indeed paid for what she'd done all those years ago – now her reign of destruction was over. It was time to stop punishing herself and her twin for what had happened. Time to pick up the threads and move on – to look forward, never back – and strengthen those very special ties that bound her to Olivia.

Epilogue

1948

England was enjoying an unusually warm spring. Daffodils bobbed their bright heads in the breeze, their vibrant yellow splashing pools of sunshine across Wimbledon Common. Delicate blossom fragranced the air, drifting like confetti into the dappled shadows, where snowdrops and primroses peeked through the long grass.

Olivia lifted her face to the gentle warmth of the sun – so different from the aggressive heat of Australia – its very kindness so much a part of England. For here the colours seemed muted, less jarring to the eye, more polite somehow. She smiled as she watched the strolling couples and the children playing in the sunshine. Memories of the war were beginning to fade, and despite the strictures of rationing, and the changes to the landscape made by the bombing, people were picking up the threads of their lives again.

She took a deep breath, grasped her cheap, cardboard suitcase more firmly, and began to walk, knowing she too must look to the future. For the threads of the past had snared Maggie and herself and entangled those they loved. It was time to weave a new pattern – one that was strong and founded on truth – one that could only be woven with the help of tough, British fibre.

The tree-lined avenue seemed drowsy in the sunlight, the houses mellow in their neat gardens, chimney smoke drifting aimlessly into a clear blue sky. It was strange how quickly she'd become used to the little wooden bungalows with their corrugated roofs, and the startling green of the tropical plants – this all seemed so alien, so old and settled after Trinity – and she felt she no longer belonged.

Olivia stood on the pavement and looked across at the house where Giles had once lived, saw the tweak of net curtains in an upper window and knew she was being watched. She bit her lip and turned away. There had been a time when Giles' mother would have rushed out to greet her, but the front door remained resolutely closed, the net curtain firmly replaced. Giles was no doubt working in the city, planning to return to his bachelor flat in Knightsbridge for a solitary evening before a gas fire. Perhaps it had been a mistake to come?

The hinges complained as Olivia opened the gate and walked down the brick path to her own front porch. As she stepped into the hall and put down her case, the sunlight streamed in with her, chasing away the shadows, but not quite dispelling the abandoned aura that clung to the house with lingering resentment.

Taking off her hat and gloves, she shrugged out of the dowdy brown overcoat she'd had to buy in London and hung it on the hook by the door. Because of the unexpected warmth of this spring day, the cardigan provided enough protection over her cotton dress. She kicked off the low-heeled pumps and padded in her stockinged feet from room to room, ignoring the memories, casting aside the darker thoughts that plagued her as she threw open the windows and gathered up the dust sheets. Maggie and Sam would be arriving tomorrow, and she needed to have everything ready for them – yet, by the look of things, it would take a month of Sundays to get this place straight.

The bedrooms were shadowy, strangely silent and empty now that Eva was no longer here. Olivia opened the window and removed the dust sheets, then sat on the bed and stared out over the roofs to the park. The eiderdown crackled beneath her, the goose feathers a strong reminder of cold nights when she'd snuggled beneath the covers waiting for the hot water bottle to warm the linen sheets. She could remember Eva feeding her chicken soup when she'd had measles. Could remember the stories she would read when sleep seemed to elude her, and could almost hear her voice in the silence that surrounded her now. Forgiveness for what she'd done had come easily – Jessie was right – Eva had tried to protect her, and by remaining silent, Eva must have suffered. It wouldn't be right not to forgive.

Impatient with her thoughts, she looked at her watch and was amazed at how long she'd been up here. It was late and would soon be dark. Time to close the windows again before the night air chilled the house any further. Olivia hurried out of the room and made a cursory inspection of the rest of upstairs. Eva's room held too many memories and there was still a lingering hint of the talcum powder she used. The three spare rooms were soulless, but she could arrange flowers on the night stands and find some prettier bed covers for her visitors. The bathroom was beyond redemption, unfortunately. It was as icy as ever, the great heavy bath set in the centre of the room like a monolith, the chain on the plug still broken, the fine web of cracks still veined in the enamel. She closed the door and hurried back down-stairs. What she needed now was a cup of tea, then she would see about lighting a fire in the sitting room.

The kitchen was gloomy, the linoleum cracked in places, the boiler on the wall a lingering threat. Olivia struck a match, turned the knob and ducked as the boiler roared to life with an explosive pop. She'd always hated the thing, but if she was going to stay a while, she needed hot water. There was no milk or sugar, her ration book had long run out, but the cup of tea was hot and welcome and went some way towards dispelling the dust in her throat. She carried it into the sitting room and after lighting the fire, perched on the window seat that overlooked the back garden. In the lengthening shadows of a spring evening she could see how neglected it had become in her absence. The lawn needed cutting, the rose bushes needed pruning and there was a forest of bindweed choking all the flowers in the borders Eva had so loved.

Turning her back on this depressing view she looked around the room she and Eva had spent so much time in, and realised for the first time how shabby it was, how dark the wallpaper and paint, how threadbare the carpet. Eva's plans to refurnish and decorate had come to nothing, and once war had been declared, there seemed little point.

'Hello? Anyone home?'

Olivia hastily put down her teacup and turned towards the door. Giles stood there, tall and straight, smart in his City suit, his hair and trim moustache gleaming in the sunlight. There was a sense of purpose in the set of his shoulders, and a return of confidence in his stance that told Olivia he was content with life.

Olivia's initial rush of pleasure was tempered by the memory of their last meeting and the rather stilted letters they had exchanged over the ensuing months. She stood, suddenly shy, her fingers tugging at the narrow white belt on her cotton dress, her tone uncertain. 'How did you know I was here?' she asked.

'Bush telegraph, old thing. Mother phoned and I got the first train.' Giles strode into the room and threw his hat on the couch. 'I hope you don't mind me turning up like this, but ...' He faltered, the confidence momentarily shaken.

Their eyes met and Olivia was saddened by the awkwardness that had grown between them. 'Of course I don't mind, you silly boy,' she scolded softly as they kissed one another's cheek fleetingly and drew apart again. 'If you hadn't come I would have searched you out. You know that.'

Giles sat down, picked up his hat and balanced it over his knee. 'Not really,' he murmured. He looked back at her, his gaze unwavering. 'It has been five months, and your letters were non-committal.'

Olivia silently acknowledged he was right – but it had been necessary at the time, for so much had happened during those intervening months, she had become almost bankrupt of any emotion. 'I had a great deal to contend with,' she murmured. 'I didn't think it fair to burden you with any of it.'

'I see.' Giles' hand wasn't quite steady as he lit a cheroot and snapped the lighter shut. He seemed to Olivia to have regained his assurance, for when he looked back at her, his gaze was penetrating and steady, his expression rather stern.

'So why come back, Olivia? You made it perfectly clear there was nothing for you here in Wimbledon.'

It was Olivia's turn to hesitate. Giles seemed so different – so distant and self-contained. It was hard to know how to tackle the thorny subject of why she had really come back to Wimbledon, for he wasn't making this homecoming any easier. 'I had to return some-time,' she said as she stood up and began to pace. 'The house must be put on the market, the furniture sold or put into storage. Mother's effects sorted through and dealt with.'

'So this is just a flying visit? You're still planning to make a life for yourself in Australia?'

His tone was tinged with uncharacteristic bitterness, his expression enigmatic, and Olivia wondered what was going through his mind. There had been a time when she could read him like a book, but this Giles was almost a stranger. 'Of course,' she said softly. 'I have family and work there, and despite everything that's happened, it's where I belong. I know that now.'

Giles nodded thoughtfully as he stubbed out the cheroot. 'The clinic's going well, according to your letters. You must be very proud – it's quite an achievement.'

Was that a hint of sourness in his tone? Olivia decided to ignore it. 'The clinic is doing splendidly, and we've even managed to equip a small emergency theatre. We've set up a series of hygiene classes as well as the ante- and post-natal side of things, and persuaded a retired doctor to oversee the morning surgeries.'

She smiled as she thought of Doc Harris. 'Poor man. He came to Trinity with plans to spend his final years out on his fishing boat, then he saw what we were trying to achieve and before he knew it he'd thrown in his lot with us. He's marvellous with the Aborigines, and the kids adore him. I think, in a way, it's given him a whole new lease of life.'

'It strikes me Trinity didn't know what hit it once you'd arrived,' said Giles with a ghost of that old familiar teasing light in his eyes. 'Must have shaken the old place up a bit.'

Olivia grinned. 'The influx of young, single English nurses certainly caused a flutter. Two of them are already courting, and Sam tells me the drovers and ringers are coming into town more regularly, so it's boosted his trade. He's even cleared out the back room behind the dining room and holds dances there every Saturday night.'

Giles must have noticed the brittle note beneath her bright tone, for he frowned. 'And what about you and Maggie?' He rose from the couch, but made no attempt to touch her, merely moving past her to stand by the window where he could look out over the common. 'I must say, I was flabbergasted when you wrote and told me you and Maggie were twins – I would never have guessed.'

'We aren't identical twins,' she replied. 'But if you look closely enough the similarities are there.' She fell silent, remembering those terrible few moments following Jessie's pronouncement.

Bewilderment and pain had accompanied the heavy silence as she and Maggie stared at their reflections in the mirror of that tiny house in Port Douglas. Without conscious thought they'd reached for one another, their fingers intertwining – re-establishing the ties so cruelly severed all those years before.

'How is it none of us realised the connection?'

His voice sounded distant, and Olivia had to drag herself back to the present. 'There was no reason to,' she said quietly, her fingers idly trawling through the dust on the mantelpiece. 'We were two young women from opposite sides of the world, with very different backgrounds.' She brushed her hands together and folded her arms tightly around her waist.

'But you guessed the connection was closer than Maggie realised?' Giles turned from the window, his face in shadow as the sun streamed into the room behind him.

Olivia tried to keep her tone measured. Talking about those days still made her emotional. 'Only in hindsight.' She shivered, despite the warmth from the fire and the thick cardigan Maggie had knitted for her. Hot tears threatened and she busied herself by emptying the ashtray into the fire and plumping cushions.

'Leave that and sit down,' said Giles firmly as he took her by the arm and forced her onto the couch. 'Here. I don't suppose you have a handkerchief as usual. Use mine.'

Olivia took the square of carefully ironed linen and dabbed at her eyes. This was more like the gruff, bluff Giles she remembered, and although he was making sure he kept his distance, the old familiarity of his tone somehow gave her renewed strength. 'None of this would have been resolved if it hadn't been for Jessie. Thank God we found her.'

'It's an extraordinary coincidence she should turn out to be Sam's mother-in-law,' said Giles from the far end of the couch.

Olivia blew her nose and balled the handkerchief in her lap. She gave him a watery smile, wishing he wouldn't sit quite so far from her. 'Not really. People don't move about as much in Queensland as they do here, and of course the population is smaller. Ties through blood and marriage are interconnected, forming a confusing genetic network that probably weaves right through every state in Australia if anyone bothered to do the research.'

The silence was broken only by the soft cooing of the pigeons in the eaves as they sat there, distanced by the length of the couch and the memories of their last encounter.

Olivia tucked the handkerchief into the belt at her waist. 'Maggie took it hard,' she said finally. 'The realisation of what Irene had done almost broke her.'

'Poor Maggie. One does have to feel very sorry for her.' Giles' voice was soft with compassion, for he'd liked and admired Maggie.

Olivia sniffed and dabbed her nose again. 'Maggie looks for pity from no-one. She's a tough sheila, my twin, and if she heard you feeling sorry for her, she'd sock you in the eye.' The fleeting ghost of a smile touched the corners of her mouth. 'But she did take it hard, and there was a hefty price to pay for what Irene did to her.'

'Why? What happened?' Giles sat up, his expression concerned.

'She wasn't right when we got back to Trinity, but it was worse after the funeral. Just as we thought she was getting better she had a breakdown. She shut herself away in that cabin of hers, eating barely enough to keep a sparrow alive and refusing to talk to anyone but Sam. He was like a man possessed. Every spare minute he had was by her side, coaxing her to eat, to talk – to cry. She'd shed no tears, shown no emotion following the day of Jessie's revelation and we both feared for her sanity.'

Olivia stood up and began to pace – it was impossible to remain still remembering those awful weeks when she and Sam had thought they might lose her. 'She refused to see me, and I can understand why. After all, I was the favoured twin – the chosen one who grew up surrounded by love and comfort – while she ... She lived through a hell I can only imagine.'

'A difficult situation,' mumbled Giles with his customary English habit of understatement.

'Far more difficult for Maggie,' Olivia said firmly. 'She had to come to terms with being rejected at birth – to being separated from

279

her twin – to being the loser in a heinous game of chance. To her it was the worst betrayal, and even though she attended Irene's funeral, it was through no sense of loyalty or regret – it was to make sure the bitch was well and truly buried and incapable of hurting her any more.'

She used the handkerchief briefly before jamming it back under her belt. 'But Maggie's made of sterner stuff than to let Irene kill her spirit. She got better – slowly, but surely – and we were able to begin to establish a closer bond.' She grinned. 'We discovered we'd both had imaginary friends as kids. That we both loved chocolate and hated carrots. That our favourite colour was blue and we were both handy with a needle. Neither of us can sing to save our lives, but we can dance any man off his feet.'

Giles grinned. 'I can certainly confirm the latter two. Eardrums and toes both shattered at some point or another.'

They smiled at one another – the first tenuous signs of the distance growing shorter between them, and Olivia experienced a flutter of hope.

'You'll get to see both Maggie and Sam if you stick around for a couple of days,' she said softly. 'They came with me, even though they're on honeymoon. I left them up in town, but they're due to visit here tomorrow.'

She saw the cocktail of hurt and pleasure, of chances lost in his eyes and turned back to the mantelpiece. Eva was staring back at her from the photograph in the silver frame. Her gaze was wistful, her thoughts unreadable. It was only now, in hindsight, that Olivia could understand why Eva had never been able to forgive Irene for what she'd done. Only now could she interpret the sadness she had sometimes seen in Eva's expression when she thought she was unobserved.

'Did you ever discover how or why Irene made such a terrible choice?'

She turned from the photograph and faced him. 'She only needed one of us – two would have been over-egging the pudding somewhat. I was kept because I was easier to handle and more likely to be attractive to our errant father. Who, by the way, sounds a complete bastard, and I hope I never have the misfortune to meet him.'

'Olivia!'

Giles' shocked expression at her ripe language actually made her smile. 'Sorry if that offends your sensibilities, but that's how I feel,' she said as she rammed her hands into the pockets of her dress and stared defiantly back at him.

'Fair enough, I suppose. But your time in Australia has certainly not mellowed you in any way. Whatever would Eva have said to such

280

language being used in her drawing room?' Giles had the ghost of a smile playing around his mouth and Olivia realised he was teasing her.

'Under the circumstances, I don't think she'd mind.'

'Oh, my dear girl,' sighed Giles as he stood and held out his hand. 'You have been through the mill, haven't you?'

Olivia stepped willingly into the warm, familiar safe harbour that was Giles' embrace. Her cheek rested on the lapel of his pinstripe suit and she heard the rapid tattoo of his heart. It echoed her own. 'Would you ever consider coming back?' she murmured into his shirt. 'We could really do with a decent lawyer in Trinity.'

'Like a shot if you were to ask me. Should never have left you in the first place.'

'That's settled then,' she whispered as she snuggled closer. His hand was stroking her back, sending shivers of pleasure down her spine. 'Giles?'

'Mm?' His heartbeat was deep and reassuring in his chest and his fingers were working their magic at the nape of her neck.

Olivia wished he would kiss her. She decided to risk this moment of pure delight by asking the question she'd come home to ask. 'Giles,' she began. 'Is a girl allowed to change her mind about something – really important – even if it makes her previous behaviour seem wanton and shallow?'

His lips were soft against her forehead, his moustache tickling her skin as he spoke. 'Wouldn't be a girl if she didn't change her mind every five minutes,' he whispered.

Olivia gently dug him in the ribs, pulled away just enough so she could look up into his eyes. 'So, will you marry me then?' she asked, the giggle rising in her throat.

'Of course,' he said solemnly. 'But I reserve the right to name the day and purchase the ring. Women are far too liberated for their own good these days, and you should be ashamed of yourself, Miss Hamilton, for being so forward as to propose.'

'Shut up, Giles, and kiss me,' she growled.

Ever the courteous, English gentleman, Giles enthusiastically complied.